My Mother's Sin
and Other Stories

My Mother's Sin
and Other Stories
by Georgios Vizyenos

Translated from the Greek by
William F. Wyatt, Jr.

Published for Brown University Press by
University Press of New England
Hanover and London, 1988

Printed in the United States of America
∞

LIBRARY OF CONGRESS CATALOGING-IN-PUBLICATION DATA
Vizyenos, G. M. (Georgios M.), 1849–1896.
My mother's sin and other stories.
I. Title.
PA5610.B49A6   1988   889'.32   87–23218
ISBN 0–87451–434–7
ISBN 0–87451–443–6 (pbk.)

5   4   3   2   I

Contents

Foreword

Baptised simply George the son of Michael in the small town of Vizó or Vizýi in eastern Thrace (near Edirne in what is today the European province of Turkey), Vizyenos (Viziinós) took his surname from his birthplace. The anonymity or double identity conferred on him by his entry into the world of letters as Georgios M. Vizyenos was scornfully noted by his mother: "Nowadays, when they write about him in the newspapers, even I don't know if it's really my own child they're talking about, or some European!" (Moullas 1980:71–72). Confusion of identity and the doubling of reality are themes that haunt the six long stories of Vizyenos and provide the mainspring for one of the most original departures in Greek, and even European, fiction of the latter part of the nineteenth century.

Born of humble parents in 1849, the young George was sent at an early age to Constantinople to work as an apprentice. His aptitude for learning attracted the attention of a wealthy Cypriot merchant, the first of a series of benefactors whose generosity enabled the always impecunious Vizyenos to live in a style befitting his learned inclinations. Vizyenos received his early education within the Orthodox Church, in Cyprus and Constantinople, before, like Paschális in "The Consequences of an Old Story," going on at a relatively advanced age to the University of Athens. (It should be remembered that Greece during Vizyenos' lifetime was a much smaller state than it is today and that probably a majority of Greek speakers at that time were born, like Vizyenos, outside its boundaries.) After only two years at Athens, he left to continue his studies in Germany at the University of Göttingen (like the narrator, this time, in "Consequences"). Thereafter Vizyenos seems to have turned himself into a polymath of some distinction. His doctoral dissertation (in German) on child psychology was published in

Leipzig in 1881, and after completing a second doctorate at the University of Athens on Plotinus' theory of beauty, he was elected to an assistant professorship in the History of Philosophy at that university in 1885.

During the course of this extended education, Vizyenos also traveled to France and England and began to publish poetry (conventionally Romantic in content and form) that won literary prizes in Athens. Between the spring of 1883 and the summer of 1884, he published, in the periodical *Estia,* five of the six stories on which his literary reputation rests. It is not known for certain when he wrote them or in what order (it has plausibly been suggested that the two set outside the Greek world were written first, before Vizyenos discovered his "true métier" in exploiting the background of his own childhood in the remainder), but none can have been written much before 1881. The sixth story, "Moskóv-Selím," may have been written during the same period but was completed in or after 1886 and was finally published only posthumously in 1895. After 1886, Vizyenos wrote no more fiction, although he continued to teach and write about psychology and philosophy. In 1892, he was committed to the lunatic asylum at Dafní outside Athens, where he died of "progressive general paralysis" four years later.

Vizyenos' brief literary career stands at a turning point in the history of Greek literature. The importance of his stories was not fully recognized in his lifetime or, indeed, for a long time afterwards, due in part to his adherence to the *katharévousa,* or purist, form of the language, which shortly after his death decisively lost the age-old battle with demotic, or spoken, Greek for recognition as the language of creative literature. Other reasons were undoubtedly his implicit rejection of militarism and Greek nationalism (he is practically the only writer of Greek fiction ever to portray a Turkish character sympathetically in his stories) and the element of complexity, bordering at times on erudition, that governs his work. The last few years have brought a dramatic re-evaluation of Vizyenos, as compromise over the language question has encouraged a new look at the *katharévousa* writers of the last century and twentieth-century modernism and radical critical approaches to literature have placed a new emphasis on the complexity and intellectual subtlety that distinguish his work.

At the time, however, Vizyenos' originality was viewed from a more limited perspective. The first years of the decade in which he wrote and published his stories heralded a transformation in Greek narrative fiction. The genre had made a late start in Greece, on the wave of the Europeanization that followed independence, and between the 1830s and the 1870s had been dominated by the romantic historical novel inspired by the example of Walter Scott and the ideological need for a new nation to reclaim a history of its own. Contemporary life was almost completely passed over, and the aspirations of the European novel at this time, whether to study the "manners" of human society (Balzac) or to plumb the depths of human nature (Zola), were absent from the Greek novel throughout this period. Although there were hints of change during the 1870s, it was not until the rumpus following the interrupted serial publication of Zola's novel *Nana* (in Greek translation) in 1879 and the belated discovery of Greek folklore as a subject of scholarly and popular enquiry during the same period that *realism* as a literary art and *contemporary life* as an appropriate object for it began seriously to engage Greek men of letters. In May 1883, the periodical *Estia* announced a competition for a "short story on a Greek theme," and in this way, Greek realism was born. Closely bound up with the contemporary folklore movement and its goal of establishing the roots of a national identity, the literary realism of the 1880s and 1890s in Greece, known as *ithografía* (the realistic portrayal of life), uses as its object almost exclusively the rural life of peasants. Often mistaken for a purely Greek phenomenon (only the relative exclusion of urban realism at this time is peculiar to Greece), *ithografía* has often been denigrated. But it is a recognizable offshoot of a trend within European realism throughout the latter half of the century, beginning probably with Turgenev and Flaubert (in short stories such as "Un Coeur Simple") and developed, with many points of similarity to its Greek counterpart, by such writers as Maupassant in France, Hardy in England, and Giovanni Verga and the youthful Pirandello in Italy. The Greek writers of the 1880s and 1890s, whose medium was the short story more often than the novel, all in their different ways come to grips with the issues raised by European realism, while modifying and experimenting with its aims and techniques as applied to their own observation and experience in Greek villages.

Among the first of this new generation stands Georgios Vizyenos, whose first story to be published ("My Mother's Sin") actually appeared in *Estia* a month *before* the announcement of the competition for a "Greek short story" in the same periodical and in many ways matches its prescription for a new type of fiction. Two of his other stories, "Who Was My Brother's Killer?" and "The Only Journey of His Life," also exploit the setting of Vizyenos' native village, and to that extent make common cause with the stories of Alexandros Papadiamantis (1851–1911) set in Skiathos, those of Ioannis Kondylakis (1861–1920) set in Crete, and the stories and novels of Andreas Karkavitsas (1864–1922) set in the outlying parts of Greece to which his duties as an army doctor took him. But not even these stories by Vizyenos (and still less "Moskóv-Selím," which only begins and ends in a Thracian landscape) are really *about* village life, and all of them move back and forth to the City (Constantinople), while his remaining stories, "Consequences" and "Between Piraeus and Naples," are set outside the Greek world altogether. It is not in fact his use of rural settings, vivid and strange though they are, that sets Vizyenos at the head of the tradition known as *ithografía,* but his acceptance of the challenge thrown down by European realism. This challenge is what really unites the writers of *ithografía,* and no writer makes as far-reaching a response to it as does Vizyenos (with the single exception of Papadiamantis, in his very different way).

Literary realism presupposes two things: a fairly literal understanding of Aristotle's definition of literature as the "imitation of things," and the implicit conviction that literary fiction may offer a way of determining and discovering what actually *is* real. The first involves, primarily, technique: the externals of the story must be consistent with, though they may also extend, the reader's experience or knowledge; the facts of the story must be plausible, its background recognizable. But no writer "imitates reality" in this narrow sense as an end in itself. The result would be mere duplication, tautology. The realist writer "copies" the visible world in order to announce or discover something about it. Zola, through the medium of a fiction that is plausible in every separate detail, propounds a theory of the mainsprings of human behavior that is based in a "reality" quite different from that we normally perceive; Hardy's meticulous fictions demonstrate the workings of the random forces of nature (the cruel "Immortals") on human lives; and so on. Vizyenos, although he stretches it considerably, never violates the first principle of realism: everything that happens is possible, if not always probable, in the world as we know it to have been in his day.

But all his stories go well beyond the *means* of realism to experiment, dangerously, with its *ends:* what happens when you cannot tell what is real any more?

All of Vizyenos' stories involve an elaborate experiment in *trompe l'oeil;* but the "game" is that of the experimental psychologist, not the conjuror. In several of the stories there is a mystery to be solved, and the narrative deploys all the tricks (and respects all the rules) of the detective story. The reader is invited to spot the clues, to disentangle a confused chain of circumstances according to rational principles of cause and effect and probability. As in the best detective stories, each of the stories presents, towards its end, a dramatic revelation for which a trail of rational clues had been laid. What was "My Mother's Sin"? "Who Was My Brother's Killer?" What were "The Consequences of the Old Story" and "The Only Journey of His Life"? What is the explanation for the strange name and appearance, half Russian, half Turkish, of "Moskóv-Selím"? And what, in "Between Piraeus and Naples," is the true explanation for the girl's father's generous invitation to the narrator?

It would be unforgivable, in an introduction, to betray the answers to these secrets, but it betrays nothing to say that the answer given in each case proves unsatisfactory as a total explanation. All the stories end with different characters possessed of different, and incompatible, perceptions of the "truth." At the end of "My Mother's Sin," it is very uncertain whether the mother, having confessed to her son and even having been absolved by the Patriarch, is aware that to us, seeing through the narrator's eyes, her true sin may actually have been committed in an act meant to atone for the sin to which she has confessed. At the end of "Piraeus," the young girl, Másinga, parts from the hero with a picture of her future that, the narrator knows from her father, is quite different from that which the latter has planned for her. In "Consequences," the play of conflicting appearances reaches its most complex form when the scene near the beginning, in which the narrator visits a girl patient playing a harp in a padded, blue-velvet cell in a mental asylum, becomes the object of successive interpretations: her former lover dies in the belief that he has seen her, in a dream, in heaven. The rational narrator is not so sure, but news comes that she had in fact died on the night of the dream. With a *frisson* of the uncanny, the narrator, and we, are left wondering. "The Only Journey of His Life" brings the worlds of fairy tale and sober fact into uneasy juxtaposition, and the journey of the title has a different meaning in each. Finally, Moskóv-Selím, the Russophile Turk who lives for the coming of the Russians, cannot throw off either half of his divided identity when the moment comes to choose between them.

The world of Vizyenos' stories, whether the story is set in eastern Thrace, at sea on the Mediterranean, or in the Harz mountains of Germany, is a world of conflicting realities and merging identities. The town from which Vizyenos took his name lies in a province that in his lifetime had been fought over by the Russian and Ottoman empires and was regarded by Greeks as belonging to Greece. This disputed identity is carried over into the story "Moskóv-Selím," whose hero is a Turk so badly treated by his own people that he learned, while a prisoner of war in Russia, to admire everything Russian. The narrator, who is of course Greek, comes upon Selím's Russian-style log cabin in the middle of the Thracian landscape, the cabin giving the whole terrain a look of the steppes; and the bond between the Turk Selím and the Greek narrator is established because Selím mistakes the latter for a Russian. In the divided character of Moskóv-Selím and the presence of the Greek narrator to whom he confides his life story, the three incompatible identities of Vizyenos' native land are brought together. A similar ambivalence or ambiguity appears in several other stories: "Killer," set in the same terrain, also cuts across tribal and religious loyalties to portray a Turkish family that mirrors the narrator's own. "Piraeus" uses a setting that is indeterminate in a different sense—as the title indicates, the action of the story takes place in the empty space between two points, and a further shift, to the mysterious riches of Calcutta, is discussed as a possibility. In "Consequences," the two principal characters are Greeks in a foreign country, fallen victim, among other things, to its Romantic Idealism and the pronunciation of Homer.

Nationality and religion were, specially for the nineteenth century, two of the most fundamental determinants of a person's identity, and each of the stories mentioned explores what happens to one's perception of reality if these potent boundaries are transgressed. Another such determinant is sex. Two of Vizyenos' male characters, the grandfather in "Journey" and Moskóv-Selím, were brought up as girls. For both, a plausible explanation is offered so that the canons of realism are not violated: the narrator's grandfather, at ninety-eight, was old enough to have been born in the days of the Janissary levy, which took male children from Christian families to turn them into a Muslim military elite; and Selím was the victim of his mother's obsessive desire to have a daughter (an inversion of traditional Greek prejudice, which also makes an appearance in "My Mother's Sin"). It was as a girl that Yoryís' grandfather learned the fairy tales for which the boy so admires him—and the telling of tales, the traditional counterpart to Vizyenos' own art, is always traditionally the prerogative of women. In a very different way, in "Moskóv-Selím," it is Selím's divided sexual identity that is responsible for the entire narrative, since everything that happens to him is the result of his father's prejudice against a boy dressed as a girl. Ambiguous sexuality appears too in "Piraeus," for the heroine is observed at the age of transition from the narrator's tomboy accomplice of childhood to the object of his incipient romantic attentions.

By setting his characters so they straddle the most sacred boundaries that determine identity for each of us and define, in consequence, our perception of reality, Vizyenos in his stories brings into question the nature of identity and of reality as constructed by reason and the senses. The uncertainties in his stories, which we may, with some excuse, project back into Vizyenos' own life, strike at the most basic premises upon which, conventionally, a rational view of reality is built. One of the consequences of transgressing these boundaries is madness; insanity and delusion play a part in "Killer" and "Consequences," as well as in Vizyenos' own life, while in each of the remaining stories at least one character is set apart by an aberration bordering on delusion. Another problematic area is the art of narrative, and it is no accident that a large place within each of Vizyenos' narratives is taken up with the telling of stories: time and again *what is narrated*—the action that moves the story forward, sets it in motion, or solves a mystery—is the act of narrating.

Frequently in the stories, a character embarks on narration to bridge the chasm between private trauma and a shared conception of "reality." But each narrative actually multiplies the ambiguities and contradictions that, for the person narrating it, it is supposed to resolve. In "My Mother's Sin," the mother's confessional narrative to her son only widens the gulf between her perceptions and his, since it is discovered that everything she has done has been the consistent and reasonable working out of an obsession incompatible with full maternal feelings towards him. Paschális' narrative, in "Consequences," of his dream in which he saw Clara in heaven, which provides the resolution of his story in his own mind, has quite a different meaning for the narrator hearing it, a meaning he dares not communicate to Paschális. The grandfather's narrative of his own life, in "Journey," which is a response to the narrator's confusion over the fairy tale world of his grandfather's previous narratives and the world of real life, in fact compounds the confusion, because this narrative, too, is part fairy tale and seems to cross the boundary into the narrator's reality at its end. The answer to the question, "Who Was My Brother's Killer?" is learned by the narrator (and the reader) indirectly as the killer unburdens himself, once again through narrative, of a different and lesser guilt.

Vizyenos' stories probe behind reality as conventionally perceived by calling into question some of its most stable foundations—the differences of sex, nationality, and religion—and by revealing the incompatible perceptions on which different individuals depend in order to retain their identity. To perceive the terrifying relativity that, in the world of these stories, lies behind "reality" is to risk losing one's identity, that is, to become insane. Those characters who do not go mad struggle to recreate identities for themselves by means of story, though often (as for Paschális, the brother's murderer, Moskóv-Selím, and the grandfather in "Journey") this is but a temporary remedy. The stories of Vizyenos can be read as a kind of *Thousand and One Nights* in which a whole series of narrators seek by telling stories to save themselves not from death but from the madness consequent on "double vision," that is, the simultaneous perception of and beyond reality. It is a dizzying, at times a disturbing, experience to read them. But alongside the psychological brinkmanship, the "pleasure of the text" in Vizyenos' case lies in a warm, understated plea for gentleness and for a humanity redeemed from the divisions on which personal and national identities depend, and in the step by step progress of a rational mind probing its own foundations in the irrational.

King's College London   Roderick Beaton

Bibliography

The following is a list of works one may consult to receive a fuller orientation to the works of Vizyenos and of early Greek (nineteenth-century) fiction.

TEXTS

Mamoni, K. G. *Vizyenou, ta Apanta*. Athens: Biblos, 1967. Contains all stories, long and short, and most of the poems.

Mamoni, K. *Bibliographia G. Vizyenou (1873–1962)*, *Archeion tou Thrakikou Laographikou kai glossikou thesaurou* 29 (1963). Contains bibliography and some earlier poems elsewhere overlooked.

Moullas, P. G. M. *Vizyenos, Neollinika Diigimata*. Athens: Ermis, 1980. Contains the longer stories, plus a long, detailed introduction.

Panagiotopoulos, I. M. *Georgios Vizyenos*. Athens: Aetos, 1954. Contains the stories, some poems, and selections from several essays.

SECONDARY WORKS

Dimaras, C. T. *A History of Modern Greek Literature*. Translated by Mary Gianos. Albany: State University of New York Press, 1972.

Mastrodimitris, P. D. "Appendix: Andreas Karkavitsas and Nineteenth-Century Greek Literature." In *The Beggar*, by A. Karkavitsas, trans. by W. F. Wyatt, Jr. New Rochelle, N.Y.: Caratzas, 1982.

Politis, L. *A History of Modern Greek Literature*. Oxford: Oxford University Press, 1973.

Preface

Many people and organizations have helped in the preparation of this translation. First, I want to thank two organizations who with their financial support made work on this project possible: The National Endowment for the Humanities provided a challenge grant, and the Kostas and Eleni Ouranis Foundation of the Athens Academy most generously provided the funds to match that grant. I am deeply grateful to these organizations, and within them Athanasios Petsalis-Diomedes, President of the Special Committee within the Ouranis Foundation, and Dr. Susan Mango of NEH, who has always taken a personal interest in translations from the Greek. I also warmly thank the Hellenic Cultural Society of Southeastern New England for its support, both spiritual and technical, and particularly Dr. Venetia Georas who read through my first attempts and provided necessary suggestions and corrections: without her the work would never have been completed. Others have helped in various important ways. Kyriake Mamone, herself editor of Vizyenos' works, helped with many of the more difficult terms. Peter Bien gave the manuscript a thorough reading and provided numerous helpful suggestions, most of which I have accepted and which have proved most beneficial. Roderick Beaton both authored the foreword, and in reading the entire work, improved the translation. Alan Boegehold, my colleague here at Brown, read the whole and corrected lapses in my English style. I am grateful to all these good friends of Greek literature for their interest and help with this work.

My Mother's Sin
and Other Stories

My Mother's Sin

◫◫◫

Introduction

"My Mother's Sin" was Vizyenos' first story published in *Estia* and is one of his best—it is certainly the best known. As with all his stories, it is presented in the first person by a narrator who, in this case, happens also to be one of the actors. Whether or not one wishes to regard the story as being in any sense "true" and hence evidence of the author's own life, it does at least correspond chronologically to events and details in the life of the narrator as that life can be reconstructed from other stories. At least some of these events, particularly as regards chronology, correspond also to periods of Vizyenos' life. It would, however, be dangerous to assume exact equivalence between the narrator and the author.

The story begins in the narrator's home town with him under ten years old. His father has died before the story begins; he has a brother Hristákis four years older than he, a sickly sister, Annió, probably only a year or so younger than he, and a brother somewhat younger even than the sister (the brother was born after his father died). Annió dies, and shortly after her death, the narrator leaves home and stays away for some time. Many years after the sister's death, his mother tells him the story of her sin, from which the story derives its title. This sin was committed three years or so before the narrator's birth, and the mother has lived with it all this while. The narrator tells us the entire story, including his mother's, in Constantinople when he must be about twenty-seven and already a man of the world and, in any event, thirty years after the sin was committed. There is no real need for chronological precision: the story of the mother's sin and its consequences covers a period of thirty years.

There is little local color, few references to places and things, and, unlike some of Vizyenos' other stories, no Turkish words and phrases. The only artifacts that need clarification are coins—the *rubiédes*, Turkish coins, and the *Konstantináta*, Byzantine coins representing the Emperor Constantine and his mother Helen—and *raki*, a spiritous liquor.

Geographical movement is restricted in the story, though much is suggested. In fact, the story is set in a village, the name of which is dramatically unknown but which was, of course, Vizýi, and in Constantinople, the "City." Within the village, though, and to a lesser, though parallel, extent in Constantinople, there is some motion. In the City, the narrator visits the Patriarchate, seat of the Patriarch of the Eastern Orthodox Church, Ioakím II, Patriarch from 1873–1878.[1] I concentrate on only two spaces in the village, the home and the church, two spaces available and normal for women at that time. In fact, almost all the action takes place in one or the other, and many of the same activities—eating, sleeping, praying—are carried on in both.

The house consists of a structure surrounded by a wall with a gate. Everything within that gate is family, everything outside it is foreign, strange, hostile: one of the points of the story is the question of what is and what is not "our own." The house itself contains an iconostasion, or icon case, in which images of the family's saints are placed and worshipped. Little in the way of furniture is described, and the only relevant pieces are the cradle and the bed. The cradle must be similar to the ones with which we are familiar, but the bed is not. In village houses, beds as such were nonexistent, and it was necessary to spread the bedding on the floor each night and fold it up and store it during the day. Any room could serve as a bedroom, but no room was set aside as such. Hence "making the bed" or "spreading the bed" was quite a different activity from what we do.

The church was, of course, the Greek Orthodox Church. Greek churches usually have high walls that frequently support a dome

---

1. Ioakím III was Patriarch from 1878–1884, and again in 1901 and following. Hence, Moullas (1980:96), who places the dramatic date of the story at 1882–1883, cannot be correct. Nor can we assume that Vizyenos is confusing the second and third Ioakíms, because the Second is referred to as dead in the story while the Third was alive into the twentieth century. Rather we must go with the dates as derived from the story itself, as in fact Moullas does when he derives a dramatic date of 1875. Ioakím II was Patriarch twice, once too early for our story (1860–1863), but the second time accords well with a date of 1875.

over the front of the sanctuary and may have aisles extending in the shape of a cross. The altar is in the sanctuary behind a screen and is visible to the congregation only when the priest opens the central of three doors, or the "beautiful gate." The service begins when the priest enters from the door on the left and ends when he goes out through the door on the right. Several hymns are cited in this story, and aspects of the ritual as well. The "Spear" is a ritual implement used during the service and is emblematic of the spear that pierced Christ's side. The screen generally has a number of icons on it, one of which must be the image of the saint to whom the church is dedicated, in this case the Virgin Mary. Other saints may have icons, each in his own icon screen (iconostasion) located in various places around the church. A place of light and life during the day, a church can be a gloomy and frightening place at night.

The church has its rituals as described in the story, and people have their beliefs. As is generally the case with a matter so important to the individual as health, various systems of healing are available in Greece. There is generally a doctor, more or less respected; there is also the Church with its exorcisms and blessings; and then there is also the realm of magic and superstition. If medicine cannot cure the illness, and if the Church cannot exorcise the devils, then magic steps in. One tries to drive out the evil spirit with exorcisms or to distract it by other means. The means described in the story are perfectly normal ones and exampled in other stories and sources.[2] The Neraides, for example, are (or were) supernatural creatures who haunted the countryside and could render one spastic or deaf and dumb. They will reappear in "The Only Journey of His Life." Some of the mother's actions, notably when she "prowled the streets asking passersby if they had seen me anywhere," are stock features in Greek folksong, in this case songs about *xeniteiá* "being abroad." "My Mother's Sin," in fact, owes a good deal to folklore and local customs and is a highly sophisticated amalgam of local color and psychological interest.

---

2. Cf. K. Papathanasi-Mousiopoulou, *Laographikés Martyríes Georgíou Vizyinoú* (Athens: 1982); and, for other folklore matters, cf. J. C. Lawson, *Modern Greek Folklore and Ancient Greek Religion* (Cambridge: Cambridge University Press, 1910), particularly 130–162 (on Neraides). A good contemporary ethnographic account of these creatures is to be found in C. Stewart, "Nymphomania: Sexuality, Insanity and Problems in Folklore Analysis," in M. Alexiou and V. Lambropoulos, eds., *The Text and its Margins* (New York: Pella, 1985), 219–252.

My Mother's Sin

We had no other sister, only Annió. She was the darling of our small family, and we all loved her. But our mother loved her most of all. She always sat beside her at table and gave her the best of whatever we had. And while she dressed us in our deceased father's clothes, she usually bought new ones for Annió. She did not rush her into school, either. If she wanted, she went to school; if she didn't, she stayed home. Something we'd never have been allowed to do for any reason.

Naturally such special exceptions had to cause harmful jealousies among children, especially children as little as my two other brothers and I were at the time these events took place. But we knew deep down inside that our mother's affection continued impartial and equal towards all her children. We were sure that those exceptions were only external demonstrations of a certain natural favor towards our household's only girl. And not only did we put up with these attentions without a complaint, we even contributed to increasing them as best we could, because Annió, besides being our only sister, had unfortunately always been weak and sickly. And even the youngest in the house who was justified more than any other in claiming his mother's attentions because his father had died before he was born, ceded his rights to his sister, and the more gladly since Annió did not become bossy or conceited on account of this.

On the contrary, she was very sweet to us and loved us all deeply. And—strange to say—the girl's affection for us increased instead of diminishing as her illness progressed. I remember her large black eyes and her arched eyebrows that met over her nose and appeared all the darker the paler her face became. A face by nature dreamy and sad onto which a certain sweet gaiety spread only when she saw us all gathered together near her. She would frequently hide under her pillow those fruits that neighborhood women brought her as a "tonic," and she'd parcel them out to us when we came back from school. But she always did this in secret because it enraged our mother, who did not like us wolfing down anything that she wanted her sick daughter even just to have tasted.

Nonetheless Annió's illness grew steadily worse, and our mother's concerns centered more and more on her.

Mother hadn't left the house since the day our father died: she had been widowed very young, and was too modest to make use of the freedom of movement that, even in Turkey itself, belongs to every mother of many children. But the day that Annió fell seriously ill she cast modesty aside.

Someone had once had a similar illness—she ran to ask how he had been cured. Somewhere an old woman harbors plants of miraculous medicinal power—she hurried to buy them. Some queer-looking stranger had come from somewhere, or one renowned for his knowledge—she did not hesitate to beg his assistance. The "learned," according to folk widsom, are omniscient. And sometimes behind the disguise of a traveling beggar there lurk mysterious beings of supernatural power.

The neighborhood's fat barber came to visit us, unsummoned and as a matter of right. He was the only official doctor in our district. As soon as I saw him I had to run to the grocer because he never went near the invalid before gulping down at least fifty drams of *raki*.

"I'm old, my girl," he would say to the impatient mother. "I'm old, and if I don't have a nip, my eyes don't see well."

And it seems he wasn't lying. The more he drank, the more easily he was able to pick out the fattest hen in our courtyard to take with him when he left.

Although my mother had already stopped using his medicines, she nonetheless paid him regularly and without complaint. She did this in the first place so as not to displease him, and also because he often maintained by way of assurance that the course of the disease was good, and exactly what science had the right to expect from his prescriptions. This last was unfortunately all too true. Annió's condition went slowly and imperceptibly, but constantly, from bad to worse. And this prolongation of the unseen malady drove our mother wild.

According to folk widsom, if an unknown disease is to be viewed as a natural affliction, it must either yield to the elementary medical knowledge of the area, or bring death within a short time. As soon as it becomes prolonged and chronic, it is attributed to supernatural causes and is characterized as "due to an evil spirit." The invalid had sat on an evil spot. He had crossed the river at night at the very instant the Neraídes, unseen, were celebrating their rites. He had stepped over a black cat which was in reality the Devil in disguise.

Our mother was more devout than superstitious. At first she

viewed such diagnoses with horror, and refused to put the suggested spells into effect for fear of committing a sin. Besides, the priest had already read the exorcisms of evil over the invalid, just in case. But she changed her mind after a while.

The invalid's condition was growing worse, and motherly love conquered fear of sin—religion had to come to terms with superstition. Next to the cross on Annió's chest she hung a charm with mysterious Arabic words on it. Magic took the place of blessings and after the priest's prayer-books came the witches' "spells."

But all went for naught. The child grew worse and worse, and our mother became more and more distraught. You'd think she'd forgotten she had other children, too. She didn't even care to know who fed us boys, who bathed us, who mended our clothes. An old woman from the neighboring village of Sofídes who had been living with us for many years now took care of us as far as her Methusaleh-like age allowed. There were times when we didn't see our mother for days on end.

Sometimes she took a ribbon from Annió's dress and tied it at some wonder-working location in the hope that the disease, too, would be tied up far from the patient. Sometimes she went to churches in neighboring villages who happened to be celebrating a saint's day carrying a candle of yellow wax that she had dipped with her own hands and that was exactly the sick girl's height. But all these things proved useless. Our poor sister's illness was incurable.

Finally when all means had been exhausted and all cures had been attempted, we reached the final refuge in such cases.

Our mother took the wasted girl up in her arms and carried her to the church. My older brother and I loaded ourselves with the bedding and followed along behind. And there, on the damp, chill pavement, in front of the icon of the Virgin, we made the bed and placed down in it the sweetest object of our concerns, our one and only sister. Everybody said she had an "evil spirit." Our mother no longer had any doubt about this, and even the patient herself began to recognize it. So she had to stay in the church forty days and forty nights in front of the sanctuary and facing the Mother of our Savior, trusting only that their mercy and compassion would rescue her from that satanic affliction that lurked within and was so mercilessly grinding down the delicate tree of her life.

Forty days and forty nights. That is how long the demons with their frightful perseverance can hold out in their invisible battle

with divine grace. After this period of time the evil is defeated and
retreats in disgrace. And accounts are not lacking in which patients
feel within their body the awful writhings of the final battle and see
their enemy fleeing in a strange shape, especially at the moment
when they bring out the sacred vessels or the "In Fear" is pronounced. Lucky are they if they have sufficient strength at that time
to withstand the shocks of the struggle. The weak are shattered by
the immensity of the miracle taking place within them. But they
have no regrets on this account. If they lose their life, at least they
gain the most valuable thing. They save their soul.

Nevertheless some such eventuality plunged our mother into
deep distress, and as soon as we set Annió down, she began with
great concern to ask her how she felt. The sanctity of the place, the
sight of the icons, the aroma of the incense had, it seems, a beneficial effect on her melancholy spirit, for, after the first few moments,
she brightened up and began to banter with us. "Which of the two
do you want to play with," my mother asked her tenderly—
"Hristákis or Yoryís?"

The invalid cast her a sidelong but expressive glance and, as if
reproaching her for her indifference towards us, answered slowly
and deliberately: "Which of the two do I want? I don't want either
without the other. I want all my brothers, all the brothers I have."

My mother drew back and fell silent.

A short while later she also brought our littlest brother to the
church, but only for that first day. In the evening she sent the other
two away and kept me alone at her side. I still remember what an
impression that first night in the church made on my childish imagination. The faint light of the lamps in front of the iconostasion,
barely able to illumine it and the steps in front of it, rendered the
darkness around us even more dubious and frightening than if we
had been completely in the dark. Whenever the flame of a candle
flickered, it seemed to me that the Saint on the icon facing it had
begun to come to life and was stirring, trying to wrench free of the
wood and come down onto the pavement, dressed in his broad, red
robes, with the halo around his head, and with those staring eyes
on his pale and impassive face.

Or again when the chill wind whistled through the high windows, noisily rattling their small windowpanes, I thought that the
dead buried about the church were clambering up the walls and
trying to get in. And, shaking from fright, I sometimes saw a skele-

ton across from me reaching out to warm its fleshless hands over
the brazier that burned in front of us. And yet I did not dare show
even the slightest anxiety because I loved my sister and thought it a
great honor to be constantly near her side and near my mother, who
would surely have sent me home as soon as she suspected I was
afraid.

So during the following nights as well I suffered those terrors
with a forced stoicism, and I eagerly discharged my duties, trying
to prove as agreeable as possible. On weekdays I lighted the fire, I
fetched water, I swept the church. Feast-days and Sundays during
matins I would lead my sister by the hand and stand her below the
Gospels from which the priest was reading at the Beautiful Gate.
During the service I spread out the woolen blanket onto which the
invalid would fall—flat on her face—so that the Host could pass
over her. But during the recessional I brought her pillow over to
face the left door of the Sanctuary so she could kneel on it until
"the priest draped his stole over her" and made the sign of the cross
over her face with the Spear, mumbling the "Through thy crucifix-
ion, Oh Christ, the tyranny has been destroyed, the power of the
Enemy has been crushed," etc.

And in all this my poor sister followed me, her face pale and
mournful, her step slow and uncertain, attracting the pity of the
church-goers and calling forth their prayers for her recovery, a recovery that, unfortunately, was slow in coming. On the contrary,
the dampness, the chill, the strangeness and, yes, the ghastliness of
those nights in the church were not slow to have a harmful effect
on the invalid whose condition by now had begun to inspire the
worst fears. My mother realized this, and began, even in the church
itself, to show a sorrowful indifference to anything other than the
invalid. She did not open her mouth to anyone anymore except to
Annió and the saints when she prayed. One day I came up to her
unobserved while she was on her knees weeping in front of the icon
of the Savior. "Take from me whatever you want," she was saying,
"and leave me the girl. I see that it has to happen. You recalled my
sin and are determined to take the child from me to punish me. I
thank you, Lord!"

After several moments of deep silence during which her tears
could be heard as they dropped onto the stones, she sighed from
the bottom of her heart, hesitated a little, and then added: "I've
brought two of my children to your feet . . . let me have the girl!"

When I heard these words, an icy shudder coursed through my nerves and my ears began to roar. I could hear nothing more. And when I saw that my mother, overcome by her frightful anguish, was falling limply onto the marble slabs, instead of running to her assistance I took the opportunity to dash out of the church, running in a frenzy, and crying out as if Death itself incarnate were threatening to seize me. My teeth chattered from fright, and I ran and kept on running. And without realizing it I suddenly found myself far, far away from the church. Then I stopped to catch my breath and dared to turn to look behind me. No one was chasing me.

So I began to come to my senses little by little and to reflect. I recollected all my acts of tenderness and affection toward my mother. I tried to remember whether I had ever been at fault toward her, had ever wronged her, but could not. On the contrary I began to see that from the day that this sister of ours had been born, I not only was not loved as I should have wished, but in fact was being shunted aside more and more. Then I remembered, and it seemed to me that I understood, why my father had been in the habit of calling me his "wronged one." And my outrage got the better of me and I began to cry. "Oh," I said, "my mother doesn't love me and doesn't want me! I am never going to church again—never!" And I turned toward home, gloomily and in despair.

My mother was not long in following me home with the sick girl. For the priest, alarmed by my cries, had come into the church, and, when he saw her, had advised my mother to remove her. "God is great, daughter," he told her, "and His grace extends over all the world. If He's going to heal your child, He'll heal her in your house as well." Unhappy the mother who heard him! for those are the formal words with which priests usually send away those about to die so they don't expire in the church and defile the sanctity of the place.

When I saw my mother again, she was more melancholy than ever. But she behaved toward me especially with great sweetness and gentleness. She took me in her arms, she fondled me, she kissed me tenderly and repeatedly. You'd think she was trying to mollify me. I, however, could neither eat nor sleep that night. I lay on my bed with my eyes closed, but I strained my ears attentively to catch my mother's every move. She, as always, was keeping watch at the sick girl's pillow.

It must have been about midnight when she began moving about the room. I thought she was laying out the bed to go to sleep, but I was wrong because after a short while she sat down and began to chant a lament in a low voice.

It was the lament for our father. She used to chant it very frequently before Annió fell ill, but I was hearing it now for the first time since then. This lament had been composed for our father's death, at her orders, by a sunburnt, ragged Gypsy who was well known in the area for his skill in composing verses extemporaneously. I can still see his black, greasy hair, his small, fiery eyes and his exposed, hairy chest. He sat inside our courtyard gate surrounded by the bronze pots and pans that he had collected for tinplating. And, with his head tilted to the side, he accompanied his mournful air with the plaintive sounds of his three-stringed viol. My mother stood before him with Annió in her arms and listened attentively and tearfully. I was holding tightly onto her dress and hiding my face in its folds because, sweet as those sounds were, the face of their fierce singer terrified me.

When my mother had memorized her mournful lesson, she took two *rubiédes* from the corner of her kerchief and gave them to the Gypsy—we still had enough at that time. Then she placed bread and wine in front of him and whatever other food was handy. And while he ate down below, my mother went upstairs and repeated his lament to herself so as to fix it in her memory. And it seems she found it very beautiful, for as the Gypsy was about to leave, she ran after him and made him the gift of a pair of my father's good trousers.

"May God forgive your husband's soul, daughter," the singer called out in surprise as he went out of our courtyard loaded down with his copper pots and pans.

That was the lament my mother was chanting that night. I listened and let my tears flow in silence, but I didn't dare move. Suddenly I picked up the smell of incense! "Oh," I thought, "our poor Annió has died!" And I jumped from my bed.

I found a strange scene before me. The sick girl was breathing heavily, as always. Near her lay a man's suit, arranged as a man would wear it. To its right was a stool covered with black cloth on which rested a pan full of water flanked by two lighted candles. My mother was on her knees swinging a censer over these objects and staring at the surface of the water.

It seems I turned pale from fright, because when she saw me, she hastened to calm me. "Don't be afraid, my child," she said mysteriously. "They're your father's clothes. Come, you also ask him to come and heal our Annió." And she made me kneel beside her. "Come, Father—please take me—let Annió get well!" I cried out between my sobs. And I cast a reproachful glance at my mother to show her that I knew that she was asking for me to die instead of my sister. Fool that I was, I didn't see that I was heightening her despair by doing this! I believe she forgave me. I was very young then and couldn't understand her heart.

After a few moments of profound silence, she again swung the censer over the objects in front of us and directed all her attention to the water in the large pan on the stool. Suddenly a small moth circled over it, touched the surface with its wings, disturbing it slightly.

My mother bowed piously and made the sign of the cross, as she did when they parade the Host in church. "Cross yourself, my child!" she whispered, deeply moved and not daring to raise her eyes. I obeyed mechanically.

When that small moth disappeared at the other end of the room, my mother took a deep breath, got up happily, and said with satisfaction, "Your father's soul has visited us!" as she continued to follow the flight of the little moth with looks of affection and devotion. Then she drank from the water and gave it to me to drink as well. I recalled then that occasionally in the past she used to have us drink from that same pan as soon as we woke up. And I remembered that every time she did this, she was lively and cheerful all that day, as if she had enjoyed some great but secret happiness.

After she had had me drink, she went over to Annió's bed with the pan in her hands. The sick girl was not sleeping, but she was not entirely awake, either. Her eyelids were half closed; and her eyes, insofar as they were visible, emitted a kind of strange brillance through her thick, black lashes. My mother carefully lifted up the girl's thin body. And while she supported her back with one hand, she offered the pan to her wasted lips with the other.

"Come, my love," she said to her, "drink some of this water to get well." The sick girl didn't open her eyes, but apparently she heard the voice and understood the words. Her lips spread in a lovely, sweet smile. Then she sipped a few drops of the water that was in fact about to cure her. As soon as she had drunk it she opened her eyes and tried to draw a breath. A light sigh escaped her lips, and she fell back heavily against my mother's forearm.

Our poorAnnió! She had escaped her torments!

Many had reproached my mother saying that while unrelated women had wailed loudly over my father's corpse, she alone shed bounteous, but silent, tears. The poor woman did this from fear that she might be misunderstood, that she might overstep the bounds of the decorum appropriate to young women, because, as I said, my mother was widowed very young. She wasn't much older when our sister died. But now she didn't even give a thought to what people would say about her heart-rending lamentations. The entire neighborhood got up and came to console her. But her sorrow was frightful, it was inconsolable.

"She'll go out of her mind," whispered those who saw her bent over and wailing between our father's and our sister's graves. "She'll abandon them to the four winds," said those who met us in the street, forsaken and uncared for. And time was needed, time and the admonitions and reproaches of the church, for her to come to her senses, remember her surviving children and take up her household responsibilities again.

But then she discovered the state in which our sister's long illness had left us. All our money had gone for doctors and medicine. She had sold many woolen coverlets and rugs, works of her own hands, for trifling sums, or she had given them as barter to charlatans and sorceresses. Others they and their ilk had stolen from us, taking advantage of the lack of attention that prevailed in our house. In addition, our supplies of food had also been exhausted, and we no longer had anything to live on.

Instead of daunting my mother, however, this fact rather gave her twice the energy she had had before Annió fell ill. She moderated or, more accurately, concealed, her grief; she overcame the timidity of her age and sex and, taking mattock in hand, she hired herself out as a "hired hand," just as if she had never known a life of ease and independence. For a long time she supported us by the sweat of her brow. Her wages were small and our needs great, yet she refused to allow any of us to work with her and lighten her load.

Plans for our future were formed and reviewed in the evening by the hearth. My older brother was to learn our father's trade so as to take his place in the family. I was destined, or rather wanted, to leave home, and so forth. But prior to this all of us had to learn our letters, to finish school because, as our mother used to say, "illiterate person, unhewn log."

Our money problems reached a peak when a drought hit the area and food prices went up. But our mother, instead of despairing about supporting just us, increased our number by one, an unrelated girl whom she managed to adopt after protracted attempts. That event transformed the monotony and austerity of our family life and introduced some new liveliness.

Even the adoption ceremony was festive. For the first time my mother wore her "Sunday best" and led us to the church clean and combed, as if we were about to take communion. After the service ended we all stood in front of the icon of Christ, and there, in the midst of the surrounding throng, in the presence of its natural parents, my mother received her adopted daughter from the hands of the priest, after first having promised in the hearing of all that she would love and raise it as if it were flesh of her flesh and bone of her bone.

The child's entry into our house was no less impressive and in a way triumphant. The village elder and my mother led the procession with the girl; then we came. Our relatives and our new sister's relatives followed up to our courtyard gate. Outside the gate the elder took the girl in his hands and raised her high above his head, displaying her for a few moments to all present. Then he asked in a loud voice, "Which of you is more relative or family or parent of this child than Michael's wife Despinió and her relatives?"

The girl's father was pale, and, grief-stricken, stared straight ahead. His wife was leaning on his shoulder and weeping. My mother was trembling from fear that some voice might be heard "I!" and would thwart her happiness. But no one answered. Then the child's parents embraced it for the last time and left with their relatives. Our relatives and the elder came in and enjoyed our hospitality.

From that moment our mother began to lavish on our adopted sister attentions such as we had not had the good fortune to obtain at her age and in far happier times. And while I shortly thereafter began my homesick wandering in foreign lands, and my other brothers endured a wretched existence living as apprentices in artisans' workshops, the unrelated girl lorded it in our house as if it were her own.

My brothers' meager wages would have been enough to relieve my mother, and they gave her the money for this reason. But she, instead of spending the money to lighten her load, acquired a dowry with it for her adopted daughter and continued working to support her. I was far, far away, and for many years did not know what was going on in our house. And before I could manage to return, the unrelated girl had grown up, been educated, provided with a dowry, and married, as if she had really been a member of our family.

Her marriage, which it seems was purposely hurried on, was a real "ball" for my brothers. The poor fellows, freed of the added burden, breathed a sigh of relief. And they were right because that girl, aside from the fact that she never felt any sisterly affection for them, in the end proved herself ungrateful to the woman who had looked after her with an affection few legitimate children have known. So my brothers had reasons to be pleased, and they also had reasons to believe their mother had learned her lesson sufficiently from that bad experience. But imagine their consternation when a few days after the wedding they saw her coming into the house tenderly cradling a second girl in her arms, this time in swaddling clothes!

"The poor thing!" our mother exclaimed, bending lovingly over the baby's face. "It's not enough that it was orphaned in the womb, but its mother died, too, and left it in the street!" And, in a way pleased at this unfortunate event, she triumphantly showed off her prize to my brothers, who were speechless in amazement. Filial respect was strong, and my mother's authority great, but my brothers were so disappointed that they didn't hesitate to indicate to their mother, decorously to be sure, that it would be a good idea to give up her plan. But they found her obstinate. Then they openly revealed their displeasure and denied her the use of their purse. All in vain.

"Don't bring me anything," my mother said. "I'll work and I'll take care of her just as I took care of you. And when my Yoryís comes back from abroad, he'll give her a dowry and he'll marry her off. What, you don't believe me? My child promised me that himself. 'Mother, I'll provide for you, both you and your adopted child.' Yes! That's what he said, and may he have my blessing!"

Yoryís was me. And I had actually made that promise, but much earlier. It was during the time that our mother was working to take care of our first adopted sister as well as our selves. I used to go with her during school vacations, playing by her side while she dug or weeded. One day we stopped work early and were coming back from the fields to get away from the unbearable heat that had nearly caused my mother to faint. Along the way we were caught in one of those violent rainstorms that in our region usually occurs after a preceding intense hot spell—or "scorcher," as the natives call it. We weren't very far from the village now, but we had to cross a river bed that had become a violently rushing torrent. My mother wanted to lift me onto her shoulders, but I refused.

"You're weak from the fainting spell," I told her. "You'll drop me in the river." And I hitched up my clothes and ran into the stream before she had a chance to grab me. I had trusted in my strength more than I should have because before I could think to go back, I lost my footing and was bowled over and dragged along by the torrent like a walnut shell. A heart-rending cry of terror is all I remember after that. It was the voice of my mother as she threw herself into the stream to save me.

It's a wonder I wasn't responsible for her drowning as well as my own. That river bed has a bad reputation in those parts, and when they say of someone that "the river got him," they mean that he drowned in that very spot. And yet my mother, faint as she was, exhausted, and weighed down by the native costume that was enough to drown even the most skillful swimmer, did not hesitate to expose her own life to danger. She had to save me, even though I was the child she had once offered to God in exchange for her daughter.

When she got me home and set me down from her shoulder, I was still very dazed. For this reason, instead of blaming my own lack of foresight for what had happened, I attributed it to my mother's labors.

"Don't work any more, *Mana*," I told her while she was putting dry clothes on me.

"Well, my child, who'll take care of us if I don't work?" she asked with a sigh.

"I will, *Mana*! I will!" I answered with childish self-importance.

"And our adopted daughter?"

"Her, too!"

My mother smiled in spite of herself at the impressive pose I assumed in pronouncing this assurance. Then she put an end to the subject by adding, "Well, take care of yourself first, and then we'll see."

Not much later I left home.

I didn't think my mother would even notice that promise. I, however, always remembered that her selflessness had for a second time granted me the life that I owed to her in the first place. For this reason I kept that promise in my heart, and the older I got, the more seriously I thought myself obliged to fulfill it. "Don't cry, Mother," I said to her as I left. "I'm on my way to make money now. You'll see! From now on I'll take care of both you and your adopted daughter. But—do you hear?—I don't want you to work any more!"

I did not yet know that a ten-year-old child, far from being able to take care of his mother, can't even take care of himself. And I didn't imagine what frightful adventures awaited me, and how many bitter draughts I was yet to force my mother to drink during that absence from home by which I had hoped to ease her burden. For many years not only did I not manage to send her any assistance, I didn't even send a single letter. For many years she prowled the streets asking passersby if they had seen me anywhere.

Once they told her I had run into money problems in Constantinople and had turned Turk. "May those who spread that rumor eat their tongue!" my mother said in reply. "The one they're talking about, he can't have been my child!" But after a short while she shut herself up all atremble in front of our iconostasion and with tears running down her face prayed God to enlighten me so I would come back to the faith of my fathers.

Once they told her I had shipwrecked on the shores of Cyprus and was dressed in rags and begging in the streets. "May fire burn them!" she answered. "They're saying that out of jealousy. My child must have made his fortune and is going on a pilgrimage to the Holy Sepulchre in Jerusalem." But after a little while she went out into the streets, questioning the traveling beggars, and she went wherever she heard of a shipwrecked person in the forlorn hope that she would discover in him her own child, with the intent of giving him her last coins in the same way that I found them abroad from the hands of others.

And yet, whenever it was a question of her adopted daughter, she forgot all of this and threatened my brothers, saying that when I came back from abroad, I would put them to shame with my generosity, and I would dower and marry off her daughter with pomp and ceremony. "What? You don't believe me? My child promised me this himself! May he have my blessing!"

Fortunately those dire reports were not true. And when, after a long absence, I returned to our house, I was in a position to fulfill my promise, at least as far as my mother was concerned because she was so frugal. As for her adopted daughter, however, she did not find me so eager as she had hoped. On the contrary, as soon as I arrived, I spoke out against keeping her, to my mother's great surprise.

It's true I was not really opposed to my mother's obsession. I found that her partiality for girls conformed to my own feelings and desires. There was nothing I desired more upon my return than to find in our house a sister whose cheerful face and loving concerns would banish the lonely sadness from my heart, who would erase from memory all the hardships I had suffered abroad. In return I would have been eager to tell her the wonders of foreign lands, my wanderings, and my accomplishments, and I would have been eager to buy her whatever she wanted; to take her to dances and festivals; to dower her; and, finally, to dance at her wedding.

But I imagined that sister pretty and likeable, educated and bright, knowing how to read and embroider—in short with all the accomplishments possessed by the girls of the lands in which I had lived up till then. And instead of all this what did I find? Exactly the opposite. My adopted sister was still young, an emaciated, ill-formed, ill-willed, and above all hostile little girl, so hostile that right from the start she prompted my dislike. "Give Katerinió back," I said to my mother one day. "Give her back, if you love me. I mean it this time! I'll bring you another sister from the City, a pretty girl, a bright one who'll be an ornament to our house one day." Then I described in the most lively colors what the orphan I would bring her would be like, and how much I would love it.

When I raised my eyes to look at her, I saw to my astonishment that large tears were flowing silently down over her pale cheeks, while her downcast eyes expressed an indescribable sorrow! "Oh!" she said in a despairing tone of voice. "I thought you would love

Katerinió more than the others, but I was wrong! They don't want a sister at all, and you want a different one! And how is the poor thing at fault if she was born as God made her? If you had a stupid, ugly sister, would you throw her out into the street for that reason, to get another one who was beautiful and intelligent?"

"No, Mother, surely not," I answered. "But she would be your child, just as I am. But this one isn't anything to you. She's a complete stranger to us."

"No," my mother cried out with a sob, "no! The child isn't a stranger! She's mine! I took her from her mother's dead body when she was three months old; and whenever she cried, I stuck my breast into her mouth to fool her; and I wrapped her in your swaddling clothes, and I put her to bed in your cradle. She's my child, and she's your sister!"

After these words which she uttered forcefully and impressively, she raised her head and fixed her eyes on me. She awaited my answer belligerently. But I did not dare say a word. Then she lowered her eyes again and continued in a weak and mournful tone: "Eh! What can be done? I wanted her better, too, but . . . my sin, you see, hasn't been lifted yet. And God has made her like this to test my endurance and to forgive me. I thank you, oh Lord." And with this she placed her right hand on her breast, raised her tear-filled eyes to heaven, and remained silent in this position for several moments.

"You must have something weighing on your heart, Mother," I said somewhat timidly. "Don't be angry."

I took her cold hand in mine and kissed it to appease her.

"Yes!" she said decisively. "I do have something heavy inside me, something very heavy, my child! Up till now only God and my confessor has known about it. You've read a lot and sometimes talk like my confessor himself, even better. Get up, close the door, and sit while I tell you. Perhaps you'll provide me a little consolation, perhaps you'll feel sorry for me and come to love Katerinió as if she were your sister."

These words, and the manner in which she pronounced them, threw my heart into great confusion. What had my mother to entrust to me and not to my brothers? She had told me all she'd suffered while I was away. All her life before that I knew as if it were a fairy tale. So what was it she had been keeping from us up till now? What had she not dared to reveal to anyone except God and her confessor? When I came over and sat down next to her, my legs were shaking from a vague but powerful fear.

My mother hung her head as a condemned person does when facing his judge in the consciousness of some awful crime.

"Do you remember our Annió?" she asked after a few moments of oppressive silence.

"Yes, Mother, of course I remember her! She was our only sister, and she died before my very eyes."

"Yes," she said with a deep sigh, "but she wasn't my only girl! You're four years younger than Hristákis. A year after he was born I had my first daughter.

"It was about the time Fótis Mylonás was wanting to get married. Your late father delayed their wedding until I had completed my forty days after delivery so we could give them away together. He also wanted to take me out in public so I could have the good time as a married woman that your grandmother hadn't allowed me as a girl.

"The wedding took place in the morning, and in the evening everybody was invited to their house. There was violin music, and everybody ate in the courtyard, and the wine jug passed from hand to hand. And your late father was in a good mood, fun-loving man that he was, and he threw me his handkerchief to get up and dance with him. When I saw him dancing, my heart opened up to him and, being a young woman, I, too, loved to dance. So we danced, and the others danced on our heels. But we danced both better and more.

"When it got close to midnight I took your father aside and said to him: 'Husband, I have a baby in the cradle and can't stay any longer. The baby's hungry; I'm full of milk. How can I feed it in public and in my good clothes? You stay if you want and have a good time. I'll take the baby and go home.' 'Eh, very well, wife!' he said, God bless his soul, and he patted me on the shoulder. 'Come, dance this dance with me, and then we'll both go home. The wine's begun to go to my head, and I'm looking for a reason to leave, too.'

"When we had danced that dance, we set out. The groom sent the players, and they escorted us half-way. But we had a long way to go to the house because the wedding took place in *Karsimahalá* on the other side of town. The servant went ahead with the lantern. Your father carried the baby, and also supported me on his arm.

"'You're tired, I see, wife,'

"'Yes, Mihalió, I'm tired.'

"'Come on, just a little more strength until we get home. I'll lay out the beds myself. I'm sorry I made you dance so much.'

"'No matter, husband,' I told him. 'I did it to please you. Tomorrow I'll be rested again.'

"So we arrived home. I swaddled and fed the child while he laid out the beds. Hristákis was sleeping with Venetía, whom I had left to watch him. In a little while we went to bed, too. There, in my sleep, I thought I heard the baby begin to cry. The poor thing, I thought; it hasn't had enough to eat today. And I leaned over its crib to suckle it. But I was too tired and couldn't hold myself up. So I took it out and laid it on the mattress beside me and put the nipple in its mouth. Then sleep took hold of me again.

"I don't know how long it was till morning, but when I felt that day was breaking—'Better put the baby back again,' I said. But when I went to pick it up, what did I see? The baby didn't move! I woke your father up. We unswaddled it, we warmed it, we rubbed its little nose—nothing! It was dead!

"'You smothered my baby, woman!' said your father and he burst into tears. Then I began to cry out and wail, too. But your father put his hand on my mouth and said, 'Shush! Why are you bellowing like that, you ox?' That's what he said to me, God forgive him. We'd been married three years, and he'd never said a harsh word to me. But he said one then. 'Eh? Why are you bellowing like this? Do you want to rouse the neighborhood so that everybody can say you got drunk and smothered your baby?'

"And he was right, God bless the dust that covers him! Because if people found out, I would have had to split the earth and enter it out of shame. But what can you do? A sin is a sin. When we had buried the child and come back from the church, then the formal mourning began. Then at last I did not cry in secret. 'You're young,' they told me, 'and you'll have others.' But time passed and God didn't give us one. 'There!' I said to myself. 'God is punishing me because I wasn't worthy to take care of the child he gave me.' And I felt ashamed in the company of others and was afraid of your father because all that first year he pretended not to be sad, and tried to comfort me so as to give me courage. Later, however, he began to fall silent and thoughtful.

"Three years passed—without eating bread that could go to my heart. But after these three years you were born. You can imagine the thank-offerings I made. When you were born my heart settled down but did not find peace. Your father wanted you a girl and one day he told me so: 'This one is welcome, too, Despinió, but I wanted it to be a girl.'

"When your grandmother went to the Holy Sepulchre, I sent twelve shirts and three *Konstantináta* with her to get me a pardon. And just look! The month your grandmother came back from Jerusalem with the pardon, that very month I began to be pregnant with Annió.

"I called the midwife frequently. 'Come here, lady, and let's have a look. Is it a girl?' 'Yes, daughter,' said the midwife. 'A girl. Don't you see? Your clothes aren't big enough for you!' What joy I felt when I heard this! When the baby was born and turned out actually to be a girl, then my heart finally returned to its proper place. We named it Annió, the same name the dead girl had, so it wouldn't seem that anybody was missing from our house. 'Thank you, Lord,' I said night and day. 'This sinner thanks you because you have lifted my shame and blotted out my sin.'

"And we loved Annió more than life itself. And you were jealous, and could have died from your jealousy. Your father called you 'his wronged one' because I weaned you so soon, and he yelled at me every once in a while for neglecting you. My heart was torn apart when I saw you wasting away. But, you see, I couldn't let Annió out of my hands! I was afraid that at any moment something might happen to her. And your father, God rest his soul, no matter how often he yelled at me, he, too, was very protective of her.

"But the poor child, the more attention she got, the worse her health became. You'd think God had regretted giving her to us. You all were ruddy and lively and active. She was quiet and silent and sickly. When I saw her so pale, so very pale, the dead girl came to my mind, and the thought that I had killed her began to take over within me again. Until one day the second one died, too!

"Whoever hasn't experienced it himself, my child, doesn't know what a bitter draught that was. There was no hope I would have another girl. Your father had died. If there hadn't been some parent to give me his girl, I would have taken to the hills and run away. It's true she didn't turn out good-natured. But as long as I had her and took care of her and cherished her, I thought I had my own, and I forgot the one I'd lost, and I calmed my conscience. As the saying goes, another's child is a torture. But for me this torture is a consolation and relief because the more I'm tormented and torn apart, the less God will punish me for the child I smothered.

"And so—and may you have my blessing—don't ask me now to get rid of Katerinió and get another good-natured and industrious child."

"No, no, Mother!" I cried out, interrupting her impetuously. "I don't ask for anything. After what you've told me I beg your pardon for my heartlessness. I promise you I'll love Katerinió as my sister and will never say anything harsh to her again."

"May you have the blessings of Christ and the Virgin!" my mother said with a sigh, "because, you see, my heart is filled with pity for the poor child, and I don't want them to say bad things about her. I don't know, you see. Was it fate? Was it God's doing? No matter how bad and slow she is, I'm responsible," she concluded.

This revelation made a profound impression on me. Now my eyes were opened, and now I understood many of my mother's actions that had at some times seemed like superstition, at others purely the results of obsession. That frightful accident had had all the greater influence on my mother's entire life because she was unsophisticated and virtuous and God-fearing. The consciousness of her sin, the moral necessity of expiation and the impossibility of expiation—what a horrible and implacable Hell! The poor woman had been tormented for twenty-eight years now without being able to put to rest the reproaches of her conscience either in good times or in bad.

From the moment I learned her sad story I directed all my attention to lightening her heart by trying to represent to her on the one hand the unpremeditated and involuntary nature of her sin, and on the other God's extreme compassion and His justice, which does not requite like with like, but judges us according to our thoughts and intentions. And there was a time when I believed my attempts were not without success.

Nonetheless, when, after a new absence of two years, my mother came to see me in Constantinople, I thought it a good idea to do something still more impressive on her behalf. At that time I was a guest in the most distinguished house in Constantinople, in which I had occasion to become acquainted with the Patriarch Ioakím II. While we were walking alone one day under the spreading shade of the trees in the garden, I laid out the story to him and asked his assistance. His high office, the remarkable authority in which his every religious pronouncement was clad, would surely inspire the conviction in my mother that her sin had been pardoned. That old man of blessed memory praised my zeal in religious matters and promised me his eager cooperation.

So after a little while I took my mother to the Patriarchate to confess to his Holiness. The confession lasted a long time, and from the Patriarch's gestures and words I saw that he was being compelled to use all the force of his plain, clear eloquence in order to bring about the desired result. My joy was indescribable. My mother bade the venerable Patriarch farewell with sincere gratitude, and came out of the Patriarchate as happy and as buoyant as if a large millstone had been removed from her heart.

When we reached her lodging, she took a cross out of her bosom, a gift from his Holiness, kissed it, and began to examine it carefully, little by little sinking deeper into thought.

"A good man, the Patriarch, don't you think?" I said. "Now at last, I imagine, your heart has returned to its proper place."

My mother didn't answer.

"Haven't you anything to say, Mother?" I asked with some hesitation.

"What can I tell you, my child?" she answered, still deep in thought. "The Patriarch is a wise and holy man. He knows all God's plans and wishes, and he pardons everybody's sins. But what can I tell you? He's a monk. He never had children, so he can't know what a thing it is to kill one's own child!"

Her eyes filled with tears, and I said nothing.

Between Peiraeus and Naples

Introduction

The story is set on a ship traveling between Peiraeus and Naples, and all the action takes place on board. The narrator meets a young girl whom he knew seven or more years earlier in Constantinople. Though both are traveling to Paris, the narrator is going only as far as Naples by ship because of his dislike and fear of the sea. The time is some indeterminate present, but we learn that the narrator, a poet of at least some renown, had been in Germany for some time prior to the dramatic date of the story. Vizyenos himself studied in Germany, and also traveled to Paris (in 1882), so up to this point, at least, the careers of narrator and author coincide. We have, of course, no way of knowing whether there are other coincidences as well; one is rather inclined to doubt there are significant ones. Vizyenos was also a poet, and in this story we have examples of his poetic activity: two of his early poems are quoted from memory by the young girl, and two prose poems—one to the setting sun, one to Vesuvius—form part of the plot of the story.

The folk element is lacking from this story, and its place is taken by classical and literary allusions to the sea-nymph, Glaukothea,[1] the goddess, Aphrodite, the Tritons, who were half-human sea creatures, and to the myth of the Tyrrhenian (Etruscan) merchants changed into dolphins by Dionysus (Bacchus). Typhon, a mythical monster thought to be pinned under a volcano (usually Mt. Etna), Ixion, forever spinning on a wheel in Hades for his attempted rape of Hera, Laélapes, spirits of storms, and the Sirens fill out the classical mythical picture. Classical allusions also include Croesus, the fabulously wealthy king of the Lydians.

---

1. There is no such ancient nymph, and Vizyenos must have mistakenly used this (quite plausible) name in place of the correct Leukothea, or Ino, daughter of Cadmus and helper of Odysseus in the *Odyssey* (5.334).

Geographical descriptions are primarily of Naples. The young girl, Másinga, however, recalls happy times she and the narrator had had in Constantinople, and a number of places are mentioned in this connection: Therapeiá, where Másinga's aunt lived; the monument to the Greek; and Tokát, the ancient Eudokia, a city in Asia Minor. The only reference to Athens is to Patisíon Street, the main artery running north out of Omónia Square. The narrator reflects that his days in Constantinople were the only happy days of his life, days spent before traveling to Germany. Vizyenos had, of course, himself spent a good deal of time in Constantinople, and if we are to identify narrator and Vizyenos, he must be referring to when he was a theological student on Hálki, one of the Prince's Islands, in 1872–1873. His first collection of poems was published in Constantinople at the beginning of 1873.

There is very little action in the story, though there is some self-deprecating humor and some rather vicious satire. We learn of the fate of the young girl and about her father's passion for poetry and his insensitivity to others, including his daughter; but again, the main point of the story is the narrator's own impressions and reactions, impressions and reactions that may strike the reader as self-centered and naive. Many regard this work as the author's weakest effort in story-writing, but it has a good deal of charm both in the narrator's candor about his own foolishness and in his sympathetic descriptions of the young girl.

Between Peiraeus
and Naples

Rio Grande was the ship's name, and the name fitted the thing: it was a large ship, the company's largest. It had arrived in Peiraeus later than scheduled. The sun had long since risen when it took on its passengers from Greece, although, according to the schedule, it ought to have left the harbor two hours after midnight.

Though I belong to that tribe of men who don't feel easy with the sea, when I set foot on the deck of that colossus, I felt a sort of fearlessness towards the watery element very like the insolence of the goat in the well-known fable to whose taunts the wolf replied: "It's not you who taunt me but the place."

More self-confident than the wolf, the sea didn't even notice my presumption. I, however, did not attribute its silence to its contempt but rather to its lack of power. The still waters of the harbor appeared to me to have lost their suppleness because of the enormous weight that pressed upon their bosom. And in the unshaken conviction that we would have a smooth sail, I successively directed tender looks at the *Rio Grande* and challenging ones at the waves. "Aha!" I said to them mentally. "You won't be able to wrap my friend here around your finger the way you do the local steamers." And secure in this conviction I began to walk steadfastly along the length of the deck.

I was to sail as far as Naples, and since we were doubtless to have good weather, I began to scrutinize my fellow passengers to see if I might find acquaintances or people suitable to strike up an acquaintance with. The voyage is long, I thought, and I'll have ample time both to enjoy the beauties of nature alone by myself and to associate with people as well. And while I was thinking thus, I spied a short man walking swiftly in the direction opposite to my own. He was wearing a low traveling cap on his head, and his eyes were fixed lovingly on the tip of the fat cigar, which he was drawing on while holding it, as it seemed to me, between his lips and teeth. "I've seen that man somewhere before," I said to myself, and I made ready to greet him. But he was totally preoccupied with his cigar and didn't notice me.

All the ship's cranes had ceased their racket save one, and it was continuing to lift trunk after trunk of different shapes and sizes on board. All were marked with the same initials, and all were carefully enclosed in waterproof containers of the same color. It appeared that some Athenian Jacob with his sons and daughters, his daughters-in-law and sons-in-law, his grandchildren and his great-grandchildren, was departing for a permanent sojourn abroad. "Lucky those who managed to get berths!" I said to myself, and I felt curious to know what numerous family it was that must consist of at least thirty adults if we suppose that there was one trunk for each of them. No such dense retinue had appeared on deck, however. I went down to the cabins at the same time to check whether I still had my berth, but neither there nor in the ship's luxurious lounge was there anything suggesting a crowd.

"Very well," I said. "After their luggage has been loaded, the army will not be long in boarding. We'll see it for sure." And I was making ready to go back up on deck when I heard the light footsteps of a woman coming down the stair, sweetly singing a lively and cheerful song to the rhythm of her footsteps. I had barely had a chance to determine the nationality of the language when I found myself face to face with the singer—not a woman, as I had imagined, but a boyish creature of barely fourteen, it seemed, a girl to judge more by her clothes than from her face and expression.

"Good morning, Jug!" the young girl cried out when she saw me, and she playfully and charmingly extended her right hand to me. I was thunderstruck at the strange greeting.

"I bet you don't remember me any more!" the girl stammered out in embarrassment, and withdrew her hand from my own, evidently regretting the indiscreet familiarity with which she had offered it.

"Good morning, Mademoiselle!" . . . I answered in the meantime, even more embarrassed than she and examining her face with curiosity.

"Of course," the girl said, pouting in the manner of small, spoiled children, "it's been a long time. It's many years now since I've been in the City, in Therapeiá. And I took one of your hands and my cousin took the other, and we made a 'jug with two ears,' and hanging in this way, one on one side, the other on the other, we walked to the edge of the Bosporus in the moonlight. At least you remember our outing to the Monument to the Greek on the top of the mountain opposite? And the fun we had at the expense of that old gypsy woman who came to read our fortunes? And she took my aunt for your wife and me for your daughter? And do you remember we went down afterwards to Tokát and visited the palace? And do you remember the lines you wrote for me? Or do you want me to say them to you? Listen:

> Where the sun gleams gold,
> all other stars refuse to shine;
> Where like a rose-bud you unfold,
> all other flowers I decline."

"Yes, yes, yes! I remember!" I cried out, preventing her from continuing my youthful attempts at verse. "And so you must be Mademoiselle . . ."

"I'm not Mademoiselle," the girl interrupted with childish indignation, "I'm Másinga!"

"Really," I said, "Másinga! The lively, pretty girl! How you've grown! And how beautifully you speak Greek now! I wouldn't have thought it possible that you could unlearn your English pronunciation. Good for you! You're a true Greek now!"

"I studied in Athens, you see," the young girl said with some pride. "I was a student at Madame K.'s for three years."

"Three years in Athens and I didn't know it?"

"And what did it matter to you to learn it? Come off it! You concern yourself about a crazy little girl, as you called me!" Then staring fixedly at me, she exclaimed: "He pretends he didn't know! And didn't you see me day before yesterday at Madame M.'s soirée?"

"So!" I said. "You were there?"

"Yes I was! And didn't you have a long conversation with my father? And didn't he give you his calling card with our address in Calcutta on it?"

"Stupid of me," I exclaimed, "not to realize that he was your father! Believe me, the name seemed familiar, but I didn't realize that it had to be your father. It was stupid of me not to look for you among the girls."

"You weren't stupid," said the girl, drawing her voice out in an ironic drawl, "but you were much too occupied with the ladies. Bah!"

And she uttered that contemptuous exclamation against 'the ladies' with the same childish candor and impertinence with which she always used to express herself about other people when she was a guest in her aunt's house on the shores of the Bosporus.

At least seven years must have passed since I had met her there, a small, very charming and playful little girl. Life's intervening concerns and cares had not, as one might perhaps think, dimmed her image in my memory. The short period during which we came to be acquainted was and probably will remain the only happy time of my life. Thereafter, exiled far from our cloudless skies, lacking friends and acquaintances, imprisoned behind the ice-covered windows of an inhospitable Germany, whenever I called to mind those idyllic scenes of happiness beside the Bosporus, I could not omit from them their most beautiful jewel, the face of my small friend, so full of life, innocence, and charm. And when I returned after many years of exile, I found everything changed, everything different; and whenever, alone and gloomy, I visited those places of children and gaiety, it was only the picture of Másinga that I found in them faithful and unchanged because she alone was not there to replace the picture in my mind's eye with a dry reality.

Today I had the original of that picture before me. But that original had in the meantime turned out very different from the image I had of it, more different than grown people generally are from pictures taken of them at an early age. That totally delicate and tender child with the inexpressibly delightful and bewitching face—her short curly locks resting on her bare shoulders and her slender arms constantly in motion—had been transformed into a stocky, boyish girl, whose masculine and impudent face expressed anything but the modest sweetness and unpretentious charm of the girlish face I remembered. In contrast to this, two thick, long braids elegantly tied with a blue ribbon provided the young girl's back with the proudest adornment of the womanly body, while her small and carefully gloved arms were weighed down by two or three valuable bracelets; valuable, too, was the pin that flashed through the narrow opening in her coat. I knew that her father, an Asia Minor Greek but married to an Englishwoman, was an immensely wealthy man and that he served in a high and very lucrative position with the English government in Calcutta. The sight of that golden weight on the arms of the not yet fully grown girl recalled the overly Anglicized Croesus to my mind.

"And so, Másinga," I asked, "is your father traveling on the same ship? I think I saw him on deck with a fat cigar in his mouth and with a cap on his head. And you've come to see him off of course, haven't you?"

"Fortunately not," said the girl. "I'm leaving with him and my mother. They've come to get me."

"Oh! That's an unexpected pleasure!" I said. "I would never have believed I'd have such luck on this voyage."

"Really? Do you really reckon it a pleasure," asked the girl, tilting her head to one side and eyeing me somewhat suspiciously, "or are you only saying that to flatter me? Look here, we'll be traveling together to Marseilles because you're going to Paris, too, or so I've heard."

"What an idea!" I said reproachfully. "To think that I'm trying to flatter you. Only it's too bad I didn't get a ticket to Marseilles! I would never have believed I'd have such company, and—I must admit—I didn't know we'd have such a large and solid ship. But I'll book a continuation from Naples on. I'll be sure to book it! Unless, that is, that vast population that will inundate the rooms will force you to disembark at Naples, too."

"What vast population?"

"Why, this deportation to Babylon. Haven't you seen the innumerable trunks they're bringing on board? I counted forty on deck, and I think there must be as many again in the lighter. I tried to learn whose they are, but it seems that the 'rag, tag and bobtail' haven't arrived yet."

"But those are ours!" the girl exclaimed, accompanying her exclamation with a resounding and oddly sweet and harmonious laugh. "There aren't any more passengers. The captain told me: we're off as soon as our trunks are on board."

"And how many are you, then?" I asked in great surprise.

"Three!" said the girl carelessly. "Three plus the servants."

"And how many servants do you have, then?"

"Ah! To tell you the truth I haven't counted them. I was in school till a week ago. But I know father has many servants. Let's go ask him how many!" And taking me suddenly by the hand she went up the ladder in a flash with me following before I had a chance to think. Her father was in fact the gentleman whom I'd recognized as an acquaintance striding the length of the deck with swift, short steps. We found him still walking, as always quickly, his hands as always behind him, his eyes lovingly fixed on the tip of his cigar, half of which now was nothing more than a white ash firmly attached to the unburned section and preserving the shape of the fat cigar. And it seemed this pleased the smoker because before removing his eyes from the tip of the cigar when he heard his daughter's voice, he carefully took the cigar with one hand and held it in such a way as to prevent the ash's falling.

I had already met Mr. P., as I've said, at Madame M.'s soirée, not, however, as my young friend's father, but as an immensely wealthy Calcuttan, who made the greater impression on me because he was unexpectedly attentive and complimentary to me, especially, as he said, because of my poetic "gift." Our second acquaintance filled the gap in the first and at the same time heightened my pleasure because of the flattering attentions he constantly lavished on me because, as he said, of my poetic "gift."

"Never was there a finer voyage," I said to myself when we parted, "a wealthy admirer, an old but very young friend, and a mountain of a ship that even the greatest tempest will not be able to budge." And in this conviction I began to pace with firm stride, happily watching the ship's proud course as, having in the meantime weighed anchor, it left the narrows of Peiraeus harbor.

*****

How many, I wonder, had come proudly onto the deck of that fortress that same morning, as I had, with their heart filled with that same conviction? And how many were not shortly forced to empty all that pride into the receptacles provided for the purpose? I at least was not slow to admit that there is not a ship in the world that doesn't dance to the tune the winds pipe and doesn't leap to the rhythm the waves beat, for, contrary to all expectation, the huge mass of the *Rio Grande* proved the lightest dancer among liners! It was, to be sure, a long, tall ship, but it was accordingly very narrow. And the sea "moves" narrow ships, as the experts say, especially when they have the wind against them as ours did!

I do not pray for a voyage under such conditions for the sensitive and easily affected. On the other hand, I do recommend it to malicious satirists and mockers, because nowhere else can they satisfy their spiteful nature in a more Aristotelian manner than by the safe but tragic sight of seasick men and women.

Here they will come upon a swaggering general. This robust and athletic man has faced death countless times in the tumult of revolts and battles, and has scorned it with that dignified pride natural to his calling. But now? Now, pitiable and humiliated, he "hunkers down" in the spot he considers safest, his cabin, pale and terrified and trembling from fright lest even his most gentle movement may again incite and irritate the sickening revolt of his own intestines.

There they will come upon a coquettish traveler. Until just a few minutes before, her admirers had still been buzzing around her. Her artful charms were so many snares for them. The deck was the huge shell on which the goddess Aphrodite was carried in triumph, slavishly attended by the Tritons, half-animal by nature, or by the Tyrrhenian merchants turned into animals through the wonder-working power of Bacchus and later called dolphins. But now? Now the triumphant beauty has been hurriedly snatched from her open-air throne and plunged into the dark flanks of Leviathan, into some stifling corner of Dante's *Inferno* where she experiences the twisting torments of an Ixion because of the foul winds in her own intestines. And she is angry and she despairs and she cries, not repenting because of her sins, but because the spasmodic convulsions, the tragic contractions and expansions of her face make her appear to the mirror opposite so ugly, so frightfully ugly!

They will doubtless encounter one who is not absent from any voyage, the disdainful one who doesn't fear the sea! He is the big talker, one whom "the sea doesn't affect" as long as the ship is at anchor, but who after a few hours' sail becomes dumber than the fish, milder than a lamb, but is still circumspect enough not to go down to his cabin where his neighbors' constant exhortations will soon force him also to take the lead in their tragicomic concert, and at that more passionately than they would have expected. And how many, many other characters wouldn't our scoffers and mockers be able to encounter in a pitching ship!

I myself do not envy their inhuman occupation, nor do I rejoice at the unbearable ordeals of my friends, my fellow passengers. I only express my personal indignation at an imperfection in human nature that, however trivial it may be, nonetheless is accompanied by serious disadvantages. Apart from the fact that it frustrates many intentions and plans for a pleasant use of time, apart from the fact that it blocks so many favorable opportunities for the forming of friendships and acquaintances, it deprives the sensitive traveler of many special, aesthetic enjoyments.

One of the greatest of these enjoyments is the magnificent sight of a tempest on the open sea. Philosophers never fail to adduce it as an example of the Sublime in their Aesthetics; and I cannot recall now what painter or poet it was who, traveling in a frightful tempest, begged the captain to bind him tightly to the tossing ship's half-shattered mast so that he could, without being snatched away by wind or waves, delight his soul with the highest spiritual enjoyment that God, for all his omnipotence, would shortly no longer be able to provide in the other world! As for the philosophers, I'm quite sure that they have never admired a tempest themselves, not even from the safety of shore. To that artist, moreover, I say: "Whoever you are, give thanks to God that he formed you with intestines less sensitive than others' are. 'Just once get seasick' and I'd see whether you wouldn't rather let the waves snatch you and drown you so as to be freed from your torments one hour sooner." I say this to you, I who during that voyage survived to hear an eighty-year-old woman renowned for her zest for living reproaching a god-fearing archbishop because he wouldn't acquiesce in what she sought of him as her confessor—namely, to throw her into the sea!

Since such things happened during my voyage, one can easily see that all my intentions, all my hopes and plans were frustrated. Not only was I unable to enjoy the beauties of nature, not only did I not contract new acquaintances, I did not see my very wealthy admirer again nor his merry daughter, my little friend. Only her voice, or rather her musical laughter, could I hear from time to time through the curtain of my door as she passed through the hall.

From the very first moment, Másinga's laugh created an oddly sweet impression on my hearing. Never did I hear a young girl laugh so melodiously, so harmoniously. Never did I know a laugh that contained so much expression, so much rhetorical accuracy and variety. The rest of us laugh as geese cackle, almost identically in every situation. In that girl's laugh you could discern not only its cause on each occasion, but also all the phases of the emotional state from which it originated and by which it was accompanied. You'd think that in her the task of laughing was not entrusted to the body's physical nerves and physiological motions, but was accomplished from beginning to end by the soul itself on the strings of some mysterious, harmonious instrument that made the girl's laugh more expressive, more musical, more ethereal than any articulate voice or rational tongue.

This phenomenon stood in clear contrast to the girl's exterior characteristics. As rough and as masculine as was her facial expression, so delicate and so wondrously feminine was her soul revealed to be in her laugh. When you saw her, you behaved towards her as you would to an immature child; when you heard her, you were compelled to imagine her as the sole ideal of mature maidenly perfection.

And so it happened from the moment I shut myself up in my cabin that I began to see and admire my little friend with my ears rather than my eyes. And it soon turned out that my ears did not agree in any way with my eyes either as regards the girl's age or her education or her experience of life. And it turned out that the ears were more accurate than the eyes. Many of the girl's words and phrases, which I had till then taken to be literal expressions of childish naivete, were found to be susceptible of metaphorical interpretation, wondrously suited to give the conditions in which they were uttered a quite different and much more weighty meaning. Her years as reckoned on my fingers proved to be seventeen and not fourteen; logic and arithmetic sided with the ears rather than the eyes; and her laugh, her silvery laugh, in the midst of the uproar of the waters, the clanking of chains, the officers' whistles, the passengers' cries and moans, her heavenly laugh was carried out over the waters like the breath of God, calming the insubordinate elements and sweetening the sleep of my suffering head.

*****

I didn't know where we were when the wind dropped and a kind of calm followed, but it was evening; that I could see from the sun's position, and from its position, I could see that in a little while we would have a beautiful and magnificent sunset. So I went up on deck as soon as I could.

A kind of misanthropic feeling had settled into my heart; a bitter, indescribably emotional complaint was on my lips. It was the complaint of a sick, loving child towards its only mother, Nature, into whose arms it is drawn by innate love just after having suffered the harshest consequences of her fickle character. So I was in a most elegiac mood. I sat apart and alone, breathing in the invigorating evening breeze and gazing fixedly towards the west, and allowing the images of my imagination to move as they willed. The sun, proud monarch of the skies, was growing larger the closer it came to the waves, and it was assuming a more and more magnificent appearance, spreading its royal purple about itself with obviously increasing show. The clouds, reddish from the impressive presence of their lord, respectfully drew in the golden hems of their black robes, like officers receiving the secret password for the night from the mouth of the king. The Hero has accomplished the tasks set him and is now headed down to rule in the Ogress's realm, taking her daughter who had been promised to him as his reward. His bath is ready and his dinner prepared. But before the golden gate of the palace closes behind them, he takes his final thoughts about his own kingdom and his subjects: he gives the requisite orders to the clouds gathered before him—"You take your water sacs and run to Egypt. The people there have planted trees. The trees have asked for rain. You know my weakness for trees: I can't bear to see them thirsty. You fill your pitchers and fly to Athens. The improvident city authorities haven't yet taken care to furnish sufficient water for the city; the thoughtless citizens throw refuse onto the streets and vacant lots; the stagnant air is filled with noxious exhalations and dust: intestinal typhus will break out soon, and the thoughtless people of Athens will be blaming me and those about me for deaths for which they themselves are solely responsible. Go! Bring rain and postpone the evil if only for our reputation's sake!"—And behold, the clouds bent down to the sea and, filling their water sacs and pitchers, were carried on the wings of the winds in opposite directions, becoming heavier and blacker as they receded.

"I do exactly the same thing myself!" someone behind me exclaimed, thus destroying the silent images of my imagination. It was Mr. P., with his hands as always clasped behind his back, his eyes as always lovingly fixed on the tip of his cigar, but standing still now. "I do exactly the same thing myself," he said, "but when I'm in Calcutta. When I'm not in Calcutta, I travel, and when I travel, I can't stand still." And without taking his eyes from the tip of his cigar he again threw himself into his usual motion, his hands as always clasped behind his back.

I must observe here that no one on the ship had seen Mr. P. sitting still, save at the dining table, and that I was perhaps the first to see him still for even a few seconds. From the moment he set foot on deck he began to move as if he were the ball of a pendulum condemned to cover in a precisely defined time the long distance between bow and stern, regularly and without cease. It would be a very pretty problem for a mathematician to determine how often on that voyage Mr. P. had covered the distance between Peiraeus and Marseilles on foot, though he had paid the company to assign this task to one of its ships.

Many Englishmen have this habit; one will frequently encounter them sailing through the Bosporus or along the coast of Asia Minor, in swift motion on the steamship, their eyes fixed on their guidebook. Mr. P. perhaps differed from them in that while they admire the beauties of the lands through which they pass in the descriptions in their book, Mr. P. literally saw nothing but the tip of his cigar, no matter where he traveled.

Mr. P.'s assertion that he couldn't stand still when he traveled was unnecessary. Anyone who saw him had to draw this conclusion. But I couldn't understand what he meant when he said that he too did the same thing when he was in Calcutta, and I didn't ask him in time. So when, in his marathon, he came back to the spot where I was sitting, I got up and fell in beside him, and, "Pardon me, Mr. P.," I said, "but I didn't completely understand what you told me."—And I began running after, rather than walking with, him.

"I meant," he answered, his eyes as always lovingly fixed on the end of his cigar, "I meant that I, too, do exactly the same thing. I do exactly the same thing when I want to think. And when I want to think, this is what I do: I direct my gaze upwards, I fix my eyes on the clouds, and I look, look, look until ideas come down as if they were a poem. As if they were a poem, because you, too, were certainly writing a poem. You were certainly writing a poem on the sunset. You cannot know how much I admire you, how much I admire you for your poetic 'gift.' "

"If he knew," I thought to myself, "how far the value of that coin has slipped with us today, he would thank God that He had given him English pounds and not the wealth of expression and poetic talent."

"I," Mr. P. continued, "I give myself over to thought very often, but I give myself over to thought very often when I'm in Calcutta. When I'm not in Calcutta, I travel, and when I travel, I cannot stand still!" And he increased the speed of his step as if he wished to express his feet's passion in their own swifter tongue. "Besides," Mr. P. continued, "what can I tell you? What can I tell you since there's nothing poetic? There's nothing poetic here because there's nothing natural. And where there's no nature," said Mr. P. with dogmatic emphasis, "there's no poetry."

"True," I said, approving the axiom, but holding Mr. P. responsible for the second term of his syllogism because he did not find nature except at the end of his cigar.

"Calcutta's another matter!" exclaimed Mr. P. all the more warmly and, in the manner of steam engines, all the more rapidly, in such a way that I could scarcely keep up with him. "Calcutta's another matter because there's nature there. There's nature there because there are plants, trees, forests, mountains, waters, comforts, and enjoyments. Do you understand?"

"I understand," I said with some emphasis because it appeared that Mr. P. doubted whether I was quick enough to comprehend his eloquence.

"Here everything's dry," he continued, "because everything is bare, old, exhausted, small, coarse. For that reason Calcutta's something else! Calcutta's something else!"

"It really must be something else," I said. "I'd like very much to get to know it."

"Nothing simpler!" exclaimed Mr. P., turning his eyes towards me for the first time. "Nothing simpler! Come visit me! Come visit me, nothing simpler!"

And Mr. P. so quickened his pace that I, who for some time had been running after him rather than walking beside him, was compelled to collapse into the first seat we came across before having the chance to thank him, because that violent motion suddenly dizzied my head and made my step uncertain and unsteady. Mr. P. noticed this, but, you see, "when he travels he cannot stand still." So he continued his marathon alone.

"Strange mixture of natures!" I said to myself a little later, unconsciously borrowing the expression from the condition (or rather confusion) that prevailed inside me. The nature of the hospitable Anatolian with his love for green grass, shady trees, flourishing plants, sweet-smelling flowers, the babbling of waters around his ivy-covered pavilion, the nature of the sensitive Anatolian who travels dragging behind him a caravan of servants and trucks all full of products of his country that he does not intend to be deprived of when he moves, this nature has been mixed up with the nature of the cool, eccentric Englishman who cannot stand still when he travels, who finds everything small, insignificant, and meaningless outside of his homeland because he doesn't take the trouble to raise his eyes from the tip of his cigar to see the nature or art about him, and who in his self-centeredness invites you from Athens to visit him—where?—in Calcutta! To travel three months in order to spend three minutes with him. Do you have time to waste or money to burn? He doesn't even think about that. He derives a fabulous annual income, and "when he's not in Calcutta, he travels." So he regards it as natural for one to spend thousands of pounds and to endure two months of seasickness in order to go to squeeze the hand of My Lord. And he will perhaps regard it as an insult if you don't accept. And if you do accept, and if you find that My Lord is traveling to the North Pole the instant you're knocking on his door in Calcutta, be assured that he's apt to regard your visit as obligated in any event, as long as from the manner in which you left your calling card there is lacking even the slightest of those English formalities unknown to us!

And while I was thinking these things, Mr. P. came and went

before me, his hands as always clasped behind him, his eyes as always fixed on the tip of the cigar in his mouth, and with a stride that made impossible the continuation of our interrupted conversation.

Not much time had elapsed, however, before Másinga appeared running towards me, lively and laughing. After a few jokes and sarcastic references to my fear of the sea, "Did you hear me?" she asked, "how I was always laughing out loud? I did it on purpose. You don't know how funny the doctor is. Whatever he says will keep you in stitches. And since Mother is a little unwell, and since, he says, he likes my laugh, he never left our cabin the whole time. Did you hear him and how he made me laugh?"

"No," I said. "Him I didn't hear, but I heard you, and my delight was all the greater. You don't know how musical your voice seemed to me, how beautiful!"

"Scoundrel!" the girl exclaimed with an expression of disbelief on her face. "So since you want to flatter me, hear what I have to say. I, too, heard you once or twice, but to tell the truth it wasn't a great delight because the music you made was frightfully dissonant! Does this please you? If it does, flatter me again!"

And as if wishing to show me how the beautiful music is made, she laughed her most silvery, harmonious laugh. And while she was still laughing, she said, "What a shame you're not a doctor! I would certainly introduce you to my mother. You see, the way she is, no one but the doctor can see her."

"What?" I said. "Is she very sick?"

"Not sick," she answered, "but she won't come up on deck till we reach Marseilles. That's what the doctor wants. And you, I'm sure, suffered so much that you can't wait to get off in Naples. And Mother wanted to meet you. Will you come visit us in Paris?"

"Listen to that!" I said playfully. "I'll come visit you in Calcutta. Your father's invited me."

"Really?" the girl exclaimed happily, and threw herself around the neck of her father, who happened to be passing by at that instant, forcing him to stop against his will. "Really, Father, will he come to Calcutta?"

Mr. P. first took care to prevent the ash from dropping from the tip of his cigar. Then, without even noticing his daughter, he turned to me and said, "Of course, I shall be very happy if you come, very happy if you stay as long as possible. I have a villa on the Ganges, a villa with a most splendid garden. With a most splendid garden and first-class stables—I put it at your disposal. At your disposal, it and my servants, my servants and my maids. There we'll talk, we'll talk at leisure. We'll spend the most beautiful days together, the most beautiful days and nights."

"There speaks the hospitable Anatolian," I said to myself, "not the self-centered Englishman." But besides the hospitable Anatolian, something else was speaking, something more eloquent, more compelling. And while father and daughter were counting the beauties and comforts of my future stay, I was imagining my star of fortune rising on the banks of the Ganges and advancing to meet me ever brighter, ever more gleaming.

When Mr. P. had ended his dithyramb about India with the agreeable epode: "Come visit me," the girl's damp eyes looked at me with a kind of uncanny brightness in which were reflected at the same time an expression of joy, of expectation, of entreaty, above all that childish wheedling that some ancient writer tastelessly named "the puppy-like character of children." To me those bewitching glances appeared as two luminous small angels that bent down from the depths of their blue heaven and in a serene voice repeated Mr. P.'s epode: "Come visit us." And since I continued silent and confused with amazement and uncertainty and didn't answer that serene invitation, "Oh yes, I beg you, do come visit us!" cried the girl, and, blushing modestly, she lowered her gaze and, taking her father's hand, began to fondle it tenderly and gratefully.

Anyone who didn't see Másinga's glances and hear her voice would laugh out loud at the eagerness with which I, who didn't have in my purse even a quarter, perhaps, of the fare to Calcutta, accepted the invitation to visit. I am, however, certain that in my place that person, too, would have done the same.

Never perhaps have simultaneous impressions of ear and eye been so congruent, so in agreement with one another, as Másinga's voice and look. Never has soul pouring out through the eyes managed to invest its immature and still imperfect body with such a warm glow that in a twinkling of an eye it overwhelemed the imperfections of the flesh, lending to the substance the timeless, the eternal form of its own perfection. Másinga was no longer the boyish girl of our first meeting on the steamship. Through the heavy and rough fea-

tures of her temporary state there shone the exact picture of that
form that had once beautified her childhood delicacy and that
would, after a short while, emerge triumphant from the graceless
ambiguity of her transitional period of life.

After Mr. P. had squeezed my hand affectionately, but without
paying the slightest attention to his daughter, and had resumed his
walk, it is hard to say which of the three of us was most happy. It
was obvious that Mr. P. couldn't conceal his pleasure from us, nor
we from him. Not only did he treble his pace, but he even let the
ash drop from the tip of his cigar, and he drew so powerfully on his
cigar that, though it wasn't yet dark, we could make out its burning
tip at a distance, like the headlamp of an approaching train.

Másinga sat beside me, silent now, and my happiness was complete. The only thing that troubled me was her father's great indifference to her and her behavior, by which he appeared to imply that
he attributed no significance to her behavior towards me. And
though up to that point I had behaved towards her as a child, I
could not now bear the idea that her father regarded her as still an
adolescent girl. Yet I was especially troubled lest the Calcutta Croesus' indifference stemmed from the conviction that neither his
daughter nor I could misunderstand his invitation, recognizing the
huge chasm that separated our social positions.

*****

Because of the length of the tempest we had endured, the *Rio
Grande* entered the gulf of Naples extremely late. The mountains
that wreathe the coastline could now only barely be distinguished
as confused, shapeless masses on the dark horizon. Scattered here
and there along the foothills, the lights of towns and villages now
disappeared, because of the ship's motion, behind some intervening
obstruction, now appeared again, like huge fireflies flying silently
and slowly along the dark sea coast. The actual harbor towards
which we were heading was still hidden behind the intervening high
bow of our ship, but as we continued to turn towards the left and
proceed into the bay, we began to glimpse the countryside and sub-
urbs of Naples on the other side.

"Here's Sorrento! There's Castellamare! Look, that's where Pompeii is! Look, there's Vesuvius!" Másinga stood by my side and
called out the names—she had visited Naples once before and felt

constrained to guide my inexperience, obviously pleased whenever I asked a question.

Naples of the ten thousand lights gradually emerged before us, rising like an amphitheater on the broad ocean front. Above it shimmered that vast red reflection of lights that usually hovers over great cities at night. The dense lights of lanterns and windows seemed at a distance like a low-flying swarm of stars, which, having strayed from their solar center, have shed their speed and animation, and are now, weary and gasping, climbing the neighboring heights of Vesuvius so as to come and beg a little fire from its inexhaustible hearth to save their lives. But the closer we got to the ocean front, the more their animation increased, the greater the effect that captivating scene had on us.

When the *Rio Grande*'s anchor thundered onto the sleepy waters of the harbor and the ship stopped moving, then it seemed as if Naples, that beautiful and richly dowered daughter of the Mediterranean, adorned in lights from its tower-crowned head to the hems of its sea-washed gown, was wearing those gold and silver wedding gowns in which, just yesterday and the day before, our mothers, decked out as brides, prayed at each step as they made their way to church in order to receive the blessing together with our fathers, those persevering and frugal suitors of days gone by.

And Naples, too, has her suitor. And he, too, melts away, burning with perseverance and expectation, one day to place his warm kiss on the marble-like forehead of his lively but too cautious fiancée. And Old Vesuvius is a jealous swain! And so he sits and observes his love, raising his head and shoulders higher than all the neighboring mountains. And he sits up all night smoking his huge pipe and occasionally moaning moans that deeply affect his neighbors.

That night his stern face was exceptionally clouded over. He was angry. Angry because a pip-squeak neighbor, the hill of Pausilipo, had had the gall to compete with the haughty giant, to take on the eagle as rival lover. And he had succeeded up to a point. And he had managed to hold Naples' attention turned towards him, enticing her feelings with beautiful music, outstanding food and drink, and frequent fireworks. And so Naples ran clapsed in Pausilipo's embrace, and Vesuvius was jealous, and he was angry, and he stamped his foot and shook the ground, and he was ashamed of his beloved's fickleness, of his weakness for her. Then his dark face

grew red and his thick eyebrows lowered and his lips parted spasmodically, and the sparks of his deep pipe shot into the air in the
violent manner he uses whenever he is angry, to stir up its flame and
to speak while he smokes. And this is what he was saying that
night:

"Look at the fickle, giddy girl! A little foam of champagne, an
ordinary, common waltz, two cheap firecrackers have intoxicated
her mind, have roused her feelings, have dazzled her perception,
and she runs lovesick to my worthless rival, Pausilipo. And she's
entranced with the favors of his little men who, however, serve only
a contractor! While I, through the divine forces that serve me, melt
nature's hardest elements, I mix them up with the bubbling lava of
my chest, and I offer her my crater overflowing—and she refuses! I
summon to a concert the dancers of the subterranean Typho and
the orchestras of the aerial Laélapes to whose music even the inanimate mountains dance, and in the midst of this symphony I offer
her my fiery hand—and she refuses! For her I fling like fireworks
the diamond balls of my fiery moans, the sherds of my heart, which
is being consumed by love's fire—and she refuses! She's a faint-
hearted woman; she cowers before grandeur; she grows dizzy before immortality! She prefers a trivial display, a momentary sparkle,
to eternity. And yet look at my choice, my faithful Pompeii! The
mud of her streets adorns the chests of princes, and with her refuse
are decked out the halls of kings. Who would remember today the
insignificant town of sailors and fishermen if it had not been true to
Vesuvius till death, if it hadn't expired writhing under my fiery
embraces? . . ."

Some such things was Vesuvius thundering to Naples, or—to be
more accurate—some such things was I whispering to Másinga
seated at my side, who, having finished her job as guide, had asked
me what the sight before our eyes appeared to me to be.

Any other girl, and perhaps even my female reader herself, either
would not have understood immediately what I was aiming at with
those imagistic excesses or, though understanding, would have pretended she didn't understand. But Másinga, just as her external appearance combined the nature of the child and the young woman,
so she had in her mind the openness and candor of childish simplicity joined with the shrewdness and delicate discernment of a
mature and powerful understanding.

"I know why you're telling me these things!" she exclaimed,

again drawing her voice out in a drawl like a little, spoiled, complaining child. "They're pretty, with imagination and poetry, but I don't like them."

"Why?" I asked. "Explain."

"Hmmm!" she responded. "Why? Because I know why you're telling it to me." And after a short silence she added in a whimpering voice, "I'm not fickle or giddy or faint-hearted like your stupid Naples! But you were always like this. You always took me for a 'crazy little girl.'"

"What slander!" I cried out with a guffaw in order to forestall the harm, but it was too late! Though the girl laughed with me mechanically, two large tears shone from the corners of her eyes! "Oh!" I said regretfully, "I beg your pardon! You're angry with me!"

"I?" she cried happily. "What an idea!" And she emitted a series of those silvery and captivating tones that God gave her instead of a laugh. "I angry with you? What an idea!" And she laughed again.

Then she continued. "Yes, I was angry! That I don't deny. But I was angry not with you, but with Vesuvius. With your Old Vesuvius, your harsh and inhuman suitor! Did you hear him? He burned one girl, and now he's trying to burn another! And after a little while perhaps another, and so on and on! Do you like that? And how then is Naples to blame if she doesn't want to fall into his snares? Did you hear him? Immortality! Such an immortality that any girl can acquire—no thank you!"

Then I realized that with my thoughtless comparison I had not only insulted the girl but had also failed to show myself in a good light. "What a fool I am!" I said to myself, not knowing how to make good my mistake.

"But it doesn't matter!" the girl said when she recognized my position. "It was a poem off the top of your head, but a poem that didn't succeed. That's why I don't like it. Another one! Make another one, even if it's in prose like that one, but different, very different! And see to it that I like it. So come on!" she cried finally in impatience, with her little hand nudging the arm on which I was resting my foolish head in silence.

"Másinga," I then said looking up, "forgive me. I'm the biggest fool in the world! I'll never again try to make poems, even prose ones."

She laughed happily then and said, "All right, then, since that's the way things are, I'll make you the poem I like myself, but not in prose. Listen!

> Ach, cruel parents
> what sacrifice do you desire
> that we propitiate?
>
> Excessive wealth
> true happiness cannot acquire
> and joy does not create.
>
> Of true lovers'
> the strong and oh! so prudent youth
> on earth suffices well.
>
> Their joy is lasting
> and, even 'neath a humble roof,
> does always with them dwell."

"So you're the long-lost manuscript of my poetic foolishnesses!" I exclaimed. "Where did you get those verses?"

"Where? From Therapeiá! Do you remember how you used to distribute them like ceremonial cookies to all the ladies? So listen! If you ask them for one of your poems now, not only will they not know them by heart, they won't even have a written copy. How many have I seen throw them away before reading them! How many have I seen read them and laugh at you, while just a moment before they were praising them with their eyes and begging you to give them written copies! But I was your 'crazy little girl.' You never even noticed me! And yet I remember by heart all the poems that came to my aunt's house; I've kept them all. It's not that I took them from my aunt secretly! But since everybody considered them worthless, she let me collect them to make a present for my father, a very pleasant one, as he said." Although the above revelations related to poetic attempts that had already long since been condemned, even by me, they struck a frightful blow to my pride. If I had learned that I had once been mocked by some mischievous lady before the world, I wouldn't have minded. But before Másinga! To be mocked before Másinga, that made me furious. And yet I had to pretend indifference. So as soon as the girl mentioned her father, I took advantage of the situation to turn the conversation to him, changing the subject imperceptibly.

"Your father, it seems, loves poetry a great deal. He's surely read many poets, hasn't he?"

"Oh yes, of course," said the girl, "many, very many. And he's read them in many languages, even in Sanskrit."

"Behold! A true lover of poetry!" I cried out with enthusiasm. "Of course! In order to enjoy as much heaven as possible in the midst of the essential banality of life. And then there's another thing. Your father's not like those ingrates who eat the fruits without thinking of the tree. Your father is also a friend of poets. Who ever heard of anyone putting an entire villa at the disposal of a Greek man of letters simply because he's a poet? It's true the villa's in India, and that the Greek poet will ride along the Ganges and not along Patisíon Street. That, however, doesn't change anything, for even if your father lived in Athens, he'd do the same thing, wouldn't he?"

"Why, yes!" said the girl, slowing her speech as if hesitant to continue the thought she'd begun. "Because my father . . . my father . . . but I'd better not say it. You'll learn about it when you come to Calcutta."

The caution in her statement and in her voice, the timidity in the girl's look, awakened in me a strange feeling of delight. Surely it concerned—but she didn't want to tell me yet—her father's love for me that had been growing for some time and, above all, certain special plans that he had formed from our acquaintance in Athens. Surely it concerned that! A girl's father doesn't simply and on the spur of the moment just happen to give a young man in Athens his calling card with his address in Calcutta written in his own hand.

"You're hiding something from me, Másinga!" I said then, warmly and tenderly looking at the girl's lowered eyes. "You're hiding something from me, but I know it already, and I'm all the happier."

"Really?" the girl exclaimed in wonder. "And how do you know it? Oh well, all the better then! You won't complain I didn't tell you. You should know this for consolation, though, that father has this good point: he never reads when he travels. He carts them with him since he can't bear to be parted from them, but he doesn't read them."

"What doesn't he read?" I asked, wondering how to take her words. "He doesn't read poets?"

"No!" answered the girl, "his poems. The poems he writes."

"What?" I cried out in amazement. "So your father writes poems?"

"He asks me if he writes poems! And didn't you say you knew it? That you knew what I was hiding from you?"

"Hmmm!" I said with a scowl. "So that was it? So our father writes poems!"

"Listen to him! Does he write poems?" she answered in a tone that seemed to be pitying me rather than my ignorance. "Listen to him! Does he write poems? Yes, and he overwrites in fact. Haven't you seen all the boxes? Some of those are full of parchments. He writes his poems only on parchment. And that isn't really the bad thing so much as the fact he wants to read them to others."

"What a disaster for me!" I thought.

"All the same," the girl continued, "this defect will surely come to some good. Surely it will be of benefit. No one dares visit us in Calcutta any more. He'll value you all the more, he'll love you all the more for being his only auditor."

*****

The *Rio Grande* had lain at anchor for some time now, and the officials had come out to check our passports. They were, however, slow to return, and contact was not allowed. There was even a rumor that it would be very slow in being allowed because one of the passengers was ill with a very suspicious disease. I was to disembark in Naples to recoup my strength after the seasickness of the long journey, but I had decided to remain on board up till the last moment before departure. Suddenly sweet music was heard from the sea, and everybody ran to the side of the ship from which the sounds came. A large Neapolitan boat was carrying one of those musical groups that beg about the ships that put into port. A wide, round umbrella inside which there shone a large torch had been tied upside down on its mast. A white-robed girl, her hair flying free, could be seen reclining lazily on its stern, more supporting herself on the rudder than holding it and working it. The sounds of the instruments were sweet and shrill, but the players could not be seen. The upturned umbrella concentrated all the light within itself and hid the musicians' faces beneath its extended shadow. Only from time to time did some ludicrous face appear, bawling hoarsely and dissonantly—*Encouragez la musique, messieurs et mesdames!*—

and the people on deck threw some coins into the umbrella. After some selections from well-known Italian operas, one of the passengers requested in a loud voice: *Santa Lucia! Cantate la Santa Lucia!* And the Neapolitans' instruments obediently responded to the command by striking up the introduction. Then in the surrounding reverent silence, that unseen chorus began as one to sing the hymn to the patron saint of Naples, very skillfully in fact, repeating after each stanza with deep emotion: *Santa Lucia! Santa Lucia!*

After the tedious fatigue of the voyage, the fears of the tempest, and the torments of seasickness, that beautiful, moving music, unseen on the black mirror of the sea and echoing through the night, unquestionably exerted a favorable, soothing effect. One might say that the good spirits of the liquid element, Glaukothea's attendant nymphs—their delicate bodies having broken through the silent waves in their rhythmical chorus—had come to console those who had suffered, to encourage the faint-hearted, and to escort those disembarking with a wish for a calmer return. The eagerness with which coins were thrown into the upturned umbrella from all sides bore clear witness that some such was the impression on my fellow passengers.

Things were otherwise with me. From the moment Másinga had informed me of her father's passion for versifying in all its details, the mania with which he tormented whatever listener he'd been able to track down, I felt that I had been plunged from the twelfth heaven of my happiness. There was no longer any doubt that his affection and attentions had only one thing in mind: to snare me as his listener. Towards this goal he had not only put his villa by the Ganges at my disposal, but he would have paid for my travel expenses and whatever else I asked if only I would listen to his verses. And what verses! And how many verses! Did you hear? No one dared visit him so as to avoid hearing them. And the vastly wealthy poet, pretending love of poetry and hospitality, managed to entice me, the foolish magpie, to India! And very advantageously for his purpose because the Calcuttan listener can claim stomach-ache after the first stanza of a poem and get up and leave. But the foreigner? The guest in the house? One who does not know the area or its language? He will be captive to the verse-mad master of the house, consigned unconditionally to his mercy and his pity. And so the villa by the Ganges will be my gold-bedecked jail. The kaftan-wearing servants will be the jailers barring all exits to me. And the beautiful days and nights with Mr. P. (Did you hear? and nights!) will pass in the hearing of his poems on parchment! That is to say, in torture in the face of which everyone else in India turned tail and fled. And yet I, I could not escape it. Másinga wanted it. She knew it was an awful thing, but that awful thing, she said, would doubt-less turn out well, undoubtedly would be of benefit. For that reason, when I heard the mellifluous Neapolitan violin and saw that white-robed girl reclining on the boat's stern, I thought I was sailing by the Sirens' land, that one of them in particular was trying with her charms and melodious voice to seduce me from my path, to entice me into her magic cave, in which I saw a frightful, green-scaled snake ready to choke me, but towards which I was hastening joy-fully because that Siren was Másinga.

*****

Almost all the passengers for Naples had disembarked. The *Rio Grande*'s cranes were still working, bringing the last merchandise on board. I had put my things in a boat, but I was still waiting on deck. During all this time Mr. P. had not ceased walking with his hands behind him, just as he hadn't stopped fixing his eyes on the tip of his cigar. He gave me the opportunity two or three times to walk and converse with him; he constantly pressed his invitation, but he didn't admit to me that he wrote poetry, although in my sounding him out I had given him many opportunities to do so.

He only said, "I give myself over to thoughts, I give myself over to thoughts a lot, and I do exactly the same thing you do. I lift my gaze, I fix my eyes on the sky and I look and look until ideas begin to come down. Doesn't that seem odd to you?"

"Very odd," I answered, "very very odd! And I wonder why the idea never came to you to write them down."

"Oh, that didn't have to come to me," he exclaimed. "I've had that idea since I was a small child. I've had it since I was a very small child, but more about that when we're in Calcutta. Now I ask you not to forget my address, my address in Paris. Hotel Continen-tal. Come and I'll present you to my wife. But come quickly. Come quickly so you can see Másinga as well one last time. Másinga one last time."

"Why one last time?" I interrupted. "We'll travel together to Cal-cutta. I'll see her in Calcutta."

"You'll not see her in Calcutta," he replied, lovingly regarding the tip of his cigar, "because she won't be there. She won't be in Calcutta because she'll stay in Paris."

"What?" I yelled, almost in a rage. "Másinga won't travel with us? She'll stay in Paris!"

"She'll stay in Paris," he continued dispassionately, "in order to enter a girl's boarding school. She'll be a boarder in a—"

"What? Boarder!" I interrupted indignantly. "But she didn't say anything to me!"

"She didn't say anything," Mr. P. continued, as if he were a life-less talking machine, "because she doesn't know it. She doesn't know it because we haven't revealed it to her; we haven't revealed it to her because it's not her business to know it, to know it before the time comes to do it. Do you understand?"

"I understand!" I said, and I said it as if I were uttering a curse between my teeth. "But what's the idea, I beg of you, shutting her up again in a girls' school? The girl's grown up now; she has all the training and education required for her sex and class. She knows four languages; she knows music, painting, handiwork; what more do you want her to learn?"

"To learn the ways of high society," Mr. P. replied, as if convers-ing happily with the tip of his cigar. "The ways of barons and counts, whose class she'll be entering, whose class she is entering as the future wife of Count Plumpsiun. Count de Plumpsiun with an income . . . widowed . . . some . . . aged . . ." The wooden machine continued talking with the tip of its cigar. I, in the meantime, was thinking that the twelve heavens had come crashing down on my poor head, and the frightful crash of the glass sherds that constantly lacerated my hearing made me so upset that I almost fell in a faint.

I don't know how long I walked with him, hearing nothing, and moving rather under the influence of some frightful galvanism than by my own powers. When I came to myself, I was exhausted, bathed in cold sweat. The versifying Croesus, however, noticed nothing, not so much because it was dark as because he hadn't raised his eyes from the tip of his cigar.

"And now, Mr. P.," I stammered, "to your health! I must go."

"I hope we meet again, and soon!" he said, and turned to shake hands, but I had left.

Everything about me seemed to be laughing sarcastically and re-peating my "to your health!"

Másinga was waiting to say good-bye to me at the ship's disembarkation platform with the light above her illuminating her face. Her happy expression, the childlike eagerness with which she hurried towards me, testified that she had guessed nothing. Nothing of what had happened, of what awaited her!

"And so," she said, squeezing my cold, limp hands, "we're agreed. You'll be in Paris before us, and you'll come to our hotel. Too bad the sea bothers you so! We could have made the whole journey together. What an awful sea, eh? How awful and crazy and stupid to make such a tempest! But hush! Let's not speak ill of it so we can have it favorable to us for the longer journey. All right? How wonderful! How beautiful! I'll jump for joy!"

And on that platform the girl continued speaking and laughing, clearly persisting in her attempt to brighten my despairing expression. But when she saw that her attempts were failing, "Oh!" she said in a low voice and with a frown. "You're crying, and I'm joking! Foolish me! But we'll meet again, won't we?" And she raised her sad eyes inquiringly to mine, and I saw two tears rolling down her cheeks.

"Yes, Másinga, I hope so."

"And you'll come to Calcutta, won't you?"

"With you, of course," I answered. "But without you, never!"

"But of course with me!" she cried, brightening up again. "Listen. I'm going to Calcutta. A little time in Paris, a little in London, and then, wish me a good voyage!"

And Másinga laughed again, and I squeezed her little hand, and let the tears flow freely, and went down without looking at the platform and threw myself into the waiting boat. The darkness was thick and only for a few moments could I pick out Másinga's handkerchief waving in answer to my own.

Then grief and indignation began to overmaster my soul by turns. I was indignant at my usual blind optimism and foolishness that inspired in me the self-deception that, in fact, Mr. P.'s attentions toward me sprang from a true appreciation of intellectual qualities, from love, as he said, "of my gift." I felt sorry for myself because now even the last vision of happiness by the Bosporus was disappearing forever behind the pitiless iron face of reality that rose up before me.

"It would have been a thousand times better," I said to myself, "never to have seen Másinga again. There would then have remained in the dead worlds of my imagination one small butterfly flitting towards me over the relics of the desolate past with the same cheerfulness and happiness with which she used to frolic when those relics were still freshly scented flowers of a poetic Paradise."

Then again I thought that perhaps everything was not yet lost. Perhaps I was betraying my duty, trampling on my happiness by not going to Calcutta. And by one leap of the imagination I found myself surrounded by India's blooming nature, inhaling the intoxicating aromas of its flowers, marveling at its broad-leafed banana trees, its huge figs, its tall palms, and all those plants and trees whose beauty and wealth have constituted the enticements and the comforts of Eden for Eastern peoples. I saw the yellow waters of the ancient Ganges flowing majestically before my eyes; the half-naked daughters of the Indians on its bank with reverent attention placing their lighted lamps on its slow waters and following the course of those lamps with beating heart and tear-drenched eyes to see whether their beloved loved them. And among them I noticed one especially—so well-known, so familiar, and so superior to the others in beauty and mind—and she, too, with her white fingers was reverently placing a small, lighted lamp on the Ganges' waters and was following its movement with her beautiful blue eyes, and she saw that no matter how far away the lamp's flame got, it did not sink, it did not go out, and she leaped up like a deer and exclaimed through her tears: "He loves me! He loves me! 'I'll jump for joy!'" And a fiery yearning inflamed my heart within my breast, and I decided firmly to go to Calcutta.

But then I imagined that girl's father sitting before me in a rich Indian pavilion beside a valuable table on which burned a tall lamp of noble porcelain decorated with those imaginary snakes and crocodiles of Eastern art. In front of us and around us lay opened the boxes I'd seen full of parchments and papyri; Mr. P. selected from them and read me the verses of his youth, written to the length of the Mahabharata and the Ramayana, but in the manner of his speech, in accordance with which the first half of every succeeding sentence was the second half of the preceding!

"Oh good and noble gentleman! Have you longed for the fame of an Indian Euripides, the 'stitcher of rags?' In your treasury you have the most brilliant strings of pearls and diamonds—are they not sufficient to delight your imagination? You have created the most beautiful poem in the world, your guileness and clever daughter—is she not enough to slake your ambition? But at least spare

me; spare one who has suffered two months of seasickness solely
and only to see her again. So wait a while, don't begin right away
with verse-sickness. Don't submit me to the tortures of Hell while
hosting me in complete Paradise!"

Then I recalled that that Paradise had been deprived of its Angel,
that Másinga was no longer Másinga, but Countess de Plumpsiun,
taught to perfection all the ways of high society, but having un-
learned the guilelessness and charm of her nature; adorned with
gold and diamonds, but having lost her liveliness and energy; rich
in all other respects, but bereft of that heavenly laugh, in place of
which now only words parted her lips, words like:

> Excessive wealth
> true happiness cannot acquire
> and joy does not create.

And I became furious with that cruel father, and I made up my
mind firmly and irrevocably and didn't go to Calcutta.

Who Was My Brother's Killer?

◫◫◫

Introduction

This story, like "My Mother's Sin," involves the narrator's own family. This time, the killing of his brother Hristákis is at issue, a killing that took place three years prior to the events described. Though there was one prime suspect, he proved to have an alibi, and as the story opens, the killer has not yet been found. The direction of the story moves toward locating the killer, but the plot has to do with situation and character.

This tale is the first of Vizyenos' stories in which Turks appear, and they appear in general in a sympathetic light, though the narrator professes a dislike for Turks. The story is set in Constantinople (the City) and at the end returns to Vizýi: in this, it is the mirror image of "My Mother's Sin" and moves in the same direction as does "The Only Journey of His Life." The characters include the narrator and his mother, together with his youngest brother Michael. On the Turkish side are the unnamed Turkish widow and her two sons, the unnamed police inspector, and Kyamíl—they form, as it were, a Turkish doublet to the narrator's own family.

A number of places in the City are mentioned, some of them quite familiar—Hagia Sophia in Turkish Aya Sofya, the famous church erected by Justinian, the Byzantine Hippodrome, which is nearby that church, Diván-Yolú, the main street of Istanbul, which ends at the Topkapi palace, and the Old Bridge, probably the predecessor of the current Galatá Bridge. Others are less familiar. Méfa-meïdáni is an area near the Rose Mosque (Gül-Cami), the church in which, as in the story, the body of the last emperor of Constantinople, Constantine XI, is said to be buried. Baluklí (which means "with fish") is the shrine of the Zoodóhos Pigí, the Virgin Mary, at the Selivria Gate, in which there is a pool containing small fish, red on one side and black on the other. Legend has it that these fish were being fried when Constantinople fell to the Ottomans in 1453, that they leaped out of the pan and into the water. There had been a prophecy in the form of an *adynaton* that if ever the City turned Turk, fish would jump out of the frying pan and return to the water.

Again, the mother functions as narrator herself at the beginning and end of the story, providing details the narrator cannot have known. Later on, the narrator's surviving brother performs the same function to bring matters up to the present. On the Turkish side, both the old lady and Kyamíl provide details, again functioning as doublets of the Greeks. There is, however, more action in this story, and the narrator himself takes more of a part in it. He is once more the central figure against whose reactions the events are inevitably seen, though he cannot in any sense be considered the protagonist; he is a minor participant and a major observer of the action, both his own and others'. Foreignness and distance are again an issue in this story.

As in "My Mother's Sin," a considerable amount of time elapses during the story, six years from the killing to the narrator's return to Vizýi, and the story moves between the City and Vizýi. It is conceivable that the dramatic dates of the episodes in "My Mother's Sin" and "Who Was My Brother's Killer?" are the same; they must at least overlap. For the latter story, however, we can attach actual dates to the events. The Russo-Turkish war, which broke out in 1877, coincided with the killing of Hristákis. Thus the search must have taken place in 1880, and the story is being told in 1883, the year, in fact, in which it was published.

There are a number of Turkish words in this story, as well as in "The Only Journey of His Life" and "Moscóv-Selím." I have left many of them to retain a bit of the color of the original. All, or nearly all, would have been familiar to Vizyenos' readers, and some are still in use in Greek today. Turkish words in general can be easily rendered phonetically from their spelling. The fricatives, however, are written in a manner not immediately clear to speakers of English: c = /dž/; as in English *judge*; $ç$ = /tš/, as in English *church*; $ş$ = English /š/, as in *shush*; and the vowel i, when following a low vowel such as a, represents a mid-vowel i, like the sound represented by the English spelling of *just* as *jist*. These words refer primarily to titles, clothes, and Turkish customs. Among them we find:

bey, a term of respect rather than a title, in principle referring to government officials or otherwise distinguished persons;

dzánun (T. [Turkish] canim), meaning "beloved" or, ironically, "my dear fellow, my dear madam";

hanúmissa (T. *hanim* with a Greek ending), meaning "lady";

eféntis (or *aféntis,* a less formal use for addressing brothers or others who merit some respect), meaning "master" or "sir" (it stems in turn from medieval Greek *afthéntis*);

Imámis, a religious official (Arabic *Imam*), having a Greek ending;

kaïmakámis, an Ottoman district governor (T. *kaymakam*), also with a Greek ending;

kokkóna, a Rumanian word meaning "lady";

pashá, a term denoting a high Ottoman official, English *pasha;*

sultán, used both for the Sultan and as a term of respect to males (feminine: *sultána*);

validé, meaning "mother" (the Validé-Sultána is therefore the mother of the Sultan, a woman of great power); and

Zaptié, the Turkish police (T. *zaptiye*).

Other words cluster around the character of Kyamíl. He was a *softás* (T. *softa*), that is, a Moslem student of religion in a *teké* (T. *tekke*), a dervish lodge presided over by a shcik. He was called *kará Sevdá,* "black passion," because of what he had done. He wore a *kaftáni* (T. *kaftan*), a long honorific robe with a sash and conical hat (*kyuláfi,* T. *külah*), while an initiate, *saríki* (T. *sarik*) and *tsubé,* turban and robe, like a vestment, when he became a saint. His mother wore a veil, *yasmáki* (T. *yaşmak*), and a *feretzés* (T. *ferace*), a robe covering the body from head to toe.

Other words are of more general meaning, and not all are Turkish:

hatíri (T. *hatir*) means "favor";

kióski, English kiosk, means a pavilion or gazebo (T. *kösk*);

musafírides, Turkish *misafir,* are guests (singular *musafíris*);

mastíha is the alcoholic drink made from mastic;

oká is a measure of weight, now abandoned in Greece but once widely used there, and equals 1.282 kilograms;

pazári is, of course, an English bazaar (T. *pazar*);

temenás (T. *temenah*) is the Eastern greeting in which the hand touches the ground, the chest, and then the forehead; and

vrykólakas is from Slavic *vrukolek* and refers to a revenant, a creature that returns from the grave.

To these words must be added the Greek words *primates,* the Greek leaders of a village; the *leptón,* the smallest Greek coin; and *Panagía,* "the All-holy" or the Virgin Mary, to whom the mother frequently appeals.

Who Was
My Brother's Killer?

"Today at last I can eat a little bread and it will go to my heart!" said my mother as she sat between me and my brother at the frugal meal that the waiter had brought to our room.

"First do it, then say it, Mother," replied my brother, teasingly, because for some time now he had often heard this good intention but had never seen it put into effect.

The mother, used to such observations from her younger son, paid no attention whatsoever to his words, but turning around to make sure the door behind her was closed, she said, "And don't let that coquette come in here again. Really, what a delight he is with his 'somersaults' and his 'leaps!'"

The "coquette" was the French servant in the hotel on the Bosporus to which my mother came to meet me, just returned from the West. His morning coat with the "tails"—a thing unheard of for a woman from the provinces—and the beardless Frenchman's constant bowings inspired in her an uncontrollable dislike right from the beginning. And the worst thing was that in trying to gain her good will at all costs the unfortunate servant redoubled his somersaults and his leaps, with the result that already in those first few days he had brought her exasperation with him to a head. She baptized him with the name of coquette because, she said, he had a feminine, that is to say, smooth-shaven, face and was unable to stand on his feet without bowing his head and shaking his tail.

After a few scornful observations of this sort, both about the unfortunate Louis' overall appearance and his clothes, my mother unconsciously stopped eating and, fixing her eyes on the window, sank little by little into thought, as was her habit.

The Bosporus flowed charmingly beneath our gaze; many long thin boats traversed its dark blue waters in opposite directions, like swallows flying with incomparable speed. My mother observed these things with expressionless eyes; and after a long silence she sighed deeply.

"Just see," she said, "how the years pass and things return! My child won't return, I used to say, he won't come back in time, and I'll die, and my eyes will remain open from their longing to see him! All day long I watched the streets and asked passers-by. And when evening came I left the courtyard gate open till midnight. 'Don't close it, Michael, he can still come back. I don't want my child to come back and find my gate closed. It's enough that he's been alone and away from us for so many years, I don't want him to come back to his village and think there's no one in the world watching for him.' When I went to bed I saw you in my sleep, and I seemed to hear your voice. And I got up and opened the gate: 'You've come, my child?' It was the breeze whistling in the street.

"So day dawned, and so day ended. Eight years passed, bread didn't go to my heart because my child won't come in time, I thought, and I'll die, and my eyes will remain open! And just look! Now that I have you near me, now that I see you, it seems it was just yesterday you went away and today you've come. And the bitter draughts I've drunk, my child, and the terrors I've suffered are as if they never were!"

At this point she absentmindedly cut off a little bread as if wanting to continue her meal. But before putting it in her mouth, she again stared through the window, saw the constantly flowing Bosporus, saw the boats returning, and with a deep sigh from the bottom of her heart, repeated slowly and sadly:

"So the years pass and things return! From the direction I feared, I suffered nothing; from the direction I felt secure, trouble came! You went to the ends of the earth, my child, and you weren't lost, but returned. But our Hristákis—he went a five-hour journey and didn't come back! . . . Eh . . . only the dead don't come back! . . .

"It was the day before Epiphany—you know how my heart is on such solemn days. I remembered your deceased father, and I remembered that on one such day before Epiphany, when you saw everybody else's children carrying sorb branches and 'sorbing' people in the street, you went and got a broom and began beating your father on the back and 'sorbing' him: 'Sorbs, sorbs! strong of body, strong of spine, full of health and strength, may strength all year be thine!' Young as you were, you knew the words. And your late father was delighted and took you in his arms and kissed you: 'Have my blessing, and may it turn out true!' And he gave you a coin and beckoned me with his finger and said, 'This child, woman, will be somebody!' How could he have known that after three months he would leave you an orphan! And how could he have known that Epiphanies would come and go and you would be suffering hardships abroad and I would be weeping all alone!

"And so it was that day before Epiphany. Michael, knowing my wishes, went to the mountain early and brought back a sorb: a large branch full of firm, green buds. 'With this sorb, *mana*, tonight we'll see our fate.' When Hristákis came home, we sat at the hearth and separated the fire into two sections, and Michael began to put the sorbs between them on the hot tile so we could see our fate. First of all he called your name, and he cut a sorb and threw it on. And as soon as he threw it, it roared and jumped and popped out of the hearth. 'Have my blessing, Michael,' I said to him. 'Tonight you've delighted my heart. If our Yoryís is healthy, we're all all right!' Next he called our my name. E! I, too, you see, did well. Next he named Hristákis—and just look! The sorb bud stayed still and motionless on the tile where he threw it, until it turned black, began to smoke, tilted a little, and burned up!—'Christ and Virgin, my child!' I cried. 'You didn't throw on a good sorb!' And I took the sorb branch from his hand and chose the best bud and opened a new spot in the fire and threw it. . . . It smoked a little, turned black, spread out, and stayed where it was! Then Hristákis laughed loudly and took a stick and stirred the coals and said, 'Mother, I'm a tough person, as you know. It's not so easy to get me to jump and run away from a little heat as it is you. If you want to see my fate, come here!'

"And he took the branch from my hand and threw it in the fire. And the sorbs caught fire and began to roar and to jump . . .

"Now, say what you will, sorbs are sorbs, I know that. And people seek their fate because it's the custom and not for the truth, that too is true. But when I think of those muffled noises and the distant rifle shots that began to be heard a few days later in the villages round about, my heart flies into my mouth and I can find no peace. The thing was clear and straightforward, but we didn't pay attention, we just took it lightly and laughed.

"While we were still laughing the door opened and in came Mitákos' boy, Haralambís. You know him. He was Hristákis' age and resembled him a lot in both height and built. While he was small he used to come to our house a lot, but when he grew up he took an ugly course, and I couldn't stand the sight of him because many times he got in trouble, and they took him for Hristákis. He was so like him, and since they were fellow workers they also wore the same clothes. For that reason, one day I lit into him—after that he never crossed our threshold again. But that evening he came.

"'Good evening, ma'am! Good health to you!'

"'Welcome, Lampí. If you're bringing me a letter, sit down and let me treat you to something.'

"'No, ma'am, I've given up the mail route. And I've come on purpose to tell Hristákis again not to let anyone else get it.' At that point my heart began to flutter!

"'And why, Lampí?'

"'Because the post is a good job, ma'am, a good job!'

"'And if the post is a good job, why don't you keep it yourself, since you've had it up till now?'

"You'd swear someone had stabbed him with a knife; his color changed and he began to stammer his words. 'Ma'am, I've gone and got the mail from the railroad station for two years now, and I've made quite a lot of money. It's time now for my friends to do it.'

"'Listen to what I tell you, Lampí!' I said to him then. 'If you made money, as they say you did—God and your soul! We don't need that kind of money. Besides, you know paper bills aren't any good any more. And the postman can't get rich any more with the last pennies that some orphan is mailing home from abroad to provide a memorial prayer in church for his dead father. As for the other craft that has been making you rich, Lampí, there's God and he'll judge you. My boy is a Christian and an honest man, and he knows how to earn his bread with the sweat of his brow.'

"That's the way I spoke to him because I knew he was a thief. And while I was talking to him, my child, a trembling came over him and his lips turned pale, and his face turned wild, like an epileptic's. Oh, *Panagía mou!* Three times he opened his mouth to speak, and three times I heard his teeth chatter, my child, but I didn't hear his voice! His face turned pale and he looked quickly left and right. And I saw the great fright and terrified expression with which he furtively examined his clothes and his right hand, even between the fingers! As if he were smeared with something and were afraid we'd see it. And after that frightful struggle—Oh, *Panagía mou*—with the voice of one who is being choked and is fighting for his life, my child, he said, 'Don't listen to people, ma'am! I'm a good person!' and he hid his face in his hands and went out and didn't even say good night! . . .

"'You see, Mother?' said Hristákis then, 'I told you and you didn't believe it. He killed a man and he's got blood on his hands. Everybody says it, and you don't believe it. As soon as you say you know something he did—even if it's only to test him—he thinks you're talking about the killing. He thinks the blood has appeared on his hands to betray him.'

"'Since you didn't see it with your own eyes,' I told him, 'why do you want to go and speak evil of him? Every lamb hangs by its own foot. And if it's true, he has God who'll judge him, and he'd better watch out. Just do me a favor and don't get mixed up in that business of the post; he surely isn't giving it up without a reason.'

"'Why don't you listen to what I tell you, Mother?' he said again. 'It's the blood that's got him! The blood he spilled on his route has turned into a ghost now and won't let him pass. Day before yesterday he had to turn back midway and leave the mail. You hear? He saw someone lying in wait for him. It was the blood for sure. They say if a man kills someone and doesn't think to wipe off his knife, the blood will either turn into a ghost to strangle him one day, or it will torment him until he admits his crime and they hang him.'

"'If you want my blessing, my child, don't upset my heart any more. And, if you want the Virgin's blessing, don't get mixed up in these things! If anyone in authority hears you, you're in trouble! Forget both the post and the postman and look to your own business, like a decent lad.'

"But your brother—you know how he was—the place wasn't big enough to hold him. I taught him a trade and opened a shop for him so he could take his father's place. But how he loved to hang around in the streets!

"'From here to Lulevurgáz,' he said, 'is a five-hour trip. Once every two weeks I'll go and I'll come: why let someone else profit from it?" 'No, if you want my blessing! I'm not letting you take the post! Promise me you won't take it because you'll make me lose my peace of mind!' 'Well, all right!' he said then. 'I'm not taking it. You just wait a month or two without a letter, and then you'll see how sorry you'll be.'

"That hit me right where it hurt. Your letters didn't come regularly because they opened them on the way. And it wasn't enough that they didn't leave anything inside, but they didn't dare deliver them once they'd been opened. So I went on without news of you and merely sat and cried. In spite of this, I said nothing to him. I've held out this long, I can hold out longer.

"When mail day came I see him coming in with the official pouch under his arm and a rifle on his shoulder. 'Now at last, mother,' he said, 'the treat won't go to someone else. When I bring you Yoryís's letter tomorrow, you'll give the treat to me. What do you say?'

"About twelve days had passed from the evening when I'd tried to stop him. It happened then, as it always does, that the prophecies of the day before Epiphany had already been forgotten. But Mitákos' son, I hadn't forgotten him. For that reason, I began to reprove him for doing just as he pleased. But you think he'd listen? He'd already taken on the job! He'd promised the primates and the Kaïmakámis!

"When I saw my words were going for naught, I gave him your letter and told him, 'You be careful now, my child,' I told him, 'not to lose our Yoryís' letter!' I can see him now! He took off his fez, kissed my hand, and left. . . . Who would have known not to let him? . . .

"The next day was the day the new bishop was to come. Church and village officials went to the station early: the schoolteachers with their children all lined up, the priests and the rest of the villagers went out about an hour's walk to meet him in person. Michael also went along with them. You'd think the village had been deserted. The time for the mail came, but I wasn't worried about Hristákis: surely he would come with the bishop's retinue. The weather was good, and I was watching at the window. When I saw the crowd returning at a distance, I fixed my kerchief and went out of the village so I, too, could kiss the bishop's hand. From the distance, the seraphim on their metal disks and the church banners shone in the sun, and behind them gleamed the crosses and the vestments of the priests. Behind and off to the side I could see the gold-saddled white steed that they had taken out for the bishop; but the closer it got, the clearer it became that the bishop wasn't on it. 'Oh-Oh!' I said to myself and anxiously hurried closer.

"'Get back, ma'am!' yelled one of the children who were running out in front dressed in their best clothes. 'Get back, the irregulars are coming! Listen, they've cut the railroad and they've taken our bishop!'

"Then my heart flew up into my mouth! We'd heard of the war, but the Russians were far away, goodness knows where, in Romania, they told us, and farther away still. And to think that now they'd suddenly cut the railroad!

"See, I said to myself, something terrible's happened to my child! My legs refused to carry me, and I stopped right where I was. The terrified crowd rushed up to meet me at that point. And the Cross and the seraphim on their disks came up, followed by the priest with the censer, and behind them, four people came up with a corpse on their shoulder, and beside them, Michael, disheveled and bathed in tears . . . 'Ach! My child! My child!' . . . Who could have thought to stop him?"

At this point, her trembling voice was drowned by her sobs and wailing.

It was the first time that day. And since I knew my unhappy mother's nature, I neither interrupted her nor allowed my brother to. Grief was flooding her loving heart, and if she did not allow it to overflow once, twice, or three times a day, she could find no peace. The frightful blow had struck our much-suffering house more than three years earlier. But my recent arrival—I, who hadn't witnessed that frightful drama at first hand—reopened the poor woman's barely healed wounds. My presence made the loss of my late brother far more noticeable, because, as my mother rightly said, it now seemed that our joy could not be complete. Though I had left only a few relatives behind, I found them fewer still now. And I could neither kiss my poor brother, nor could he rejoice at the return of his so long-awaited brother! And so the poor woman wept and told that sad story as if it had happened just the day before.

And do you think she forgot her misfortune when her flood of tears had relieved her deeply sorrowing heart a little? Far from it. Sorrow for the murder of our beloved brother was succeeded by implacable wrath at the murderer.

"Every so often," my brother told me privately, "I thought she was beginning to forget Hristákis, but never have I seen her forget his killer."

During that entire time, she had left neither the bishop nor the *Kaïmakámis* a moment's peace in hopes they would find her child's killer for her. At first, it was thought he had been killed when he happened upon the battle during the attack on the station at Lulevurgáz. But this was soon found to be impossible. Those coming to receive the bishop found that the station had been abandoned by the local authorities two days earlier, after which time all communication with the Capital had been cut, and that the Russians had taken possession of the place without a fight, but only about the middle of the preceding night. Our poor brother had been found during their disorderly retreat, by the highway bridge, far from the village, and dead well before the Russians arrived. So he hadn't been killed accidentally or in an engagement. But neither was it possible that he had been intentionally killed by soldiers or brigands because the former would not have left the corpse unstripped, the latter, the mail pouch untouched. Every investigation ended with the obvious conclusion that the killing took place from ambush with no intent of robbery. For this very reason, my mother kept insisting that the killer be located and punished. It was the way in which the disreputable former postman had deceived the unsuspecting youth into taking over his dangerous job that provided her investigations their leading thread.

"It can't be otherwise," she kept saying. "The murderer must have been angry with him, and he must have known it. Otherwise the murderer couldn't have ambushed him on the very first day he took over the post. So it's sure to be someone from our village or from one of the surrounding villages. When they took the former postman to jail, I thought God had judged. But after two days they let him go because it was found he was in our village at the time of the killing. Who knows? Perhaps they were lying. . . . But now that you've come at last, my child, don't leave your brother unavenged. Don't look at me like that and say nothing! If I didn't have living sons, I'd cut my hair, I'd put on men's clothes, and with my rifle on my shoulder I'd hunt out the killer's trail until I had avenged my dead boy because you see, my child, our poor Hristákis can find no peace. He only writhes in his tomb whenever he feels his killer walking the earth. And he feels him, my child! Even if he's at the ends of the earth he feels him, as if he were trampling on his heart! For that reason—revenge! We must have revenge!"

Anybody who did not know this most gentle mother prior to her son's death would have taken her, perhaps, for a woman of harsh and cruel character; for I myself now found it difficult to discover in her that boundless humanity that made her have pity and feel compassion for even inanimate nature and that caused her to be unable to bear the sight even of a slaughtered hen. Though it's true that in saying retribution she really meant "justice," she did not understand that this "justice" would be meted out only by the dispassionate hand of the law and without her own personal satisfaction. "Let me see him hanging," she used to say. "Let me drag down on his rope, and then let me die!" So hideously desirable did revenge seem to the love of this simple, uneducated woman!

The arguments of cold logic with which I sometimes tried to cool the impulses of her heated heart evaporated before reaching their goal like small drops of water when they fall upon a violently flaming furnace. And so it happened that day as well. When, after lengthy instruction concerning the position of individuals vis-à-vis public justice, I promised her I would leave no stone unturned in finding and punishing the criminal, she said with a certain fierce satisfaction, "Yes! Let me see him hanging, let me drag down on his rope, and then let me die!"

But suddenly there was a knocking at the door, and, with obvious displeasure, she saw the smooth-shaven face of the servant respectfully peeking out from behind the door. "What's up, Louis?" I asked him as he came in.

"A Turkish lady," he answered, bowing before my scowling mother, "a Turkish lady to see you."

"To see us? It can't be! You must have made a mistake, Louis. Go! We don't know any Turkish lady." But while I was sending him away in this manner for my mother's sake, a disturbance was heard in the hall and sounds of people arguing. Louis bowed again as deeply as he could in order to persuade me that we were indeed those asked after. But suddenly the door opened with a frightful clatter, hitting him from behind and causing him to fall on his face, and an old Ottoman lady, almost completely unveiled, threw herself at my mother's feet with sobs and tears. It seems that the servants outside had tried to bar her entrance, and she, in desperation, had

forced the door. The astonished Louis managed to pull himself together and, with his kicks, chase away the exceedingly tall, white-
turbaned *softás* who was timidly following her. But my brother
stepped in when he saw him, reprimanded the servant, and with
great joy led that thin, pale Turk into the room as if he had been
his closest friend.

"It's our Kyamíl," he said to me by way of explanation, "and this
must be his mother."

My mother finally managed to extricate herself from the Ottoman lady's embraces, and staring up at the *softás'* pleasant face
with a strange affection, she asked him, "Are you Kyamíl, my child?
And how are you? Well? Well? I didn't recognize you in that outfit."

With tears in his eyes, the Turk bent over and, taking the hem of
her skirt, kissed it and said, "May God grant you many good things,
Validé! Day and night I ask him to cut years off my life and add
them to your own."

My mother seemed extremely pleased. Michael was going out of
his mind with joy, directing thousands of questions and attentions
sometimes to that tall, thin man in the green robe and sometimes
to his mother. Only I and Louis remained speechless and confused.
Finally, taking my brother aside, I said, "Come on, cut out your
laughing and tell me what's going on around here. What are these
people to you?"

"I'll tell you in a minute," my brother said laughing still harder,
"in a minute. Go, Louis! Two coffees, and quick! But see here, don't
make them like those European slops of yours again! A-la-Turque,
and without sugar! Do you hear?"

And with this he went with me into the adjoining room. "He's a
Turk our mother tended in our house for seven months when he
was sick. And she's his mother, who's come now to thank her." My
brother said this with a laugh that caused me great astonishment.

"A Turk our mother tended for seven months when he was sick!
Since when has our mother been a nurse to Turks?" I asked, scowling with indignation.

I must note that Michael was in the habit of making jokes about
our mother's excesses, the more happily as he paid for them eagerly
and without complaint from his own purse. Nothing delighted him
more than to mimic our mother acting under the influence of some
excess of affection, the components of which he twisted comically
in a way altogether his own. The patience of our good mother, who

laughed along herself as often as she heard him, ingrained this bad habit in him all the more deeply. For this reason, when he saw me indignant at what I had heard, he said, "Listen to what I'm saying. If you mean to take everything so grumpily, I won't tell you anything. You'll ruin my story. Better to leave it for another day so you can have a hearty laugh, and mother can laugh a little, since she hasn't had a really good laugh for many days now, poor thing."

"Come on!" I said then. "Mother seems very happy with the visit, and she's completely occupied with her Turks, and I can't stomach them. So tell me the story till they finish their coffee and we're rid of them."

"O.K., listen," he said. "You know how worried mother was when you left. And it's not enough she was worried, she didn't leave anyone at all in peace. Someone's passing by, she stops him in the road; someone's come from somewhere, she goes and asks him: has he seen you, has he news of you? You know her. Early one morning we were gathering melons in the field. All at once she sees a traveler passing by. She doesn't let him go about his business, but runs to the fence.

"'May the hour prove favorable to you, uncle!'

"'Many years to you, ma'am!'

"'You coming from Europe?'

"'No, ma'am, from my village. And where's this Europe?'

"'Well how should I know? It's where my son is. Have you heard them saying anything about my son?'

"'No, ma'am. And what's your son's name?'

"'Do you think I know, myself? His god-father baptized him Yoryís, and his father, my husband, was Mihaliós, the tradesman. But you see he's got ahead in the world and taken a name from learned circles; and now, you see, when they write about him in the newspapers, I don't even know myself if it's my boy they mean or some European!'"

"The story, Michael! The story about the Turk!" I interrupted impatiently.

"Hold on, there!" he said. "The story came after the conversation. After the conversation, you see, Mother went and cut the biggest and best melon.

"'Won't you take some fruit from our garden, uncle?'

"'No thank you, ma'am, I have no place to put it.'

" 'No matter, uncle, I'll cut it up and you can eat it here.'

" 'No thank you, ma'am, but I have a stomach-ache.' "

" 'Come on, please, do me a favor. You see, I have a boy in foreign lands, and I have an aching heart. And since I can't send it to my boy, you eat it since you're a foreigner. Perhaps he'll find one from someone else.' "

"The man lost his patience. '*Dzánun*, that's all very well for you, a Christian. But how am I to blame if you have a son abroad so that, fasting as I am, I have to stuff this cholera into my stomach? You think I'm tired of life? I have a wife who's waiting for me, and I've children to support. But if you're bound and determined to make use of that melon, send it to Old-Múrtos' inn. There's a foreigner near there who's been wrestling with death in a fever for three weeks now. As soon as he tastes this cholera, believe me, he'll escape his fever, and his fever will escape him.' "

"For heaven's sake!" I said to him. "Are we done with the anecdotes? Get on with the story now!"

"Hold on there!" he answered teasingly. "You think we're in Europe where they sell meat without the bones? I'm telling you the story as it happened. If you don't like it, forget about it. Let's go see the *hanúmissa!*"

"I wish you could've been there," he continued then, "to see Mother when she heard this. 'Christ and Virgin, my child!' And the melon dropped from her hands and flattened like a pancake. And she arranged her kerchief and took to the road. That is to say, she took to the planted and fallow fields in a straight line to get there as soon as possible. I knew her ways and let her go. But when she'd gone a short distance and saw I wasn't following, she turned back angrily and shouted, 'What are you gaping at there, you wretch, you? Eh? You waiting for me to tell you to get a move on?'

"Who could dare not to follow her? I wouldn't have put it past her to crown me with a lump of dirt. So I left my work and fell in behind her. No way you could keep up with her! Nettles, ditches, fences—man, she didn't see any of them. Nothing, except Old-Múrtos' red roof that stood out in the distant fields.

"When she got close, her legs began to shake, and she sat down on a rock. 'Christ and Virgin, my child! How come you didn't tell me there was a sick man around here?'

" 'And why should I tell you? You a doctor so you can heal him?

And besides, Pappadémos, the priest, who had heard of him, didn't go see him because, he says, he's a Turk, and Turks don't pay for the last rites.'

"'Turk, you said?' she cried, and her color began to come back a little. 'If he's a Turk—glory be to Thee, Oh Lord! I had a fright it might be our Yoryís!'

"'Too bad I didn't tell you sooner, Mother, so you wouldn't have ruined everybody's fields and made a sieve of my feet with the nettles. In your rush, you made me take off barefoot.' But she, in the meantime, had started toward Múrtos' inn.

"After I'd fallen in behind her again and was going to jump over a ditch, I hear someone moaning. I turn and I see a tall Turk down below, his face pale, his eyes red. Though all my life I've been quick to laugh, I've never laughed at a sick person. That day I couldn't contain myself, as you'll see. On one side there was a shrub, on the other a wild artichoke. And the Turk, who was thrashing about and raving between them, turned to the bush and made *temenádes* to it and spoke to it tenderly and was acting lovingly toward it. He turned to the wild artichoke and gnashed his teeth and made his eyes wild and raised his hand, cursing and threatening to cut its head off! His big words on the one hand and his weakness on the other were enough to make you split with laughter. But when Mother came and saw me, she was so angry I thought 'God help me!'

"'Why're you standing there and laughing, you idiot? Eh? Why're you standing there and laughing? The man's fighting for his life, and you're enjoying it? Get him out of there! Load him on your back!'

"'For God's sake, he's half again as tall as I am! How do you expect me to load him onto my back?'

"'Get him out of there, I tell you, or else!'

"You think I dared not do it? So I grabbed the crummy Turk, and she loaded him onto my back and we set out. Old-Múrtos was warming his belly in the sun outside his inn. When he saw us, he laughed deep in his throat and yelled out, 'Hey there, wouldn't you better pick up that dead donkey over there, so 'least you could get money for his hooves 'stead of wasting your breath carrying that pestilence to your house?'

"I didn't answer, because, you see, I didn't have enough breath for jokes. But Mother, you know Mother. She read the riot act to him for his callousness!

"When we got him home, we unrolled Hristákis' bed and laid him in it. Hristákis, God rest his soul, was at that time on his horse making the circuit of the villages in the province with his wares. It was before he opened his shop. And when he learned we had the sick man in the house, he went and hung his hat in our aunt's house in Kryoneró. Mother had always been after him for his unsettled habits, and he, God rest his soul, was looking for a reason to move out and live the way he wanted to. Seven months we had the invalid in our house, seven months he didn't cross our threshold, until Mother was forced to send him with me to the City before he was completely cured."

"And how did he land in our village?" I asked. "And how did he happen to get sick?"

"Hmmm!" said my brother, scratching his head. "Even I know that only sketchily. You think Mother would let me ask him as I wanted? 'We're human beings,' she said, 'and human beings get sick. Woe to him who has no one to look after him! And who knows? Perhaps this very minute our Yoryís is sick in a foreign country without anyone of his family by his side! So don't sit around and ask for details about the fellow, just heal him first!'"

"Kyamíl is a fine, a very fine person, the poor fellow," my brother continued, "and many times he broached the subject of his own accord to tell me how he got sick. But every time he tried, the fever seized him again."

At this point, our mother interrupted by coming in with her guests. The short and somewhat stout Ottoman lady had her snow-white *yasmáki* in order and was holding her long, black *feretzés* most decorously; beneath its border you could barely make out her pointed, yellow shoes. But Kyamíl, with his pale, sad face—the characteristics of which seemed to me so mild and sweet—now made such a deep impression on me that he gained my affection by assault, so to speak. This did not escape the attention of my mother, who knew my hatred for Turks. For this reason, fixing her gaze lovingly on him while she presented him to me, she said, "Poor Kyamíl is a very, very good fellow. He even eats the boiled wheat mixed with sugar at memorial services; he even drinks holy water; he even kisses the priest's hand. What won't he do—all to get well!"

His mother's eyes filled with tears. As soon as I directed two or three words to them in their language, they began to load me with prayers and blessings, with praises and eulogies, those well-known excesses of Turkish etiquette. But my mother, abruptly cutting off the torrent of their rhetoric, said, "Now sit down and let's see what we'll do. The *hanúmissa,* my child, has a son in the *Zaptíe,* where he's one of the chief investigators. I told her the disaster that befell us, and she'll get him to find the killer for us. The poor woman! You don't know what a good person she is! Too bad I didn't know enough to come to the City earlier! I'd have already had him hanged three times and would have found peace from this quarter at least!"

The Turkish woman understood a bit what was being discussed. "Yes," she said, "and my son, the *eféntis,* and your servant, Kyamíl, and I, your slave, we'll go right up to the Sultan's doorstep, but we'll never let your case drop. They've had it under the carpet up till now for sure, and that's why the killer hasn't been caught. My son the *eféntis* is an investigator with the police, and even if the criminal splits the earth to enter it, he'll find him again."

"And for nothing," continued Kyamíl in his pleasant voice. "It won't cost you a *leptón!* My brother, the *eféntis,* will set matters straight with one stroke of the pen. And, if God wills, I, too, will go to the provinces for the investigation. When the child of my *Validé* was killed, it's as if the *eféntis,* my brother, was killed. There must be retribution!"

The eagerness of both produced indescribable happiness not only in my mother, but also in my brother and even in me, since, I now thought, good deeds even toward heathens had not been lost in vain. For some time we discussed the subject, and I, who had completely despaired of discovering the killer, both because of the length of time intervening and because of the disasters caused by the war that had befallen our province after the murder, was not slow to be convinced that it was still likely that justice might be accorded our unfortunate, dead brother. So it was quite natural that I now began to treat kindly the only persons able to assist us in fulfilling this duty of ours. As soon as the old Ottoman lady noticed my attitude, she said, "And now, my *Sultán,* give the hotelkeeper the keys. From today on you are my *musafírides.*"

This was completely unexpected. Turks, especially in the larger cities, not only do not live under the same roof with Christians, they can't even stand living in the same neighborhood. So what was this? Another of their many slavish courtesies? But no, the old woman wasn't speaking for form's sake.

"You're a learned man," she said to me, "and you know God's law. Even if I had only a span of land in the world, and I knew that the blessed woman who tended my fatherless child for seven months in her own son's bed was here as a stranger, and I didn't give her my headrest to set her foot on—wouldn't God close the gate of his pity to my prayers? Wouldn't he remove his blessing from the works of my hands? Wouldn't he turn his face away from my sacrificial lamb? Come, my sweet one! Don't make me commit a sin!"

Kyamíl intervened and, kissing the edge of my clothing, said, "Don't take it amiss that we didn't come get you sooner. We learned you were here, and we've been looking all over for two days to find you. We went to all the inns one after another. We sifted the whole city of Constantinople. But we, simple people, are like oxen. It stands to reason that a gentleman like yourself travels in the European way and stays in a hotel. Now that we've found you, it can't be otherwise." And, turning toward my mother, he said, "Isn't that so, my *Sultana*? We've already agreed to it. That wretched coquette won't ruin your disposition any more. For your sake, I pardon him the kick he gave me, but we're not staying around here any longer. Isn't that so?"

"Yes," said my mother, "we're not staying, if Yoryís agrees also. Listen to that, the wagtail striking my child, my Kyamíl!"

Then I realized that, while I was listening to Kyamíl's story from my brother, the remaining three had plotted against the hotelkeeper and the unfortunate Louis. At that point the old Ottoman lady struck up an Eastern entreaty: "I will sit outside the door of your lodging for seven days; seven times each day I will kiss the threshold of your door; seven times each hour, etc."—and I seven times lost my patience. The invitation, however, seemed to me favorable for our case. For this reason, I allowed my mother to do as she pleased.

Scarcely half an hour had passed before the Ottoman lady and her son departed in true triumph, leading my mother and my brother with them as if they were the most sought after spoils. As for me, neither my affairs nor my disposition allowed me to change my lodging. So I declined to accept their hospitality as they offered it. I did, however, promise that as soon as I had completed my preliminary activities with the appropriate authorities regarding the search for the one who had killed my brother, I would visit them at length each day in their house.

This task did not take long, for, where the law does not exist save in the good will of the individual authorities, either even the simplest case drags on interminably or the most complicated is finished in a moment. To be sure, it wasn't possible to finish our case in so lightning-like a fashion, but already during the first days of my consultations with the ministry of police many arrests had been ordered in our province, and the son of our dear Ottoman lady, the investigator, all zeal and dedication, had set out from the Capital accompanied by my brother and supplied with full power to investigate those who had been captured and to chase down other suspects. We didn't allow the impatient Kyamíl to go along, both because of his precarious health and so that the two old ladies would not be left totally alone.

"And now that we've put the water in the ditch," my mother said to us a few days later, "come along, my child, and spend the day with us. We're home all day because we've finished our tours. And where my child Kyamíl didn't take me! And where the *hanúmissa* didn't take me! First of all we went nearby here to Hagia Sophia. Next they took me to Mefá-meídáni where I worshipped at the tomb of Constantine. You ought to go there too, my child! On one side they have the Moor who killed him, all covered with Lahore fabrics and rugs. On the other side, the poor king himself with only one small lamp over his grave! And we went to a mosque and saw on an old tree the chain where the hand of Justice hung. And we went to Baluklí and saw the fish that came to life in the pan the day the City was taken. And over the Gate that was taken we saw the letters the angel wrote that day, supposedly for the City. 'The wors-wors-worst.' We saw them, but, illiterate that I am, I didn't read them. And why should I read them, my child? Don't we see every day what's happening to the City? And where didn't we go! And what didn't we see! But now that we've seen everything, I'm beginning to worry again. So come every day so I can see you—may you have my blessing—and tell me all about how our case is going."

The Ottoman widow's property lies on *Diván-Yolú*, the now broad but no longer most picturesque street it once was, not far from the square of the Byzantine hippodrome. It is clearly an old building of a once prosperous family, for while the adjacent properties appear mercilessly truncated by the widening of the road, the

Ottoman lady's is distinguished by a forecourt, narrow now, which allows those seated on the balcony to look out over its low wall and see everything in the street, surely a remnant of former spaciousness. Behind it has a beautiful little garden with high, ivy-covered walls and a small pavilion on one side. It is to these walls, principally, that it owes the miraculous preservation of its greatest part from the great fire, which had burned down the entire neighborhood beyond that road. A portion of the side of the wall opposite the pavilion—which had collapsed, it seems, during the conflagration—had been repaired in a makeshift fashion and allowed the addition of a small door through which the house acquired a new means of communication with the outside that was far shorter for one coming through the vast ruins from the ministry of police. This spaciousness in depth, however, was nullified by the loss in width that the house had suffered during the conflagration, because economic difficulties had not allowed reconstruction of the damaged side: half-burned planks, attached as a temporary measure, left the rooms on that side wide open to every wind and completely uninhabitable.

And yet there was room in that house not only for the old Ottoman lady and Kyamíl, not only for the *Eféntis* with his numerous family, but also for my mother and brother, and indeed for all those relatives close and distant who came to visit me, for as soon as the trusty Kyamíl sniffed out a relative, he hunted him down until he found his dwelling and transferred his things to his mother's house, even if by force. And the old Ottoman lady rejoiced at this because, as she used to day, "Even the entire world is not room enough for two evil people, while a thousand good people can enjoy themselves even in a walnut shell!"

Such was the house in which I spent the greater part of my day for almost four weeks, going back and forth regularly each day. I could hear the old Ottoman lady's greetings from her latticed windows even before I knocked on the door on *Diván-Yolú*. My arrival was awaited from the balcony. But my appearance caused an uproar in the house like that of many birds flying up at the appearance of a cat in front of their large cage. It was the cries of the *eféntis'* wives, children, and babes, who leaped up and fled to their harem in disorderly haste out of fear I might see them without their *yasmáki*. Kyamíl, in his small, snow-white *saríki*, his long, green *tsubé*, with his pale and likable expression, almost as tall as the wall of the forecourt, regularly opened the gate for me with that sweet, sad smile on his lips as he bent to the ground in the deep and heartfelt *temenás* of welcome. The two old women always had one of the sweets I liked ready for me, or some fairy tale, which I liked even better. The Ottoman lady was especially delighted with me because, she said, though I was wise and learned, I had not become a faithless infidel but believed with all my heart—in fairy tales! She found fault with me on only two counts. First, that I could in no way bear to hear anything about the wonders of magic, and second, that I had not yet consented to spend one night under the roof of her humble dwelling. It did not prove possible for us ever to agree on the first, but we did finally compromise on the second.

We expected the arrival of her son the investigator any day now. He had already sent some twenty suspects to prison in Constantinople, whither he had transferred our case in order to be free of the influence of local authorities. "When the *eféntis* arrives," I told the old woman, "I will sleep at your house that night. I'll need to be brought up to date on many things." Three days later, if I'm not mistaken, the investigator returned. My brother, who had returned the day before, gave me many examples of his harsh efficiency.

"So tomorrow I'll come after sundown," I told them, "when the *eféntis* will also be here. Don't expect me earlier."

The next day, mounting one of those ponies that are for public hire by the Old Bridge and not sparing the sunburned and bare-legged driver who, bathed in sweat, ran the entire distance by the tail of his swift and obedient horse, I reached the house much earlier than I had said. For this reason, I was not surprised this time not to hear the Ottoman lady's greetings from behind her latticed window. But when the gate opened and I saw before me a small Turkish boy staring stupidly at me, and not Kyamíl's pale face as he made his great *temenás* with his perpetually sad smile, I felt somehow strange and disoriented. Other than the child, no one appeared in the courtyard. I entered the flagged and cool ground floor—again not a soul. I called out somewhat impatiently for my mother, my brother, but no one answered. The small door at the end of the ground floor that led into the garden was, contrary to custom, slightly ajar. And since I could not go upstairs before being sure that the harem had withdrawn from the "salon," I approached it hesitantly and, peering around it, looked into the garden.

There, by the high, ivy-clad wall and half in the shade, were seated my mother, the Ottoman lady, and another old woman in rags and bare-headed, to all appearances a filthy *romiokatsivéla* or Greek-speaking gypsy. Seated at a higher level than the others, she held a sieve on her lap over which the Ottoman lady and my mother were bent; it appeared that they were trying to understand something with obvious amazement and perplexity. After a long silence, the gypsy said with authoritative emphasis, "As I say, the killer is near you; he moves about you; don't seek him far away."

"Aha," my mother said with triumphant joy. "So he's been caught! It must be one of those the *eféntis* sent in chains. I forgot to tell you that the suspects are in the City."

"I told you not to tell me anything unless I ask you, otherwise you'll ruin my spells!" said the Pythia of the crossroads indignantly, and she shook the sieve forcefully; within it was heard a noise as of beans striking against one another.

"Come now, don't be angry!" said the Ottoman lady. "Let's give them another toss. Count them again."

"Hmmm!" said the prophetess. "Three and the truth! Good! But as I told you, don't tell me anything. The beans will say the thing, whatever it is. Look here, dear—the killer, I'm taking him out again." And taking a black bean from the sieve, she tossed it over her head and, uttering a curse over her shoulder, said, "Now, the two of you count them and I'll ask them."

My mother took the sieve, poured the beans out onto her apron, and, placing the sieve back on the gypsy's knees, began to put the beans back in one by one, counting them with a care and accuracy that perhaps no miser ever used when counting his priceless pearls when about to entrust them to the hands of others.

"Are they correct?" asked the gypsy, tossing her gray locks over onto her shoulder blades.

"Yes!" my mother answered. "Exactly forty."

Then the gypsy took the sieve and, casting a familiar glance over the beans in it, shook them two or three times as if wishing to awaken the mantic spirit slumbering deeply in them and cried out in a most commanding manner, "A man has been killed, who can have killed him? Three for the wolves, three for the thieves, three for the fleeing irregulars' band, three for his secret enemies, and forty-one beans in hand." And while chanting these words, she separated the beans into separate piles of three, apparently attributing to each triad a different position and quality. "Three the thieves, three the wolves, three the fleeing irregulars' band, three for his secret enemies, and—forty-one beans in hand!"

"How many beans did you count, dear?"

"Forty," said my mother.

"And forty there were," said the gypsy. "But the killer entered, and there are forty-one. You see, I've bewitched him, and I can bring him into my sieve from the very ends of the earth."

When the two women had assured themselves of the miraculously increased number of beans, the prophetess shook the sieve repeatedly and, with the skill of a prestidigitator, tossed the beans high into the air three times, and three times caught them again in her sieve without a single one falling out. Then, placing the sieve on her knees and bending over it, she began, as it seemed to me, to examine carefully the relative positions of the beans. My mother and the Ottoman lady also studied them with great reverence.

"Look!" said the gypsy after a long reverent silence. "Here's the killer and here you are. No one is as close to you as he and your children are. That's why I tell you not to look for him in the City, not to look for him far away. It will be some compatriot of yours, someone of your own."

The great curiosity with which I was following these goings-on apparently caused me to forget that I had been a spy up to this point and to press somewhat too heavily on the door into the garden. Before I realized this, the door opened with a creak, and I was caught red-handed standing behind it.

"Bah!" exclaimed my mother, astonished at my unexpected presence. "You here, my child? And why didn't Michael come tell me? What good is he, the wretch?"

Both my mother and the Ottoman lady appeared somewhat unpleasantly surprised by the way they had been caught in the act, and neither could find any way of hiding things from me any longer. As I've said, they were aware of my war against superstitions and especially sorceresses. Just a few days earlier, I had rudely chased one away who had persisted in seeing my fate. And they had obviously chosen this out-of-the-way corner for their divinations for safety's sake. Their complaints against my brother revealed that they had posted him at the gate to guard against my arrival, and that he had betrayed his responsibility in allowing me to come upon them unannounced. The sly Pythia divined the way things lay as soon as she saw my scowling face, and, gathering up her beans and her sieves, she sneaked out hastily through the garden's other gate like a wet cat. Without a doubt she had had the foresight to be paid in advance. The confusion of the two gullible women and their lack of skill in finding some ready motive to justify themselves made me regret my indiscretion. For this reason, I pretended complete ignorance of what had happened:

"Buying needles, Mother?" I asked with complete indifference.

"Yes, my child," my mother said with some hesitation, "let's say we're buying needles to mend lies. And when did you get here?"

"Just now, Mother. I just came."

"And where's that rascally Michael? Why didn't he come tell me?"

"I don't know, Mother. There's no one in the courtyard except the child who opened the gate for me."

"Well, who knows where he can have got to this time. The place isn't big enough to hold him."

The Ottoman lady continued to look at me askance and suspiciously with a smile of disbelief on her lips, waiting for the outburst of my indignation at what I had seen. But instead of any reproach, which would have been useless now anyway, I pretended I had seen nothing.

"Let's go inside then," she said. "The *eféntis* will be along soon also."

Then again there was heard over our heads the usual noise of the retreating harem. Obviously, its denizens had up to that point been glued to the windows over the garden, following in reverent silence the gypsy's sievemancy.

We had just repeated the usual greetings and courteous gestures when the *eféntis'* arrival was announced from without. Only with great difficulty could I recognize this gently brought up Turk in the European clothes, because the provincial sun, while it had faded the more prominent surfaces of his clothes by bleaching them, had tanned his pale face in such a way that you couldn't see where his cheeks ended and where his dark and carefully trimmed beard began. As laconic as our greetings had once been in the offices of the *Zaptié*, the official's rhetoric today was so free-flowing, so artful, that I was uneasy as to the effectiveness of his mission.

"Leave us alone," I said to the women. "The *eféntis* will have painful details to recount to me that are unsuitable for your nerves."

The women left. The *eféntis* scowled. "Details," he said. "I could, in fact, recount frightful details to you. I don't do it so you won't be pained excessively, learning how many crimes I have on my conscience! The result of my mission is in any event very painful, and you must know it. It's zero. Failure. Failure as regards our case, for, though my investigations brought many crimes to light and many criminals will receive punishment for their wickedness, our brother's killer has not been found. Either he must have been killed during the disasters that subsequently befell the province, or it must be the postman whom the deceased replaced. That postman will cause me to lose my mind! I find him the manifest perpetrator of many crimes, I find him most likely guilty of the murder of our poor brother, but I am unable to find him himself! I'm unable to apprehend him! As soon as I arrived this morning I gave the strictest orders. I'm almost certain he's hiding in the Capital. You know the story. The old lady looks for the flea in her quilt and it's sitting on her spectacles. Don't say anything to the *Validé*, however. I said the same thing to Michael, too. When she asked me early this morning, I told her that my position forbids me to say anything until the court decides. The poor thing. She didn't say anything, but I'm afraid she perceived my failure."

I have already said how much, at first, I had distrusted even these more drastic activities of justice in this case, on the one hand, because of the long time that had intervened, on the other, because of the plunder and slaughter that had taken place in the province. Who knows whether the killers had not been punished for their wickedness by God, they alone justly killed among so many innocents in that general disaster? But when a little later I came to know the *eféntis*, I changed my mind, and along with the others, I hoped that his zeal would satisfy the law and aid us in fulfilling our sad duty toward our beloved, dead brother. The investigator's report, by not trying to conceal a failure greater than the one it admitted, caused those hopes to vanish forever. Nothing remained any more save to moderate the effect of this news on our mother, putting her off as long as possible. The unfortunate *eféntis*, sincerely disconsolate, agreed with me that we should abandon all further pursuit, especially when I assured him how my heart was torn on account of the innocent people who were suffering in their confinement as suspects during his rigorous investigations. As regards the former postman, our case would gain nothing through his capture, since his alibi had already been proved many times in court.

I thought that my mother was waiting outside the room, impatient to learn the *Eféntis'* news. But when I got up and peered through the door to see, I spied her at the bottom of the stairs reproaching my brother Michael in a low but very vehement voice. After a moment he ran out of the house, full of agitation.

"Don't let me see you coming back without Kyamíl!" my mother shouted after him.

"What's up, Mother?" I asked when I saw the great anxiety on her face.

"Nothing, my child, nothing." And she went into the kitchen without asking anything about our case, so preoccupied was she, it seems, with Kyamíl's absence!

It was the first time I had seen the *eféntis* in his house. After his numerous struggles on our behalf, it was right that I should appear as courteous and grateful to him as I could, especially since I saw how despondent he was at the fruitlessness of those struggles. So I sat down beside him, and we began chatting in a friendly manner on various subjects, mostly political. When in the course of our conversation I asked him what he thought of the party of the so-called Young Turks in Constantinople, he got up and closed the door of the room.

"I, my friend," he said, "belong to that progressive party." Then, taking a key out of his pocket, he opened the built-in closet behind the door and, continuing to talk, said, "It is my humble opinion that the conservatives are stagnant, and stagnation is not progress."

And with this, he took a tray out of the cupboard and set it down before me on the divan. On the tray there were a "Kilo," two glasses, and several plates of pistachios, raisins, and sweets. "I mean, you see," said the *eféntis* as he sat down opposite me, "I mean let's leave behind the old and rusted past and let's become imbued with new spirit, new ideas."

And while saying this, he filled the glasses in front of us with great skill. Then I realized that the new "spirit" with which the Young Turks were imbued was—alcohol! I knew that many of the *eféntides* drink in secret. But never could I have imagined that anyone could drink about an *oká* of *mastîha* in such a relatively short time, and without water at that!

When they came to call us to dinner and I watched that good man bouncing from one wall to the other, I then understood why the party to which he belongs moves only crab-wise on the road to progress, and a desire to laugh came over me. But when I saw the Ottoman lady's gloomy expression, my mother's troubled face, when I saw that some hidden disaster was causing them not even to notice the *eféntis'* slurred speech, a kind of mysterious force threw my heart into confusion! Obviously something more distressing than the *eféntis'* drunkenness was going on. The hour passed, but neither my brother nor Kyamíl came to dine with us. The oppressive silence that each of us maintained increased my anxiety the more, and since my mother refused to answer the questions in my eyes, I stopped eating and asked her:

"Where's Michael, Mother?"

"He'll come right away, my child," she said in a sorrowful voice.

"And Kyamíl?" I asked again.

My mother put her fingers to her lips and nodded to me in the name of God to be still! The old Ottoman lady, her dejected head bowed in indescribable sorrow, did not raise her eyes, but she shook violently at hearing her child's name. Then, pulling herself together and vainly trying to smile, she said, "Don't ruin your appetite, my *Sultan*. It's nothing. Kyamíl went out and is late in coming, but it's nothing."

"The Lord be praised!" I said then with a sigh of relief. "I was afraid he'd been taken ill. Since he's all right, he'll surely come any minute now."

"The Lord be praised!" repeated the old lady with a deep sigh. And as if she were excessively hot, she opened up her *yasmáki* more than she had ever done in my presence and began to fan herself with one end of it. Tears filled the large but somewhat sunken eyes of the old woman whose oriental beauty was still faintly visible on her withered face.

"And that my son is so strong," she added then, "again the Lord be praised!"

"It's only that he's a little pale," I said to her by way of encouragement. "Otherwise he's a strong lad."

"Strong," she sighed. "Strong, but what good is that! Inside he has the worm that gnaws at his heart! And if it ever goes up to his head—God save everybody else's children and, afterwards, my own! God save even you yourself, my *Sultan!* '*Kará Sevdá*' they called it," the old woman continued sadly, "and *kará sevdá* it is because it has blackened the hearts of many mothers, it has sent many young men to the black earth below! The *Kokkóna* told me the story of your fellow villager who took poison at Psomáthia because of Xanthúlis' daughter, and they made a song of him and sang it in the streets. . . . God save my child!"

I knew the story of our villager. From her hint I inferred poor Kyamíl's disease. His pale face, his dreamy eyes, that sad something in all his being, the intermittent fevers, his constantly failing health should have made me figure it out. "So Kyamíl loves and isn't loved in return?"

"And without hope that he'll ever be loved," sighed his mother, "because the bitch is married already!"

"Ah!" I said, "that I don't like. We must help Kyamíl forget her."

The unfortunate woman broke out into entreaties, prayers and blessings, praises and encomia, all excessive in the oriental manner, but all in fact coming from the bottom of her heart. "If you do this favor for me," she said finally, "I'll be your slave, I'll sweep the threshold of your house with my eyelashes!" Then she began to tell the story.

"It was before there was a tobacco monopoly in the City. My Kyamíl wasn't the sort of lad to become a *softás* and sit around all day with his arms folded as you see him now. He had a partnership in a tobacco shop, the likes of which you've never seen. His partner sold at retail in the City, and my child made the rounds of the countryside and bought wholesale from tobacco farmers. There in the country he became acquainted with a landowner's son. My Kyamíl was such a sweet lad that everybody loved him. But the landowner's son loved him very much—better it had never happened!—because Kyamíl loved him a lot and brought him to the City, and they went to the *Imám* and he opened a vein in each, and each drank the blood of the other and they became *kankardásides*, blood brothers. Since they were so fond of one another, 'Come, I'll make you my brother-in-law!' he said to him. 'I have a sister on our farm— beauty of beauties. Once you've seen her you'll lose your mind.' Eh! My Kyamíl was young, too, and he was good, and he was deserving. But the girl's father—he loved him, I don't say he didn't love him—but he didn't want him as a son-in-law. You see, he was one of those *sultans* born from the Sultan's slave girls, and he wanted her to pick some *bey*, some *pasha*. But the young people had fallen in love, and the girl—damn her!—loved Kyamíl so much that the old man was forced to bite his lips and be silent, no matter how touchy and proud he was. Nazilé was his only daughter and he didn't want to cause her pain. So they gave pledges and were engaged. If only we'd thought to marry them then and bring them to the City! But you see, in the meantime the Monopoly had come into being, and they shut all the tobacco shops everywhere and left many people out of work. And Kyamíl, aside from the fact he lost so much money, he had no job either. So he went to his father-in-law to get work doing one thing and another on the farm together with his brother-in-law; and he decided to move to the country himself for the sake of his fiancée, who now didn't want to be separated from her father.

"'Kyamíl, my child,' I told him, 'fruit that clings tightly to its tree isn't ripe yet. And a girl who can't leave her parent's house isn't ready yet to be a wife.'

"But Kyamíl, because he loved her, did what she asked of him. When the time of the marriage approached, Kyamíl and his blood brother mounted horses to come to the City and do some shopping. The railway was nearby, but the young men loved horses, and they really wanted to ride into the City on horseback, with gold buttons on their jackets, with pistols in their sash, with rifles on their backs. So they set out with money in their wallets. They reached the Lulevurgáz Bridge, the same bridge where your poor brother was killed later on. The bridge, as the *eféntis,* who saw it, told me, is narrow and high; the river is deep and swift; one bank is bare and the other covered with many wild willows and other trees that merge with the forest that begins at that point."

The drunken *eféntis* was not in a position to refute the correctness of the description, because for some time now he had been asleep, stretched out by the table and snoring.

"They had just reached the middle of the bridge," continued the old lady, "when my son Kyamíl saw a flash in the willows and heard a rifle shot! And before he had a chance to think, my child, his companion fell wounded! And Kyamíl's horse shied and veered to one side and broke through the railing and fell into the river with my child! May God protect us all from the evil hour! Who knows how many hours he wrestled with death! But you see it wasn't his destiny. The horse was found killed, but he got away. I thank you, Lord! And the way he got away, again glory be to Thee, Lord! Three days he didn't know where he was. When he came to a little, he discovered he was in a mill. The current had dragged him that far all entangled in the horse's reins! And if the miller hadn't had time to pull him out at the very last moment—but so be it! And the miller wasn't a very nice person, but so be it, because when my child came to his senses, he realized that the miller had taken his wallet from his sash. But he didn't say anything. He would have given it to him anyway of his own accord. So he thanked him as best he could and took to the road to go to his father-in-law's farm to see if his blood brother had been hurt and to bring the news. But when, half-dead, he got to his door, he didn't let him in. He only turned his face away so as not to see him and said, 'You let them kill your blood brother without emptying your rifle; and you come to my house without the killer's head in your hand? You coward! You traitor!'

"And he shoved him out and closed the door! Without life in his body, without a penny in his pocket! Who knows in what field his bones would be lying scattered now if he hadn't had the good fortune to land in your village, and if there wasn't this sainted woman, the *Validé*, your mother, to shelter him in her house and to look after him. We Turks say that all Christians will go to Hell; but when I think of the good thing your mother did I say to myself, 'If this Christian lady doesn't go to Paradise, I don't know what Turk will go!' So be it! The will of God, no one knows God's will!

"All that time my child was lost to me. We learned that the killing had taken place, but the *eféntis* wasn't yet in the *Zaptié*, and the *sultan*, Kyamíl's prospective father-in-law, replied that he hadn't seen him again. So we wrote him off as dead. When your brother came and brought him to me so terribly thin and as pale as death, it seemed to me that he had come from his tomb. And the great joy I felt on that day, my child, may God grant such joy in your life! In fact, much time passed, but finally my child got well. When he got well, he got up to leave.

"'Where will you go, my child?'

"'To my fiancée, Mother, to my father-in-law.'

"'And why will you go to such a father-in-law, my child? Let him be hanged!'

"'No, Mother, it can't be. He has to learn I'm not a traitor, not a cowardly person. I have to talk to him.'

"So he got up and left. After two or three weeks he came back without my expecting him. But he went one man and returned another! Where he went, what he did, he didn't say a word to us. But, as soon as he came, he fell onto his bed with the fever. It was January.

"Didn't I tell you, my child, not to travel in the winter? Just look, you're sick again!'

" 'Better to have died from the winter, Mother, than to have suffered what I've suffered!'

"That's all he told me, and he gave me the pledges that we sent the sultan's daughter when he became engaged to her. Then I understood his illness! The bitch had got married and had taken someone else! May she get hers from God! She's responsible for what's happened to my son! You see what's become of him! From his grief, he enrolled as a novice in the *Teké* here near us, and he goes every Friday and eats opium with the dervishes and kneels down with them and moans until his insides are bloodied, and he beats his chest until they drag him in a faint from their midst. And if this were all, no matter, because the sheik, the leader of the dervishes, loves him very much for this, and he told me that one day my child will become a saint. But an evil that comes on him every once in a while will make me lose my mind! You've seen how calm and sweet and quiet he is. That's how he became after he'd learned his love had got married, even more so than before. But from time to time you see him grow wild, and a restlessness comes over him and he's too big for his clothes, and he doesn't know what he's doing! Just like today. While we were out back in the garden with the gypsy, he rushed suddenly into the house like a madman, grabbed something from the closet, and went out and left. We didn't see him. But Michael whom we set to watch in case you came saw him and opened his arms to stop him. But it was as if he'd seen the devil in front of him. He let out a curse, you see, and knocked Michael down and went out and left! That's why my child didn't open the door for you today, and that's why you didn't find anyone to greet you. Because when Michael recovered, he took off after Kyamíl in hopes of catching him, but he couldn't. And he came back to tell us what had happened and went out again, hoping he might even find him somewhere near the sea. . . . God protect my child from the sea!"

And the old woman sighed and allowed the torrents of her tears to flow freely!

I had imagined that evening's meal one way, and it ended another. On one side, brutally drunk, snored that zealous, energetic investigator who up to that point I thought was the model of a temperate and dedicated public servant. On the other side, sunk in the extremities of misfortune, wept the old Ottoman lady who for so many days had been preparing to celebrate the evening of my stay with her with all manner of Turkish amusements and who, tonight, did not find consolation even in my mother's tenderest ministrations. And Kyamíl, the abstemious, the sober Kyamíl, who even drank holy water and kissed the priest's hand, and thanks to whom principally I had begun to forget my dislike of Moslems, was suddenly presented to me as belonging to the most fanatic sect of wailing dervishes, as an unfortunate man whose wits, perhaps from his unlucky love, perhaps from excessive use of opium, had become unsettled and who, for this reason, experienced periodic lapses. And yet, for a moment, I contemplated going out myself in search of him. But aside from the fact that I didn't know where to go, I immediately thought of his modest and respectful character, and I imagined how harmfully his weakened nature could be influenced by the idea that he had me, too—one whom he honored and respected to such a high degree—as a witness to his misfortune. But since time was passing and neither my brother nor Kyamíl had returned, I said to the women, "I have an idea. Michael surely must have found Kyamíl; but Kyamíl is shy, and after what's happened, he'll refuse to come into the house because I'm here."

"That must be it!" said my mother. "Perhaps they're walking around outside in the street waiting for the light in the 'salon' to go out before coming in. Come, my child, so the *hanúmissa* won't worry any longer, come let me show you where you'll sleep."

After a few vain attempts to console the wretched Ottoman lady, my mother led the way, holding a small oil lamp, and I followed her. "We've made you a bed in the *kióski*," she told me as we came down the stairs. "You're a light sleeper, and the children wake up early and make a lot of racket. That's why we made your bed in the *kióski*."

When my mother opened the door to the pavilion, a sweet smell of burning aromatic wood greeted my nostrils. Everything in the small house appeared extraordinarily well arranged. But the dejection that I felt upon entering it did not allow me to look around at all. A vague anxiety, a hidden premonition of some unforeseen disaster, had taken hold of my heart. It was for that reason that, when my mother began to question me about the *eféntis'* report concerning my brother's killer, I was, I still recall, very vague and brief and caused her sorrow without intending to.

For a long time after my mother left, I still sat cross-legged on the red coverlet of the low sofa, leaning toward the faint light of the pitiful lamp, trying to distract my thoughts and the lifelike pictures of my imaginings by reading some book, the name of which I can no longer recall. But the objects of mental vision intervened between me and the book, far brighter than its pages, and my reading during all that time was no more than a mechanical wandering of my eyes over the lines on each page. Two or three times I lay down on my perfumed bed with my eyes forced tightly shut, but in vain. The odor of musk that my hand-embroidered pillows exuded, so intoxicating, so sleep inducing, was not strong enough to lull my agitation to sleep. Poor Kyamíl's story unfolded in lifelike images before my closed eyes. How sociable and charming the solitary, the taciturn, and for this reason, now wearisome, *softás* must once have been! He who had, counter to all expectations, acquired the love of one of the *sultánides* who are the haughtiest members of Ottoman society in spite of all their advancing poverty! And what a friendship that must have been! What brotherliness! Undoubtedly the young *sultan* had found in this a happiness much greater than ordinary, and being a good brother, had hastened to make his beautiful sister also a participant in it. At one point I imagined Kyamíl, secretly and blissfully in love with his future fiancée, experiencing emotions and feelings so unfamiliar to his compatriots and yet so natural to his sensitive heart; at another point I imagined him master of his spirited horse, galloping by the side of his blood brother, wearing the picturesque outfit of provincial youth, bright colors and weapons flashing; and after a little I saw him in frightful confusion crashing down together with his bolted horse from the great height of the bridge and desperately wrestling with the creature's panic, with the fury of the violent currents, with death, as his mother said, until, exhausted and worn out, he allowed himself and his already dying horse to be drawn along—like as not caught in the stirrup straps—a plaything of the raging waters. And then I saw that hateful egoist, the inhuman *sultan,* who so pitilessly closed his door to the half-dead suitor of his own daughter! And then again the unfortunate Kyamíl cruelly abandoned at Old-Múrtos' Inn, tor-

mented by fever and yet exposed to the chills of the night and the
heat of the day because of his poverty, in his delirium asking for
pity from a bush, perhaps his fiancée, and threatening to butcher a
wild artichoke, perhaps the killer of his blood brother! And how
could the unlucky young man find the killer? And how could he
avenge his blood brother? And did he find him? And did he get
revenge? And if he did avenge his fiancée's brother, why then did
she abandon him, since she ought to have loved him twice as much
for that? Surely Kyamíl's gentle character was not up to fulfilling
the fierce duty of harsh, bloodthirsty revenge. And sooner than
commit a crime to satisfy the heart of his brutish father-in-law, he
preferred to kill his own heart forever, ruining all its happiness.
Perhaps it would have been better if he hadn't made himself an exception; if he had behaved as a true Ottoman, avenging his blood
brother in accordance with that barbarous custom that, among
members of his race, is condoned by the law and that even among
Christians has not yet been successfully abolished, even by the most
humane religion on earth.

Such pictures and such thoughts were occupying my mind when
the sound of footsteps in the entrance to the pavilion made me leap
up suddenly from where I sat. As I came in I had seen some bedding
on the ground there. Clearly the one for whom it was intended was
coming to bed. Perhaps it's my brother, I thought, and opened the
door. In the half-darkness of the entryway I could dimly make out
the tall, thin shape of Kyamíl, with his phosphorescent white turban that almost touched the ceiling of the room.

"Do they know inside that you've come, Kyamíl? Your mother
was very anxious," I said, trying to conceal my own anxiety.

"It's all over now!" said Kyamíl in an unimaginably strange tone
of voice as he stood there motionless. "The evil's over now. Now
she'll find peace, and I'll find peace, too!"

"Bravo, Kyamíl!" I said, encouraging him to follow me into the
room. "I know you're a sensible fellow. I know that this will be the
last time now."

"Yes," said Kyamíl with conviction. "The last!"

But imagine my surprise when I got a look at his appearance as
he came into my room! His pale face, onto which was reflected the
white color of his *saríki* from above and from below the green of
his robe, had the appearance of a long-dead corpse! His lips were
livid, his eyes lifeless, his motions like the motions of a corpse act-

ing under the influence of some mysterious galvanism. And the constant flickerings of my lamp's faint light as they moved uneasily in waves over him made his appearance chillingly frightful, like the appearance of some ghastly specter! I don't know how I managed to preserve my presence of mind. But I still remember with horror that I embraced him and kissed him to encourage him. So great was the pity I felt for the unfortunate man! When he had calmed down a little, he took a deep breath and said, "Now it's over! Now I'll find peace." And he uttered an indecent oath against some third party, calling him an insulting name.

"It's not enough he killed my blood brother," he said then, "it's not enough he ruined my happiness and my health, but he was beginning little by little to poison even the wretched life that remained to me!"

And when he saw that I had nothing ready to say to him, he said, "I know. You're a learned man and you'll laugh. That's why I haven't told you anything, up till now. But the *sheik* of our *teké* is more learned than you; he's a saint. And whoever does his word does the will of God. Three years now the *vrykólakas* has been pursuing me. No one saved me. Every time I went to a festival, I found him before me; to the *pazári,* I found him before me; until he drove me to despair and I gave up my job and went and became a *softás.* It's a good thing I did! Because our *sheik,* the one I was telling you about, he saved me. May we have his blessing! 'Pay no attention to the one who resembles the murdered man,' he told me. 'The *vrykólakas* is only a wineskin stuffed with blood. Bring me a black-handled knife so I can read it to you; and when you see him again, make a hole in him so the blood will pour out! He'll never appear before you again.'"

Then I observed with horror that his hands were bloodied and his clothes stained. Cold sweat poured over me! "Oh! Kyamíl, you've shed blood!"

"No! It's only the blood of the *vrykólakas,* of the man who was killed."

"And who was the murdered man whose *vrykólakas* this was?" I asked, trembling in all my limbs.

"The one who killed my blood brother," he answered.

"And so who killed your blood brother's killer?"

"Who else had the duty but me?" said the Turk with such pride that I loathed him.

"What! Such an awful thing!" I stammered out then, rather mechanically and unintentionally.

"Hmmm!" said the Turk. "Isn't it written in your scripture? You stab, you get stabbed! The devil that casts the bullet for the killer casts one also for his avenger. So listen. Perhaps you don't know that my blood brother's killer put me in danger for my life, caused me to be robbed by a miller, to be chased away by my father-in-law, to end up sick in your village. Learn the rest now that I'm telling you this. As soon as I came to the City from your house and felt better, I took my rifle and went back to the miller who pulled me half-dead out of the river.

"'You stole a purse from me,' I told him, 'with five hundred florins; you saved for me a life that isn't worth five *parádes*. You who spend so much time at the river's edge, you surely will know who killed my blood brother the day you pulled me out. Look, I've got my rifle cocked! If you tell me, I make you a present of what you stole from me! If you conceal it, you lose your life!' That's what I told him, and I did the right thing. The miller was a cowardly receiver of stolen goods, and when he saw the straits he was in, he said, 'Promise you won't do the killing in my mill and I'll point out your man for you.' I promised. 'So hide back in here,' he told me. 'A man is sure to come along with the mail sack under his arm and his rifle on his shoulder. He's the young sultan's killer. His name is Haralambís, Mitákos' son. Every two weeks he crosses the same bridge you and your horse fell from.'"

My ears roared loudly, I could barely hear him.

The Turk continued: "But even before I had time to hide, in came the dog exactly as he had been described to me. I had the trigger cocked, but I'd given my word, hadn't I? I was afraid he might guess something and make me break it. So I went out and headed for the bridge. 'He'll pass by this way,' the miller had said. I waited for him there in the same spot where he stood when he killed my blood brother. There I watched him as he approached the bridge. But since it was winter and the branches had no leaves on them, and since he suspected something, he took fright before getting to the height at the middle of the bridge and turned back and began to run. I took off after him with all my might, but he was too quick. Twice I shot at him, twice the dog fired back as he fled. 'Very well!' I thought. 'Wherever you go, you'll pass this way again!'"

Aha! So that was the haunted blood that my unfortunate brother told my mother about, the blood that met the killer on the road and made him turn around and resign from delivering the mail! My hair stood on end; my limbs shook like leaves in the fall; I was barely in control of my senses.

The Turk continued. "Two weeks passed, two weeks I kept watch for him. It was in the time of the war. The local *Kaïmakámis* had cut the Lulevurgáz railway and had given the order to leave for the City; I didn't budge. If one more night had passed, the Russians would have killed me. But God protected me and sent me my man."

Cold sweat was running in rivers from my forehead. I recall that twice I lunged at him to squeeze his throat, to stifle his confession in his larynx. But I was thunderstruck with horror. And while inwardly I thought I was moving, externally I remained inert, like a person paralyzed.

The Turk continued. "This time I was well hidden, and so as to remove his every suspicion, I let him cross the bridge. And when I saw he had come down to the bank and had bent over for a drink of water, I waited still another minute so as not to make any mistake. . . . And then I fired. . . ."

"Oh! Wretch! You killed my brother!"

At that point a confused sound was heard in the garden, from which I could distinguish the voice of my younger brother shouting, "There! He's sleeping in there!"

Flames from torches and lamps shed a bloody light on the ivy on the wall, and the gleam of swords and rifles advanced through the small door toward the pavilion. It was the police! My door opened with a crash, and my brother was the first to come in.

"Let them take him!" he cried. "He's a killer! He killed Mitákos' Haralambís! He killed our fellow villager before my very eyes!"

The room filled with night watchmen, firemen, and police bailiffs. Kyamíl, rooted to the spot, let them tie him up without any resistance, without emotion. Then the officer leading this throng stepped forward and greeted me politely: "What a coincidence, sir!" he said. "What strange coincidence brings you to the killer's house?"

Only then did I recognize him. I had become acquainted with him during my comings and goings at the Ministry of Police. He knew our case. And he had been remunerated for his every effort to bring it to a successful completion. So I took him aside and explained to him that the Kyamíl who was regarding us coolly and dispassionately had previously killed my brother, thinking he was avenging the killer of his blood brother, and had tonight also killed the postman, who was being sought as a criminal by the police, under the impression in his delirium that the postman in the flesh was a demonic apparition that had come to pursue him.

The officer squeezed my hand in sympathy and led the prisoner away.

Very early the next day and at my repeated urging, my mother left that loathsome house and went straight to our village. It would have done no good for her to learn the truth . . .

*****

It was about three years from that night when I entered our village for the first time since having left it as a child. Many recent disasters had intervened and overshadowed that old one to a certain extent. But the nearer I got to my house, the more its mournful story emerged from the depths of time, and the fresher it became. My coach was now driving by a collapsing, abandoned house. Anyone else would have felt a deep melancholy sadness if, returning after a long absence, he found deathly silence where he had left a merry, noisy life, ruin and abandon where he had left prosperity and ease. But in me the closed windows, the gaping walls, the overgrown courtyard, the unfenced garden open to every pillager somehow produced a strangely satisfying impression. It seemed to me I would have grieved if that house had continued to flourish. It was the Mitákos' house, the house of Lampí, the former postman. And it was impossible for me not to regard that postman as responsible for the killing of my unfortunate brother. The actual killer had gone mad before my eyes during the very first judicial inquiry as soon as it had been ascertained whose heart had been pierced by that bullet that he directed at the killer of his blood brother. But as the target of that bullet, which had been fired out of blind retaliation, Mitákos' criminal son had with wicked cunning substituted my poor brother's chest, who had the misfortune of resembling him not only in height and carriage, but also even in dress. It had already been proved that it was only on account of this that he had wanted to persuade my guillible brother to succeed him in his job, and it was known that he was so certain about the result of his loathsome cunning that he had even maliciously predicted the very hour of my brother's death!

When we arrived in front of our house, I was astonished to see a filthy, ragged, barefoot dervish emerging from the courtyard and running to open the carriage door.

"Amán, sultaním! Kokkóna bílmesin!"

My body shuddered in horror! Those were the only words that Kyamíl uttered when, in full court, he became deranged and fell fainting before my feet!

"In the name of God, my sultan, don't let the *kokkóna* know!"

And the repugnant sound of his voice, a sound that one would think had come from some deep grave rather than from a mortal mouth, so shook my nerves that when I threw myself into the arms of my mother, who had run up to meet me, an indescribably weird mixture of loathing and pity filled my heart. In this way I entered the courtyard, turning my back in the direction from which I supposed that loathsome object was following me.

Along the other side of our house the garden gate was open. In this garden there still flourished an apple tree in whose shade my brothers and I had once played so happily. But those loud shouts, our childish laughs, are no longer heard there. Eternal silence reigns under it, and a white stone cross, in front of which a lamp burns constantly, bears witness to the sanctity of the spot. There lies buried my much lamented brother. There in tears I directed my steps. The brightest roses, the choicest flowers decorate his resting place. Our garden was at one time very neglected. Now it is full of flowers that appear to have sprouted in great numbers from that grave and to have spread, little by little, up to the farthest corners of the garden.

"Poor Kyamíl tends all of them!" my mother whispered sadly.

Again my hair stood on end. And, my lips violently quivering, I turned toward the one of whom she spoke and said, "I order you not to set foot in our house again!"

"Oh, the poor fellow!" my mother cried out in indescribable sorrow. "Who are you saying this to, my child? The poor fellow neither hears nor speaks any more! He's out of his mind, poor thing!"

Kyamíl fixed his lusterless eyes on the far away horizon like one who does not comprehend at all what is going on around him. On his head he now wore a dervish's green-banded *kyuláfi*, which made him tall to a ridiculous degree. Around his bony body hung the ragged *kaftáni* of the monastic rank to which he belonged. His elbows showed through the tears in his clothes, but he had around his waist a bright leather belt, which bore on its buckle a large, choice stone, an onyx of Mecca. And his face, whether from the untroubled state in which he now lived or from the action of the sun, appeared healthier than before.

"Damn them!" said my mother as she looked at him with pity. "They've made him a saint! After he went crazy they made him a saint! And they kiss his hand, and they bring him food, and they bring him clothes, and they want to take him to the *Kaïmakámis'* house. But he doesn't eat anything but dried bread, he doesn't wear anything but what you see, and he sleeps on the ground in the hay barn. And he doesn't want to go away from me no matter what they do to him. It's only when they upset him a lot, only when he's distressed, that he lets out a strange shout, 'In the name of God, my sultan, don't let the *kokkóna* know!' Other than that he doesn't know anything! Poor Kyamíl!"

And while she was saying this, I reflected on her earlier wild rage against the killer, her protest that our poor brother was disturbed in his grave every time his killer trod the ground, even if at the ends of the earth, and my body shuddered at the thought that that very killer was walking each day over his victim's grave, and I shuddered lest the poor woman be told. It would kill her!

"Nonetheless," I told her, "if you chase him away yourself, I'm sure he'll leave and go with his own people. Do me the favor and chase him away from our house."

"What are you saying?" she cried out almost in tears. "Once in a while I think of that coquette who gave him a kick and chased him out of our room, and I wish I had an arm long enough to reach from here to the City to strike him one on his girlish face. And you tell me to chase him away myself with my own hands? He left his mother and came to me, you see. He carries water, he goes to the mill, he takes the bread to the bakery, he digs the vines, he cleans the courtyard, he cultivates the flowers over our Hristákis' grave; he even wants to light the lamp with his own hand! And so you see, how can I chase him away after I looked after him for seven months in bed, like my own child? I hope the one who caused him such misery gets his from God! Come, if you want my blessing, my son, leave the poor fellow with his misfortune, and now then, tell me—has the killer been found? Has it been possible to find out who he was?"

"No!" I said, as I looked at him standing before me. I had considered what she had told me about him. Comparing the crazed man's goodness with the loathsome cunning of the former postman, I could not determine which of the two was my brother's killer!

The Consequences of
the Old Story

Introduction

This work is the only one of Vizyenos' stories that is set in an area other than Greece and the Ottoman Empire. To be sure, "Between Peiraeus and Naples" is set on a ship in the Mediterranean, but "Consequences" is placed in a totally unfamiliar and foreign environment, and there are only references, and one flashback, to Athens. Within Germany the story begins with the narrator in Göttingen studying psychology: the whole story, indeed, is a study in psychology. While in Göttingen, he witnesses the mournful scene of a girl crazed for love in the local insane asylum. From there he moves to Clausthal to visit his closest school friend, Paschális, who likewise has had an unfortunate experience in love. The story concerns two Greeks abroad and derives part of its power from the fact that it deals with Greek *xeniteiá,* the homesickness and loneliness Greeks feel when away from home, a theme much treated by Vizyenos in his stories. As in "My Mother's Sin," spaces are important, with the oppositions/identifications being light/enclosed space/female/blond versus dark/open space/male/black. The room in the insame asylum is the antithesis of the mine in Clausthal.

The narration takes place in the present, but it refers to events that took place a number of years earlier. Those events, we are told, happened in 187–, and we know that the narrator and Paschális had graduated from the gymnasium in the Pláka (on the northeast slopes of the Acropolis in Athens) two years earlier. Because the narrator had spent some time at the University of Athens, we may assume that that year was the year preceding the year of the story. Both students came from an area under Ottoman control and thus were "Turkomerites" who had come to Athens to complete their education. Paschális was subsequently supported in his studies in Germany by a wealthy Greek from abroad, just as Vizyenos himself was, in fact, by the wealthy G. Zarífis. The narrator does not record the source of his own financial support.

Because the story is set in Germany, the mythology is German as well. Thus Goethe's *Faust* is referred to by the learned doctor in Göttingen, particularly the Walpurgis Night scene (*Faust* 1.3835–4222) with its *stríngles,* "witches," and *Kallikántzari,* "demons," these last both creatures of Greek folklore, not German. The German poet Heine is referred to in a sardonic manner in connection with the mine. Parody also abounds, as in Wolkenhaar's (means "Clouds-hair") sermon, which is a parodic version of the Western story of St. Francis and the birds, or St. Anthony and the fishes, taken up in German folk tradition, for example, in *Des Knaben Wunderhorn.*

Like "Between Peiraeus and Naples," this story deals with poetry. The narrator does not claim to be a poet here, but he does criticize others who do, and more importantly quotes a bit of poetry in Greek translation. The most famous poem quoted is Goethe's "Über allen Gipfeln," of which I give three versions here. (1) The German original:

> Über allen Gipfeln
> Ist Ruh,
> In allen Wipfeln
> spürest du
> Kaum einen Hauch;
> Die Vögeln schweigen im Walde.
> Warte nur, balde
> Ruhest du auch.

(2) Vizyenos' translation:

> ἐπὶ πάντων τῶν ὀρέων
> ἡσυχία βασιλεύει:
> ἐπὶ τῶν κλαδίσκων πλέον
> οὔτε φύλλον δὲν σαλεύει.
> τά πτηνὰ ταῖρι ταῖρι
> κοιμῶνται σιγὰ κ΄ εὐτυχῆ
> ὤ, καρτέρει, καρτέρει,
> καὶ σὺ θὰ κοιμᾶσ΄ ἐν βραχεῖ.

and (3) Longfellow's translation of the Goethe ("Wanderer's Night-Song ii"):

> O'er all the hill-tops
> Is quiet now,
> In all the tree-tops
> Hearest thou
> hardly a breath;
> The birds are asleep in the trees:
> Wait; soon like these
> Thou too shalt rest.

The Goethe poem is itself a translation or rendition of a poem by Alcman, *Fr. 34*, (D. L. Page, *Lyria Graeca Selecta* [Oxford: Oxford University Press, 1968]):

> εὕδουσι δ᾿ ὀρέων κορυφαί τε καὶ φάραγγες
> εὕδουσι δ᾿ οἰωνῶν φῦλα τανυπτερύγων

The poem said in the story to be a translation of the German poet is a version of the first stanza of Goethe's poem, "Kennst du das Land wo die Zitronen blühn," from *Wilhelm Meister*. In that work, there are five songs, the first two sung by the mad Harp Player, the others by Mignon, a child of mysterious origin. The poem about the brook is the girl's (that is, Vizyenos') own, called "Anemone," and was written on August 27, 1882 (P. Papachristodoulou, *Archeion tou thrakikou laographikou kai glossikou thesaurou* 14 [1947−1948]:304, cited in Moullas 1980:84). It is ironic that an author should put one of his own poems in the mouth of a character in one of his stories. Compare "Between Peiraeus and Naples" again in this regard.

Homer is quoted by the German doctor, and I have left the passages as Vizyenos wrote them. The joke is in the pronunciation, for a Greek would have pronounced the lines quite differently and would have found the German pronunciation both difficult and absurd. Germans pronounce ancient i-diphthongs such as /ai/ and /oi/ as in English *buy* and *boy,* whereas in modern Greek they are /e/ and /i/ as in English *bed* and *bead;* Germans also pronounce /ei/ as /ai/ as they would in native German words; ancient u-diphthongs are pronounced with /v/ between vowels and voiced consonants, but as /f/ before voiceless consonants in modern Greek; ancient /d/ and /g/ are now voiced spirants, /d/ having the sound of the English

/th/ in *the*—I render them here /dh/ and /gh/; many ancient sounds, more or less correctly pronounced by the German, are now simply /i/, as with /ee/ (for ancient *eta*), /oi/, /u/. The German cannot pronounce the aspirates, so renders ancient /th/ as /t/ and ancient /kh/ as /k/, whereas in modern Greek they are fricatives, with /th/ having the sound of /th/ in *thin*, and /ch/ the sound of /ch/ in German Bach. The German's voicing of /s/ to /z/ is simply wrong, but correctly represents what Germans did (or do) actually say. It will be noted that Vizyenos (or his editor) was not completely consistent in his renderings; I have not corrected him but have noted the inconsistencies.

> Aïén aristóïaïn káï yupéerokon émenaï pántoon Toïtónon
> Eèn aristévin kè ipírohon émene pánton Teftónon

"Always to excel and surpass all Teutons." The original has *allon*, "others," instead of "all Teutons," and represents fatherly advice given to Glaukos by Hippolochos (*Iliad* 6.208) and to Achilles by Peleus (*Iliad* 11.783).

> Áï gàr Tsóü te páter, káï Ateenaïee káï Ápollon
> Toïoútoï déka moï zumfrádmones áïen Akaïön
> É ghár Zéf te páter ké Athinéi ké ápolon
> tioúti dhéka mi simfrádhmones íen Aheón.

"Father Zeus and Athene and Apollo, would that I had ten such councillors!" This said by Agamemnon of Nestor in *Iliad* 2.372.

o tróozas iázetaï, would now be *o trósas iásete*, "the one who wounds will heal," and is a proverb quoted in the *Mantissa Proverbiorum* 2.28. *Odoússeous* is the German's pronunciation of the name Odysseus (with incorrect accent), pronounced in modern Greek as *Odhiséfs*.

> aktéen poluphloïsbóïo talássees
> aktín poliphlísvio thalásis

"Shore of the loud-roaring sea." Here there is an error in recollection, for the line as given will not scan in dactylic verse. In *Iliad* 1.34 we find the metrically correct *thína* for *aktéen*. But the accent of "loud-roaring" on the *-oio*, incorrect for Greek, is correct in a German metrical rendition that ignores the position of the Greek accent.

hiémenos káï kapnòn apotroóskonta noeézaï heès gáïees
iémenos ké kapnón apothróskonta noïse ís yéis

"longing to see the smoke arising from his homeland" (*Odyssey*
1.58).

Húïes Akaïoón is now *íes Acheón* and is the frequent "sons of
the Achaeans."

Poïkilomíteen (error for *poïkilomeéteen*) is now *pikilomítin* and,
as an epithet of Odysseus, means "of many wiles."

Polúplangton is now *políplangton* and means "much wandering."

This tale is Vizyenos' longest and most ambitious story. Though
not much in accord with modern tastes, it is nonetheless—it seems
to me—more successful than many have held in the past (for example, Moullas 1980:114).

The Consequences
of the Old Story

I was studying in Göttingen at the time, a small town in Hann-
over that is as obscure and insignificant from every other point of
view as it is distinguished and famous for its Augustan Academy,
for in its intellectual firmament there once rose, and still today glit-
ter, the most brilliant stars of German learning.

I had passed my first winter in Germany "wrapped in the prover-
bial five cloaks," but still always shivering and warming my hands
with my breath. And I beg my Athenian reader not to laugh at me
for this confession. Let him save his Attic salt to season his witti-
cisms with when he is given the agreeable opportunity of living,
even for only a few weeks, with a temperature of 32, I mean thirty-
two degrees Réaumer, not above zero, if you please, but below; to
see the moisture in the air settling in thick layers of wondrous, thou-
sand-shaped crystals on the glass and metal surfaces of the house;
to hear the snow creaking under his footsteps, as if it consisted of
hard, sharp, noisy steel filings; to be covered with frost over his
entire body like a flour-covered miller from bodily perspiration as
it freezes on his clothes; to see the ice hanging from his mustache,
taking the shape and the dimensions that the icicles hanging from
the downspouts and the roof tiles in Athens had during the winter
before last, and then, "Let him come and we'll talk about it"!

I, too, used to the scorching heat of Greece, once found insolent words with which to make fun of a poet "by the grace of God" because of his exaggerations about cold, which I then thought contrary to nature. But during that winter of 187– in Göttingen, I fully understood and then some the phrase, "May your breath freeze in your mouth" because that frightful cold froze my own breath not in my mouth, but in my very lungs! And when the following spring came and went, and when the summer was more than half over, I still coughed, coughed, coughed! Finally the stifling heat of August set in, and my illness began to go away. But the dust, the evil exhalations of the still Athens-like streets of shabby Göttingen, were not very suitable for hastening a complete cure. For this reason, it was judged necessary for me to have a change of climate.

My doctor at that time was the—now deceased—Court Councillor Herr H***, an old man most learned in Homer and (according to the philologists, for this reason) most celebrated of the internists in Germany, director of the general hospital, professor, etc., etc., but above all famous as the author of the well-known *Physiological Pathology of the Nerves*, to the study of which he had devoted his entire life. This specialty of his in nerves was the principal cause of our close acquaintance, not only because my cough had become a kind of nervous affliction, but also because his field of inquiry bordered most closely on my own studies in psychology.

"Every other disease," he said when I first visited him with a letter of introduction from the late Professor H. Lotze, "puts us in touch only with the body, that is, the material substance. Our therapy, consequently, is based only on the animal, that is to say the mechanical, chemical, physiological forces of matter. Things are otherwise with diseases of the nerves. Nervous diseases 'are special,' or at least, according to your teacher, 'are accompanied by related' diseases of the psyche. Consequently, our therapeutic method cannot make its speculations without the assistance of that unknown factor Psi, that is the psyche. So what can more naturally be expected of us than to discover in the final results of our speculations, if not the entire nature of this unknown Psi, then at least all its qualities? And if not all at once, at least little by little? For this reason I most fully commend your intent to attend not only my class at the university, but also my psychiatric lectures and demonstrations at the mental hospital. In this institution you will have cause to think on many, many psychological questions. And in my philhellenism, I wish you at their conclusion: '*Aïen aristóïaïn kaï yupéerokon émenaï pántoon Toïtónoon.*'"

Needless to say, that commendable intent was not realized during my first academic year, and still more needless to add that the good and virtuous old man's tongue-twisting wish would never be realized. I have already described how I spent the winter semester. When the spring term had progressed a bit, I began to attend his lectures in the city, but after a short while I was forced to give them up, because regularly, and always after fifteen minutes of suffering in the midst of that deep reverent silence with which his many listeners meticulously wrote down every syllable of Herr Professor's teachings, suddenly that violent coughing would come over me, so violent, so continuous, that my fellow students, in spite of their courtesy and tolerance for foreigners, were forced to drive me away from the lectures with the usual hissings and shufflings of feet.

I never attended the psychiatry class because of the distance, even though I was eager to become acquainted with the Prussian insane asylum, which was famous for its organization and originality. For that reason, when on the morning I went to my doctor's house at the appointed hour for him to examine me once again and to advise me definitely where I had to go to regain my strength, I was not much displeased when I learned that, in spite of his appointment with me, Herr H*** had been forced to go unexpectedly to the insane asylum, having left orders to tell me that he requested that I meet him in his private office at that institution.

The Prussian government's spacious and architecturally excellent philanthropic institution lies about ten minutes south of Göttingen on a most charming hill among green lawns and shaded gardens, furnishing to the view of the beholder the most picturesque landscape around that city. Its management is entirely independent of university authorities; the only link connecting it with the medical school was the unquestioned expertise of Herr Professor H***, who by leave of the directors taught applied psychiatry there as well. The institution is endowed with large estates, the cultivation of which is entrusted to those of the mentally disturbed whose psychic powers, having been crippled by the weight of disasters and the efforts of life's struggle in large cities, need only spiritual refreshment and activity more conformable to human nature in order to regain their former vigor. But even the tasks within the asylum are discharged mainly by the less afflicted of its occupants. Thus even the sextons were from among the mentally ill, and, what is most remarkable, even the preacher during the period of which we speak. He was a most reverent man and most expert in Holy Scripture, Wolkenhaar by name, graduate in Theology, who always composed the most brilliant sermon from the pulpit but rarely managed to proclaim it to its end in the institution's chapel. His witless flock, though it consisted of human beings, did not—as one might have expected—preserve the proper silence during the sermon and did not always behave with the requisite decorum. Very often the silly laughter of some madman interrupted him in the middle of the most lofty passage of his discourse; sometimes again some idiot's editorial comments startled him, and that always during the most passionate parts of his homily. Then Wolkenhaar lost his presence of mind and the continuity of his text; he went wild. And after a few moments' agitated thought about what to do, he snatched the weighty tome of the Scripture under his arm, went out through a side door into the kitchen yard, and there, quickly assuming a most majestic stance amid the cackling of hens, the grunting of pigs, the whistlings and peepings of ducks and geese, he declaimed his masterpiece with enormous rhetorical skill and with touching devotion and reverence from beginning to end!

I don't like digressions in stories; but since I have made an exception as regards Wolkenhaar's illness, allow me to add how it affected me.

"A more consistent affliction you won't find very often," the professor of psychiatry told us one day. "He tolerates all manner of hubbub in animals, but he cannot abide the slightest disturbance on the part of humans. Obviously there still remains in him a dim consciousness that regard for the high and important is the natural duty of mankind alone. And instead of allowing poor Wolkenhaar to run away from a pulpit truly worthy of him, it would perhaps be more sensible always to substitute each time the simple animals of the kitchen yard for his witless audience."

My reader will be astonished. I should like to say, however, that those words made me blush from shame right up to the tips of my ears, because I recalled some repeated scenes in the highest educational institutions of our free Fatherland, scenes in which yours truly sometimes played a very active role, and I found that the professor's proposal would have been more justly applied to the foolishness that prevailed among us rather than to those poor creatures who in the end could invoke in their own defense the extenuating circumstance that they were bereft of reason. I beg your pardon, however, for the digression. From our institutions of higher learning, through a most natural chain of ideas, I go back to the insane asylum.

When I traversed the shaded road that spiraled up the landscaped hill for the first time and arrived in front of the neo-Gothic façade of that splendid structure, I thought for a moment that I had strayed from my course and had found myself unexpectedly before a stately country mansion in which a large gathering lived in joy and gladness. Voices of singers, sounds of various musical instruments, came from its high windows and mingled with the songs of birds that contended with them in the thick foliage of the shade trees. One hearing those concerts neglects to ask why such cheerful windows are covered with iron bars like the windows of prisons, why the walls of the grounds are so secure, against those inside rather than against those who perhaps were intending to broach them from without. Behind those lofty walls, instead of the gloomy, the hopeless, the evil plotting silence of prisons and jails, resound the most cheerful laughter, the most lively conversations of the— perhaps very happy—inmates, and I could hear the familiar sounds of all kinds of gymnastic games in the open air.

The doorkeeper allowed me to enter only after many questions and repeated formalities. In spite of all my assurances that I was a sane person, he behaved very suspiciously towards me, obviously because of those very assurances, because I remember he said: "The most reasonable people in the world are precisely those who try in every way to get into the asylum."

When, finally, through splendid staircases and still more splendid corridors I was led into the office of Herr Professor H***, "I'm glad you've come!" exclaimed the good old man. "Let's go and I'll introduce you to the director. He's a very good and wise man: he's the father of all of us in here."

The blood in my veins suddenly stopped flowing. Those words and the courtesy with which he pronounced them inspired a strange suspicion; inexpressable horror stopped my tongue. What business had I with the director of the asylum? So, perhaps my chest isn't my only problem, I thought in a flash, and wished that the doorkeeper had never allowed me entrance into the asylum.

"A very sad illness," said the professor, somewhat taken aback by my silence, "very sad, even if a 'poetic' illness, called me here so unexpectedly and made me neglect my patients in the city."

The galleries through which we were passing seemed to be spinning around and around and around about my head! The professor waited in vain for me to speak.

"We are about to examine, to study," he continued, "an unfortunate young lady from the Duchy of Baden; a victim of love's despair. I am sure it will interest you greatly to be present during the examination. What do you think? It will be your first psychiatric lesson. That's the main reason I left instructions for you to come."

Glory be to God! So they weren't about to examine me! "Many thanks, Mr. Court Councillor!" I said. And I breathed forcefully and deeply as if instead of weak lungs I had the great bellows of a smithy in my chest!

"I have to study her condition before the madness returns," continued the professor, "and it would have been boring for you to wait by yourself. After the session I'll examine you and tell you what's necessary as regards your trip."

I breathed deeply again and tried to appear as calm as possible. But I did not really calm down until I saw with what difficulty the director consented to allow my presence during the examination of his patient. That small-eyed and grizzled descendant of the Pygmies brought up his objections so outspokenly that for a moment I felt myself personally attacked.

"Don't misunderstand my humane colleague," Herr H*** said to me over the director's head. "He can be neither philhellene nor philhomerist. In general he has no special liking for anyone of sound mind. For twenty-five years now he has been living and associating only with his children, that is, the insane. His goodness is immeasurable, it's without limits, but it doesn't extend beyond the walls of this building. I'm sure that your visit doesn't disturb the sick girl at all, but, you see, the director also has, naturally, other more general reservations."

And lifting his hands and eyes like a praying child,

"Aï gar Tsóü te páter, kaï Ateenaíee kaï Ápollon
toïoúti déka moï zumphrádmones áïen Achaïón!"

cried out the old man, casting the glances of a rapturous lover at the director's ugly face.

After several conventional civilities to that little man—who was a cheerful as he was hard to win over and who, it seemed, tried to hide the misfortunes of those entrusted to him with the same concern and love with which parents conceal the defects of their own children from the eyes of the world—the three of us went to visit the patient. After we turned the first corner in the hall, the director bounded like a shot, but as silently as a hare, up a narrow, side stairway from the top of which I thought I saw the sun's rays coming in. The professor and I stood in front of the adjoining door. After a few moments of waiting in silence, the director came, opened the door for us, and said, "Come in. She's completely calm." He behaved as if he were admitting us to the sanctuary of some church.

The place that we had reverently entered was large, a room almost circular in shape, its height about equal to its diameter and lighted only by a glass-roofed dome. It had no windows, nor could it, because the walls of this room up to half again the height of a man were lined with a kind of thick, soft padding in the manner of those headrests all of silk that adorn the rooms of the wealthy. The thick-piled velvet that covered this padding was a gentle blue color and was picked out in regular rhomboid patterns by studs that, thought driven in deeply, scarcely showed because of the thickness of the padding. The bare portion of the wall above this padding was white. The thick rug on the floor was green, while the woodless and, as I noticed later, air-filled, rubber chairs and couches had the same color as the wall decoration: a blue inexpressibly soft and truly calming so that you couldn't tell whether this or the colors of the glass dome was the reason that the light in that room produced such a pleasing, relaxing, and indeed soothing reaction on the senses and the nerves. No means of circulating the air could be seen anywhere. And yet when we entered that windowless room, I thought we had come out into the open air, so pure and cool was the atmosphere in there!

The room's unfortunate occupant did not appear, however. So the director, after a few moments of silence, went to the end of the room and, placing his ear against the soft surface, asked in that loving voice with which parents call those dearest to them when they are sick: "Is it all right, Fräulein?"

A section of the blue covering noiselessly opened up in the manner of a door, and a girl, with flowing hair and dressed in white, emerged from it, pale, but smiling and lovely.

"Come in! Come in, please! Take a seat and pardon me while I adjust my hairpin."

And entering the room, she raised her snow-white arms and busied herself—but in vain—in gathering together her rich, golden blond locks.

"Oh, let it be!" she said at last scornfully, and let her hair fall on her shapely shoulders. "Since he's not here to see me, let it be! But don't be in a hurry, please, so I can present my future husband to you. He went out digging to get diamonds for our rings, our engagement rings. Big diamonds! He'll want to find very big diamonds, that's why he's late in coming back. But don't you be in a hurry. He has a sharp pick, and he's a clever person. He'll go to the center of the earth, but he'll find them and come back."

And taking a chair and coming towards me as if we had known one another from childhood, she said, "Tell me, please, tell me in all seriousness, how hot is the center of the earth? As hot as this, like my hand? Or like this, like my cheek? What do you say? Like this? Or like that?"

And taking my hand in a familiar fashion, she brought it up to her fevered cheek and fixed her blue eyes on my own, awaiting my reply.

"Hotter," I stammered in confusion, "much hotter!"

"So much the better!" the girl cried out happily and sprang up like a gazelle from her seat, clapping her tiny hands. "So much the better! He was cold when he left me, and he'll come back to me all fire! All love! So don't be in a hurry, please; wait to see him. Do you want me to sing something so the time doesn't seem so long?"

In a flash she went into the next room and returned, carrying a gilded Italian harp. Then, choosing that spot under the lighted dome from which the most and purest light came in, she positioned herself rather coquettishly under its rays and began to strike the strings of the instrument as happily and as animatedly as if she were the happiest girl in the world. At first she played nothing other than products of her imagination. After a while, though, she began to sing more sadly, accompanying with the charming and languid tones of her instrument the still more charming and languid notes of her voice:

> That it's gloomy in the woods,
> is the thick branches' plan.

> That my lover loves me not,
> I've known since time began.
> Ach, and Vach, and that means woe:
> but parting causes pain,
>   and love rocks to and fro
>   like a skiff upon the main!

At this point she suddenly broke off her playing and, turning to the director as if she were completing a conversation that had already begun, she said, "And send me my nurse, Anníka, so I can write him a letter and tell him openly and clearly." Then, taking up her instrument again, she began to sing in a more sentimental tone, moved to the verge of tears:

> Do you know the green seaside,
> where the lemons are in bloom?
> and there beneath the shade
> golden oranges perfume?
> There, there, in Paradise's green land,
> with you I want to travel hand in hand!

But having reached the end of the German poet's well-known stanza in such a rush, and even before completing the notes accompanying her singing, she suddenly broke off again. Tossing back the clump of her yellow hair that had come to rest on her bosom, and shaking her beautiful head in such a way that her silky locks gathered any which way on her back, she said: "Curse those who write songs, since no one of them suits me! Not one! Not one! Not even the one I wrote myself, even that one doesn't suit me!" And drawing her delicate fingers over the sweet-sounding strings of the harp as if she were caressing them, she said with childlike pride, "And yet it has beautiful music, very beautiful music! So beautiful that no one has written it yet. So pardon me if I sing it without a score."

And now, dear reader, don't expect from mortal pen that I can represent to you the deeply moving scene of which we were the mournful, astonished witnesses. Perhaps some perfected form of phonograph could manage instantaneously to transcribe one by one and preserve the individual notes of that sad music in such a way that it could be read by others as well. But read only, not sung. The demonic force that engulfed us like a magic spirit of life and that inspired the imaginative and improvised arrangements of those notes that were at the same time so simple and yet so inexpressible, the melodic and yet dramatic nuances of each individual line, of each word—yes, of each individual syllable through which she made us see before us with a shudder, alive and moving, those scenes only faintly, only figuratively hinted at in her composition—these things no machine manufactured by mortal hand, no musical genius can repeat or imitate even remotely.

But the sad frailty of her posture, the indefinably desperate expression on her face, and at the same time the special facial movements with which she accompanied the sounds of her voice and the tones of her instrument—what camera, or what superhuman painter's skill could transcribe them! I say nothing about genius in writing because the fact that even in this most feeble recounting I am forced to separate the elements of music and physiognomy, things that in nature are so inseparably united, reveals most clearly, I think, the descriptive imperfection of any written account.

For this reason I trust to the imagination of my sensitive reader, and I remind him only to reflect on the mournful purpose of the building in which we found ourselves; the special design of the room, its colors, the artificial charm of the bright rays by which the poor girl was illumined, her beauty, which was already now beginning to fade, the singer's attire, and the remarkable range of passion through which her voice and her facial expression passed from the idyllic serenity of the first line to the blackest despair of the final sounds of her song. All these things I leave him to imagine, so that he may comprehend the powerful emotion our hearts were constantly under during those moments and may judge concerning the enormous power that the following very simple verses exerted over us:

> A rock up in the hills
> in silent revery—
> A brook right by its side,
> sings out an air so free.
>
> An anemone's sweet blooms
> from out the rock are sent;
> she tries so hard to grasp
> what is the song's intent.
>
> And she bends out more and more,
> and she stoops to identify

what is the song he sings,
that hurrying passer-by

He sings about two arms
longingly opened wide,
which await him night and day
on a golden ocean side.

"Oh I wish that it were I
whose arms will him enfold!"
And down she bends to touch
the racing waters cold.

But stooping in this way,
the rushing water's brim
plucks all her little leaves,
and sweeps them off with him!

Now she stands bare,
with tear-drops in her eye—
"Oh why, Oh why, Oh why
did I love a passer-by?" . . .

The director all this while was consulting with the professor by
means of glances and whispers. But the tears of all three of us I
think had been flowing silently for a long time now. The farther the
song progressed, the more agitated the girl became. And when she
reached the final line, her thin, rosy fingers, as if they had been steel
picks, all at once snapped the strings over which they had been
moving. A deathly silence prevailed for several moments after
which the girl suddenly stood up, and, leaning on her instrument,
fixed a piercing gaze on the surface of the room as if she were looking through it far, far beyond. And, as if addressing the border
guards of her country: "Shut the gates," she cried out like one in
danger. "Throw the foreigners out and shut the gates! They're
killers of hearts! They're triflers with love!"

At a sudden kick from the girl, the instrument flew up into the
air and fell in front of us making plaintive sounds with its broken
strings. The crazed girl cast a mad glance full of loathing and hate
at us and dashed to the opposite side of the room as if seeking to
get away. But she collided with the soft façade of the wall and fell,
or rather rolled up, in front of it with her back turned towards us.

The director silently locked the door through which we had entered and, taking the instrument with him, nodded to us to pass into the next room, the one from which the young girl had come when she had welcomed us. When we entered this room, he locked this door, too, in this way shutting the unfortunate girl in the round room. I then understood why the walls and the doors of that room were thickly padded in the same way, and why the seats in it consisted entirely of air-filled rubber and were for this reason very light and soft. The unfortunate girl was seized at intervals by a dangerous madness, and she had to be protected from likely suicide or even simple bruises because of her forceful and blind collisions with the walls and the furniture! Silent and morose, we passed through the adjoining room and a third smaller than it. I didn't think to look around, but I believe that those rooms didn't differ essentially from the room just now described. When we emerged into the hall, we found ourselves beside the narrow side stairway that the director had gone up before he let us in, presumably so as to assure himself from there of the patient's condition. That simple surmise of mine was now strengthened by the fact that the two doctors ascended that same stairway so pensive and abstracted that neither noticed whether I was following or not. There could be no doubt that they went up to keep an eye on the mad girl's movements. The guard who was, it seems, always on watch there, came down after a little to look for me, but I had neither the desire nor the spiritual strength to be the witness any longer of such frightful, heart-rending misfortune! My mind was occupied with bitter, melancholy thoughts; a heavy sadness filled my heart to overflowing; my tears flowed unchecked. I mentally compared what the unfortunate girl must have been like perhaps just a few days earlier and what she was today! And I wept for her youth, her beauty, her unhappy parents' bereavement, and I wept at the cruel inhumanity of nature that built on the weakest of foundations that mechanism of the human mind that was as wonderful as it was exceedingly delicate. And the more I thought, the more furiously, and more bitterly I gave vent to my silent complaint against this stepmother Nature. Nothing, I thought to myself, nothing good has she given us that doesn't share in the property that a single moment alone is more than enough to change it into an evil two and three times worse! From the simple grace and suppleness of the limbs of the body up to the most intricate functionings of our god-like spirit, not one single benefit has she given us that is not overshadowed by some flaw following upon it!

Behold the worm of the earth. What more lowly, what more defective creature could anyone imagine? And yet—would you believe it?—Nature has behaved towards the worm more lovingly than towards the self-styled king of creation!

Imagine a man deprived of hands and legs—what a danger that loss is! What a pitiable and ugly sight for the eyes! How difficult his struggle to survive! But his mother Nature couldn't care less! Yet cut the worm in two and you will see with what efficiency and loving kindness she will hurry to complete the cut-off part, to erase the slight deformity, to make two worms of the pieces of the one! Behold the ore in the earth. Could anyone imagine a more lifeless object? The attraction with which its atoms are drawn to one another, the mathematical accuracy with which their only very dim understanding constructs their simple, uniform, and regular thoughts, i.e., their crystals, is so elemental, so invisible, that for the explanation of their effects the physical sciences have been forced to separate these properties from the atoms that possess them and to characterize them with the general and incomprehensible names of electricity and magnetism, attraction and repulsion. But confuse the feelings and thoughts of ores, that is to say, damage the angles and faces of those crystals and place them in the midst of the constituent substances that nourish them, and you will see with what eagerness Nature supports those insubstantial internal operations so that they can reconstruct the damaged parts with the same mathematical exactness as before. But when the structure of a man's mind is damaged, when a spring is broken or a wheel stops in that machine of the mind that the Greek people have so characteristically called a "clock," then Nature proceeds to inquire what spider has lost its tenth leg so she can put it on again, what lizard has grown tired of its aquatic life so that instead of gills she can fashion suitable breathing organs for it, new, firm lungs, and so on and so forth. But that beautiful young girl, the highest perfection of Nature's creation? She leaves her prey to her misfortune and doesn't even hasten to take her back, to join her with the original elements from which she had formed her so imperfectly, but presents her as a sight all the more pitiable and heart-rending to mankind because we have a clear conception of our supposed superiority and perfection!

Such were my thoughts as I walked about in the hall of the insane asylum until the professor came and led me to his office. My suspicions concerning the unfortunate girl were not illusory. "It's not enough," the old man said with evident sadness, "that these diseases are incurable, but they're also of no use for the enlightenment of science. The evil does not have its roots in the nature of nerves, which is known to us, but in that unknown factor Psi, that is the psyche. We cure nerves only. Here we have the destruction of feelings and mental images—may the guilty party find his just punishment!" And, reassuming the mental composure of his calling, the old man took the stethoscope into his hands. This meant that he had drawn the curtain before that sad scene forever.

*****

"I've made arrangements to leave today, Herr Professor; where do you recommend I go?" I asked the doctor after he had recorded in his notebook the satisfactory result of his examination.

"Where else than in the Harz! I haven't changed my mind. 'O tróozas iázetaï,'" said the old man, and he said it as if he were conferring mentally with some Homeric Asclepiad. Then turning towards me, "The Harz mountains are not far from here," he said, "and that is the principal reason for their good climate and beautiful surroundings, but at the same time also for their winters, which are sometimes bitter and harmful to foreigners. That's why I say 'o tróozas iázetaï.' But be careful, young man!" he added, shaking his forefinger. "Be careful! I allow you to go up as high as you can on gleaming Parnassos, not, however, to the snow-covered peaks of our Harz. On them violet-wreathed Muses and radiant Apollo you will not find, but only *Stríngles* and *Kalikántzari* and all those medieval demons that inspired in our great classical, our most Homeric, Goethe, that cold, dark section of Faust that—better he hadn't written it!"

"No matter what, Herr Court-Councillor," I told him, "I must go up to Clausthal. I don't know the area and you see with what difficulty I manage German. Everywhere else I would feel frightful loneliness, I would suffer from homesickness. While in Clausthal, as I told you, I have my fellow countryman, my classmate."

"There we are, he too; he's like all patients," exclaimed the professor as he got up from his chair. "I tell him that something is harmful to his health, yet he comes back and asks my permission to do it with the idea that, if he does it with my permission, it won't hurt him! But that's the failing of all my Greek friends"—he added then with a smile—"from Odysseus up to your worship. You can't be separated from one another. You can't forget that you're abroad. And when you're abroad, wherever you run into a fellow speaker of Greek, even if he's from the other end of the world, there is your fellow countryman, there in some sense is your fatherland. And so you make, as they say, 'a village,' and you spread out your 'shepherd's cloak' and sit down and talk and talk and talk from morning till night. And when it finally gets to be evening and you return home, then, if it happens you aren't living in the same house, you each sit in the corner of your window, like '*Odoússeous*' on the '*aktéen polouphloïsbóïo talássees,*' '*hiémenos kái kapnon apotroóskonta noeézaï heès gáïees.*'"

Then assuming a dignified seriousness, he said, "In any event, '*Húïes Akaïoòn*' (sons of the Achaeans!), what suited the '*poïkilomíteen*' and '*polúplangton*' Odysseus so poetically doesn't suit you. You say you still have trouble with the language. Here's a chance to practise. Make a virtue of necessity. Live as long as the good weather allows in Osterod or in some other village in the Harz, one of those I recommended to you day before yesterday, but live as a German with Germans, and you will see how much it will benefit you both from the point of view of language and of health."

"And Clausthal, Herr Professor, isn't it a healthy city?"

"Clausthal again!" exclaimed the good old man impatiently. "I don't doubt that you are '*hiémenos kapnòn apotroóskonta noeézaï!*' Of course you wish to see the smoking hearth of your fellow countryman. Go, and you will remember my words. You don't need another guide to find him. Wherever there is a chimney constantly smoking, knock on the door: that's where your fellow countryman lives. I remember a Greek fellow-student of ours once. What I and my late brother spent for the warming of our stomachs and, unfortunately, of our heads, the Greek spent twice as much to keep the stove in his room constantly glowing."

"But surely, Herr Court-Councillor, they don't light stoves in Clausthal now? We're in the month of August!"

"Hmmm! Hmmm!" said the old man pensively. And as if he had grown tired of me now: "I don't know; perhaps yes, perhaps no. That, however, is of no interest to us since there is no question of your going there. A short hymn, one halleluiah, and we're done!"

While we said good-bye, the doctor enumerated once again the villages that he allowed me to choose for my stay, but I went straight to the station for information about train departures and to get a ticket for—Clausthal.

"After so many recommendations from your doctor?" you'll say. Yes! after so many recommendations! In my bosom I was carrying the fifth letter from my beloved Paschális who was once again imploring me not to prefer any other place for a change of climate and giving me the most favorable information concerning the weather. For some time now such beautiful weather had prevailed in Clausthal that its residents could not remember having seen its like in many years. I did not say anything about this to the doctor, however, because I wanted to surprise him by writing the unexpectedly pleasant news from the spot itself, that is from Clausthal.

Paschális was my dearest friend from school. We were classmates and had graduated together from the gymnasium in the Pláka only two years earlier. He, too, belonged to the ranks of those learning-starved youths from enslaved Greece who through all manner of tribulations and deprivations manage to save a skimpy sum of money and go, at a relatively ripe age, to what is for the East the source of light, "the famous Athens," in order to drink deep from the sacred springs of civilization and education. Consequently he was the most diligent, the most morally upright student in our class. The frugality with which this young man lived in Athens was unbelievable. Kleantheian the toils in the midst of which he completed his gymnasium studies. Weekdays he was free literally only during the hours of instruction; the rest of the day he was exhausted with giving private lessons left and right—in return for pitiful remuneration—to such students as for the most part other private tutors had despaired of because of their inattention and slowness. He had to study and to learn his gymnasium lessons at night. And it's a marvel that he not only learned them excellently well but even had time left over to go to his washerwoman's house and prepare her daughter for the teachers' examinations. "The teacher is taught," is a proverb that all such young men have on the tip of their tongue. And Paschális as a matter of fact derived no great benefit from his washerwoman if not in the sense of that proverb and the small cost of his washing: an insignificant benefit for which the unfortunate youth paid in the end very dearly, because once that ungrateful student had seduced her teacher into love's mighty net, she sent him away with unsurpassed callousness, for no other reason than he was more chaste than his rival! In any case no one else knew of this incident save me, because I was witness to his sighs and tears. The rest of our fellow students regarded Paschális as a person who had never entered love's school and would never enter it. After the conclusion of his gymnasium course, study in Germany was assured for him on the one hand through the justly acquired goodwill of his teachers and on the other through the well-known beneficence towards industrious but impecunious students of one of those Greeks from abroad who promote learning without drawing attention to the fact. Never will I forget the way we celebrated the joyful arrival of that message. Paschális was determined to pay for this party himself, and to pay in a striking and worthy manner. For a long time we discussed the plan for our "blow-out"; finally it was decided, in accordance with his principles, to "combine the pleasant and the useful." We were both in a short while to go to Germany, to become Germans. And who can become a true German until he's been baptized in beer? But we did not yet know what that fabled drink was, the distillation of barley and straw, the drink that was tending even in the middle of Athens to elbow out the life-bringing wine, the joy of mortals and gods! So let's enjoy ourselves by learning what beer is. "Let's combine the pleasant and the useful!" said Paschális.

After many furtive looks about we sneaked into Berniudákis' beer parlor, purple with embarrassment. We had just graduated from the gymnasium and were entering a tavern for the first time. When we had pressed into the farthest corner of that barbaric cellar, Paschális took six ten-leptá pieces from his pocket and counted them out: they were all he had, his entire fortune.

"These," he said, "on the altar of friendship! But you order, since you manage these things better."

After a little while the waiter placed two glasses of beer in front of us. For a long time we looked at them silently, deeply moved. Finally we clinked our glasses and brought them to our lips. Paschális' eyes suddenly opened wide and, as if instinctively, exchanged with my own a glance of dumb amazement. A strange grimace of unexpected disappointment wrinkled his face, a grimace that seemed the exact reflection of the expansions and contractions of my own face. That lukewarm, yellow liquid inspired in our taste buds strong suspicions as regards its true origin. But our emotion was great, and neither of us expressed what he was thinking at that instant; placing our glasses down in front of us, we looked at them for a long time with silent caution and disbelief. Whereupon suddenly Paschális got up in great agitation, grabbed his cap, and gave me mine. I took it and got up too. Paschális quietly placed the *leptá* "on the altar of friendship" and proceeded towards the exit like a dog with its tail between its legs, very purple and very ashamed. I followed him, still not knowing why. It was only when we were out in the street that I learned that the reason for all that agitation and for the premature breaking off of our party was the entrance of Mr. N. into the tavern! Mr. N. was the teacher who was without exception mocked and hissed by all his classes, in whose presence even the worst student there during my time would have thought nothing of smoking his cigarette, even during class. And Paschális was grown up then, dear reader, with a mustache that rivaled that of Mr. N.! But it seems that Paschális, as a poor "Turkomerítis," had been taught from a very early age to respect his teachers. And please don't take him for a man of limited intelligence because of this. Goodness isn't dullness. Paschális was the smartest and most practical of all of us because while the rest of us after a while, when we were students, began to squander the most valuable time of our lives, causing disturbances in the squares and boulevards of Athens, giving political speeches, bawling about Phalanx, and for this reason getting cold showers from Fire Department pumps, getting beaten up by "street toughs" hired by the ministry of the time, and in the end day-dreaming in the prisons of Garpolás, smart Paschális, although he was free to stay two years at the University of Athens, was studying in Germany, and was studying the science most useful for Greece, mining and metallurgy. In the beginning he had been enrolled at the University of Freiburg and from there wrote me praising that good but small institution, extolling the good behavior of even the most unruly students the minute they set foot on university grounds, admiring the professors' activity and industry; above all, however, hymning the kindliness of those wise teachers, who, through their consorting and associating with their students, either as honorary members of the latters' associations or through constantly receiving and entertaining them in the bosoms of their families, quietly bring about the greatest part of the moral education of that battle- and bottle-loving youth.

But while I was still in the middle of my spring semester in Göttingen, Paschális also moved nearby to the Harz mountains, for as soon as the word got out that Germany's Iron Chancellor, in the centralizing craze of his political theory, proposed to transfer the

flourishing mining academy in Clausthal to Berlin, Paschális hastened to move to the former so that, before the disaster, as he wrote
me, he would benefit from the double advantage of theoretical and
practical studies, since around Clausthal there are, dependent on
the academy, many different mines and smelting works in which
students work as a matter of right, practicing under the immediate
supervision and guidance of the government's most important mining engineers and metallurgists. And as a matter of fact, the small
town of Clausthal is the child and nursling of these installations. Its
population consists only of the personnel of the mines, the metal
works, and the academy.

About two hours after my discussion with the doctor I was on
my way to that city, and I arrived at Osterod after a train ride of
several hours. From there the journey into the mountains is effected
by means of the mail coaches familiar in Germany, drawn by four
horses on the steeply ascending highway. Clausthal lies high in the
Harz, very high. And the ascent towards it, winding for the most
part, offers the traveler's eyes one enchanting sight after another of
most charming valleys, thickly shaded forests, snow-capped peaks
in the distance, sunny upland plateaus, fierce defiles and sheer
rocks; with the babbling of the brooks flowing below, the roars of
the waterfalls splashing down from above, and all that variety of
color with which autumn's hand brushes and varies nature's clothes
just prior to removing them one after another. Moreover, the calm
of that day was something rare in Germany! Light breezes, perfumed with the sweet-smelling pitch of the pines, played about,
shaking the blue curtains of the coach's windows, giving life to the
travelers' faces, recharging the blood within their hearts and lungs.
The sunburned postman, the white insignia of his rank on his black
leather cap, incessantly cracked his whip, and he took his shining
trumpet from under his arm at the first appearance of some village
on our road and trumpeted most charmingly several melodic stanzas of the postman's popular call to announce his approach. The
mountains about us wondrously echoed back the final notes of his
calls. But as we got closer to the village, the drowsy music of the
echo was eclipsed by the loud cries of the geese that hurried to
welcome us with wings spread and necks stretched forward; the
grunting of pigs eager to make a free passageway for us and retreating in thick phalanxes, their curly tails, with which they greeted us,
raised in the most military manner; and finally the lively cries of the

merry children, running to meet us, running to hang on back of the coach. Even the horses were excited. The higher we climbed, the nimbler and more spirited they became. The coach had ten seats but we were only four passengers. So even the horses had reasons for being happy during that journey.

We reached the charming, forested plateau in the middle of which Clausthal lies just before sunset. And as we were emerging from those thick forests, and while the coach was moving slowly up an incline, a pale face suddenly peeked in through the open window by which I was sitting; a hot and in fact feverish hand nervously squeezed my own. It was Paschális, who had come out to meet me in response to my telegram from Osterod. Paschális, in miner's uniform, with his student "helmet," on the visor of which shone two crossed silver hammers, the general symbol of miners and mineralogists. Even before the driver noticed him and stopped the horses I found myself outside the coach and in the embrace of my dearest friend.

More than two years had passed since we had seen one another. And though Paschális had always been pale and anemic, as is normal in a youth who attended to his body so sparingly and so unsparingly overworked his intellect, I had never seen him so pale, so weakened, whereas in those cool mountains, among comforts incomparably more humane than those in Athens, and after so many hymns of praise about the climate in which he lived, I had expected to find him full of life and vigor. And yet here before me I held him, dumb from emotion, and I squeezed him repeatedly in my embrace and with a shudder felt the heat of his dry lips, the fever of his sweating hands, I, who, in spite of all my illness and the fatigue of the journey, moved in that life-giving atmosphere so light, so strengthened!

"Paschális, my brother, you seem a little unwell!" I said to him after our long and repeated embraces.

"Ah, bah! It's nothing," he said nonchalantly. "I'm always like this."

"Strange! I expected to see you fat and ruddy as can be in this pure air."

"Oh!" said Paschális with a melancholy smile, "you expect things that are incompatible with our profession. The pure air is for people like you who come on purpose to breathe it in, not for us who live all day like moles in the bowels of the earth or breathe in the poisonous vapors of the metals in the metal refineries. And besides, I've had a touch of insomnia lately—I was so anxious. I expected you every day."

As he emerged from the forest the postman began to trumpet the sweetest stanzas of his song, obviously because he was announcing the arrival not so much to the inhabitants of Clausthal as to his children and his wife. We followed the coach at a distance, arm in arm.

"Let him go," said Paschális. "You won't lose anything. He'll bring your things for you to my house. We all know each other here; besides, I left orders at the post office."

After a short while the meadows around Clausthal unfolded before my eyes like broad and very thick green carpets. High, isolated chimneys, rising up here and there, drew my attention: without a doubt they belonged to the mines. The roofs of the city, barely distinguishable in the distance, looked like fields of red earth recently plowed in the middle of the light green of the plateau. But the houses couldn't be seen yet because they lie lower than the meadows, in the basin and on either side of the small stream that divides the city. The setting sun was robed in wondrous majesty, gilding the peaks of the heights opposite; a distant harmony of bells, like the dying sounds of music, reached us from the slopes around us on which could be faintly seen white herds of cattle returning home. At still greater distances the forest-clad slopes of the mountains were turning blacker and blacker; a white fog was beginning to drift over them. And above them the highest peak in the Harz, "Snowcap" in the local idiom, was changing from white to an ever brighter shade of red, rivaling in the beauty of its colors the well-known radiance of the Alps. After a short while the chirping of the birds grew still; the sounds of the bells died away; the breezes dropped; not a leaf stirred. A strange feeling of religious awe gripped my heart in the presence of nature's grandeur. Indescribable emotion bound my tongue. Paschális continued to squeeze my hand and look at me with inner satisfaction at the deep impression that the scenery was making on my senses. Finally he broke the silence:

> On every mountain, every hill,
> the air is calm and still.
> On every oak and every fir
> no leaf or branch does stir.
> The birds in twos and threes

sleep silent and in peace—
Oh, now endure the test,
you, too, will soon find rest!

These melancholy lines of the great German poet, unexpectedly declaimed by Paschális in this way, in Greek, with a deep passion and true perception of their meaning, caused in me that mysterious sweet shudder and brought to my eyes those tears that do not come to me often, save under the influence of unattainably lofty thoughts and immeasurably deep feelings, but even at that only when my soul happens to be suitably disposed.

"He wrote them up there," said Paschális, pointing out the snow-capped peak of Vruk. "You see that black spot? That's the hotel where he spent the night. On its walls the date and his signature are still preserved. It must have been an evening like this when he wrote those lines. So clear, so peaceful."

"And so you often have such enchanting evenings on the Harz?"

"Very often, no. But now is the time for them. For quite a while we've been living here as if in Paradise. That's why I kept insisting that you hurry your coming."

"And you weren't afraid I'd bring the bad weather?"

"Not so much as that you wouldn't catch the good weather. You have no idea how fickle the old man up there is, him with his perpetually white cap. How perverse! So see you sleep well tonight and rest up from the journey. I think it wise to visit him while he's in a good mood."

"What? You mean right away tomorrow?"

"Yes! Yes! We've got to flatter him; it's our only tactic to make him prolong his kindness. What do you say?"

"I'm not so sure," I said, referring not so much to the manner in which he spoke as to our own abilities.

"Of course, of course!" continued Paschális with a teasing smile. "When he sees that this new worshipper of his does not resemble us profane and vulgar folk who climb him solely and only to dirty his cap, that within that pale forehead there gestates an ode in his praise, then surely he'll behave towards us as he should. In that respect he's like all the 'greats.' But in any event pretend that you admire him starting right now, that you don't know where to begin your praise of him. Then I promise you much joy and instruction on the Harz."

"So, always the same?" I exclaimed laughing. "Always the pleasant inseparable from the useful? Have you forgotten the fiasco in Berniudákis' 'beer parlor?'" At this the two of us laughed heartily.

"But," said Paschális seriously after a moment, "now things are different. Now we're not merely about to mimic foreign ways, to learn how the tragicomic scenes of Germanic drunkenness are acted out, but to come to know the locations in which the most sober dramatist of this country imagined the most magical and extravagant scenes of *Faust*."

"That's true. I had forgotten that the 'Walpurgis Night' scene takes place on the Harz. Is the spot nearby, then?"

"There! High up there is the plateau on which he set the orgies and the dances of the witches on Walpurgis Night; and in front of it there gapes that chasm to an amazing depth, which even to this day is called 'the Witches' Cauldron.' Nearby it is not, but it's certainly closer for us than it is for the Americans who cross the ocean to visit it."

In this way we went down into the village, which was by now visible to us, I absorbed by the grandeur about me, my eyes fixed now on one, now on another scenic wonder; and Paschális greeting passers-by for me as well, but always with his protective gaze on me, eager to name the landmarks for me, to enumerate the special beauties of each, as if there did not exist a span of earth in those mountains on which his foot had not trod. And he entered into the role of guide all the more gladly because, since we had for a long time been in regular correspondence, we had little special news to share with one another.

The houses of Clausthal, except for the scientific institutions, are distinguished neither for their size nor for their beauty. The streets through which we passed were analogous to the buildings on them. Inclines and descents are frequent and unavoidable in mountain villages. All these were remarkably well cobbled, however. In fact, in spite of all our inattention and the dimness of the roadside oil lamps, we rarely hit against bumps and never fell into a hole. The greeting of passers-by seemed strange and original to me, because in Clausthal you will meet no one on the road without his addressing you, "Glück auf!" even if you are quite unknown to him. At first I thought that they pronounced the German "good day" so idiosyncratically as to deform it to the point of misunderstanding.

But when I was convinced that they were saying nothing other than "good luck," I asked the reason.

"That, you see, is a consequence of our calling," said Paschális melancholically. "Good day and good night when said to a miner would be bitter irony. Day doesn't exist for those who spend it in the gloomy night of the underground, nor night for those who pass it working under the light of torches and lamps. For this reason don't ever wish them any such thing, unless you wish to remind them of their misery. In every situation wish whomever you meet good luck. All of us here have need of that wish."

"But what does it mean, then, sir?" I asked, laughing at the seriousness with which Paschális had begun to invest the question.

"Oh!" he said, more melancholically still. "The wish doesn't mean what many people think it does: good luck and dig up some diamonds! good luck and discover some vein of gold! But for the poor miner it means: good luck that no underground vault collapses and crushes you! good luck that the gasses in the mines don't catch fire and burn you! And so on."

In this way we reached his house, and "Good luck!" we greeted the mistress of the house, who was waiting by the door. That is, good luck that in the next minute they do not announce to you that you're a widow, that you have no children! In this same house Paschális had seen to it that lodging for me was provided, a thing that was most comforting both in name and in fact. It had been a long time since I had slept so comfortably, so satisfyingly, as that first night in Clausthal. Perhaps my exertions had contributed to that, because we had barely finished dinner when I "hit the sack," I was so exhausted from the trip.

But oddly enough I had had enough of sleep well before day actually broke. And though I had long since heard people up and around in the house, since it was still so dark, I preferred not to get up. Finally Paschális knocked loudly on my door and came in, drenched from head to toe.

"Hey, brother!" he exclaimed in astonishment. "You still sleeping? It's noon!"

In fact I had slept deeply not only all night, but also half the day! And I wasn't so very unhappy about this, but I was unpleasantly shocked when I drew the curtains on the window and found that my room was no brighter than it had been up till then. The rain was falling as from a myriad of taps; a thick mist covered every-thing; the heavens were black as pitch! We were in the very clouds!

"And now?" I asked to Paschális, astonished at the unexpected change.

"Now—'God have mercy and pity on us,'" he answered, hanging his hands and his head like a man without hope. "Too bad you didn't come earlier! When I went out early this morning to go to the mine nothing seemed suspicious yet. And just see what a state of affairs in the course of a few hours!"

"So we won't climb Snowcap today?"

"Today!" exclaimed Paschális pitying the naiveté of the question. "Ask instead whether you'll be able to stick your nose out the door for a week or even two, much less think of Snowcap! Why didn't you come sooner?"

At the time I thought my good friend was joking and trying to frighten me because I had not obeyed his wish and come sooner. So I sent him off to put on dry clothes without attaching any meaning to his prophesies. We did not, however, stick our nose even out the window that day. The next day the rain stopped, but a thick white fog saturated the atmosphere, hiding even the rooftops opposite from our sight. I opened the window for a few moments, but was forced to close it again: the fog came into the room and was as quickly soaked up by every woolen cloth and by our clothes as if they had been fashioned of the prophet Aaron's wonder-working fleece! The fog was followed by rain and very strong winds, and the rain by fog, and the fog by rain! And in this way for eight days Paschális' prophetic powers were triumphant. The weather became excessively cold, and I began to cough more violently than ever. The result was that I didn't even dare stick my nose out of the curtains of the bed.

In spite of all this, however, Paschális continued to go out regu-larly every morning. Even though he was on vacation as regards his studies, for his practical training he spent the first half of the day sometimes in the washing rooms and crucibles of the metal works, sometimes, however, in the very bowels of the earth entrusted with the oversight of the works or himself digging as a simple worker. I shall never forget the extraordinary impression he produced in me every time I saw him returning from the mines. With his broad-brimmed hat on his head, the special miner's torch hanging below his chest, with his leather apron around his buttocks, and his gleaming pick on his shoulder, he looked to me like one of those kindly creatures of Germanic folklore to whose hands is entrusted the production and surveillance of the treasures of the earth. His thick eyebrows, his long, thick, jet-black beard, his extremely pale face, his eyes sparkling animatedly from the depth of their sockets, and the superhuman nervous energy lurking beneath the translucent skin of his long thin fingers continually strengthened that impression to the point of actual self-deception. But the witty, bantering, and teasing nature of the playful demons of mining seemed to be vanishing from Paschális' spirit by the day. The longer the bad weather continued, the more melancholy and silent he became.

Finally the horror outside got so bad that precisely on the fifteenth of August, following the example of the rest of Clausthal, we put our stoves in operation. More tedious days I have never lived through! The rain lashed the windows incessantly; the wind whistled madly, threatening to shake the roof off the house; and from time to time it rushed so suddenly, so fiercely down the chimney that all the smoke came back through the stove, filling the room and my eyes. And I then recalled with tears the "desiring to see the smoke rising up" of my Homer-quoting doctor and regretted bitterly that I had not obeyed him. Then the nights began. A wilder thing no one can imagine. Our house was built on the downhill side of a height on which arose some tall oaks in a clump with two or three aged pines beside them. The raging wind had once felled one of the oaks and shattered it; the shattered portion—about two thirds of the tree—still attached to its original trunk and forming a right angle with it, extended the tips of its branches up to our house, touching the roof with its dry leaves, right over my bed. When the gales howled, whistling through the needles of the pines, roaring through the thick foliage of the oaks, rustling through the dry branches of the fallen tree, they sounded, right on my roof, like frenzied satanic concerts, so fierce, so frightfully weird, that even the dullest person would have been unable to listen to them without losing his sleep. And when someone loses his sleep under such conditions, what mad ideas come to increase the turmoil in his soul! I could not forget the *Stríngles* and the *Kallikántzari* and all those demons with which the professor in Göttingen had tried to frighten me if I should go very high up in the Harz. And yet there nearby me I now had the plateau on which those monstrous, grim distillations of Hades celebrated their horrible rites! Nearby was the "cauldron" around which the hideous and half-naked *Stríngles* danced, with their filthy hair flying in the wind, throwing into it now the heart of a young girl who had been deflowered, now the twitching limbs of a new-born babe!

Moreover the scraping of the dry leaves over my head sounded like the fingernails of phantoms of the dead trying to push aside the roof-tiles and come into my darkened bedroom and touch me with their cold wet shrouds! And so my heart was in turmoil, and I strained my ears, without wanting to, and heard the thumps and tumults of the rain, the whistlings and howls of the gales, and constantly thought that through that frightful roar of the winds wrestling with the trees I distinguished the confused sounds of the moans of people being throttled, the wails of women being ravished, the whinings of children being exposed, and above all these things the sardonic laughter, the sharp cries, the shrill howls of all those personified passions that were the malicious causes of those rites taking place in the darkness! . . . I relate this after the passage of many, many years, and yet—strange to relate!—I seem to see the scenes, to hear the cries, anew and a chill shudder runs through my nerves from head to toe! . . .

*****

At first Paschális made every effort to make our evenings at least pleasant. In his study he had carefully arranged a small but choice collection of ores and minerals, so he spent hours on end eagerly explaining to me the reasons for their bright colors, the causes of their strange shapes, the magnetic or electric reasons for the arrangement of the crystals of each, their chemical composition, their classification, and their properties with such incomparable ease and joy that there, too, as he used to say, the pleasurable was joined to the useful. But as these lessons began to come to an end and as most subjects of conversation became exhausted, while the weather continued to get worse, so Paschális, as I said, continued to lose his liveliness and cheerfulness of spirit.

Clearly that chill, damp, dark atmosphere affected his nerves more than mine and more than I had supposed at first, because for some time not only had he not gone out for his mining practice, but he had even given himself totally over to a kind of sullenness and sadness so silent that it began to trouble me. The landlady presented the matter as nothing unusual for him and assured me that it would pass as soon as the weather improved. And yet the bad weather continued; the rain fell mercilessly. Paschális appeared to be suffering from dreadful insomnia and got up the next day, even after the calmest night, still more exhausted and despairing than he had the morning of the day before! Frequently I tried to divert him as I had before with anecdotes, stories, or scientific questions, but now it was in vain. Just when you thought he was following with the greatest attention, then it turned out that he was daydreaming, lost in thoughts and imaginings about which he declined to talk.

One chilly and yet somewhat less blustery evening after dinner, after we had carefully stopped up the last cracks in the windows with old newspapers, we were sitting—as usual—in his room, he in his brown tassled nightgown, daydreaming on the sofa, I next to the stove and near the lamp, leafing through the new edition of Carl Vogt's *Geology* and thinking how the doctor in Göttingen would rebuke me after he read the letter I had written him today. Then I recalled—I don't know through what chain of recollection— Paschális' old love affair with his laundress' daughter in Athens, and I wondered to myself how it had not occurred to me to speak to him of this before. Not because I suspected that that unfortunate love could bear any relation to the young man's present condition; no, but because it was a subject well suited for us to joke about, to laugh at, to cheer ourselves up with. I was moreover also surprised that Paschális had never mentioned the subject to me, not even in his earliest letters. Nonetheless, without raising my eyes from the pictures in the book in my hands, I said, "But Paschális, you haven't told me anything about Evlalía yet—"

"Damn her to hell!" he broke in to my astonishment, bolting upright in his chair and dropping the red tassle of his nightgown with which he was wont to play when daydreaming. Then, like a man recovering from a deep dream, he fixed his wide eyes on my own and shouted, "What? You, too? What made you think of that dirty—?"

"I don't know," I said, trying to conceal my astonishment. "I'm sitting here looking at the palaeontological illustrations in this book. How ugly and monstrous those creatures were which enjoyed Creation's virgin beauty, Nature's first bloom, before the noble heart of man, for which alone they were destined, had a chance to enjoy them!"

I shall never forget my agitation when I lifted my eyes from the book in order to get the response—which was slow in coming—and saw Paschális! The posture of his body, the position of his hands, the paleness of his face and his livid lips, and above all the expression in his eyes presented the picture of a helpless man who, having suddenly received a fatal blow and still under the sway of pain and terror, is at a loss how to avert a second, death-dealing blow!

"Don't!" he cried out after a long struggle. "Don't strike that chord!"

His voice had burst out as if the iron hand that had been choking his throat had suddenly let go! The book fell unnoticed from my hand. Getting up from my chair in great distress, I went over and sat next to him on the sofa.

"Brother, Paschális, you astonish me!" I told him in a tender tone, taking his fevered right hand in both of my own. "What's the matter?"

"I'm in pain! I'm in pain where you touched me, you cruel, heartless fellow! Why do you say it in parables? Isn't it clear enough? Don't I understand it? I do! As newly formed Creation was, so was my heart: full of virgin beauty, full of vigor and life. But who enjoyed it? Who rejoiced in it? That loathsome, monstrous creature! And do you suppose she could appreciate those things? No! She wallowed in swinish fashion in the most tender emotions, the most divine feelings of my heart, and when she had had her fill, she polluted it with her poison, she muddied it with her conduct! She rolled around in it like a filthy pig! She debased it! She rendered it an unworthy seat of the noble, the beautiful, the sublime, for which it had been destined!"

"But in the name of God," I said thunderstruck, "who are you saying all these things about? About Evlalía? I would have staked my life that that old story was totally over and done with by now!"

"Oh!" he said after a short hesitation. "The 'old story' is over and done with, but the 'consequences' remain! . . ." And he pronounced these last words with such desperate sadness that I no longer doubted that the cause of his present situation was that unhappy love affair. But why? The catastrophe had happened well before he left for Germany, and, however dreadful the shock to his heart had been, Paschális had endured it with remarkable courage and dignity while his blow was still recent. It is true I had contributed not a little to this, in that I had accustomed him to scorn that base and unworthy female, principally because I thought that by so doing I would make him emerge more quickly from the spiritual discouragement and depression into which the first rush of his misfortune had plunged him. That's what I thought and what I accomplished. Paschális not only regained his self-control after a short while, but even when I jokingly asked him in the midst of his instructions, while seeing him off on the steamship upon his departure: "And what are you leaving for your 'intended'?" with a bitter, scornful smile, "My contempt," he answered. This contempt was presented to me today increased to a very great degree. And yet his spiritual discouragement and despair had not only not been overcome by it, but was now so great, so incommensurate with what it had been that, till just a moment before, I would not have been able to imagine that the present Paschális had any relation with the Paschális of old or was his intensified continuation. And what was the cause of this intensification? What were the "abiding consequences of the old story?" Perhaps Paschális had not emerged from the slime into which he had slipped so chaste and pure as I had hoped? Perhaps in that untimely love affair he had not behaved so prudently as I had thought? Vague, frightening suspicions inflamed the turmoil in my imagination as they leaped forward one after another in the dark recesses of my brain.

In the meantime Paschális was silent, abject and humiliated like the most pitiable convict in the world. His facial features were painted so eloquently with a kind of bitter remorse, and he spoke so expressively through his tear-filled eyes, that the sight of him moved my heart deeply.

"Paschális," I said to him finally and with an unaccountably trembling voice, "brother Paschális, have you by any chance withheld anything from your story? Why do you do me this injustice? What secret did I ever have that I didn't entrust to you entire and without reservation? How can you want me to share in your pain, to take the portion of it that belongs to me, when I don't know it? Come now! Don't be so selfish with your misfortunes when you're so communicative of your happiness. All right? Otherwise I'll suppose that I did not share in your every joy up till now either, as I had the right as a friend, as your brother. Because we've been brothers now for a long time, haven't we, Paschális?"

Paschális at first seemed uncertain, but then, moved by my words, he threw himself with sobs and tears onto my neck. I squeezed him affectionately in my embrace, and for a long time we wept silently. Finally he pulled away, took a deep breath, and said, "Oh forgive me! Forgive me for my weakness! For such a long time I tried desperately to bring you to my side, for such a long time I waited for you to come, and for this one thing alone: to open my heart to you, for you to see its bleeding wound. And I had such courage, such confidence as long as I didn't see you. But now that you're here, now that I have you before my eyes every day, I don't know what makes me so cowardly, so faint-hearted! Perhaps a state of nerves made worse by the bad weather, but perhaps, perhaps, the magnitude of my guilt! . . . And yet, I don't have any other confessor hereabouts. You must be my confessor! Who knows? Perhaps tomorrow will already be too late. You see how my strength is receding and wasting away under the frightful weight of the disaster. Forgive me! An unrestrainable desire overwhelms me, a desire for rest and peace. I'm tired, I'm exhausted now. I crave sleep, sleep, sleep. But I haven't tasted sleep for a long time. The winds in heaven grow still, the waves of the sea find rest: only I, only I cannot sleep! You wonder. You're astonished. I'm not surprised. Listen and judge."

And bowing his head as if trying to gather his recollections, he fell silent for some time. Then, without raising his eyes towards me, he asked, "Do you recall what bitterness and anger I carried in my breast when I left Athens?"

"Yes," I said. "I recall that you had not yet completely calmed down, and yet—"

"You should know," he interrupted, "that in my chest there no longer beat the bold, the optimistic heart of a young man, but a trampled chaff, a bloody rag barely and forcibly saved from the filthy nails of a hyena."

"Those are the great exaggerations of your present thoughts," I said. "As for me, neither did I then nor do I now accept that a cheap woman's behavior can damage the worth of a pure heart."

"I don't know how you mean that," said Paschális skeptically. "But diamonds and pearls, when once they are set before swine and are chewed and trampled by them, become unsuitable to adorn even the most humble head, let alone to be raised to the height of a queen's diadem."

"And can't I wash them," I asked with a laugh, "so they become again as they were at first?"

"Oho!" said Paschális sternly. "You can wash 'physical' jewels and clean them. But 'moral' ones? What about feelings and thoughts, the heart's only treasures? With what acid, with what soap will you wash away that moral filth, I ask you? Better not to roll them in the mire so as not to soil them in the first place. You soiled them? Their stains are indelible! However"—he then added, suddenly falling into a very sorrowful tone—"it's no longer a question of that! Do you remember my first letters from Freiburg?"

"Yes," I said, "I remember them."

"You were still in Athens and didn't know anything about the Germans. I described to you the professors' courteousness, their affection for students, their hospitality to foreigners, especially their fondness for Greeks. Do you find I exaggerated?"

"No, on the contrary."

"Among those good men who were especially fond of me," said Paschális lowering his gaze, "was, best of all, Professor M., a man unique in his field."

"Yes," I said. "You wrote me about him. I remember his name."

"I wrote you of his virtues, his importance, and all the inestimable good things with which he enriched his science. I never mentioned to you one good thing, the most precious of all, which adorned his house and all of Freiburg. I never wrote you that he had a daughter."

"No!" I said, sitting up with a start. "The last thing you wrote me was that in the meantime he had lost his wife. Isn't that right?"

"Yes. And while that loss closed his hospitable house to the rest of my fellow students, I was always welcome. I can say I was entertained more heartily than ever. The old man's loneliness, especially during the winter nights when he couldn't go out, made him feel all the more compassion for me because of my own loneliness."

"But the old man had his children," I said. "He had his daughter, didn't he?"

"Yes. He had Clara. But you know what it means to be an old professor, especially a German one. Clara was his only child. A warm, lively young woman—perhaps a little uppity because of her ideas and her reading, but full of music and poetry, full of imagination and feelings. The old man was by nature dispassionate and indifferent toward anything that wasn't his subject. I, with my heart disappointed so young, the wings of my imagination already clipped, and possessed only of a dispassionate mind devoted exclusively to my studies, suited him better than any other. I'm sure of that. I owed that extraordinary partiality of his to my devotion to science but perhaps also to my reserve towards his daughter. In this I differed from the rest. Clara was a young woman of extraordinary beauty, and she was also the city's 'darling.' By common agreement the readiness of her spirit, the simplicity of her heart charmed all who knew her. Perhaps she was a little flirtatious. But not by nature. Surely not! The undivided attentions, the constant flattery naturally turned her head a little. Moreover, she deserved it; it 'became' her. Whenever they had a formal soirée at their house, no one paid any attention to the professor's woman guests; all laid siege to Clara, all competed to see who could first secure favor for himself, be it only for a moment. She, however, emerged from these repeated assaults with wondrous skill, always victorious and triumphant, but also always more bewitching, more lovely, than before. I usually passed the whole time at the party with the older people; I never flirted with her or danced with her. But I experienced an inner pleasure when I saw her being successful, being adored. I experienced a kind of pride; she was the treasure of the house that honored me with its trust. And yet my German fellow students envied me. One of them, my closest friend, confessed this to me. 'Clara's ideal,' he said, 'is not "four-eyes, bushy eyebrows, pasty face!"' She didn't tell them these things in so many words, but at the appropriate time and in the appropriate manner, so that no one would feel insulted. But they suspected my closeness to Clara's father. They concluded from that that I was more familiar with the girl than it seemed. Clara, however, never behaved flirtatiously or coquettishly or ostentatiously with me as she did with them. This was natural. Since I was always serious, always reserved, she too behaved with me in a more serious way and with greater modesty. It seemed she respected me. And that made me as happy—as happy as I could now be after what I had experienced. Later, much later, she took me by surprise. She gave me a suspicion, a hint—a very tangible hint.

"There had been a performance of Wagner's *Flying Dutchman* in the theater. The actor who played this part appeared, as usual, dressed in black, with black eyes, black hair and beard, and so pale and mournful that many thought they recognized me on the stage. After a few days the subject came up somehow, and Clara told me . . ."

"But what did she tell you?" I asked him when he suddenly fell silent.

"That the ideal of her imagination, her heart's desire, was . . ."

"What?" I asked again after waiting in vain for him to continue. Paschális reddened suddenly like a guilty child, and with thick tongue, said, "The Dutchman! The Flying Dutchman!"

"He's every German girl's ideal," I said, pretending not to have noticed his confusion.

"Yes," he said, taking courage, "especially of blondes. I had heard it many times before from other girls and it didn't seem strange. The way in which Clara said it, however, the circumstances under which she said it, left no doubt. From her confusion the poor girl could say no more. And it came on me—like a shock . . ."

"And why so faint-hearted again?" I said with a laugh. But he suddenly opened his eyes wide and said, "You don't understand why? The girl wanted love!" And as he pronounced those last words he looked furtively about and lowered his voice as if he were afraid the walls would hear him.

"Eh! And so what if she did?" I said with a light laugh.

"And so what if she did?" he repeated, astonished at the lightness with which I was treating the subject.

"Yes!" I said. "If she wanted love, where were you?"

"I was there," he answered sternly and harshly. "But I—what love did I have to offer her? The scourings of my washerwoman? I tell you, she was the queen of girls, she was the worthy object of the world's adoration. You're a strange one! A heart opens up before me, a spotless receptacle of God's blessing—and you want me to fill it with pigs' leftover slop?"

Then for the first time I really understood why Paschális had begun by comparing his cheated feelings to pearls cast before swine. But I found nothing to answer him with right away, and he continued in a calmer tone, "From that moment on, in spite of her father's kindly complaints, I began to go to their house less frequently. And when I did go, I was very careful to avoid her. While her mother was alive the thing wasn't very difficult. There were many guests, and as they were her admirers, they tried with all their might to keep her occupied among themselves. But when Mrs. M. died, things suddenly changed. The house was emptied, closed. A poor distant relative of the professor's, the only one surviving, was taken on as Clara's nurse, or rather her companion. But Clara was no longer that cheerful, lively, and spirited girl for whose supervision at one time her mother's watchful gaze had been deemed insufficient. Clara became suddenly thoughtful, melancholy, guarded, weighing even the least syllable before pronouncing it.

"Right after her mother's death I tried to break off my evening visits. But the old professor one day expressed a complaint that cut me to the quick: 'Now that I'm bereft and lonely,' he said, 'it's not right for you too to abandon me, you who know better than anyone what it means to be alone.' So I went; rarely at first, then more frequently, but always avoiding every occasion on which I might find myself alone with Clara. She, I think, did the same. She did not speak to me as before even in her father's presence. But during those winter nights she sat opposite us for hours on end without a word, her eyes fixed on the embroidery in her hands, but listening intently and following with interest the dry and cold subjects of our conversations, a thing that she would never have done before. After that first, clear hint about the Flying Dutchman I don't think we exchanged a word in private. And there was a time when I thought the matter forgotten. I believed I had misunderstood her words. That sudden upset in Clara's life, however, her inconsolable tears at her mother's death, seriously harmed the girl's health. When winter came and the water froze and everybody put on their skates, both the doctor and her father prescribed skating for her, an activity that she had once liked very much. But her grief was recent, her revulsion at the slightest diversion great: for many weeks she did not appear on the ice. I—you remember I wrote you—had begun skating the previous winter. My health demanded outdoor exercise. That second winter I was still inexperienced, so I practiced in an out-of-the-way corner. The expanse of the ice was great, and I hoped I would remain unobserved. But the first time Clara was persuaded to come to the ice, she found me right away. And when she discovered me, she didn't leave that corner again. You mustn't think she stayed there with me from the start. But as soon as she made a turn on the ice, she came back to my corner. Her friends of course hurried back to tie on her skates, to be her 'cavalier,' to skate with her, but she accepted nothing. I was practicing to learn those great bow-shaped figures. You know how difficult they are, how dangerous. So I fell down on the ice frequently in that distant corner. But as soon as I fell, Clara—you'd think she was observing unseen nearby—came to see if I was hurt, to help me begin again. Finally:

"Don't be so standoffish,' she said. 'You'll never learn them by yourself. Come on, let's try them together.' So we began to skate hand in hand."

"I can just imagine the other students," I said.

"The other students, you understand," he said with a show of some vanity, "when they saw that unconcealed partiality, they bit their lips. And they slunk away as you would expect, one after another. It was Sunday, and we stayed on the ice three hours. The other girls had a new 'cavalier' every minute but no one offered to skate with Clara again. The matter was clear. They did it because of me. To insult her. And though this did not bother her at all, I was now all the more obliged not to leave her without a 'cavalier.' Besides, even with the loss of her color and animation, Clara was the most beautiful, the most charming skater. It was no longer iceskating we were doing. It was flying through the air, through the void. So light! So swift! . . . "

Paschális broke off for a moment and rubbed his bulging forehead with his pale hand as if trying to warm its contents.

"When the ice was new and clear as a mirror," he said, "and our flying bodies, so close to one another, were reflected in it, and deep within it appeared the azure color of the sky, and I saw its white clouds receding beneath my feet with the speed of our flight, my heart somehow began to swell up again, my imagination began to grow warm and regain its wings. I thought I was being carried aloft, above the clouds, above the firmament. I was being carried by the wings of a heavenly cherub with a flight so swift, so sensual, that my senses were constantly intoxicated with delight; they grew dizzy from the speed, became confused, swooned, abandoned me! And then only my soul continued to fly, as in a dream, to fly with the angel, up, up, up to the throne of the Almighty! There in that dazzling light, there among the angels burning incense and chanting, it seemed to me that I fell on my knees before the steps of His throne, and with tears asked God to punish me as harshly as I deserved, but to give me a heart, a new heart, its feelings intact, a heart pure and undefiled, worthy of Clara, worthy of the beauty and the virtues of Clara! But then suddenly we reached the end of the ice at that out of-the-way corner, and we stopped to catch our breath. And always, always, before my prayer was heard, the dream was interrupted! The flight came to an end."

Paschális stressed these last words with great moral indignation, as if he were convinced that the realization of his prayers failed each time solely and only because the expanse of ice came to an end before his soul's yearnings reached the ears of God.

"Whenever we stopped," he continued after quite some time, "Clara asked me about our island. She wanted me to describe scenes of our life at home. Above all, however, she delighted to hear from me the adventures of my life. To hear me recount the deprivations, sufferings, difficulties, and obstacles with which I had had to wrestle until I succeeded in assuring my education. She wanted these things in all their details; she listened to them with the greatest attention; and she sighed at my hardships, and tears constantly came to her eyes. . . . Then my plans and hopes for the future—What I would become; where I would settle down; and when; and happy, happy those who were waiting for me—who would see me again with the certainty that never, never again would they be parted from me . . . and—Why do you want me to tell you details that tear at my heart? After that first admission about the Flying Dutchman it's true she never told me anything so clearly. And that first time was principally the result of her childish naiveté, her directness and candor, for which she now was inwardly ashamed and which she regretted. But what need was there? Her constant swings from animation to daydreams, from joy to sorrow, from laughter to tears, without cause, without reason—and then her change in color, the expression in her eyes, her unfinished sentences, her half-stifled sighs. . . . The thing was obvious. The girl loved me. . . . I knew it—without anyone telling me. . . ."

"And what about you . . . ?" I asked gently when Paschális had recovered from the emotion that that confession had caused him. For some time he didn't answer. Then, raising his tear-drenched eyes to heaven:

"Oh!" he said with indescribable anguish, "he asks if! . . . If ever Christian loved his spiritual salvation, I loved Clara! . . . The better I came to know her," he continued then with lowered gaze and voice, "the more virtues I found in her, the deeper the love in me! But the more she was exalted and magnified in my estimation, the greater was the difference between her and that rubbish to whose level I had abased my love, the baser and less worthy did I appear now before Clara. I'm afraid you can't understand my position at that time no matter how I describe it to you. Imagine a love as warm as the sun, as bright as the sun, as pure as the sun—the sun of that first, that virgin Creation. But oh! That sun did not rise over virgin soil, energetic and eager to produce the first wealth of growth in equal proportion to the beneficent influence of the light and warmth it received. The heart onto which Clara's love shone was earth plundered, stripped, laid waste forever. It was warmed, yes. But in such a way as to feel with deep, burning sorrow that *if* it hadn't been deforested, *if* it hadn't been desiccated, it would flourish now as the most sweet-smelling, blooming paradise of feelings. It was lighted, yes. But—and this is the worst of it—only so as to see and compare its barrenness, its ugliness, and its degradation to the richness and the beauty and the splendor of Clara's heart! Oh why was I so foolish? So stupid? Why dissipate and debase the treasures of my young heart? What a heart! So sensitive! So rich! But so inexperienced! So heedless! It did not husband prudently the abundance of feelings with which God had endowed it. The excess of love in it oppressed it; the flood cramped it! It needed to overflow, to find relief. And when that cheap girl came before it, it did not ask, it did not think, to be sparing. Sparing! And was that possible? It believed it was loved. The more it gave, the more it would get. And so I poured all, all the treasures of my feelings into that base heart, into that unworthy, that filthy receptacle, in order to get . . . disgrace, degradation! I deified debasement, I worshipped vileness! Now what lofty thought can I have for Clara that I haven't degraded by thinking it of that other one? What beautiful thought that has not already been defiled through association with her? Nothing, nothing either sacred or holy was left to me that had not been defiled by having been offered first to her! . . . But I loved Clara—Oh, I loved her! I adored her like my God! And precisely for that reason I could not act disrespectfully towards her, to sully her. Not even to his most distant friends does a man offer flowers whose petals have fallen and been trampled. To the Gods, however, to the Gods they offer only the best, the perfect ones, only the choice and untouched. So how could I offer Clara a shabby heart and threadbare feelings? How could I accept a love like God's blessing and offer in exchange the scrapings, the slops of that . . ."

And Paschális stared at me challengingly and bluntly, awaiting my answer. I knew that that mocked and sullied love of his had been as chaste and sincere as it had been fiery. In fact I knew his goodness, and sometimes even teased him for his excessive sense of propriety. But the unique moral strictness that was revealed to me today, his fears that I would not be able to understand his position vis-à-vis Clara, "however he represented it to me," made me feel ashamed of myself somehow and unable to answer. The thing had come so unexpectedly in any event. When, after having decided to open his heart to me, he began his preamble with such sorrow, such despair, I was immediately prepared to her something horrible, something astonishing. For a moment I had forgotten his character. Not much was needed for Paschális' moral derangement. Conflicts of emotions, however trivial they might be according to the ideas of others, always caused a dreadful disturbance in his soul. As happens with many nervous constitutions, the excitation had indeed come on him in a flash, as from an electric spark. But with him the explosion did not follow instantaneously, the emotion did not pass, as happens with an empty and useless firecracker.

Moreover, in him, things of this nature were not soothed through time; on the contrary, they intensified. But they intensified insidiously and unseen, revolving in his mind and gaining strength particularly because of a dialectical method of thinking peculiar to himself. The result was that literally no one could foresee the final outcome of any disruption in Paschális' feelings if one relied only on general psychological experience. So one can understand to what a pitch of perplexity I was brought by that unexpected turn and his peculiar dialectic. His arguments against himself were not the work of a temporary emotional excitement. Paschális was repeating once again and out loud what he had weighed and reckoned perhaps a thousand times in silence and to himself. Of this I could be certain. If the arguments appeared somewhat defective, if he uttered them always cloaked in concrete forms, this arose precisely from the fact that he was choosing piecemeal and selectively from a much more logical and complex chain of reasoning only those links by which he thought he could render his position more readily comprehensible to me. Needless to say, he did not succeed in this as he wished. Nor did this escape Paschális, because when he saw into what perplexity his words had brought me, he waited no longer for me to answer him but, again lowered his voice and his eyes, said:

"I had renounced the sweetest, most ethereal happiness that a mortal could ever dream of in this world—but it had to happen. Because morally 'I was not worthy,' 'I did not have an abode in which to receive my God,' I had to remove myself from his path. I had to avoid Clara's company. You know the strength of my will.

For months on end I did not set foot in their house. I did not see her. The old man complained repeatedly, as was natural, but—I say it with shame—I resorted to lies. And sometimes with one excuse, sometimes with another, I avoided him until out of vexation he gave up on me and no longer talked to me. Now my misfortune was frightful. The road that led to Clara had been closed by my own hand, and it had been closed for good! What I suffered during that long, long interval is indescribable. I had imposed on my will more than it could bear. I had submitted myself to a superhuman sacrifice greater than any heroism. One day I suddenly got a letter—I had been expecting it—it was from Clara."

And Paschális placed his hand on his heart, perhaps to show me where the letter was, but perhaps to reassure himself that it was as always where it belonged. Then catching his breath again, he said, "It didn't say anything! Nothing! Not even as much as she had told me with that first allusion to Wagner's Flying Dutchman. But I discerned many, many things. . . . The words were damp with tears—ostensibly for her mother, her dead mother. She longed for her, she wrote me. She longed to be with her—in heaven! On earth she had no friend—after she had stopped seeing even me—no one! I joined my tears with hers on that letter. I cried all day, but I didn't answer. I don't need to tell you I wrote. I wrote an answer, but I burned it. Then I wrote another, and I took it to the post office. But at the last moment I caught myself, I didn't drop it into the box. I tore it up. I had a frightful headache all that day. In the evening, about sunset, I went out to get a little air. I was as if mad, and yet I had the presence of mind not to take the public promenade. It was likely we would meet. I went out of the city, took a lonely road—I did not really know where I was going. There—you'd think it was a secret agreement, an extrasensory understanding of two hearts—there came over me a burning desire, an uncontrollable longing to see Clara! To see her even if once only, and then to die. It was impossible to go forward.—It would have been better had I turned back!—But no, my mind conquered; my will triumphed again. I continued on my path. But I had barely taken five steps—and there was Clara before me! Clara—no! Her ghost! Her shadow! She was so pale! So changed! How did she get there? And why? I don't know. But from that time, I think, dates that violent longing that comes over me, exactly as it did on that day. And whenever it comes over me, wherever I am, wherever I happen to be—I shudder as I say it to you!—Clara is there before me! Clara—no! Her ghost! Her soul! . . . That evening, however, it was Clara. I barely had a chance to see her before I held her fainting—in my arms! . . .

"We didn't stay together long"—Paschális began speaking again, still abstracted with the thoughts into which those recollections had plunged him.—"no, we didn't stay long. And yet, when we thought about returning home, it was late, very late. The moon had long since risen without our noticing it. We had entered the nearby woods and were sitting on the dried trunk of a felled tree near the little waterfall at the edge of the meadow. When I got up and looked about in the misty light of the moon, I distinguished in the distance the black figure of a person who was watching there, like a motionless shadow. It had been watching us all that time and, like a silent shadow, it followed us into the city. When we entered the first lighted street, it approached us and withdrew Clara's arm from my own. It was Clara's relative, her companion. Then I realized that the girl had not gone out alone, that . . ." and Paschális, whose voice had been becoming by degrees weaker and weaker, then fell silent, as a sick child does in the middle of his story, sweetly falling asleep. Paschális had not fallen asleep, but the expression in his eyes, the slight twitches of his facial muscles, the imperceptible openings and closings of his lips, bore clear witness to the fact that the sweet emotions of that meeting were passing once again before his sorrowful soul, as in a very sweet dream.

"I was the happiest man!" he said with a deep sigh. "The happiest and at the same time the most wretched! . . . While I had Clara by my side, while I looked at her, while I listened to her, I was overcome by a kind of sweet intoxication, a magical ecstasy. I felt myself a stranger to the world, above the world. I did not think about the moral laws that govern it. I didn't care. But when we parted, when I found myself alone in my room again, then I reflected on what I had done, and it seemed to me that, having dreamed in the light of Paradise, I was waking up in the darkness of Hell. Each kiss on the maiden's lips now presented itself to me as a frightful desecration. And the mere recollection of her embrace reduced me to ashes, as a flame does a dried twig! It was as if I had sullied holy things, had corrupted the sacred!—I, a sinner and unclean! How that chaste girl would loathe me if she knew with what kind of person she had to deal! What remained then of my manly resolve not to act disrespectfully toward Clara? And what remained of morality? I must confess! I had to reveal it to her: the love that she thought new and original was an unnatural copy, merely the echo of the true love that was squandered where it ought not to have been! And so I sat down and wrote a letter, a long letter. And I told her. I told her why, and I gave her to understand that a man like myself was not worthy of love from her but deserved scorn and repugnance. But when I sealed the letter, I realized that I had over-looked Clara's goodness of soul, the forbearance and tolerance of her inexperienced, childlike heart. And I thought that no matter what accusations I leveled at myself, Clara would forgive me. Be-cause of her love for me, she would forgive me. And if she did for-give me, oh! if she did forgive me!—cursed be the moment when that cruel idea came to me!—I considered that, if she did forgive me, if she continued to love me in full awareness of my moral deg-radation, she would become a participant in it, and she, too, would be degraded. And then that ideal height, upon which till that mo-ment I had so reverently gazed at the object of my adoration, would vanish. My love for her would be diminished. And I tore up the letter! I burned it!"

Paschális shuddered at the sound of his own voice. His right hand jerked spasmodically backwards, as if now making the move to save the letter that he had failed to make when he had taken it with the aim of destroying it.

"The day began to dawn," Paschális continued with a wild bit-terness in his words and facial expression. "They were still sleeping in the house. And in the streets a profound stillness reigned. Only within me did agitation and confusion prevail. Agitation and con-fusion in my soul. Agitation and confusion in my room. The moral man within hated me, loathed me, could no longer live with me, sought his freedom. I was guilty, I couldn't deny it. And as if I were preparing for his departure, I gathered my books together, tied up my things, nailed my boxes shut. And, before there was time for my breakfast to be prepared, I departed from Freiburg for good.

"Bismarck's plans concerning the Academy at Clausthal had al-ready been made public and had made many metallurgy students hurry there in the middle of the semester already in progress. That fact served to hide the true reason for my hurried and unexpected departure, or rather escape, from Freiburg. You remember I wrote you from here without your expecting it, and I told you that the imminent transfer of the Academy caused me to hurry my coming to Clausthal. That was really the weakest, the most serviceable reason. The real and main reason, you now know, was the ending of the quarrel between me and the moral man within; it was the decision to save Clara. Oh, what a harsh and cruel salvation!

"Upon my departure from Freiburg I had left instructions with one of the porters at the university to arrange to send my separation papers to me in Clausthal. Two weeks later when I got the university envelope here, I found in it also a letter with my name on it but entrusted to the university authorities for forwarding to me since my address was unknown. The handwriting was completely unknown to me, and yet—as if my heart had foreseen it!—the letter was not from a stranger. It came from Clara's relative, Mrs. B. Mrs. B. reminded me of the evening meeting of Clara and me, which she had arranged; she set forth the grave reasons why, unknown to the professor, she had ventured on that desperate step. She cursed the hour in which she had harmed the girl instead of helping her, and begged me in the name of God and my conscience to burn her letter, but to hurry and console Clara if I didn't wish to become the killer of the most innocent being in the world. The letter had been written in haste and in a way that revealed the writer's very great agitation. It was dated ten days earlier! In order to avoid the added difficulty, the authorities at the university in Freiburg had, it seems, put off sending it until my papers were ready. I answered on the spot and directly to Clara. With tears I sought her forgiveness for my cowardly flight; I begged her to write me. I promised to return. But it was already too late—she had died! Two or three days later I got this letter . . . it was from her father." And choked by his tears he unlocked the drawer of a small side table, took up the letter, and began to read it with a trembling and choking voice:

"'Dear Paschális! I am discharging a sad duty, writing to you myself, to report to you the arrival into my hands of the letter that you so kindly wrote to my poor Clara. An unforeseen evil has wished to bereave me of the only support of my feeble old age and has deprived you of a friend who, I am sure, would have regarded it her good fortune to answer your letter. I ask you to join with my own your prayers to the Almighty on behalf of—'"

Violent sobs choked off his voice; large tears flooded his eyes. He covered his face with his hands, weeping bitterly and moaning.

"And I'm the unscrupulous one," he wailed through his sobs,

"the villain who bereaved the unhappy father, the one who deprived him of the only support of his feeble old age! I'm the abominable one who withered the tender lily of innocence with the poison in his heart! I am the profane one who with his noisome breath extinguished the sacred lamp at the hearth of holy love! I am the cause, the perpetrator of Clara's death! Oh, my God! My God! How could you tolerate it? How could you endure it? For her to die, and me, the wretch, the scoundrel, the thoroughly abandoned, to live? That the life of life should be destroyed and that I should live, I whose thousand years would not be worth one moment of Clara's life!"

And weeping and wailing with a frantic frenzy the poor fellow beat his breast and tore out his hair! The catastrophe was indeed frightful, the despair, just. All consolation would have proved pointless and vain. Furthermore, I lacked the requisite spiritual calm. The story had moved my heart deeply, and Paschális' situation would have moved even the very rocks to tears. For a long time he continued berating himself with desperate bitterness, with the tenderest names calling upon his dead friend, begging for forgiveness with such moving expressions, with a heart so shattered that he would have moved even the most pitiless and heartless judge to pity, if it were a case, in fact, of his being judged for an actual murder.

After several vain attempts to calm him, my hand somehow came upon the letter that he had let fall on the sofa. I took it up and read it to myself. I read it once, I read it twice, and the more I read it the stronger became a suspicion, at first faint—a secret hope in my heart. Perhaps not everything had yet been lost, perhaps nothing had been lost! If I understood this letter well, absolutely nothing!

"Paschális, brother Paschális," I said with repeated insistence, "did you answer this letter? Did you ask what Clara died of? Did you go to Frieburg?"

"How could I go or write," he said after a long while, "without causing a new catastrophe? How could I appear in person, or answer that unhappy old man without telling him the truth? And how can I tell him the truth since his wound is still so recent? To tell him that I am his child's killer, I, the man of his choice! The man he trusted! That would kill him, without a doubt that would kill him!"

That hope of mine had now strengthened to certainty. Paschális had been outmaneuvered! He had been outmaneuvered by the letter's ambiguous style. I sat down right next to him, bringing the letter close to his eyes: "Paschális," I told him reproachfully, "don't act like a child. Read the letter again. It doesn't say anything about Clara's death."

"What do you mean it doesn't?" he shouted as he grabbed the other end of the letter and put his index finger on the last line. "What do you mean it doesn't? Don't you see? 'Join with my own your prayers to the Almighty on behalf of her'!"

"We join together in our prayers to God," I said calmly and gravely, "not only on behalf of the dead, but also on behalf of the living. Your sobs just now prevented me from hearing the end of the letter. If I had not read it myself, I would have been deceived just like you. And I'm sure you, every time you read it, are so carried away by your sorrow that you don't at all consider the artistry and ambiguity of the old professor's words and sentences. The letter is truly artful and ambiguous, and not only does it not say anything about death, it does not even speak about illness. For the first it is too weak; for the second, too grandiloquent. One does not expect such a thing from a professor no matter how pedantic one supposes him to be. Because look. 'Evil' will not always mean Death. As a matter of fact, death is never an 'unexpected' calamity. Moreover, 'this or that has wished to bereave me' in German doesn't always mean that it bereaved one in fact. Many times it simply means 'attempted but was forestalled,' just as in our language. Then, in the case of the dead, we don't say pray 'on his behalf' so much as we say pray 'for his soul.' So why attribute only the worst meaning to the professor's words? Why suppose he's speaking of Clara's death, or even her illness?"

Paschális snatched the letter from my hand.

"No! No!" I continued eagerly. "It wasn't his intention to tell you the one or the other. His intention was to tell you a third something. And to tell you so equivocally, so ambiguously that you would cease your contacts with his daughter sooner than you would have if he had demanded it simply and openly. And he succeeded in this aim of his most fully and cleverly."

Paschális, holding the letter in front of the light of the lamp with hands shaking spasmodically, let his astonished eyes scan it as sharply, as penetratingly, as if it were a question of discovering what was said underneath the professor's letters or hidden in the very texture of the paper.

"But where is it then?" he finally shouted with impatience. "Where is what you say?" And without raising his eyes he moved his finger over the lines like a child reading.

"Haven't you found it yet?" I asked, getting up. "Bring the letter here." And I forcibly snatched the letter from his hands. "Listen," I told him:

"'I am discharging a sad *duty*, writing to you *myself*, to report to you the arrival into *my hands* of your . . . letter . . . to . . . Clara.' That means: I report with sorrow (and it's a matter of indifference to me if it is also to your sorrow) that *I* read your letters. My duty as a father forces me to prevent their coming into the hands of my daughter, who has proved so poor in spirit as to 'go crazy' over a simple 'schoolboy.'"

Paschális bolted up like a man startled in his dream by a loud noise. "Listen on," I told him impassively: "'An unexpected evil *has wished* to bereave me etc., and has *deprived* you etc., in your letter, etc.' and so to the end. He means that my very best student, Paschális, having been found out to be *unexpectedly evil*, tried (but did not succeed) to deprive me of my child, carrying her, albeit as his wife, to the other end of the world, although he knows that I have no other support for my feeble old age. By doing this, however, the lover, the evil Paschális, has deprived himself of the right even to be a friend of Clara's, for whom—I don't deny it—answers to his letters (if he had continued to be honorable) would have been a blessing during the sad hours of her bereavement; they would have been a consolation, the only one left her on earth. Now that she is deprived of your consolation, at least pray with me that the Almighty will console her."

This interpretation of Mr. M.'s letter had a striking effect on Paschális right from the start. When he grasped where my suspicions tended he became very agitated. With trembling hand he nervously held on to the other edge of the letter and, with anxious eyes, alternately looked at the letters and my face. But after a while he imperceptibly withdrew his hand, turned his eyes away, drew back. And when I finished my explication I was astonished to find him lying on the sofa, indifferent, and paying no attention to my words. This was not the result I had expected. I continued to support my interpretation, however, with an eagerness that was now feigned. Mrs. B.'s silence after her only letter, her urging Paschális to burn that letter, furnished me with a powerful argument. Surely, I said, this woman is no longer with Clara, is no longer living in the professor's house. Her collaboration, her presence during that evening meeting, revealed to the strict father, goodness knows how, brought about her discharge. Otherwise she would have written, she would have written if only to announce Clara's death. And in conclusion: "Do you see, Paschális," I said, "what a terrible thing preconception is? It kept you so long deceived. It tormented you for nothing. It condemned you to silence and inactivity, surely to Clara's great sorrow."

Paschális calmly raised his eyes, looked me over from head to toe pityingly and, spreading his lips with bitter irony, said, "You've certainly become an expert critic! In such a short time! A clever interpreter! Göttingen can do that, you see. I congratulate you! Save your erudition, however. You'll need it to misinterpret—I mean interpret—the classics to little children." But after a short while he again hung his head in despair. "Ach! my friend! my friend!" he said, "you're trying to console a wild, unconsolable grief: I know it. Your pity for me makes you resort to all plausible arguments. If you knew Clara's father as I do, if you had read Mrs. B.'s letter, if above all you knew my soul's communion . . . if you knew this, I'm sure you'd have no doubt."

"Communion with whom?" I asked, surprised by his manner.

"With Clara," he answered portentously, "with Clara's soul! I told you how it happened the evening of our meeting, how a wild, uncontrollable longing to see her came over me and how suddenly there she was before me, in a spot where I would never have expected her. From that moment the same thing has happened to me many, many times. I don't mean to tell you that I ever forget Clara. But when the weather gets bad and the air is damp and the atmosphere dark and my melancholy seizes me, then I can think of nothing, nothing other than Clara. All day, all night, nothing. And as I recall to memory all the events of our love, that longing to see her suddenly comes over me, to see her as she was on one occasion or on another, and—you won't believe it—she presents herself to me exactly as I imagine her! Yesterday, you saw what a frightful night it was, what ferocious winds, what a confusion of the elements. Those are my worst nights. The howling of the winds, the moaning of the trees, the rattling of the windows banish my sleep and terrify my heart and don't allow it to find peace, like a deer hunted on all sides. The events of that mournful story do not return to my memory of themselves, but my soul is driven towards them, is driven unsparingly and mercilessly as if by howling dogs and cracking whips, until it runs through them all, once, twice, and thrice. And it runs through them not in order, but randomly, as it is driven and in the direction it is driven, from the first moment when I debased myself before that cheap whore, up to the last, when I murdered the angel of love! And so it was last night. I had reached that point, worn out and exhausted with the frightful, merciless conclusion that I am the most wicked, the most abominable person in the world. There, out of the gloom of my dark imagination, like a rising star, arose Clara's pure, spotless face! How loving! How tolerant! How compassionate! Can it be she hasn't forgiven me? Never! Surely she bears me no grudge. Surely she's praying on my behalf, is praying to appease my Judge, my Maker! At that point suddenly there came over me that fiery longing to see her with my own eyes as she prayed." And shaken by a violent shudder, he said in a trembling, barely audible voice, "As I longed for her, as I longed for her, so she appeared, so she was present before me: beneath the azure sky; under the sweet light of Paradise; in her white angel's dress; with her blonde hair flowing down her back; holding her golden harp in her tiny hands. Why do you shudder so? I'm giving you only a faint idea! Because how can I describe to you her blue eyes, her proud glance? And the sounds of her harp, the music of her voice. Why are you startled? Why do you shudder so? Oh! If you could only have seen her, as I have! What would you do if you had but once seen her, since you are so moved by my mere telling you of her?"

This description shook my heart to its foundations. Throughout his entire account a chill shudder had begun to run through my nerves. I myself had seen the poor fellow's vision a few weeks before with my own eyes! I had seen it in the round, azure room in the mental hospital in Göttingen! Now my eyes were opened. The crazed girl was a victim of despair in love, they told me. She was from the Duchy of Baden! I think, as a matter of fact, that I had also heard my doctor pronounce the name M. in a low voice and pityingly. It was the name of Clara's father. What an unbelievable coincidence! What an unexpected event! And the unhappy father's letter—that, too, is now more comprehensible. His daughter wasn't dead, but she was much more than sick! And so it was for this reason that the old man wrote in so guarded a manner, revealing a misfortune less than death to be sure, but too frightful to be named, too desperate to be characterized as a sickness!

And while I tried to hide the real reason for my distress, leaving Paschális in a misapprehension that was doubtless more salutory for him than the truth, I wondered to myself how I could possibly have failed before now to observe the bond that connected the misfortune in the mental hospital in Göttingen with the one before my eyes! But so it usually happens whenever we seek to discover the truth not as it is, but as we want it to be.

*****

After my unfortunate friend had completed his description of his vision, still under the influence of those emotions that he had experienced in its presence during the previous night, he remained for some time motionless and silent, like a man fatigued and exhausted from excessive toil. But on his wasted face there no longer resided that wild, alarming sadness. The telling of his catastrophe had relieved him. The sweet recollection of the girl who was interceding on his behalf comforted him. The fever in his nerves had ceased; only his eyes remained still raised in ecstasy. But this ecstasy was the ecstasy of a man praying internally and penitently, not of a soul terrified and trembling before its own specters. It was as though a mysterious, supernatural delight gave his eyes their excessive brightness.

"She's dead!" he murmured after a long silence. "She's dead! My heart tells me."

"Yes, Paschális, she's dead!" I said tenderly. "It was fated. We all die."

"But my heart tells me," he continued in rapt enthusiasm, "that she did not die entirely. Our souls still communicate with each other. You see, they were predestined one for the other. My own, in the frenzy of an untimely passion, risked its destiny and lost it. In this way our early union was frustrated. But up there . . . oh, up there I shall bring her a heart cleansed in my tears, purified through penitence. And we shall be united forever, forever!—What is life?—Besides, I feel it. My soul is impatient, and it toils untiringly, trying to shatter and break through the material shell that restrains it. Its wings have grown large, and strong . . ."

Outside the windows of the room, in the deepest silence of night, was suddenly heard the night watchman's deep-sounding horn and his hoarse command. Today in Clausthal, just as in the middle ages, the night watchman still walks slowly around the deserted streets all night long, like a black phantom, with his horn on his back and the dim lantern in his hands, announcing the passing of the hours and ordering those who happen to be awake to put out the light and to bank the hearth fire carefully to avoid a conflagration.

Midnight had long since passed, but when I went up to my bedroom I was still so shaken that, in spite of the calmness of the night, sleep did not come to me for hours. That charming and beautiful mad girl, whom I—perhaps at first because of my illness, thereafter perhaps because of my constant anxieties about Paschális—had driven so far into the depths of my memory, now engaged my imagination all the more insistently because her initial impression on my mind had been so vivid. That sad scene to which I had been an eyewitness upon my departure from Göttingen now presented itself before my memory unchanged—what am I saying?—more vividly, sadder than on that day. It was truly astonishing the intensity with which, and the different light under which, all those details of my visit to the asylum emerged before my mind's eye. The concern and devotion with which that kind director ushered me in, the noiselessly opening and closing doors, the room's round shape, the sweet azure color of the coverings of the walls and doors, the thick carpets, the type of furniture, and above all the unfortunate Clara's extraordinary emergence from within, dressed in white and with hair flowing loose, with the blush of hysteria on her cheeks, her beautiful blue eyes with their childish, naive gaze, unconcerned about the neglected beauties of her sex, without awareness of her dreadful calamity, without suspicion of the sorrow into which her cheerfulness plunged our hearts. . . . And then there was the charm of her conversation; the bewitching coquettishness with which she took her seat in the favorable light in front of her flashing harp; the unrivaled skill with which her delicate fingers called forth the harp's bewitching notes; and then the music of her voice; the meaning of her songs, now so clear; the fiery execution; the dramatic passion; the nervous excitement; and then the crescendo of despair; the outburst of anger; the attack of madness! All these things, all of them, came back to my memory, and they came back, as I said, much,

much more vividly, more heavy with meaning. But when I called to mind the comparisons I had made in the corridor after that visit—my bitter complaints against Mother Nature as apparently unloving towards us humans—their repetition was in some sense opposed by the secure, spiritual certainty with which Paschális just a short while before had accepted his meeting with his dead friend in eternity. And I no longer envied the insignificant advantages of insects and crystals, but sitting up in bed I thanked God that he had endowed the heart of his thinking creatures with the sweet, consoling hope of life after death. Perhaps even the unlucky Clara, too, in her lucid moments of understanding, enjoyed the benefit of this same consolation.

The next day Paschális again got up before me, as always. But when I came down to the room in which we usually took breakfast, I found him playing happily with our landlady's small children. He was dressed in his miner's outfit and was sitting before the open window, in the light of the warm and brilliant morning sun.

"Beautiful day today!" he shouted when he saw me. "Good morning!"

"Good morning!" I said with a laugh, because with this greeting he had shunned the Clausthal natives' "be lucky."

Paschális, playing with the blonde hair of the little girl seated on his knees, said, "The coffee's cold, but all the better—drink it down as fast as you can and get ready to go out."

"And where're we going?" I asked, marveling at the beneficial effect the good weather had worked on his disposition.

"To Caroline!" he said significantly. "To Caroline!"

"To what Caroline?" I asked in confusion.

"To Clausthal's great mine," he answered, laughing at my confusion, "with a depth of thousands of feet, with an extent of many square miles, with railways in its tunnels, with a river inside, and, most remarkable of all, barges on the river. It's worth the trouble to see it."

I hurried to drink down my breakfast, which was in fact cold. "I'm at your service," I told him. "Get up! Let's go!"

"Oho!" shouted Paschális. "The way you are?"

"And do you suppose I brought Sunday clothes to wear to visit Caroline?"

"Wait a little," he said. "The landlord will bring them for you.

He worked all night last night, I understand, and he'll surely come to sleep his hours. He'll give us his miner's outfit for you to wear. Otherwise you'll get in a mess just like your friend Heine."

"And what happened to Heine?"

"He visited the same mine with the clothes he was wearing. As long as he was down below in the dark it didn't show, but when he came out into the light and saw the condition of his clothes, he shouted in astonishment, 'I've known many Carolines in my life, but not one of them was this filthy!'"

And we laughed at the anecdote about the ironic poet, and the children laughed with us, not understanding, but simply in sympathy. Meanwhile the time was passing, and instead of the landlord, his wife came in and announced with concern that unusual and pressing work would keep her husband in the mine till noon.

"Every obstacle's to the good!" said Paschális. "Come another day. But I've got to hurry—something must be going on down there." And with a song on his lips he went out to look for his tools.

His unexpected cheerfulness and playfulness startled me somewhat. It had been many days since I'd seen him cheerful and lively at all! Was it then the result of the weather only?

"Good-bye! Till noon," he said as he left after a little while. "And be ready for our outing to Snow-cap. We've no time to lose."

"What?" I said. "An outing right after such rains? We'll drown in water and mud! Besides, just yesterday you were still sick!"

"There's a teacher for you!" said Paschális, pretending he hadn't heard my last words. "He expects to find water and mud on mountain peaks! We don't have mud around here, my boy, nor water. The slopes don't let them stop for even a moment. And they don't stay in the gullies long; they vanish into the ground at intervals and fill up the large, underground reservoirs and lakes that feed all the springs and brooks and rivers of the surrounding plains."

And attaching his miner's lamp to his belt and engulfed in his broad-rimmed hat, he squeezed my hand nervously and bid me farewell with, "Glück auf!" As he left I saw the shining pick on his shoulder flashing in the sun's rays, and an inexplicable longing urged me to run after him, to squeeze him in my embrace, not to let him bury himself in dark, damp galleries of the mines on that brilliant day. But I thought on the other hand that perhaps his beloved job could dispel his morose thoughts more effectively. I wish

I had obeyed the impulse of my heart! About noon he came. Alas! He didn't come. They brought him—they brought him dead!

The continuous, violent rains, seeping in through the pores and holes in the earth, had filled the underground spaces over the mine to overflowing. All night the miners labored to drain off the water that had flowed in, but its unusual weight had caused it to seep in and it had soaked one gallery, causing it to collapse. Dozens of men were buried under its debris. The first of the victims brought out was the unfortunate Paschális. He had not been crushed by the debris, but had been found dead very close to the collapsed area. The autopsy revealed that the poor man had died from a heart attack. That organ was described by the doctor as weak for some time already. The shock he experienced at the moment of danger occasioned the final disaster!

Even before I recovered from the crushing blow that the loss of my dearest friend dealt me, and in the midst of wailings and lamentations echoing on all sides through the entire grieving city, a letter was delivered to me from Herr H***, my doctor in Göttingen. I guessed the nature of the contents. But the astounding catastrophe before my eyes offset the bitterness of the professor's reproaches for my disobeying his advice. I read through his illegible threats in absent-minded haste and, in fact, with annoyance. It would be a matter of real indifference to me if I died after that day as a consequence of my disobeying the doctor! I had seen my bosom friend once again; I had comforted the sorrow of his brotherly heart as much as was humanly possible; and far from our beloved fatherland, far from his loving mother, far from relatives and friends, I, at least, was there to close his lifeless eyes and to tend his corpse. But when I reached the end of the doctor's threats and advice, two or three lines, as a postscript, carelessly and hastily jotted down attracted my complete attention. "By the way, you might like to know," wrote the good old man, "that the unhappy girl whom it chanced we visited together in the asylum on the day you left has been released from her sufferings. She died during the night of the day before yesterday with the hope on her lips that she was going to find her future husband. An unusual ending for diseases that have their seat only in the unknown factor Psi, that is to say, the psyche!" The night of the day before yesterday! Precisely the night that the unfortunate Paschális had seen her in a vision in the heavens! Before her God! What a supernatural coincidence! Truly the souls of these unfortunate lovers had been still communicating with each other! . . .

*****

    Three days after these events the evening coach was leaving Clausthal, heavy and slow. Most of the passengers crowding it were representatives sent from round about to take part in the public funeral for the victims of that ill-omened day. Downcast and gloomy, we maintained a deep, sad silence in the coach. When we went up the slope towards the forest, the postman did not trumpet his usual farewell. The sun had not yet set, but after the day's violent wind the sky threatened one of the Harz's rainiest nights. Dark clouds, motionless, covered its entire expanse. The last birds, like silent arrows, were flying to hide in their nocturnal refuge. The tall, black trunks of pines and firs stood out in the misty distance, motionless and huge, like shadows of mourners. The dead calm usual before summer rains prevailed. You'd think that even inanimate nature was grieving with us. A little before we entered the forest darkness I leaned out the window to see the lofty "Snowcap" once again. A cone-shaped beam of purple-gold rays shooting from the west colored its white peak, picking out the hotel on it, but only for a moment. A flood of tears dimmed my eyes.—This is where Paschális and I had passed by! This is where he had pointed out the hotel to me. What a difference between this evening and that one! And yet the same silence, the same calm! I thought what a wild, stormy turmoil must have prevailed in the unfortunate young man's heart on that magic, calm evening when we met. Repeated shudders ran through my body. How true that mournful poetry was! How physical its affect on me! And how quickly, how quickly, alas, its sad promise had been fulfilled. Tears again flooded my eyes. The lines returned spontaneously to my lips:

> On every mountain, every hill,
> the air is calm and still.
> On every oak and every fir
> no leaf or branch does stir.
> The birds in twos and threes
> sleep silent and in peace
> Oh, now endure the test,
> you, too, will soon find rest!

The Only Journey
of His Life

◫◫◫

Introduction

"The Only Journey of His Life" contains the narrator's recollections of events that took place when he was quite a young boy, first in Constantinople where he served as an apprentice tailor, and later in his home town. We have, of course, no way of knowing when any of these events are assumed to have occurred, nor do we know at what age the young boy experienced them. We know from "My Mother's Sin" that he left home at an early age, and we must imagine that he cannot have been much older at the time of his return home. From the story, we learn that he was an impressionable young man, one who easily believed in stories told him by others: this same characteristic seems to have stayed with him for life, for in "Who Was My Brother's Killer" he is represented as still being interested in fairy tales.

The story is full of fairy tales, some of them of wide currency in Greece, such as that concerning Phókia and King Alexander, and of a type widespread in European folklore, particularly the tale of the princess and the young tailor-boy. Others, such as the legends of the Dogheads, of the land where the sun bakes bread, and of the petrified men, are perhaps not as widely circulated. Nereids, spelled by Vizyenos, Neraids, are lineal descendants of the ancient Nereids, daughters of Nereus and lovely spirits of the sea. In modern legend, however, in addition to their occasional beneficent activities, they are baneful sprites that can maim or blind the unwary who cross them in any way. The grandfather's wrestling match with the angel corresponds to the general Greek belief that death is a wrestling match, usually with Charos, the spirit of the underworld and successor to the ancient Charon, ferryman of the dead. This wrestling match was imagined to have taken place on a marble threshing-floor.[1] No really good geographical details of Constantinople are provided, but we do get a glimpse of Vizýi in this story, as we do also, to some extent, in "Moscóv-Selím." The acropolis of the place is mentioned, the *baïra* (T. *bayir*, "hill"), from which one could see both the immediately surrounding countryside and the *túmbes*, the mounds, of the Odryssians—the inhabitants of eastern Thrace during the classical period. In spite of the meager description, one does get a good feel for Vizýi.

There are but three characters in the story: the narrator, both as narrator and as young boy, his grandfather, Yoryís (this is Vizyenos' own name, as we know from "Who Was My Brother's Killer?", and his grandmother, Hrusí (she is also called *Hatzídena* because she has visited the Holy Sepulchre in Jerusalem; *Hadzi-* is merely the Islamic *Hajji*, one who has visited Mecca). The story begins in Constantinople (the City) where the young boy is engaged as a *kálfas* (plural *kalfádes*, T. *kalfa*), "apprentice" to a *mástoris* "master" in the *esnáfi* (T. *esnaf*) "guild" of tailors. The master has his workshop in the *kebetsi-han*, one of the hans, or inns and workshops, in the *tsarsí* (T. *çarşi*), bazaar or business district, of Constantinople. From there he often takes bundles to the palace, that is, the Topkapi Palace, where the Sultan's mother, the *Validé-Sultána*, lives. The *kislár-agá* (aga or guard of the women) or harem eunuch leads him to a room in which he is offered various sweets, such as *mohalebí*, *buréki*, and *baklavá*. Other Turkish terms connected with this phase of his life include:

> *daërédes* (T. *daire* with Greek plural ending), "apartments" (plural);
> *giaoúr* (T. *gâvur*), "infidel";
> *sultaním*, *sultan* plus *im*, a possessive suffix, means "my sultan";
> *apherím*, "bravo," Turkish *aferin*, usually accented *áferim*;
> *piadés*, *piyade* in Turkish, a small boat;
> *kaïki*, a boat (T. *kayik*); and
> *teziáhi* (T. *tezgah*), a "workbench" or "counter."

---

1. On all this folklore one may consult K. Papathanase-Mousiopoulou, *Laographikes Martyries Georgiou Vizyenou* (Athens: 1982), and M. Alexiou, "Modern Greek Folklore and its Relation to the Past: The Evolution of Charos in Greek Tradition," in S. Vryonis, ed., *The Past in Medieval and Modern Greek Culture, Byzantina kai Metabyzantina* 1 (Malibu: Undena, 1978), 221–236.

There are also geographical references to the Dolmabachtse, the new palace across the Golden Horn; the Edirne-Kapusu, or in English, Edirne-Kapi, which is the gate leading to Edirne (Adrianople); Salyvria, which is the gate leading to Salyvria; and the Paraporti, which must be the gate that was once part of a monumental Roman gate but is now high in the wall and of course unused.

A number of Turkish words and institutions are also referred to in connection with the narrator's grandparents in Vizýi:

halédza or *galedza* is a kind of wooden shoe;
imam is a Moslem religious leader;
mendéri (T. *minder*) is a low sofa or divan;
pehliváns (T. *pehlivan*) is a "wrestler";
servéta is a Turkish hat, like a *sariki*, a turban; and
tsuréki (T. *çörek*) is a kind of bun, or bread.

A number of other terms are used in connection with the *Yanitsarió*, the *Pedomázema*, during which Turkish authorities went to Christian communities and forcibly took young Greek boys for service in the corps of Janissaries. The grandfather is ninety-eight at the time of the young boy's return to Vizýi, which must have been in about 1865. If we assume that boys of about ten were taken, then the grandfather would have been in danger of being selected in about 1777. Words used here are:

fermáni (T. *ferman*), an order from the Sultan;
izámis, or *nizamis* (T. *nizam* "order"), a Turkish soldier of the regular army;
kavádia, not a Turkish word, a man's long, heavy cloak;
kavúki (T. *kabuk*), a kind of tall hat;
tselátis (T. *cellat*), the executioner; and
vrákia, a kind of trouser formed by gathering material around the waist and fashioning a kind of knicker.

The Only Journey of His Life

No one of their promises created so attractive an impression on my childish imagination as the assurance that in Constantinople I would sew the garments of the king's daughter. This was when they enrolled me in the honorable calling of tailors.

I knew very well that "princesses" have a certain extraordinary weakness for tailor-boys, especially when these boys know how to sing praises of their attractions while stitching the "silks" with which they deck out their charms.

I knew that when a princess falls in love with her tailor, she doesn't fool around, but falls hard; and she becomes ill; and she takes to her bed; and she's on the verge of death; and no doctor can cure her, no sorceress can restore her to health—until finally the princess calls her father and tells him straight out: "Daddy dear, either the tailor-boy who sings so beautifully, or I'll die!"

The king has no other child. What is he to do? He puts his crown on his head and goes to the tailor-boy's feet and cries out to him: "She's in God's hands and your own! Do me the favor of taking my daughter. Do me the favor of being my son-in-law. But come, first show me some daring deed so I won't lose my reputation, being a king as I am."

To the tailor-boy it seems that a bitter medlar has stuck in his throat and he can't swallow. The truth is, however, that he has nothing to swallow because even the spit has dried up in his throat. So afraid was he when he saw the king with his crown!

The king with his crown pats him on the shoulder and asks him to tell him in no uncertain terms: What worthy feat can the tailor-boy do? And with secret pleasure he waits to hear that his presumptive son-in-law is able to bring down a lion live from the mountains, or to kill a dragon, or to conquer a kingdom.

In the meantime the tailor-boy has taken courage, but this does not make him sufficiently crazy to go out and "mix it up" with wild animals in order to be his Highness's son-in-law. The tailor-boy is in general a peaceful person. And since he manages better when he sings than when he talks, he answers the king singing and tells him that he is worthy and able "to sew wedding gowns without seam and stitch."

The king, not much moved by songs, says to himself: "Very well, you rogue! I'll prove you're fooling my daughter since you haven't even a penny's worth of bravery in your heart!" Then he looks at the tailor-boy with evil in his eye and says, "Very well, master son-in-law! So stitch me forty wedding gowns suitable for a princess, and see that I can't pick out a single seam or a single thread anywhere! But see to it you have them ready tomorrow morning early before the sun comes up, because otherwise . . . I'll cut off your head!" And the king with his crown isn't kidding at this point. The proud man has made a decision to kill the tailor-boy and give his daughter to some big shot!

Luckily the tailor-boy knows his job and isn't worried very much. He is—some say the son, others, the grandson—of the nereid. And he has a thimble that he never takes off his finger, a thimble with a secret compartment in it. All that evening he eats, drinks, and enjoys himself. Round about midnight, when the *mástoris* and the *kalfádes* go to bed, he removes the thimble from his finger, takes out a golden hair that he has hidden away in it, and burns the tippy-tip of the hair in the flame of the lamp. The golden-haired nereid appears there before him.

"What's your trouble, dearie?"

"This and that," answers the tailor-boy, and he tells her the story.

The golden-haired nereid had given her word to save him whenever he was in danger. She claps her delicate hands three times, and—just look!—forty little nereids, all dressed in white, each one more beautiful than the other! Each one places the most precious fabrics in the world in front of the little tailor, singing sweet songs and making flirtatious motions in the air.

The tailor-boy cuts, and the nereids sew; and they sew and sing and joke and tease the tailor-boy, at times so flirtatiously, so excitingly, that if their mother weren't right there, they would certainly have driven him to distraction. But the golden-haired nereid watches them, directs them, and spurs them on to finish the gowns before the cock crows, before the sun comes up.

The nereids barely have time to leave when there's the king entering with the crown on his head and his executioners right behind him; he's coming to kill the tailor-boy! But as he comes in he sees the forty wedding gowns without seam and stitch hanging on a line, and his eyes are dazzled. The gold and the pearls that are stitched on them are worth the whole of his mangy old kingdom! The king with his crown bites his lips. He takes the tailor-boy by the hand, leads him to the palace, and gives him to his daughter. That's the end of the story.

*****

My grandfather told me all these things, and he told them as if they had happened only yesterday, as if they were happening all the time. I still remember even today with what pride I entered Constantinople for the first time as a new recruit in the *esnáfi* of tailors; I reckoned that after a few days I would be driving out through the same gate I was now entering on foot, triumphantly accompanying the most beautiful princess to my village. My grandfather intimated this to me. And since Grandfather was for me the most widely traveled and worldly wise person I knew, I believed his words completely.

Several months had passed after my arrival, however, and nothing had been accomplished yet. It's true that my master was head tailor to the *Valide-Sultána,* and since I was the youngest of my fellow pupils, he regularly sent me to her palace by the Bosporus, sometimes carrying a big "bundle" on my head, sometimes carrying the silk and gold-tasseled "sack" with his account books in it. So I often went through magnificent corridors and through dark passageways, and I entered into the fragrant and enchanting *daërédes* of the *Valide-Sultána's* harem. But the persons I came in contact with there were primarily the black eunuchs with their broad mouths, their great teeth hideously flashing between fleshy lips, who cast the kind of fierce glances that made me shudder from fright. Sometimes they—the princesses doubtless—wanted to express some special satisfaction to their tailor-boy. Then the most frightful black would take his most frightful whip and with a nod to me would take the lead. I followed him with my eyes on the ground. A second black with a second whip followed on my heels. Accompanied by those two executioners in this way I proceeded into the interior of the harem in which, however, I saw nothing besides the floor, which in places gleamed like the best dance floors, in places was covered with priceless carpets.

But if I didn't see, at least I heard women's voices and laughter and coarse jokes and obscene insults directed at the *kislár-agá* who was walking in front of me and shouting at the top of his voice for the sultana's maids and odalisks to run and hide at my approach, and pitilessly striking with his whip those who dared to peek out from behind the doors and curtains to see a male person so near them. The moor behind me protected me, on the one hand, from being carried away by the women who were secretly and noiselessly following behind, and on the other, watched to see I didn't dare lift my eyes from the floor and desecrate with my *giaúr's* gaze the sacred victims destined one day to be sacrificed to one of their great master's momentary whims.

It was in such a state of emotions that I would finally reach my destination. But what do you think awaited me there in the farthest room where the blacks left me, closing the door behind me? Some rosy, blond princess ready to throw herself from joy into my arms? Nothing, absolutely nothing, in the room. Inside the wall with which this room communicated with another, though, a wooden cylinder awaited me to caress and pat as if it were my sweetheart, constructed in such a way that it rotated in place on a vertical pin without letting you see around it into the next room. As soon as I caressed it, I heard a very, very delicate voice from the other side of the cylinder: "You've come, my lamb?"

"Yes, *sultaním*."

The wooden cylinder turned on its axis and now I saw a small door on its other side, which made it look like a cupboard. Aromatic oil, musk, ambergris, and all the perfumes of India wafted from behind that grill. Surely my princess was in there! I would open the door anxiously and be greeted from inside that small turning cupboard by a sweet-smelling and appetizing *mohalebí*, a *buréki* or *baklavás* or some other very sweet thing of the kind that, though it has no tongue, as soon as you see it you feel that it is saying over and over, "Eat me." Which is exactly what I would do, of course, without any further formalities.

One day I had just completed this pleasant task when that delicate voice asked me if I wanted anything even better.

"No, *sultaním*, I don't want anything better than you."

"*Apherím*, my lamb! Are you tall, tall?"

I was getting ready to tell her that I was so small that I could get into that little cupboard, close the grill, give a twist to the cylinder, and appear before her eyes like a *buréki*. But the black eunuch who had in the meantime come in without my noticing him uttered an obscene insult from over my head and choked my voice in my throat.

My poor princess had to get her answer from his fierce, frightening mouth!

"Tall, eh? Ha ha ha!" shouted the *kislár-agá*, laughing a sardonic laugh. "He's still so short, I had to order a new bench for him to stand on so I could hang him at the height of your eyes." Then he nodded for me to follow him.

Now, if the *Validé-Sultána* had happened to have, as certain kings of Asia once did, a skilled scribe at each door of her palace who

was directed to set out everything that happened around him in a
rich style of writing, I do not doubt that each of them without exception would have noted in his chronicle that I came out of the
harem on that day, as always, with one eunuch in front, scaring the
odalisks away from my sight, and with another eunuch behind,
warding off those trying to catch hold of my clothes and drag me
off from behind. I assure you, however, that from the moment that
terrifying moor said he had ordered a "new bench" to hang
me—from that moment—the floor of the room in which I was
standing suddenly gave way beneath my feet and I plunged into a
silent, dark abyss with the dizziness of head and faintness of heart
that we experience when dreaming that we are falling, falling, falling from the immense height of a sheer cliff in order to escape the
danger threatening our life in the person of some monstrous
pursuer.

I cannot give exact details about how I found myself back in our
workshop. Some of my fellow apprentices said that I had lost my
way in my terror, others that I had lost my mind as well. I let them
make their jokes. It was only when those who had themselves carried bundles to the palace before me got up and began to babble
how they, too, they said, had eaten sweets from that round cupboard that revolved around its pin, and that the room with which
it communicated when turned was not the princess' drawing room
or bedroom but the harem's pantry, and that oh! so sweet voice was
not that of my love the princess but of the oldest eunuch in the
palace—only then did my feeling of pride rebel, and I quarreled
with them all, reaching such a pitch of discord with them that from
then on I didn't even talk to them.

That I never set foot in harems again goes without saying, for,
though I was much saddened by the thought that my princess was
wasting away behind that round cupboard by the banks of the Bosporus, I was equally unable to understand why, after all, she hadn't
sent her father to seek me for her husband as all the princesses my
grandfather knew had done.

After that sad disappointment the vile and tedious monotony of
the working life and the apprentice's difficulties with the basics of
his craft seemed to me two and three times heavier. Under their
weight I began to get sickly and thin, shut up there inside Stam-
boul's *tsársi,* behind the iron gates of the *kebetsí-han,* toward the

lead-covered domes of which in my desolation I no longer directed the enchanting sounds of love songs but the wails and moans of a child's heart-consuming homesickness!

Above all I began to loathe my master. He was a small, sickly old man who, all the while he was accompanying the squeaking bites of his greedy scissors with the ridiculous movements of his toothless jaw, never ceased observing me over his big round glasses lest perchance I stretch out my numbed leg a bit or straighten my exhausted spinal column ever so little.

One day, either from weakness or obstinacy, I persisted in transgressing that sacred canon of tailorly decorum so consistently that I had the honor of being introduced for the first time to the "silent mistress," that is to say, the stick that lay by my master's side. That roused my indignation to impiety. I remember very well that in my obstinacy I began to complain and bitterly to blame God Himself because He had had the idea of sewing with His own hands that celebrated leather tunic around Eve's nakedness and thus giving a start and a beginning to the tailor's trade. If I had been God, I said to myself, I would have left my Eve as I had created her. What harm could the poor thing do, I wonder, naked as she was? In fact, I think she would have been even more beautiful. Besides, as long as the master-God kept the woman in Paradise, that is to say in His house, He left her naked, but when He decided to load her for all time on poor Adam's neck, to send her out into the world, then He dowered her with finery. Don't you see what harm He's done? With His own hands He established that most miserable of all guilds, the tailors', condemning me to sit here cross-legged and bent over from dawn till the dead of night. And He established the worst of all customs, of having fathers dower their daughters not with inner virtues while they have those daughters at home, but with outward luxuries when they load them on their fiancés' shoulders.

I'm sure I would have innocently uttered these last pedantries then and there if a familiar voice hadn't called my name from below and suddenly interrupted the flow of my lugubrious thoughts before they attained their definitively logical formulation.

In spite of all the admonishments pronounced to me over and over again by my mother—that a trade was a golden bracelet that I ought to sacrifice everything to acquire, that a rolling stone was no good for a foundation, and the like—I continued to send messages (at that time I didn't yet know how to write) begging her to call me home or to set me to learn a more humane trade. And though I did not have many hopes of success, I still hoped that I might at least be free of that master in order to breathe the purer, freer air outside the *tsársi* and the *hans*. Above all I had the secret desire to join the ranks of the head tailor of the sultan's harem at *Dolmá-bahtsé*. He lived on the Asiatic shore of the Bosporus, opposite the aforementioned palace, where, I thought to myself, the princesses would hear me when I sang and would either get in their *piadé* and come or would nod from the window for me to swim over to find them. You see, in spite of all my misfortunes, I still could not get the princess out of my head, because, as I said, I had complete faith in my grandfather's words. He was to me the most widely traveled, the most experienced, of men. And if I couldn't put my hands on some princess here in the city, my grandfather in the end would lead me to where those princesses who fall in love so easily with their little tailors are to be found. Grandfather must surely have seen them, must have known them; very likely he himself had fallen in love with one of them even though the poor man was neither a tailor nor a famous singer. So when I heard that voice calling my name, I jumped for joy because it was the voice of Thímios, my grandfather's servant.

The room in which we worked was a *tzamekiánion,* that is, a small loft constructed, like a swallow's nest, high up between two domed arches that form the end of the stone colonnades built around the *hans'* court. One ascended from the colonnade to the loft by means of a narrow ladder, the top of which rested against the very floor on which we sat and worked. So barely a moment had passed from the time I heard my name when Thímios' head began to appear from behind this ladder's rotten railing. My presentiment was confirmed—Thímios' serious eyes were looking for someone among my fellow apprentices. I didn't wait for him to call me; I didn't wait for him to come all the way up the ladder to convince myself that my senses hadn't deceived me. I leaped up from my place like a captive bird that finds the door to its cage unexpectedly open.

"Grandfather is wrestling with the angel!" said Thímios while still climbing and without any introductory formality. "Grandfather's in his death throes and asks for you. Come, let's go quickly, because, see, if you don't get there in time, he'll die and his eyes'll stay open." And, leaning on the ladder head, Thímios gave his words an added weight, nodding toward me like a man who has no time to wait.

I don't know whether it was the tone of his voice, the seriousness of his look, or the content of his words that contributed most to my agitation. I only remember that for a long while after Thímios stopped talking I stood motionless and stunned in the same spot I was in when he uttered his first words. And I remember that chill shudders repeatedly shook my nerves because of them.

Grandfather was wrestling with the angel! That surely wasn't a good thing. But Grandfather was asking for me, too. That was still worse! That must mean that Grandfather couldn't handle the angel by himself and was calling for me to help! This childish thought came to me because I used to wrestle with Grandfather, leaping onto his back and his tall shoulders, especially when I came on him sitting on his *mendéri* by the hearth. During those boisterous battles Grandfather always declared himself defeated and always recognized me as stronger, and he introduced me formally to those present as his *pehlevánis,* that is, the professional wrestler the pashas habitually keep around to wrestle with anyone who would boast that he was the strongest in the land and either throw him down or cede his place to the victor. So since I once so proudly bore that title, it seemed perfectly natural to me that Grandfather, not knowing how to handle the angel by himself, sent for me, his *pehlevánis,* to help him knock his opponent to the ground and then very likely myself to take on that frightful contest of life and death! . . .

And how could I manage it? And where would I wrestle with the angel? On Grandfather's *mendéri,* or on the marble threshing-floor? "No, no, no! I'm afraid! I don't dare!" And my knees began to knock from fear, and, returning to my place, I was stooping to sit down, when I suddenly thought that this was my only good opportunity not only to free myself from my master's hands but also to have the chance, while there was still time, to ask Grandfather in what part of the world he had come upon the princesses about whom he spoke as if he had eaten, drunk, and conversed with them.

But the master? Let's see what the master had to say! Would he let me go, I wondered? Why, just an hour ago he was assuring us that all we apprentices were his inalienable possessions, and would he let me get away from him now? Oh, disaster! I ought to have thought of that right off!

The moment Thímios came into our room the master let his scissors drop noisily on the *teziáhi* in front of him and, pushing his large spectacles from his eyes onto his wrinkled forehead, he braced his hands challengingly on his hips and continued darting very threatening glances at the one who dared to enter his autocratic kingdom in this way without any preliminary formality. My fellow apprentices were all sympathetic, yet no one dared budge or raise his head. All these things were bad omens: of course he wouldn't let me leave.

"His grandfather is wrestling with the angel!" Thímios said to him, and he let his sad face droop still lower. "His grandfather is leaving us behind, and asked to see the boy. It's his last wish, you know."

The master, whose wrath appeared to be reaching its highest pitch, was already opening his spasmodically quivering lips to curse, as he usually did during the fierce outbursts of his anger. But Thímios' last phrase, uttered with a certain mysterious respect and in an altered tone of voice, acted like magic on that harsh, inhuman old man. His inflamed face calmed immediately, the provocative stance of his body collapsed suddenly, and with a benevolence that I was seeing in him for the first time, he stretched his hand toward me for me to kiss. This was my permission to leave.

Confusion and inexperience made me believe at that moment that, just as he knew how to subdue my grandfather's untamable bulls with his stentorian voice and steely hands, so Thímios had the mysterious power to charm from a distance and tame the wildest master's savagery. But from what I can conclude today, that unexpected change was provoked by the religious reverence commonly owed to those about to die.

The eagerness and reverence with which even the most ill tempered of men among us heeds the last wish of the dying is truly remarkable. Perhaps it is believed that those who do not contribute to its fulfillment call down heaven's wrath upon themselves. Perhaps—in accordance with that most philosophical folk morality—each avoids doing what he doesn't want to have happen to himself. What is certain is that so long as the departing soul still has any desire unfulfilled, it cannot break free and depart from the body that is now foreign to it, but hovers moaning and complaining on the dying man's lips; it is considered horrible, and stigmatized as impious, if relatives and friends don't hurry to do everything in their power to prepare an easy and pleasant departure for the soul from a world to which it no longer belongs but to which its last wish still binds it. And indeed it can be infallibly determined from the expression that the dead man's face assumes when he breathes his last whether this has happened or not.

It is for this reason that extraordinarily moving, sometimes heart-rending, scenes take place by the dying man's bed. Here the prodigal son and the thoughtless daughter, whose frivolous conduct have angered the strict father and excluded them from the family circle, are commended by their now helpless mother to the father's clemency, and he, sobbing, opens his loving arms to them again to the accompaniment of fresh outbursts of weeping on the part of those present. Here the stepmother, from time immemorial most hated among the Greeks, upon being entrusted by the dying father to the love of his child from his former wife, finds in that child the warmest, the most devoted care. Here long family disputes are settled; festering hatreds between brothers are wiped away; enmities even of the most deadly sort are resolved between relatives and friends. Here, in sum, members of the family, including even the most distant, come together from the ends of the country for the same purpose—not from malicious or impious expectation of material inheritance, but because their souls, being closely connected by nature to the departing person, are instinctively drawn to meet with him once again while he is still among them in the earthly world and to exchange their last spiritual kiss. The reason is that (it's there for all to see) the soul, flying up together with their prayers and blessings, is going to the place where those members of the family previously dead are to be found. So this partial separation is a general meeting with those souls, is an indirect communication between the living and the dead. Soon the departing soul will be amongst those dearest ones in heavenly realms and will be surrounded by them and asked if he saw their loved ones on earth and how they were. So anyone having even the least respect and love for his own dead must not be absent from the bed of his dying relative. If anyone of the family cannot be present for that final meeting, either because he is gravely ill or because he is abroad, too far away, those present carefully avoid making mention of his name lest the dying man happen to hear and want to see him, for in that case, if the longed-for person does not get there in time, the eyes of the corpse will remain half-closed awaiting his arrival, even when the life in them has long since been extinguished.

And that is what Thímios really meant when he told me that, if I didn't arrive in time, Grandfather would die and his eyes would remain open. For that reason, when I had got over my initial confusion and had obtained permission to leave and was riding out of Constantinople's *Edirné-Kapusú*—not on a gold-bridled "steed" but "tucked on the rump" with Thímios on Grandfather's camel-sized horse, squeezing with both hands not the blond princess that I was to have led to my father's house but Thímios' red sash from fear that I might slip and crash down from the animal's very thin haunches—I thought about nothing, worried about nothing so much as that we might not reach the village in time and poor Grandfather would die and his eyes remain open.

That long-legged horse ran as fast as the doubled load and the pitiful condition of the roads allowed him in his old age. Morever the road we had to cover was long, and Thímios had left Grandfather, already on the verge of death, the day before yesterday. Grandfather surely could not hold out wrestling with the angel all that while. His ninety-eight years had long since bowed his manly stature. Surely, surely, the angel would knock the poor man flat on the ground before I reached him, and Grandfather would die, and his eyes would stay open!

Thímios didn't direct a word to me except whenever he thought to ask if I were still sitting on the horse's haunches. It seems that he was obsessed by the same thoughts as I was, because he didn't stop lashing the horse to run as fast as possible.

Under such circumstances, it wasn't at all unlikely that he would soon ask without there being anyone on the horse's haunches to answer. Fortunately Thímios suspected this in time. So he undid a portion of his many-looped red sash and wound it two or three times around me and his waist at the same time. Safely attached to him now in this way, as if I were some inanimate object or other of the sort that country people usually carry tightly bound inside their sash, I continued that extraordinary journey, the impressions of which I have never forgotten.

It was fall, and it had already begun to get really dark; the now chill wind whistled through the forest's sparse trees, disturbing the shivering sleep of their half-bare branches from which countless leaves were being whirled onto the ground, sighing mournfully. On such nights the moon, appearing at intervals from behind the dark clouds and increasing nature's fierce melancholy with its deathly pale shades, instead of consoling, fills the traveler's heart with indistinct fears and repeated tremors. The wildness of our journey was increased by the abnormal speed with which our tall horse passed by the objects on either side of the road before I had a chance to make out their dubious shapes and to quiet my fearful heart. Thímios' unbroken, solemn silence, the fact that the journey had been unexpected, the goal for which it was taking place, the manner of that incredible ride during which half of me was hanging from Thímios' sash and half of me was being rocked on the horse's haunches—all these things, while they kept my childish heart in constant anxiety, kindled my imagination to the point of hallucinations.

During that night I don't think I stared at strange configurations of clouds—some above the wind, some being borne along by it—without filling them out with the aid of the moonlight and my predisposed imagination into a huge pair of wrestlers risking all in their struggle. The one with his white, many-pleated drawers blowing in the breeze and with the wide, embroidered sleeves on his shirt was undoubtedly my grandfather. The other with his long, flowing, loose hair, with the white wings on his shoulders, with his scaly breastplate around his chest and the fiery sword in his bare right hand—he was surely the angel. I had seen him so many times on the left door of the sanctuary in our village church. Poor Grandfather! How could he win against such a terrifying opponent?

Whenever, wearied from fatigue and extreme nervous tension, I leaned my head on my shoulder and closed my eyes, I dreamed that Grandfather was stretched out full length in Grandmother's parlor wrapped in the elaborate shroud that she had brought from Jerusalem, with the icon of Christ on his chest and with yellow candles placed in the stiff fingers of his crossed hands. Basil, sage, amaranth, and myrrh and all the other flowers they use to deck out dead old men covered Grandfather from his waist down; the censers and two large candles had been placed high up on either side of his head and were burning; between these two candles a schoolboy was sitting on a bench and was bent over a book, reading the psalter in a loud voice and ostentatiously wearing his already tendered compensation on his shoulder: a red embroidered kerchief knotted at one

end. The pillow under Grandfather's head was one half of that silk
pillow that Grandmother had showed us proudly so many times,
saying that it was the very pillow on which she and her husband
had stepped some ninety years earlier when they were married in
the church. The things with which Grandfather's pillow was stuffed
were one half of those flowers and blossoms, no longer recognizable, with which the guests sprinkled them as newlyweds as they
left the church. The mourners' shrill laments, enough to move even
the most apathetic person to tears, represented my grandfather as
the best, the most virtuous of men. So why is his head not resting
calmly on the pillow? Why does not that divine peace prevail on his
face, that deep, dreamy expression that one usually finds in old men
who have gone to sleep forever in peace? With his pale lips he's
whispering, you'd think, a most mournful complaint! Beneath his
thick, white eyebrows his eyes—open, staring at the door—radiate
a dull crystal glow! Who is he waiting for? Who of his loved ones
was poor Grandfather still hoping to see when he died and his eyes
remained open?

Shaken by the horror of the dream, I woke up and, straightening
my numbed neck a little, leaned my head toward the other side and
fell asleep again.

Then it seemed to me as if much time had passed since Grandfather died, that they had already buried him in a grave in front of
the church. The grave was there newly dug, but Grandfather was
not lying in his coffin; he was sitting on the ground leaning against
the white stone cross in the moonlight. At the foot of the cross, a
small oil lamp was burning and a censer was smoking; there was a
small, honey-glazed *tsuréki* by his side and an earthenware jug full
of old red wine. But Grandfather, with his round *servéta* low on his
forehead and his white eyebrows lowered, did not seem pleased by
these things, had no desire to touch them; instead, he kept his
mournful gaze fixed on the road and was looking, looking, looking,
as if he were waiting with increasing impatience for someone to
come. Then suddenly, as if his patience had now run out, Grandfather shot up from his seat, very, very tall, and the cross against
which he was leaning rose up with him. But it was no longer the
cross; it was that white, camel-sized horse of Grandfather's on
which I was returning to the village—unsaddled, unbridled, thin-
ner, and fiercer than ever. Grandfather leaped onto its back, and
the horse hurled itself madly into the air, its eyes fiery, its distended

nostrils steaming, its unruly mane waving. Horse and rider appeared to be running toward me with an expression of indescribable rage and vengeance. But although both were being borne along on the wind, I could hear the horse's galloping hooves and feel the shock of its tread just as if I were sitting on its back. Grandfather's big *servéta*, undone at one end and unwound, was spread to the winds and shaking. It rendered his appearance so incredibly terrifying that the closer he and the horse came, the more my distress increased. My heart tightened, my mind spun, my senses left me. I tried to shout for help two or three times, to ask for pity, but my voice was stifled. Yet when I let out a cry of terror under the sway of frightful anguish, then it seemed to me that a large millstone had been removed from my chest—because I woke up.

Needless to say, I did not dare to doze off again after such emotions. Besides, it was about dawn by now, and I thought that we would be entering the village in a little while.

It was, however, past noon when we dismounted in front of Grandfather's house. Without saying a word, Thímios headed for the stables to attend to the exhausted horse. I went into the flagged ground floor, not making a sound as I opened the door. A deep silence reigned throughout the house. But everything about me was unchanged; everywhere the same cleanliness as before, the same order, the same exactness concerning the placing of each household implement, including even a broom decorated with multicolored felt straps. Only Grandfather's shoes, which were always dusted and "sheeny," they alone weren't there in front of the door of the room in which the old man usually spent the day, their toes facing the entrance. Their absence made the house appear empty to my eyes, deserted, abandoned. Grandfather was gone! And since I could not suppose that he was gone on some journey, a mournful premonition caused the tears to come to my eyes. . . .

Suddenly, from the depths of the basement, on the right, where the pantry door was open, I heard my grandmother's voice grumbling. I perked up my ears and listened. Grandmother was grumbling, as usual, while she was arranging the utensils and, at the same time, berating someone.

"Eh? You want me to keep feeding you? You want me to keep feeding a drone, you lazybones! Your legs, why did God give you legs? To run around after me and get under my feet? Git! Go to work, loafer, because now I'll shake your fur, ah!"

And from the noise that her *halédzas* made on the flagstones I gathered that she was running in pursuit of someone to effect that threat. Then out of the pantry door darted the household cat, running with all its might, its tail lifted high and with an expression in its eyes that seemed to be saying to me, too, "Every man for himself!"

Oh!—I thought to myself—poor Grandfather's dead and, since Grandmother doesn't have anyone to quarrel with any more, she's taking it out on her cat!

At that point Grandmother appeared as well, grumbling as always, but with her arm raised and the spindle in her hand.

I shall never forget the expression on her face and the position of her body when she saw me in the house so unexpectedly.

"Oho!" Grandmother exclaimed after several moments of silent astonishment, and she let the spindle fall to the ground and slapped her knees with both hands. Then, bent over in this way and with her hands on her knees, she stared at me again, dubiously, and—as if informing her heart—said with true delight, "Our little rascal's back!"

I rushed to bury myself in her embrace. But Grandmother suddenly frowned and looked at me as if she were now uncertain about my identity.

"Well where are you coming from, you wretch?" she asked with a reproachful look. "Eh? Where're you coming from? From the moon? Or maybe you've eaten all the Jews' sulphur and you've come to bring me such a yellow face? Oho, for shame! Oho, may you roast in hell, murderess! Oho, oho, oho! Eh? Why're you standing there like a man swinging on the gallows? Get going and bring a little water, quick!" And Grandmother grabbed me and put a jug in each of my idly hanging hands. I took them mechanically but didn't move.

I knew that no one ever crossed Grandmother's threshhold without being commandeered by her for some job. But I thought that after the manner in which I had been called and the purpose for which I had come from Constantinople I ought to be informed of what had happened to poor Grandfather in his struggle with the angel. So I stood there holding the jugs unwillingly and wondering how to broach that subject after his wife's behavior and the reception that had been accorded me, his ally. But Grandmother, not used to such procrastination in her orders, yelled, "Why're you standing there, you weakling? Eh? Why're you standing like that? You afraid your kidneys'll fall? Ooh! May you roast in hell that you wanted a shirt and collar from me! Useless! Wretch! Loafer!"

In such situations Grandmother was like those mechanical instruments that, when fully wound up, must play out their music right to the final note. The only difference was that no one waited to hear Grandmother's music to the end. So as soon as she began her preamble as above, I grabbed those jugs tightly and hurried out in the direction of the spring. My obedience did not, however, suffice to interrupt her. Grandmother's tongue continued its tune goodness knows how long after I left because, when I came back, she was grumbling even more loudly than she usually did without some reason. That's why I didn't hesitate at all when she took the two full jugs from my hands and replaced them with two empty ones, but ran to the spring most eagerly now, so as to appease her.

"Where's Grandfather, Grandmother?" I asked respectfully when I came back after a little while and found her in a good mood, probably because there wasn't any other chore handy for me.

"Where is he, you say? Where is he?" she exclaimed, wound up now to a higher pitch. "He went and left me! The loafer! The bum! The useless! The sluggard!" and so on, "the . . . the . . . the . . ." right to the end.

Grandmother, I thought to myself, will have the gall to ask Grandfather to come out of the grave to do the chores with which she had saddled him while he was still alive and will send him back to his pit again in the evening!

"Now that he has no job, I wonder what poor Grandfather's doing?" I said then in a low voice, sort of talking to myself.

"Why he's sunning himself!" Grandmother broke in, tuned to a higher pitch. "He's sunning his belly! The glutton! The drone! The good-for-nothing! The . . . the . . . the . . " again right to the end.

Strange thing! I thought. So she spies on the man even in the other world to see what he's doing!

"And where's he sunning his belly, Grandmother?" I asked, timidly now because I imagined her capable of knowing whether Grandfather was sunning himself in the warmth of Paradise or in the furnace of Hell.

"Why, up on the *baïra,*" she cried, flaring up again. "Up on the

baïra! Don't you know him? The fool man! The bum! The worthless! . . . the . . . the . . . the . . ." This time I didn't wait for her to
finish. I ran out of the house without saying a word.

The *baïra* is the rocky hill to the north of Grandfather's house on
which the acropolis of the place had been built, but on whose Pe-
lasgic walls now rise the Turkish government house and some
houses of eminent Ottomans, creating a most picturesque sight
with their variety of colors and the irregularity of their styles. These
buildings protect the south side of the hill from the north and east
winds and, by collecting and reflecting the direct rays of sunlight,
provide a warm refuge even during the winter. Whenever he got
sick of Grandmother's litanies, Grandfather slyly stole away and
clambered up that steep rock to sit high up in the sunlight for a few
hours. Grandfather justified his choice of spot with the assurance
that, together with the warmth up there, he also enjoyed the charming sight of the panorama of the country. Everyone knew, however,
that Grandfather went up that high because that was the only place
Grandmother, on account of her rheumatism, was unable to go and
collect him.

So I hurried up there, to the highest point on the acropolis, and
there, in his usual, well-known spot, I saw Grandfather sitting in
the sun with his circular *servéta* around his head and wearing his
snow-white *vrákia*. (Grandmother didn't let him wear his felt trousers except on holidays and her name-day.) In his hands Grandfather held a sock—Grandmother's, I suppose—darning it with large
boxwood needles, which he knew how to fashion and use so skillfully. For a moment I thought I was still dreaming.

But the pebbles and sod of the steep slope rolling down beneath
my hurrying feet drew the old man's attention. As soon as he raised
his eyes from his work he recognized me:

> "Little Yoryí, who's your love
> That all day long you're singing of?"

That was the couplet with which that excellent old man always
greeted me with open arms.

This wasn't another delusion. It wasn't an apparition. Granddad-
dy's knocked that angel down and beat it, I thought to myself. What
joy! What delight!

"You went to the City, my dear," said Grandfather when the embraces and kisses were over and my tears had dried. "You went to the City. Did you see many people?"

"Yes, Grandfather. I saw the Salyvrian gate with the *Parapórti* way up there and with some mills that have wings and turn with the wind!"

"Forget that!" said Grandfather. "Did you go by the land where the sun bakes bread? And did you see the Dogheads?"

"No, Grandfather! I didn't see them. Where are these Dogheads?"

"There, a little this side of the land where the sun bakes bread," said Grandfather, noting the "this side" on the horizon with a demonstrative gesture as geographers do who have visited the areas about which they are instructing. "In front they're people," Grandfather continued, "and in back, dogs. In front they talk, and in back they bark. In front they fawn on you, and in back they eat you! So, my dear, it's better you didn't go."

"Oh! certainly better!" I said. "It's a good thing they didn't eat me and I went to the City in a *kaïki*. And, Grandfather, you should see the sea! Like this, full of water up to the top! And in the water, the boats! Fssssss! Fsssss they go with swelling sails!"

"Forget that!" said Grandfather again. "Did you go by the sea's navel and see the water turning around and around and around, like when your grandmother the *Hatzídena* stirs the pickling-brine in the copper pot, and there's a hole in the middle?"

"No, Grandfather, I didn't see it!"

"Och! My dear! So you didn't see anything?"

"Where is it, Grandfather?"

"It's there, a little bit this way," said Grandfather, pointing at the horizon. "There where Fókia is, Alexander the Great's mother. Did you see her at least, did you see her?"

"No, Grandfather! I didn't see her!"

"Ach! my dear," Grandfather sighed more deeply, "you didn't see anything! Anything!"

"What's Fókia like, Grandfather?"

"Like this," said Grandfather gesturing as if he had Fókia in front of him and was marking out her limbs anatomically. "From the navel up she's the most beautiful woman, from the navel down she's the most frightful fish. She sits at the bottom of the sea. But when she sees the shadow of a boat passing above, she makes a hop! and comes out on the surface; she makes a hop! and grabs the boat with her hand and stops it. And then she shouts to the captain and asks him: 'Does Alexander live and rule?' Three times she asks him, my dear, and when three times the captain says he lives and rules, she lets him go and he goes about his business. If he says the king isn't alive, she sinks him and drowns him!" And turning Grandmother's stocking over and shaking it in such a way that the darning ball fell out, Grandfather showed me how boats go down, and added: "That's why, my dear, it's better you didn't see her."

"Oh, certainly better, Grandfather! Because, see, how could I go to the City if I drowned? Grandfather, you should see how big the City is, and all the different kinds of people who are there and *hanúmisses* and princ——"

"Forget that!!" Grandfather broke in again, as if I were talking about cheap and common things. "Did you see the place where the petrified men are?"

"No, Grandfather, I didn't see it!"

"Ach! my dear, you didn't see anything in your life, nothing!"

"And where is it, Grandfather?"

"It's deep in a forest," said Grandfather like a man pulling together his recollections, "in a cave. Just as you come in from this side you see all the people who've turned to stone. There's a witch in there, and whenever she sees anyone passing by and falls in love with him, she entices him to come in there and she turns him into stone and she has him put over there so he won't get away from her. Whenever she wants, she takes the immortal water and she sprinkles three drops onto his head, and then in an instant the stone softens and turns into a man more handsome than before. Then she sits and eats and drinks and has a good time with him. When she's through having her fun, she looks him straight in the eyes and turns him into stone again. That's why, my dear, it's better you didn't see her!"

I had never doubted that my grandfather was an experienced, widely traveled man. But still I, too, was coming back from the longest journey—after the Holy Sepulchre—from the City. I had seen so many, many things. So I thought that I was bringing with me enough narrative material to engage the old man's attention, if not his wonder, for a few days at least. But when I heard him utter that "Forget that!" so dismissively and scornfully, interrupting my most important subjects as if they were nothing to him and replacing them with his own stories, so wondrous and so unknown to me, I cowered in shame beneath the magnitude of his inexhaustible knowledge of the world and didn't dare say anything more.

After a long silence during which I sensed Grandfather gloating at my inexperience, I again looked up at him. "You must have taken many trips in your life!" I said to him. I pronounced the words with an admiration that was greatly tinged with flattery.

Grandfather was taken by surprise. Clearly my question had come on him unexpectedly. For several moments he looked at me like a man silently protesting some slander. Then—"I?" he said, "I? Journeys? Your grandmother, the *Hatzídena!*"

The pronunciation of these words hinted at an entire story. But since I gave no sign of understanding its meaning, Grandfather filled in the story in a low voice:

"Once—before she was *Hatzídena*—I said to her, 'Dear, I've promised to go to Sarakinós, to the festival of the Virgin.'

"'Go, of course. Of course you should go,' she says. 'Eh? What do I need you around here for? What do I need you for? To sit around and keep an eye on me?"—And lowering his voice still further, the old man added expressively, "'Etcetera, etcetera, etcetera.' Very well," he continued then, "I up and made all the preparations, my dear. I shave, I put on my finery, I saddle the horse, I make the sign of the cross to mount the horse—and there she is, up she comes." And lowering his voice so that it could barely be heard:

"'Come on now! I hope you hurt, and I hope you suffer! Where do you think you're going?'" Grandfather said mimicking Grandmother's mannerisms, "'Eh? Where're you going?'

"'To the Virgin, my dear, to Sarakinós.'

"'You bum, you'll leave the cow to go to the Virgin? You bum (etc., etc.), you're thinking about the festival. But the cow, the pregnant cow, you're not thinking about her? She's in her week, and you're not thinking about her?'

"Now, I wanted to tell her a thing or two," said Grandfather, resuming his own manner, "but, you know her, she wouldn't let me get a word in edgewise. When I saw that I wasn't getting anywhere: 'Very well, my dear,' I say to her. And I threw in the towel.

"'What about other people? What will they say? You've made preparations and bought the candles and the oil and the incense! And the horse? What will the horse think, now you've shod it and saddled it? The horse wants a run!'" Grandfather winked his eye expressively at me and waited for me to catch on. And he waited in vain.

"Don't you understand?" he exclaimed finally. "The quarrel was for the quilt! My dear, I lifted her up, sat her on the horse, and sent her to the festival with her brother."

"And you, Grandfather?"

"My dear, I kept watch in the stable for the cow to give birth. And not only did the beast not give birth," he added then, as if blaming the animal for the failure, "it ruined my luck as far as journeys are concerned, and after that, whenever I made a move for a journey, some obstacle turned up in my path!"

"How, Grandfather?"

"Eh!" he said, at a loss how to associate his bad luck regarding trips with the cow's belated delivery. "Even I don't know that. But if your grandmother the *Hatzídena* is mixed up with it—you try and figure it out! How she pulled it off, my dear, how she fixed things up for you—it's enough to make you go out of your mind! Every time I got ready to take a trip—either some animal was giving birth, or the bees were flying away, or someone was sick, or a *musafíris* was coming. You'd think she'd ordered them all, my dear, the very moment I was crossing myself to mount the horse!

"All the years we've been married, I made the preparations and she took the trip! So to Redestó; so to Silivría; so to Mídeia; so everywhere. One trip, my dear, one trip I planned secretly, I kept it for myself. For years and years I collected the money and I hid it wherever and however I could. I'd collected fifty thousand *grósia*, and one day I'm in a good humor and I call your grandmother. Whenever I was in a good humor I wasn't too much concerned about her. So I say to her, my dear, decisively, like this: 'Hrusí! I've made up my mind to go on a trip, so see there's no animal ready to give birth, or sick, or needing anything, and see no *musafíris* comes to the house, because, you see, I'll break his legs!" And Grandfather made as if he were admiring himself for how he'd pulled it off. "I wish," he said to me, "you'd seen how frightened she was! Not a word! And that's what I wanted. My dear, I send for my confessor and he comes and I confess; I call your grandmother before me and I write all my property in her name. I call my fellow villagers and I get each one to forgive me, because you see, my dear, that journey is the longest journey in the world, and we're all mortal.

"The next day I take the horse out and make the sign of the cross to mount. Your grandmother—she still wasn't *Hatzídena* yet—peeks out from the doorway to see me. Me—I'd made up my mind! Look! If she'd found anything to put in in my way, I wouldn't have paid the least attention! Your grandmother knew it: she didn't say a word. That's what I wanted. When I made the sign of the cross to mount, I said to her: 'Look, Hrusí, we're all mortal! You forgive me, and may God forgive you!' Then, my dear, she burst into tears," said Grandfather, as shaken as if the thing were happening that very moment before his eyes. And trying as best he could to act out his wife's great sorrow, he said half-crying:

"'Ach! I wish I'd never lived! I wish I'd never survived! Poor, unfortunate, wretched me! I'll lose my mate! My husband! My master!'"

And Grandfather, astonished at those ornamental names, said, "That, my dear, I hadn't expected. The whole world could collapse—I'd made up my mind. But when I saw your grandmother, my wife, crying, my heart sank! How could I leave her and go away to the ends of the earth?

"'I've made a sacred vow, dear, to go to the Holy Sepulchre,' I tell her. 'What can I do now? If I don't go, we've committed a sin.'

"'If you've made a sacred vow, Husband, aren't we husband and wife? We're one. Whether you go or I go, it's the same thing.'

"Tears in her eyes!" said Grandfather, changing the tone of his voice. "What can I say? I put her up on the horse, my dear, and I send her off to the Holy Sepulchre with her brother."

"From then on," said Grandfather, slapping his palms as if shaking the dust off them, "from then on I didn't try to take any trips."

"And everywhere you traveled, Grandfather, the long trips you took—you must have taken them before you married Grandmother, right?"

Grandfather took up his handiwork again, a sad smile on his lips.

"Before they gave me to your grandmother the *Hatzídena*," he said lowering his eyes, "I wasn't a boy!"

"What's that, Grandfather? Were you a girl?"

"You can say I was a girl, my dear," said Grandfather with his sad smile, "since even I thought I was, and everyone believed it."

The words made a curious impression on me. Grandfather was holding woman's work in his hands and in spite of his manly bearing—his carefully shaved face, the smartly trimmed mustache above his upper lip—the general expression of his face seemed to me at that moment to contain much that was effeminate and womanish.

"Yes, yes, my dear," said Grandfather with a sigh, becoming suddenly pensive, "all of you are living in golden times now, in golden times! You travel whenever you want, to whatever lands you want. And in any event, my dear, you know what you are. As for us, we lived in unfortunate, unhappy times! Our mothers used to kneel before the icons, my dear, and weep to the Virgin either to give them a girl or to kill the child they had inside them so they wouldn't bear a boy."

"Why, Grandfather?"

"Because every so often, my dear," said Grandfather still more gloomily, "the *Yanitsarió* came out—huge, terrifying Turks with their high *kavúkia* and their red *kavádia*—and they made the rounds of the villages under arms with the *imám* in front and the *tseláti* behind, and they gathered up the best looking and smartest Christian boys and made Turks of them."

"Why, Grandfather?"

"To make them Janissaries," said the old man, indignantly. "To make them like themselves; so they'd come back to the country when they'd grown up and forgotten they were Greek to slaughter their very own parents who bore them and to violate their very own sisters who'd sucked the same milk!

> A curse upon the hour
> on April's first bright day
> When the *Izámi* marched out
> And took the boys away!"

Grandfather sighed after reciting this and wiped away his tears. "For that reason," he continued then, "when I was born, my dear, and they baptized me, they called me Yoryiá, that is, they gave me a girl's name, just as they named children Konstantiniá, Thanasía, and Dimítro at that time—all boy children, my dear—with girls' names—and along with the name, they dressed me up in girls' clothes. In all the years thereafter, my dear, I didn't go out of the door of our house more than once a year, wretched little girl that I thought I was. When I got to be about ten my father—God rest his soul—grabs me one day, sits me on a stool, cuts off my long braids, takes off my skirts, and says:

"'Look here, Yoryiá, from now on you're Yoryís, you're a boy.

From tomorrow and thereafter you're a man, Hrusí's husband, the girl you play dolls and jacks with every day.' That was all he told me, and he dressed me in boys' clothes. The next day, my dear, the violins and lutes came, and they took me to church and married me to your grandmother."

"How, Grandfather? You were so young!"

"Yes, my dear," said Grandfather, wondering himself. "I didn't even know how to tie my new *kavádi* yet, and they even gave me a woman to command! But," he said then scowling, "it had to happen. They couldn't hide me any longer, and the *fermáni* said the Janissaries could take only the unmarried. So they married me 'in pomp and circumstance,' and so, my dear, instead of some Janissary getting me, your grandmother got me."

"Which means, Grandfather, that you never took even a single trip in your life! Unless, perhaps, you took one before you got married?"

For several moments Grandfather seemed at a loss regarding how he ought to respond. Then modestly lowering his gaze, he said, "What can I tell you, my dear? Before I got married I did take a trip, but—what's the good of it?—that one also stopped in the middle. It remained unfinished . . ."

"How, Grandfather? When?"

The old man laid his handiwork to one side on the ground, and straining his gaze toward the horizon, he seemed silently preoccupied with viewing the landscape that stretched out before us. The sky was cloudless, the sun low on the horizon. The height of the spot on which we were sitting afforded the viewer a vast and yet easily embraceable panorama.

Around the base of the acropolis and immediately beneath our gaze lay the houses of the town in confused clumps; in their courtyards one could see men, women, and children busily bringing their fall produce into the storerooms. Immediately around the city one could see the vegetable gardens and the old trees that were now losing their leaves around the broken fences and the last harvesters loading the late-ripening vegetables onto their wagons; nearby there burned and smoked the useless chaff of the now abandoned threshing-floors. Beyond, extending in a large arc came the country's most fertile fields, in which, however, there no longer swayed the heavy ears of grain like the surface of a yellow waving sea, but flocks of sheep and herds of cattle grazed there as they slowly returned to the city, consuming even the last green plant. In the farthest distance on the horizon the local vineyards, they too empty and abandoned after the harvest, enclosed this huge picture like a giant picture frame. The bright variety of fall's last colors, the brooks that at frequent intervals streaked the land, the groups of trees and houses that stood picturesquely by their banks, the tombs of the Odryssians rising up here and there like huge, cone-shaped mounds, not only broke up the flat monotony of the plain's features, but also gave that endless picture an extraordinary, wonderful unity and variety.

And yet I can still recall that, as I gazed upon that most pleasant of sights, a certain, secret anxiety tugged at my heart, a certain mournful foreboding. You would think that life, once so vigorously blooming in that land, was now withdrawing slowly but steadily into nature's innermost recesses; and that the brilliance that remained on its visage was nothing other than the final, ultimate smile on the lips of one about to die.

After Grandfather had spent some time silently and absentmindedly contemplating this view, he fixed his gaze on one of the most distant conical mounds far away on the horizon and, pointing with his finger, said, "Do you see that *túmba* there, my dear?"

"Which one, Grandfather?"

"There, that one, taller than the others, there where the face of the earth ends."

"I see it; it's touching heaven with its top, Grandfather."

"*Aï hak!*" said Grandfather, pleased with my answer. "Heaven's resting on it, isn't it?"

"Yes, Grandfather! The earth ends there and heaven begins."

"*Aï hak!*" the old man cried out still more pleased. Then, fixing a proud look on me, he said, "I managed to travel over there."

And he pronounced the words in so boastful a manner that I didn't know right away whether Grandfather had managed to travel to heaven or to the *túmba* on which heaven seemed to be resting.

Grandfather continued. "We can see the *túmba* from our window; from an early age I saw it and got a 'yen'—a great desire—if it were only possible to go there, to go to the top of the *túmba,* to enter heaven. But look, I was a girl! How could I go out in the streets?

"When my father cut my hair and put a *kavádi* on me and they suddenly made me a boy, they began cutting up papers to braid into wedding wreathes. At one point I give them the slip and go out into the courtyard. I had the journey on my mind and only the journey."

After a silence during which Grandfather appeared to be gathering his recollections, he said, "Outside the henhouse there was a plank with some sticks nailed across for the hens to walk on to get to their nests. I had had my eye on it from the beginning. I'll lean it against heaven's glass dome, I thought to myself, like a ladder; I'll climb up, make a hole, and go in. So, my dear, I take the plank on my shoulder, and if they see me, let them report me.

"I go out of the courtyard, turn right, and—I'm off! If anyone saw me, how could they know I was Yoryiá, Syrmas' daughter? It was as if I had come into the world for the first time. So even Hrusí, your grandmother, started chasing me away with rocks when she saw me dressed like this in a *kavádi*. It's not that she recognized me, but she always harassed the boys in this way from the beginning. As for me—I'm off. Who could keep me from such a journey? I go out into the gardens, I enter the fields, I cross the river, my eyes fixed on the *túmba,* and—I'm off. I go a mile, I go two. But—what do you think, my dear? The farther I go, the farther away the *túmba* gets! The closer I get to heaven, the higher it rises! Ah! That, my dear, that did me in. I had already been tired for some time, but I hadn't realized it until I saw that the edge of heaven was constantly moving farther away from the *túmba* where I had reckoned to find it. Then I lost my desire and I realized that I was tired, that I was hungry, that the plank I was carrying was as heavy as lead, that it had begun to get dark, and—what was the use, my dear? I turned back then and left the journey unfinished!"

"Because, you see," the old man added immediately, "in addition to everything else, I also thought about my father. He—God rest his soul—wasn't like your grandmother the *Hatzídena.*"

"How, Grandfather?"

"Hmmm," he said with an expressive smile, "your grandmother, my dear, thunders but she doesn't rain. My father rained but didn't thunder! That's why I turned back, my dear. It was the only journey of my life," the old man added reflectively, "but it remained unfinished."

"And the things you saw and know, Grandfather?" I asked then in the greatest perplexity. "The land where the sun bakes bread, near where the Dogheads live—when did you go there, Grandfather?"

"Oh!" he said. "I didn't go there. My grandmother told me about that when she taught me to knit."

"And the middle of the sea, Grandfather, where Fókia comes out and grabs ships, and she asks them about King Alexander—didn't you go there either?"

"No, my dear! My grandmother told me about that, too."

"And the cave, Grandfather, where the witch is who turns men to stone—didn't you go there, either?"

"No, my dear! My grandmother, she told me about those things, it was my grandmother."

I cannot describe how my disappointment increased in intensity at his every response. So all my great idea about Grandfather's journeys, all my esteem for him and my trust in his knowledge of the world and his experience, was suddenly limited to the stories, that is to say, the fairy tales that he'd heard from his granny at an age when the poor man had the naiveté even to believe that he was a member of the female and not the male sex! Despair and indignation possessed my heart.

"And the princesses, Grandfather? So you didn't see them either with your own eyes? And you didn't eat and talk with them?"

"What princesses, my dear?"

"You know! The ones that fall in love with tailor-boys, and they become lovesick and they send their father the king with the crown to go and beg one of them to be his son-in-law: don't you remember you told me this? Don't you remember the golden-haired nereid and the white-gowned nereid girls, Grandfather, the ones who sing and laugh and joke and sew wedding gowns without stitch and seam?"

"Ach, my dear!" the old man said then sadly. "I heard that from my grandmother when she taught me to embroider and sew! But, my dear, I don't think she saw them with her own eyes, either."

That dispelled even my last illusion! So it wasn't a princess who awaited me behind the round cupboard in the wall in the *Validé-Sultána*'s harem! And it wasn't she who gave me those fragrant sweets, but some filthy, wrinkled, wide-mouthed old moor! My fellow apprentices were right!

But then, the hardships and the torments that I endured and that I was destined to endure in the sweet hope of returning to my village one day with a princess at my side, had they been wasted, had they gone for naught? Very well, Grandfather! If you ever see me pick up a needle again, say I'm a girl and don't know it! And I was getting ready to pronounce that inward thought, at the same time reproaching Grandfather because he had been responsible for my going to the City to suffer in vain. But when I looked up and saw Grandfather with his dreamy gaze still fixed far away on the top of that conical mound from which he had once hoped to enter heaven, some inexplicable, mysterious force made my tongue stick to the roof of my mouth.

The sun had sunk much lower in the west. Every creature, every sign of life was withdrawing silently and slowly toward the interior of the village. The face of the landscape appeared more melancholy to me now, sadder. My heart shuddered once again. Between the appearance of the scene and the expression on Grandfather's pale and withered face as it was illumined by the last rays of the sun, there existed such a similarity, such a close affinity!

Poor Grandfather! I thought to myself. He wrestled with the angel and beat him without my help, but he's so worn out and weak that if he has another bout in the shape he's in, no one can save him.

"It's begun to get cold, my dear," the old man said suddenly. "Come on, let's go."

Silently, I gave him my arm and, supporting him as best I could, I accompanied him to his house.

That night it was in fact very cold. On the morning of the next day a thick frost lay glistening on the withered leaves that covered the ground in our garden. As soon as I woke up I ran to my beloved grandfather's house. But what a difference between yesterday and today! A large number of relatives and friends was crowded solemn and silent in the courtyard, in the ground floor, and in Grandmother's "salon," in the middle of which Grandfather lay at full length. He looked as if he hadn't woken up yet. A profound serenity reigned on his face. A supernatural radiance, like a smile gradually vanishing, played on his facial features.

Pale, silent, motionless as if turned to stone, Grandmother sat by his side with her hands folded around her knees, her grieving eyes fixed on Grandfather's face. The poor woman! What wouldn't she have given to keep him from that journey! Because Grandfather's smile was the radiance that his soul drew along behind it as it departed for heaven. Poor Grandfather was now truly completing "the only journey of his life."

Moscóv-Selím

▣▣▣

Introduction

"Moscóv-Selím" is Vizyenos' last story, published a year before his death when he was confined to an insane asylum at Dafni. It appeared in the 1895 April and May issues of the journal *Estia*. It could have been conceived and begun as early as 1881, but clearly it either was not complete or was deemed thematically difficult (or unsuitable) for publication in *Estia* with the other stories in 1883–1884. Certain themes—such as the Turkish character, boys raised as girls, cruel fathers, local color, and Turkish words—appear in earlier stories and thus unite "Moscóv-Selím" with them. My own feeling is that the story was conceived by Vizyenos as part of his short-story program but that he was prevented from publishing it earlier—whether by himself or by others, we cannot know—for reasons given in the introduction to the story. He cannot have completed it before 1886, since that is the dramatic date of the story as indicated by the reference to Battenberg's dethronement in Bulgaria.

"Moscóv-Selím" is unique in a number of ways. It is totally set near Vizýi, yet very little of the action takes place there; the narrator is really a recorder here and takes only a very small part in the action of the story; the protagonist, Selím, is a Turk who has settled near Vizýi but whose military career carried him over a large area for a number of years. Though a Turk, Selím professes a paradoxical love for Russians, the archenemy of Islam and the Ottoman Empire. At the age of eighteen, Selím enlisted in the Turkish army and went off to fight in the Crimean War (1854), participating in the battle of Silistria and then being posted north to the Carpathians in Rumania. He served for seven years. When Herzegovina revolted from the empire in 1862, he again joined up and served for two years. In 1875 Herzegovina again revolted, and again Selím enlisted, fighting in the battle of Alexinać, the headquarters of the Serbian army that the Turks took in November 1876; and later in the heroic defense of Plevna against the Russians. He returned to Turkey after the war, probably in early 1879.

The story lacks any folk tale elements, though Selím is, like the narrator in other stories, apparently prone to believe in imaginings. The only mythological note is the one quasi-poetic reference to the fog as Tithonus' bed; and the only reference to poetry is Selím's reciting of a Persian poet's lines about two souls. "Moscóv-Selím" is allied, therefore, with "Who Was My Brother's Killer?" both in this regard and also in the physical description of the two Turks. There are in this story as in "The Only Journey of His Life" a large number of Turkish words, and here they are used more conversationally and refer to a wider range of things than in that story: it seems clear that the narrator has overcome his dislike of Turks.

amán means "woe" and is a common Greek exclamation even today. The Turkish word is *aman*.

âmín, "so be it," is from Hebrew originally (T. *amin*).

askéri is the army, and the *Seraskéris* is the Minister of War (T. *asker* and *serasker*).

baïrámi is the Islamic feast of Bayram, a festival following Ramadan.

baïráki (T. *bayrak*) is a flag, and therefore the *baïraktáris* is a flag bearer (T. *bayraklar*).

dértia are "griefs, troubles," (T. *dert*).

dovléti means the government or the state (T. *devlet*).

duniá means "the world, this life" (T. *dünya*).

etzéli, ecel in Turkish, means "the appointed hour of death."

grósia are Turkish coins worth 1/100 of a pound, and in turn worth forty *parádes*. Neither coin is in use today, though both words occur meaning "money" (in larger or smaller amounts) in contemporary Greek proverbs.

haïri, hayir in Turkish, means "good, prosperity," usually in wishes that something may turn out well.

haláli, also used in current Greek, means "granted as a favor," and is the Turkish *helal* "lawful."

harassó is Russian, not Turkish, and would be transliterated into English as *harasho;* it means "good."

harémi is of course English harem (T. *harem*).

Insalláh means "thank Allah" (T. *inşallah*).

Kaïnárdza is a spring, and means "hot spring," *kaynar-ca*.

kalpáki is a round hat, frequently worn by Slavs and Tatars (T. *kalpak*).

kismét is of course T. and English *kismet,* meaning "fate" or "destiny."

karézi means "enmity, hate."

konáki is any large house, usually official (T. *konak*).

*komboló*ï, a Greek word, denotes "worry beads," a string of beads.

merhaméti means "mercy, pity, compassion" (T. *merhamet*).

meterízi is a fortified position or rampart (T. *meteris*).

múftis is a judge (T. *müfti*).

Rum (T. *Rum*) refers to a Greek under Ottoman suzerainty.

selamlík are the men's quarters in a Turkish house (T. *selamlik*). Vizyenos is in error when he records that women's wailings were issuing from the *selamlík*.

Seraskéris—see *askéri* above.

suvarídes are Turkish cavalry soldiers (T. *süvari*).

teskerés is a "permit" or a "pass" (T. *tezkere*).

tsapráz-diván means "an embroidered cover for a divan." Clearly in the story, however, it means "attention, service."

tsaús, çavus, in Turkish, is roughly our "sergeant."

tsibúki is a kind of pipe, a hookah (T. *çubuk*).

tsizvédes are the small containers in which one brews Turkish (Greek) coffee (T. *cezve*).

yúzbasi corresponds roughly to our captain and is the Turkish *yüzbaşi*.

Moscóv-Selím

I wish I'd never met you on my path; I wish I'd never known you in my life! You gave my soul enough grief to drink, you simple, strange Turk. As if the sorrows caused it each day by the fates of my fellow Greeks weren't enough! But what happened happened. Your sorrowful, gaunt face, with its deep, mournful look disturbs

my sleep, frightens my solitude. Your doleful, trembling voice ech-
oes plaintively in my ears—I must write your story.

I don't doubt that the fanatics of your race will curse the memory
of a "believer" because he opened the sanctuary of his heart to the
unholy eyes of an infidel. I fear that the fanatics of my own race will
reproach a Greek author because he did not conceal your virtue, or
did not substitute a Christian hero in his account. But don't worry.
Nothing will be detracted from your merit because you entrusted
the adventures of your life to me; and I shall never be conscience-
stricken because, as a simple chronicler, I valued in you, not the
inexorable enemy of my nation, but simply the man. So don't
worry—I shall write your story.

*****

The summer was almost over, and it was near evening. After a
ten-hour ride on horseback through mostly waterless villages, we
arrived at V., the seat of a county in eastern Thrace. We could already distinguish the dark masses of fallen Byzantine towers on the
high acropolis, and above the red-roofed buildings rose tall and
slender the two or three minarets of the town, brilliantly white in
the bright light of the gently setting sun. We had only a few kilo-
meters to cover in order to reach the end of the journey before us,
and we had to water the horses so they could, in the local idiom,
"digest" the water before reaching their stable.

"Shall we water them here?" I asked my companion when I
caught sight of a small brook flowing by before us.

"No, we'll water them at Kaïnárdza a little further on. It's not
exactly on our road, but after such pains it's worth knowing Kaïnárdza. It's excellent water. It bubbles up from inside the rock."

After a short while we turned off the road and, through a series
of small hills that were mostly in shadow but were without exception picturesque, we reached the place that my companion insisted
I know.

In fact Kaïnárdza is a most delightful spring to see. It owes its
Turkish name to the fact that as it bubbles up it presents the spec-
tacle of a violently boiling cauldron. Its ice-cold waters, so clear that
they could be liquid diamonds, rush phosphorescent from the
depths of a very white limestone rock with a charming, mysterious
shushing; thick and swift and tireless, it was as if they were waves

of magical, life-bearing subterranean spirits that Lady Mother
Earth with everlasting tenderness sends forth from her bosom with
instructions to pour out onto the broad plain and nourish the
many, many plants and flowers wilting under the summer sun's
deadly shafts.

And so there bloomed along the length of the blue and chattering
stream a long, verdant oasis that formed a smooth landscape from
which deep green rushes and reeds stood out along the water's edge,
beloved haunt of the "fair-winged maiden" and many other variegated insects and butterflies. Stubby, bushy wild willows rising in
clumps here and there furnished, it seems, an evening refuge for a
flock of doves. The evening breeze brought us their sweet, moaning
love songs, while a predatory hawk resting high up on a dry branch
of a lightning-blasted plane tree lay in wait for the merry, sweet-
songed larks, which were sending forth the last song of that day,
invisible in the heights of the sky.

The endless fields around the oasis had already surrendered their
treasures to the threshing-floors of the villages surrounding the
small town V., and consequently the countryside as far as the eye
could see appeared empty and abandoned. Only the shepherd's
flutes could be heard in the distance as they led their flocks to the
folds for the evening milking.

The heat of the day had been excessive; and since the waters that
flow from the northern slopes become stagnant along the eastern
rim of that huge basin, the fog that usually rises during the morning
and evening had begun to cover that barren expanse to the horizon,
merging heaven and earth in that direction.

When, having drunk from the cooling spring and washed, I let
my gaze wander over that landscape, I thought that I had been suddenly transported to some small oasis on the steppes of southern
Russia. A small cottage built on a small hill at a distance from the
spring, and barely discernible behind the thick foliage of two tall
beech trees, contributed wondrously to increasing that momentary
self-deception. That cottage, made of logs stacked up rather than
intertwined, was an obvious imitation of the poor dwellings that
the Russian peasants call *izba*.

Even the chimney of such cottages is constructed of rough pieces
of wood; and since at that moment a wisp of white smoke was
climbing up from it and was weaving itself around the leaves of the
trees:

"Who lives here?" I asked my companion, who was native to the region.

"Moscóv-Selím," he answered without interest.

"He must be some Russian who stayed here after the last war."

"Quite the opposite. He's a local Turk. They captured him and took him to Russia and he didn't do us the favor of not coming back. The man's got seven souls!"

"How seven souls?"

"This is how: He's been mixed up in the wars for twenty-five years now and the black crow can't find him."

"And what's he doing here now?"

"He tends this small garden and sells his produce. He's also got a cow and chickens. Then, too, he plays the coffeehouse keeper: he boils tea. He's a crazy man."

"How can he be crazy," I asked, "when he lives so sensibly?"

"Yes," he said, "but didn't you hear me say they call him Moscóv-Selím? He's got a passion for Russians. At first the Turks tried to get rid of him; they took him for a traitor. Later, though, they came to realize he's a little touched and they let him go. He has no desire to see them: he's looking for the Russians to come, he says, and that's all. The Turks, on the other hand, come here and eat and drink and have a good time with him and make fun of him."

And before he finished his sentence—"There he is!" he cried out. "There's the Moscóv-Selím I've been telling you about. He saw you with your *kalpáki* and boots—he's surely taken you for a Russian. You wouldn't believe how he watches for the Russians to come and how much he's teased and made fun of on account of that."

A tall, erect man, in fact, appeared from that cottage and approached us with firm steps. He seemed well beyond middle age. His long legs, in spite of the dryness of the soil, were plunged up to his thighs in high soldier's boots of the sort the Cossacks sold to the natives by the tens of thousands in the days when they left Thrace. Did they really love the place so much that, since their feet were no longer allowed to tread that sacred earth, they left their shoes behind instead? Or did they love money so much that they preferred to go back from Turkey with lighter feet and heavier purses? I don't know. The only thing certain is that Moscóv-Selím's shoes could no longer serve as representatives of Russian feet on Thracian soil. Their soles were so worn that Moscóv-Selím's own soles had long since replaced Russian leather.

By contrast the Turk was wearing a bright red sash around his waist, the countless folds of which, like successive swaddlings, covered and distorted the upper part of his body from his underbelly to above his breast. This made Moscóv-Selím's bearing all the more comic, especially since the cloak that he wore over his sash and shirt was obviously an old soldier's topcoat that still had two or three carefully shined Russian buttons on it and still preserved the traces of worn-off braids on the neck and cuffs. Moreover, on his head Moscóv-Selím wore a Turkish soldier's tall fez, which lacked the tassle, though, and which was tied around his temples with a thin green kerchief. No stranger outfit could have been created, not even for those locals having foolish pretensions to modernism.

"*Dobro-doide, bratushka!*" the Turk cried as he approached in evident excitement. That is: "Welcome, brother!" And while I was returning his greeting according to the Turkish fashion, he clicked his heels, assumed a military stance, and returned my greeting like a Russian soldier.

"How are you?" I asked. "Are you well, are you well?"

"Couldn't be worse, Thank God!" he answered.

And taking my hand in his bony palm he shook it forcefully and passionately. Then he leaned over to my ear and asked in a low voice and with what I sensed was affectionate familiarity:

"*Moscóv? Moscóv?*"

I stared at him in astonishment. He, however, closed one eye and nodded expressively, as if wishing to say, "Don't worry. Even if you don't admit it in the presence of this third party, I nonetheless know you're Russian and I'm very happy because of that."

"Not *Moscóv!*" I answered with annoyance. "Not *Moscóv.* *Christián, Rúm.*"

Now that he had been harshly deceived in his expectation, Moscóv-Selím's tall stature sagged in all its joints so that from that moment the man became shorter by a span at least.

Moscóv-Selím must have been more than fifty, but because of his bearing and his black hair he appeared much younger. Though very thin in the rest of his body, he had a well-developed head, a regularly protruding forehead, and only the flesh of his face appeared paler and slacker than natural. One would think he had just recovered from a long illness. His trembling and colorless voice and his deeply sad glance created a contrast with his manly posture. Above

all, his large eyes were most appealing, crowned by regularly arch-
ing, very thick eyebrows.

It's strange how some people, previously unknown to us, can
sometimes captivate us at their first appearance without our knowing the reason; can engage our hearts without our knowing from
what cause, for what end. This was what happened to me in the
case of the appearance of Moscóv Selím.

He captivated my affection and interest by a frontal attack, so to
speak, in spite of the absurdity of his outfit. While my companion
led the horses around by the bridle so that they could catch their
breath a little after their run before they drank, I tried to learn from
Selím whether poverty or some other reason made him live there so
that, as he said, he "couldn't be worse." He, however, skillfully
avoiding an explanation, invited me to have a coffee and asked me
where I was coming from and what I knew about a new Russian
incursion into Turkey. And I was glad to sip the coffee there by the
bubbling springs of Kaïnárdza, but as to what he asked me concerning the Russians, I really did not know what to answer that would
be pleasing to my host.

So I skirted these shoals as best I could, and now again attacked
him with all manner of questions. He answered them all with such
a clever conciseness that instead of slaking, he increased my curiosity still more to learn everything about this man. I had really
formed only one conviction about him, that his jumbled attire had
nothing in common with the ordering of his ideas. What my companion had said, that Moscóv-Selím was a crazy man, seemed to
me in the final analysis an insult to me myself. The man had only
one peculiarity, that he valued certain things in an unexpected way.

"Have you seen much of the world?" he asked me as I made ready
to mount. "Have you been to Russia?"

"Everywhere but Russia," I answered teasingly.

"Eh! So then you've never been anywhere. That's why you left all
those places and came back. Just go to Russia once and you'll see
you won't have the heart to leave it."

"How so?" I asked with a smile.

"We can't talk now," he said. "You've watered your horses, and
it won't do for them to stand; you've got to mount and run them a
little so they can digest their water."

My companion and I mounted, spurred the horses, and didn't

exchange a word till we reached our stopping point. The Turk engaged my imagination. I wanted to spend a little time in the large village of V. for rest and relaxation from the labors that had for some time so engaged my spirit that they didn't allow me undisturbed sleep. Recognizing this, my hosts withdrew right after dinner under the plausible excuse that, exhausted from my long ride, I needed rest. And they were not mistaken. But—who would believe it?—that night, the night during which I hoped to get my fill of sleep after such exhaustion, was the very night I was destined to pass completely sleepless!

The appearance of the Turk by Kaïnárdza with his peculiar outfit and his Russian cottage, so insignificant, so ridiculous if you will in any other circumstance, managed that night to capture my fancy to such a degree that, unwillingly and resisting, I counted the long hours of the night forming all manner of conjectures and drawing conclusions concerning that likeable, sad, and at the same time strangely manly character. Crazy he is certainly not, I said to myself. Nor is he some unhappy creature whose mental derangement is already presaged by his obsessive Russophilia. Truly some shadowy mystery—perceptible through his sad and dreamy eyes—appears to possess his internal life.

But how clear his conversation! How dignified his bearing! Faced with his manly behavior one forgets his ridiculous harlequin clothes and overlooks his passion for things Russian. He's like a proud stag that, even though his skin has been torn by the hunting dogs and even though he bears the fatal wound in his flanks, nonetheless still holds his head high in his final refuge. But what was it, then, about this strange Turk that stole my sleep and ruined my rest? Annoyed chiefly with myself rather than with the Turk, I got up from my bed before dawn, and, having put on my clothes noiselessly and as best I could, I took the road leading to Kaïnárdza.

When I arrived at the spring, I caught sight of Moscóv-Selím sweeping the courtyard of his eccentric house. I think he also caught sight of me standing by the spring in the half-light, but he was neither surprised at my early appearance nor did he show any particular hurry to approach me this time. Dawn was already dyeing the horizon purple, and the breeze and the cool of the morning had driven away the weight from my head. I drank from the spring and was invigorated. Then slowly turning towards the Turk's cottage I greeted him courteously, and, "They tell me you brew good tea 'in the Russian way,'" I said to him, "and I've come to try it. I'm very fond of tea when it's brewed 'in the Russian way.'"

Since the others tease him for his Russophilia, I said to myself, let me begin from that point, too, to see where we'll end up.

The Turk straightened up with dignity, barely returning my greeting with a slight motion of his hand, and, fixing his large eyes full of sorrow and surprise on my face, "Vae!" he cried out. "What did the Russians do to you that you don't like them? If only we had a little Russian tea for you to drink, for me to drink! Please come in and sit down."

I glanced surreptitiously through the open door of his cottage and said, "I see you have a samovar: it appears your tea's ready."

"Don't ask for any," he said. "I never had any to be ready. That samovar you see I ordered myself, and they made it here as best they could. The tea I brew in it isn't for you. I brew it this way only for solace when I'm thinking. When I sit here by myself, I like to hear the water bubbling. Don't you believe me?" And he went in and brought out a tin box to show me its contents. A pleasing aroma of thyme, mint, sage, and other local healing flowers and plants assailed my nostrils.

"Like the samovar, so the tea," I said. In fact that vessel, welded clumsily and crudely with pieces of old tin, resembled a Russian samovar as much as Selím resembled Russian soldiers. And if Selím himself—I thought to myself—resembles a Russian as much as his tea does, there's no danger that Turkey will turn Russian in the end.

"Please, in the name of your God, sit down," Selím repeated. "I'll brew you a good coffee, and I've also got fresh fruits and milk for you. You'd think your guide had told me you'd come back so we could talk. Sit here on this stool. You see that meadow down there covered with fog? There are places in Russia like that. Eï! Blessed Russia!"

While Selím was speaking he unhooked a basket full of ripe fruit from the low ceiling of his porch and set it before me on a little stool. Then he went in to brew the coffee and bring the milk. The larks contended with one another as they rushed up in groups into the sweet-smelling atmosphere. The bubbling of the boiling waves of the spring came echoing sweetly up to me; on the branches of the beech, the sole turtledove left from the morning feeding was moaning because of its loneliness. Cheerful light from the east was gilding the tops of the hills on the left and was spreading over the awakening streams like a morning smile on the lips of a fair maiden. How could I have been so deceived yesterday evening? What does this charmingly musical, warm, sweet-smelling landscape have in common with the dumb, dry, gloomy scenes of northern climes? It's true that in the farthest distance of the landscape before me a bed of very white fog still spread over the marshy plains. But isn't that whitening bed Tithonus' airy couch from which rosy-fingered dawn just recently arose? After a few moments the goddess' attendants, the breezes, snatch up its spidery woven linens and lacework on their wings, and the bed no longer impedes the insatiable vision of southern peoples. Did the morose, sunless lands of Scythia ever have such sights?

"I've heard you were a captive in Russia," I said to Selím as he returned with the coffee and milk. "I pray God that you never again see such misfortune."

"Stop your blasphemy!" cried the Turk in surprise, and almost let the *tzisvédes* drop from his hands. "If you wish me well, wish me a captive in Russia!"

"I can't figure you out!" I said in astonishment.

"It seems strange," he said, "because you don't know my story. In the same way it seems strange to the others, too, even though I haven't said it to them openly and clearly. To you I've said it. So be it. If you wish me well, wish me a captive in Russia."

Selím sat down on the sill of his cottage's narrow door and stretched his long legs towards me with the indifference about such things that characterizes his fellow Turks and in such a way that I was able to see the soles of his feet peeking out through his worn shoes. The upper portion of his body occupied more than two-thirds the height of the door. The dark interior of the cottage served as a backdrop against which the Turk's variegated and singular dress and the pallor of his face stood out all the more. It was then for the first time that I actually observed the expression of his eyes from close up. Never had I seen eyes so profoundly and so expressively reflecting some vague, sad disposition of soul that people usually call "heartsickness." When Selím understood that as I sipped at my coffee I was inquiringly studying his face, he lowered his eyes and, with a melancholy smile, said, "Something happened to me because of your worship—a great wonder!"

"May it be *haïri*," I said to him in accordance with the Turkish idiom.

"*Insalláh* it is *haïri*," he answered, and then after a short silence, added, "My heart beat when I saw you yesterday evening. I thought you were Russian. Don't ask me what made me think so. When I saw that you weren't going to be a Russian, 'strange thing,' I said, 'such a good man and you aren't Russian.' You were in a hurry to leave, and I, as you can imagine, was in an even greater hurry. And yet, after you'd left, a feeling of regret came over me because I couldn't detain you; a desire to see you came over me, to talk with you—a great wonder! As soon as you passed with your horse I fell in behind you like a hunting dog. But I was ashamed to call out to you; and you, no chance you'd turn around and look! So be it! I asked in the village and learned who you were. 'God grant *haïri*,' I said. 'That's why his aura drew me after him. So if he's like that,' I said to myself, 'he'll come back to Kaïnárdza on his own. It cannot be otherwise.' And I was so sure you'd come back that it didn't seem at all strange when I saw you today."

"It was an understanding of our souls," I told him. "I, too, couldn't rest before coming back to see you."

"Really?" cried Selím with childish joy. "So it's a true saying that two people can be such strangers and yet their souls are brothers!"

And lowering his voice slightly, Selím recited the Persian poet's lines with religious veneration:

"From the darkness of the earth
a hapless soul regards the sky;
it spies a soul among the happy stars,
which looks at it with loving eye—
Each of them knows they're one at heart,
but cruel Fate keeps them apart!"

Selím resumed his former manner and continued, "You're a learned man. Come, tell me, in the name of your God! Isn't it true that even the rocks that are in the earth, if they found someone to tell their *dértia* to, would be lighter?"

"Very true," I told him, somewhat disconcerted by Selím's manner of thinking. "Very true."

"That's what I think," said Selím, "because I feel my heart growing heavier and heavier from *dértia,* to the extent that once in a while it seems it's become a rock. Aside from the cold water that bubbles up from the lifeless rock, I have no one to whom I can entrust my grief. But even the water, you see, sometimes doesn't want to listen to me and talks to itself more than I do, chatterbox that I am, and before I turn to see it, it has gone by and left."

"If I can hear your *dértia*, Selím-agá," I told him, "I promise to stay right here motionless, silent. What hidden pain do you have in your heart?"

"I don't have anything hidden to tell you," he told me then, "or any *dértia* that others couldn't hear as well. But for others Moscóv-Selím is a person all but mad. What do you expect me to tell them? How do you expect them to understand me? That's why when I heard about your worship I felt a sense of relief. Such a man, I said to myself, will be good like the Russians. If you tell your pain to him, it's as if you told it to the whole world. In this way no one can accuse me any more of being a coward, or a traitor, because, as I hinted to you earlier, I have made a decision to do it. If ever the Russians once set foot in Turkey, I'll go over to their side; I'll be their ally; I'll go to their country and I'll not come back. Am I right? Am I wrong? You'll understand when you hear my story."

Here I must admit that I wronged Selím even if only in thought. Though it's true I could in no way anticipate the cause of his sorrow, the way in which he entered upon the subject was so clearly connected with the fixed idea of Russophilia that people attributed to him that I was momentarily afraid I had fallen into the trap of some monomaniac and had condemned myself to hear things undeserving of serious attention. Yet I thought again in a flash that the one speaking to me was a Turk: that is to say, he belonged to that race whose most striking characteristic is its deep contempt for everything that does not agree with its religion and traditions; its blind, fanatical devotion especially to those preconceptions whose object is preserving racial vanity and dignity; and above all its acceptance with stoic indifference of the twistings of fate both in national and in personal affairs. And so it would be interesting from most points of view to learn what reasons made Selím deny or reject his racial character.

After sitting for some time deep in thought, as if he were trying to gather his strength, Selím lowered his eyes modestly and began to relate in a voice as weak and quavering as if it came from a broken musical instrument: "I was born of beys and had a wealthy family. I also had two brothers from the same mother. But since I was the last and we didn't have a sister, my mother, God rest her soul, not only was unwilling to release me from the *harémi,* but she even dressed me as if I were a girl. You see the poor woman wanted to deceive herself and console her grief because she didn't have a daughter of her own. I was a child of twelve and still had long hair, reddened nails, painted cheeks, and wore girl's clothes. My mother—God forgive her!—was all the more proud of me as it became clearer that I alone resembled her in everything. While I was little, I put up with being painted and decked out like a doll. But as I grew older my aversion to women's attentions began to grow strong. That caused my good mother great sadness because the poor thing saw that I was impatient, that I couldn't wait to fly out of her hands. Our father I saw very rarely: he was a proud, strict man and didn't visit the *harémi* often. He never took me onto his lap to fondle me: you see it turned his stomach to see me with long hair and girl's clothes. He never gave me anything, and he always addressed me with derisive nicknames. Yet he was also a brave man; he had a great love of horses and weapons and made fun of womanish things. In my heart I worshipped him, and I wanted to become like him, an armed horseman, the more passionately the more they persisted in keeping me in the harem!

" 'I see that you don't love me,' my mother told me one day while she was stroking my hair. 'Poor child! You don't know it, but your father has another wife now, and he doesn't even want to recognize us any more! If you go with him, too, I'll die! You know that?'

" 'But Father's also got a beautiful steed!' I said then, like a child. 'He's also got gold pistols in his belt, and that's why he's got a new wife, too. . . .'

" 'Very well,' my mother said, after she had thought for some time in sadness. '*Baïrámi* isn't far off, my lamb. If you'll love me as much as I love you, I'll buy you pistols then and whatever else you want. Only give me your word that you won't be indifferent like your brothers.'

"As I said, I must have been a lad of about twelve, and I think aside from the milk I drank at her breast, nothing could have so devoted me to my mother as the promise that she would take off my girl's clothes and give me pistols to wear. Love—I felt a boundless love for her; and only because of that love was it possible for me to be kept transformed and imprisoned so long. But from the moment she gave me to understand that Father scorned her in favor of another, there is no way I could have shown her my love any more than I did. I never left her side. I never disobeyed her words.

'When you love me,' my mother—God rest her soul—told me many times, 'I don't feel the others' scorn. Look at your brothers, they've taken after their father: they have no heart in their breast. Only you are like me. God bless you!'

"*Baïrámi* wasn't long in coming, and I suddenly found myself a little soldier with my stiff *fez*, with green embroidered vest and trousers, with gold embroidered leggings, and in accordance with my mother's promise, two small pistols in my silk sash.

"I all but jumped for joy. The first thing I did was run to hug my father. He won't make fun of me any more. Now he'll like me. But I felt a despair to equal my joy when he saw me: the expression on his stern face changed, and he said I didn't know how to walk like a boy!

"I used to say to myself, 'If Father doesn't love me like my older brothers, my girl's clothes are to blame.' So I expected he'd take to me now that I dressed like him, was proudly riding my little horse, and was going to school. Not at all. I was always the incapable, the coward, the loathsome. No matter what I did, I was always wrong. My heart was crushed when I saw there was no way Father would love me. And not only that. He grew angry when he saw that my oldest brother wouldn't let the middle one mistreat me.

"On the other hand, when my mother learned all this, she tried to keep me near her that much longer in the *harémi,* with the excuse that she was teaching me my lessons. She was from an important family and was an educated woman. I, too, wanted to be with her now and then because I saw that she was unhappy and that it was a great consolation to her when we were together and she could tell me all the bitterness she'd had to swallow from her husband's second wife. My heart dripped blood when I heard these things, but I decided never to quarrel with anyone, never to stand up for my mother on account of the injustice she suffered. My only desire was that my father love me. So I did what I knew pleased him, and above all I tried to be like our older brother, for whom the old man had a great partiality. He resembled our father to a tee, but he was a very gentle, soft-hearted young man. Many times I heard him praise me to Father; many times he tried to insinuate me into Father's affections—it proved impossible. I was now a young man of eighteen and had never heard a kind word from his lips. Then one day they came to levy soldiers, and my eldest brother's lot came up.

"'I'm happy, very happy,' Father said when they brought him the news. 'The *Seraskéris* is sort of a relative of ours, and since it was your *kismét* to be a soldier, I want you to become important in military affairs. I'll send the *Seraskéris* a letter and you'll do as I command.'

"My brother turned pale, and as he stood with his arms crossed in front of him he shook like a leaf. Father, as I said, loved him more than the others, but he was a strict, hard man—what he wanted had to be.

"'There's nothing to be afraid of,' Father continued. 'If it's written for a man to die from lead, he can go hide at the bottom of the sea, he'll still die from lead. I hear the drum pounding outside—the draftees are getting together to celebrate. Come on, go join your comrades.'

"Sweat was dripping from my brother's face; his eyes were profoundly gloomy. Father did not turn to look at him. If I hadn't put my hand under his armpit in time to hold him up, he would have fallen in a faint then and there. Father turned his face away, got up from the *mendéri,* and without adding anything, without saying good night, went to the *harémi.* Never at any other time had he gone to the *harémi* so early.

"It was about mid-afternoon; the drums were coming closer and closer: voices were heard; 'Long live the Sultan!' Viols and lutes were heard outside our door—they were coming to get him. My brother collapsed on my neck, hid his face in my chest, and with sobs that tore at my heart said in a deep and despairing voice: 'I'm not going! They'll kill me in the war. I'm afraid to go!'

"'Don't despair, *aféndi,*' I told him, 'there's still time before you go; Father can still buy you off; and if he doesn't do it, I'll go in your place. Don't be frightened.'

"The racket reached the stair; the green *baïráki,* the conscription flag, appeared first, with the new draftees behind. Some were drunk with wine and opium; some were drunk without having drunk anything. All, however, appeared happy, even if they weren't so at all.

"'Come, brother Hasan,' shouted the flag bearer, a short, fat man with an evil reputation. 'The Kingdom gives us a week's leave to enjoy ourselves as we like before we enter the *askéri.* Come. And if you've got your eye on some pretty Greek girl, or if you have a *karézi* with any of the *giaúrs*—come, now's the time to give vent to your passion. Whatever anyone does now, all is forgiven.'

"My poor brother! He resembled my father in appearance, hard and fierce on the outside, but no one could believe how soft, how gentle he was at heart. And they were coming to take him as their leader in floggings and killings, in the thefts and woman-chasing they were counting on doing!

"The viols were playing downstairs on the ground floor; the servants had all gathered in the drawing room; my brother was yellow as wax. The *baïraktáris* took him and spoke to him privately. If it had been me, they would never have taken me with them. But my brother had no will power. When he saw them all with such false courage, you'd think he'd surrendered to their will. He hung his head and followed them. No matter, I said to myself, let him go party with them. He'll take courage. Since father wants it, there's no way he won't go as a soldier. That night he didn't come home to sleep; and since my other brother had contrived to leave with them, I, as the youngest, could not leave the *selamlíki*. The drums thundered all night, and twice I sent the servants to see whether they hadn't got him horribly drunk. He was all right until midnight.

"In the morning, early, I went out to get him because I had seen my other brother come back alone and go to bed. I hadn't gone far, and there's the *baïraktáris* with five or six draftees on his heels, heads hanging, and 'This wall's mine, that wall's yours,' they were so drunk.

"'Where's my brother Hasan?' I asked him.

"'He went to the devil!' he bellowed hoarsely. 'He left his company and went to the devil!'

"I was getting ready to go on when I saw the servant of a wealthy youth. 'Last night my brother was with your master,' I say to him. 'Do you know where he is now?'"

"'He's still with him,' he answered and slyly winked one eye.

"'But where is he? At your *konáki?*'

"'God forbid!' he says. 'What do such fine-feathered friends want with a cage?'

"'I'm in no mood to listen to your disgusting remarks!' I say to him. 'Can you tell me what happened to my brother?'

"'I can,' he said rudely. 'He's a deserter.'

"He didn't have time to finish the word. I grab him by the Adam's apple with such force that his eyes popped out of their sockets like eggs. 'Dog,' I said, 'take back that insult or I take your life!'

"'*Amán, amán,*' he moaned, half-choking, 'let me go and I won't say it. I haven't told anyone else.'

"'Come here, wretch,' I told him, and I dragged him into the house.

"'It's not my fault at all,' he said. 'I'm a servant and I did what they ordered. I got the horses ready and waited for them outside the village; your second brother brought all the other necessities. Didn't he tell you he helped him get away? It must have been two in the morning when we sent them off.'

"I closed a florin in his hand, and told him, 'Look here, if I learn that you've blabbed anything—you're a dead man!'

"Two or three hours later I was standing before the military council and was giving an oral deposition: 'Since my eldest brother is needed at home, I am here to take his place in accordance with the right that is given me by law and local custom.'

"Our family esteem was high; my father, if he'd wanted, could have bought my brother off. So the council didn't spend much time on details: the secretary erased Hasan's name and entered mine. I gave the oath to the Sultan and the flag, and on the way out the door wondered how to report the matter to my father. The old man was a proud, haughty, eccentric man: he considered life as nothing when compared to his reputation. In the eyes of the world I had preserved our reputation: no one had the right to call my brother a deserter since I was the new recruit. But Father? Father reckoned things in his own special way—how, I wondered, would he take what had happened?

"While I had these things in mind and was coming down the stairs, up comes a postman and dashes into the courtyard of the administration building. His horse was swimming in sweat—Royal decree: the new recruits are to set out this minute for Adrianople. They called me back and detained me, and they sent out to collect the others.

"At that time I didn't yet know what a soldier was. 'Just a moment,' I begged of them, 'let me dash back to say a final farewell to my mother.'—'Impossible.' The faces of all were solemn: the officer who came for the draft—God protect you! The postman had come from the Capital; they asked him the news; in a short while everybody knew: the nation was at war with Russia—the Crimean War was beginning.

"With list in hand the captain penned the new recruits one by one in a stable—they'd thrown me in there first of all. You'd think one of us had killed his father the way he looked at us. Whenever I think of him now I think I've not hated, I cannot hate, anyone in this world more than that scoundrel!

"'Just one minute! One minute! We're talking about life and death. No one knows if we'll ever come back. Just one minute to kiss my mother's hand, to get her blessing!'

"'Impossible! Impossible!'

"When they brought us out into the courtyard for departure, I spied my second brother in the crowd that had come to say good-bye to its relatives. He didn't know what I'd done in the meantime and was astonished that I was standing in the ranks with the new recruits. When he came up to me, he said: 'Father gave me a letter and a purse to give to Hasan; he told me to tell him that he sends him his blessing from the bottom of his heart, for him to be a son worthy of him and not to cause him shame. He wanted to come himself to say good-bye, but the thing came very suddenly, and he was afraid his heart wouldn't stand it and everyone would say that he was sad because his son was going as a soldier. Where's Hasan?'

"'You know very well that the *eféndis,* my brother, is where he ought not to be,' I said, 'and he's there with your connivance. But, as you see, his place isn't empty. And if you don't want to get your-self into a lot of trouble this time for the dishonorable favor you did him, listen to what I tell you. The police will be sent after the deserters with strict orders to capture them. Since you know their hiding place, run save our brother. No one knows he's a deserter, because before they started looking for him I made the request and was accepted, as you see, in his place. So tell him to come back right away so it won't be learned he left to escape and so our fami-ly's honor won't be damaged. To Father say I kiss his hand with tears, and I ask him to give me his blessing; tell him I asked Hasan to let me go in his place. I know how much Father loves him, and I didn't want him to be deprived of him in his old age.'

"I had managed to tell him these things when suddenly the trum-pet sounded. We two brothers embraced with tears in our eyes— who could tell if we would see one another again! The trumpet sounded once again, the officers mounted.

"'Take this ring,' I said, 'and give it to my mother.' How I wished she were some poor woman like those who were here embracing their sons in the crowd so I could see her once again before leaving, to hear a blessing from her holy lips. But she is a *hanúmissa,* daugh-ter of a great bey, she cannot go out of the *harémi,* and they didn't let me go see her! 'Give her the ring! When she sees the diamond flash in the gold, let her remember me, let her think she sees her son.'

"The trumpet sounded a third time. In front of the main gate an *imámis* slaughtered a sheep and blood was sprinkled in our path; then he raised his hands to pray in his heart and to bless us. In that deathly silence the drum was suddenly heard quick and fierce, the green flag was raised, and we all shouted from our hearts: 'Long live the Sultan!'

*****

"So I entered the military just as I was. It's true that right from the start I didn't find things as I had imagined them; but no one can tell me I ever neglected my duty. Even the captain who'd enlisted us—a man, I tell you, whose nose, if you should grab it, would drip poison—even he after a two or three days' march began to look favorably on me. I don't want to tell you one by one all the things that came into my head all the while the Crimean War lasted. I have made *halálí* to my master the Sultan my toils and deprivations and hardships, *halálí* all the blood that was shed before Silistria; I have made it *halálí* to him as a mother does her child the milk she suck-led him with. One thing only sat in my heart like a rock—it was the very first thing that embittered me, the thing I cannot forget. You see, when we'd chased the Russians out of Silistria, it was dis-covered that I had a bad wound that could not heal itself as my others had. So two people lifted me up and took me inside the for-tress, to the hospital. I must have lost a lot of blood, because I fainted and for many days I wasn't myself at all. When I began to see a little and to understand what they are saying around me, I hear my name being mentioned repeatedly in the mouths of two or three of those who were sitting near me. I pay closer attention—it was an account of how I had received my wound rescuing our flag from the hands of the enemy after our flag bearer had fallen and the cowardly captain had left us and fled when the enemy sur-rounded us. I think that from that moment I got better from that account alone rather than from salves and bandages. Better to have died then and there with that happiness! A doctor—I think he was European—gave me to understand that they had written our mas-ter the Sultan, and he would place a medal on my wound as soon as I get well and can get up, because I'm a good fighter. But you'd think all these things were frauds to make me get well as quickly as possible.

"When my wound was healed and I left the hospital, I saw the yellow captain, the deserter—I wouldn't have recognized him! The *Seraskéris* had advanced him three grades and hung a shiny medal on him because he'd rescued the flag from the hand of the enemy! As soon as he recognized me, he nodded for me to come over to him. 'Today,' he said, 'a detachment is going north to build fortifications; you'll go along, too, to dig and carry dirt! And better not let me catch sight of you around here again.'

"This was my reward and my medal!

"The European doctor explained it to me. The three-grade promotion and medal had been sent by our master the Sultan for the one who had rescued his flag from enemy hands. But that poisonous captain was a relative of one of the *Seraskéris'* favorites, and not only was he not punished as a deserter, he was even decorated and promoted! With the blood shed by me the very moment he was fleeing!

"While I had been recovering, I had thought of writing my father that even I had managed to accomplish something in the war, and I was sure that, now at least, he would help get my promotion. He was a man who loved bravery and courage; the *Seraskéris* was a relative in any event, and what my father had promised my older brother when he was drafted he could do for me now. But when I learned what it means to have the *Seraskéris* as a relative, I said to myself, 'Who wants it? Better to be first in doing my duty in the line, knowing that no one other than God and my *kismet* will protect me, than have such patronage. Who knows? Maybe in the danger of battle the devil will put the thought in my mind that the *Seraskéris* is my relative, and I will betray my duty, become a deserter! And after that the *Seraskéris* can order the medal and the stripes for me, his relative, while the hero who rescued the government's honor and the religion's flag will not only remain without reward on account of this, but will even suffer contempt the same way I did. He'll have the same luck I did, from whose hands they took sword and rifle and replaced them with basket and shovel! No! I know what poisonous bitterness there is in this injustice. I don't want anyone else to drink it! If I'm to gain advancement, I want to gain it through my merits, and not out of favor and patronage.' Such considerations prevented me from writing my father

then. Better if I had written! Who could know? At least they would
have had news that I was alive, for from that moment on everything
for me went so awry that it was not possible to send a letter
back home.

"Seven whole years I served the king then; I didn't have seven
parádes in my belt when they gave me leave to return home. And I
don't say that by way of complaint. We and our families, our life
and our possessions are the property of our master the Sultan, and
it is *haïri* and bliss when they are expended in his service. But the
Sultan out of pity and compassion for his people has ordered that
every soldier is to be returned and left at the door of his house in
the same condition in which the *dovléti* took him from that door.
What did you expect me to do, me, whom they left almost naked
and barefoot, twelve days' journey from my home town?

"I don't want to tell you all I suffered before reaching my house.
Three or four times imperial officials—the animals—all but threw
me in jail because they didn't know how to read the paper I held in
my hand and took me for a bandit; three or four times they tried
to kill me as a spy. Finally, I—who went into military service so
proud, so dedicated, and with such golden hopes—I came back to
my home town humiliated and scorned, not with the medal that I
had earned in the fire of battle, but with wounds in my chest and
with a beggar's sack under my arm. Surely my master the Sultan
would never have wished these things, and I was not obliged to
suffer them. And yet . . . would that this had been the only disaster!

"When I entered our courtyard, no one recognized me; but believe me, neither did I recognize anyone, and the buildings themselves had become unrecognizable. In my days, wherever you
turned to look the things you saw would tell you that a strict master
gave orders there, one who loved order and beauty and peace. Quite
a different matter now. The fountain in the courtyard had dried up;
the rings on the door had grown red from rust, and there was no
one standing with folded arms at the entrance to the house ready
to open the door for his master as once there had been. The servants
I heard only as they shouted brazenly and exchanged insults and
laughed as if possessed; but there was no one to appear, to see, to
go, to announce! Anxious and with a heavy heart and troubled
sight, I went up the stair of the house and found myself in the drawing room where Father once used to sit at that hour. No one was
inside. In spite of all this a great weight was lifted from my chest

and I breathed a sigh of relief. His weapons hung on the wall: his *kobolóï*, his *tsibúki*, the things he used once to have about him, were there. Nothing's happened to Father! And in my joy I didn't wonder that all these things were somewhat dusty, and I didn't notice my old servant, who was rubbing his eyes in front of me in order to be sure whether it was me in fact or whether he was dreaming.

"'It's me, Sakírbaba,' I told him. 'Why're you staring like that?'

"'Great is God and great the Prophet!' cried the old man, all astonishment, and the staff he was leaning on fell from his hands. 'If you're my master Selím, strike me and take my soul. Was it for this God lengthened out my days? For me to live to see you in your maternal home with the beggar's sack under your arm?'

"'It's nothing, old man,' I told him, 'it's nothing. I could have come back still worse than what you see. God willed it this way. If a man serves the King and Sultan our master faithfully and worthily, can he come back to his house better?'

"'A thousand times I wish it weren't so. A thousand times, child of my soul, I wish you hadn't done this service to the kingdom, so that my eyes wouldn't have seen those things they've seen up till now!'

"'It was written, Sakírbaba,' I told him then. 'Where's my brother Hasan? Where's my father? Go give the news to my mother in the harem, have them send me my clothes and heat water for the bath. And tell Hasan, if he wishes, to keep me company in the bath. Find him and send him to me. You hear?'

"'Oh Selím, Selím!' the old man said then, and you'd think his voice had fainted in his chest. 'I wish I could! With the sacrifice of my life! So you don't know anything?'

"'What do you expect me to know? You're the first person I've seen in our house after all these years.'

"'Then it's best that God threw me in your way, and no one of you father's people met you, and you didn't meet him himself, for they'd poison your heart, not only with what happened, but also with what didn't happen.'

"'But what happened, then?' I asked him. 'Speak quickly. I see that what happened is a disaster! What happened?'

"'What didn't happen,' said the old man then, 'is what your father and his young *hanúmissa* say—that you're the cause, you're to blame for what happened. What did happen, though . . . Great is

God and great the Prophet! Don't despair. Sit down on the *mendéri*. I'll tell you as long as my shattered heart holds out; I'll tell you. Don't tremble! Sit down. No one comes here, no one hears. From the time your father foundered the ship, no one of the slaves asks about anything here, no one stands *tsapráz-diván*. God took him from his enlightenment; they have bewitched your father, my child, and he's moved into the harem for good. The man you knew! And he's given his beard into the hands of the young *hanúmissa,* your stepmother.'

"'Sakírbaba!' I said to him then. 'Why do you torture me so cruelly, why do you tear my heart bit by bit as if you were my worst enemy? Some great disaster has happened in this house: tell me right away so I will know. Leave off these women's doings and bewitchings.'

"'Ach! Child of my heart!' the old man exclaimed and began to weep. 'Your brother Hasan . . .'

"'My brother died? Ach, my God! My God!'

"'Would that he had died,' the old man replied, and the flood in my heart was checked so I could hear.—'Would he had died, as so very many masters have died in the arms of their family when they completed the days the Creator wrote for them the moment he gave them a soul to enter the world! Would he had died as even my own brave son died on the soil of the Crimea with sword in hand for religion and the Caliph so we would have the consolation that now he enjoys grace and beauty among the flowers and blossoms of Paradise! Ach! Ach! Master of my soul—Hasan, your brother, they killed him! . . . They killed him most unjustly!'"

Selím's voice died in his throat as he recounted these things. His tears flowed.

"I don't have to tell you," the Turk continued after a long silence, "what a thunderbolt this was for my heart. I confess that up till that moment I was shaking in fear that I might learn my mother was suffering, that something had happened to her. And when I heard of my brother's death, I inwardly thanked God for pitying me to the extent of sparing me my mother at least. I told you how I parted from her, I told you how much I loved her, how much her life depended on my love. But when I heard that my brother had been killed, and father considered me responsible for the disaster, grief and shock turned me to stone there on the spot.

"The old servant was a good soul. He loved us with all his heart.

It was he who used to take us out into the street when we were small, he who took us to school and brought us back. Our mother also used him as her confidant whenever she wanted to know how Father was treating us, whenever she wanted to send us a message or send us something when we had grown up and it was not allowed us to enter the harem. For this reason, too, he was devoted more to us and Mother than to Father and his new wife. When he was able to control his sobs, I was then able to learn what had happened in our house since the time I had left and gone away. I'll relate it briefly.

"As soon as we new recruits had left—hurriedly, as I said—my father presented himself at the tribunal and charged my brother Hasan with being a renegade, with being a deserter! The judge and the *muftís* assured him that Hasan could not be a renegade, since as his brother I had formally made a disposition and had taken his place in accordance with law and custom.

"'I have witnesses,' my father persisted, 'that my son, who was obligated to military service, escaped to the mountains with a comrade during the night and has still not returned. Who has the right, the legal right, to take the place of a deserter? And a drafted one at that? But from the moment he ran away my son has been a deserter; and since I cannot possibly endure such a disgrace to my family, I demand that my son be apprehended like every other deserter, that he suffer double the punishment, and that he be forced to execute his duty in chains! Think of it! Enemy feet have trodden on the soil of our master the Sultan, and a young man, who up till now grew up with the good things our *aféndi's* compassion grants us, who grew up under my example, deserts and runs away? If you don't send the *suvarídes* after him, if you don't apprehend him, I'll report the crime to the *Seraskéris* himself. As for Selím, his brother— he could replace some girl in her responsibilities, but not my Hasan in the war! Whatever he did, he did on his own account. I neither tolerate anything nor accept anything. He cheated the law and concealed the deserter; it's your obligation to punish him.'

"The fiercest and the most bloodthirsty troopers were sent to the mountains where they supposed Hasan and his comrade were hiding. It didn't take long to find them; but the young men were armed and resisted. My brother's comrade had influential means and had the assurance that, whatever he did, he had nothing to fear; it was enough not to be caught as long as the kingdom needed soldiers.

For this reason they resisted from the high rocks and wounded a trooper. Then the others leaped after them like dogs, barricaded the young men behind a rock and, when their bullets ran out, made an attack sword in hand. The one young man was able to get away unnoticed down a ravine; they found my brother leaning against his rampart, covered with blood, killed. The bullet had pierced his forehead as he was aiming.

"When news reached my father he showed no sorrow. 'It's God who's triumphed,' he said. 'Let the others learn their lesson as well. What's written does not become unwritten. It was his destiny to die from lead. He didn't go to war and was lost in vain. Go dig his grave.'

"'But as soon as they'd buried him and his place in the house was empty, your father began to change,' the old servant said. 'He who had been so strict in his *konáki*, who had such concern for his properties; he who had never put drink to his lips, now became so you'd weep if you saw him. He neither knows his possessions nor cares for the house. He just sits from morning till midnight with a bottle of raki in front of him, he sits like a coiled snake in the harem.'

"'Your second brother married and left five years ago. Your step-mother found a way to persuade him to write whatever property he had over into her name. You know how it is. She has no children, and from the moment the disaster with your brother happened, she's done nothing but assure your father that you induced him to take to the hills in order to wound his pride; to show him that the son he loved was not like him; to become an obstacle to his future, to his progress, and other such things, and worse. And he believes them because he hears nothing else. If only you were able somehow to see him in the harem now, an old man with snow-white beard, as he sits and watches the slaves she brought him dance naked in front of him, as he lets them kiss and fondle him and sing him the songs she taught them, solely and only to make him addicted to drink and debaucheries until he closes his eyes, so she can marry another her own age.'

"'Oh! My poor mother!' I said then. 'I can imagine the poison she has to drink because of all these things—my good mother.'

"'As for that, have no concern,' said the old man, sunk deep in thought. 'She—God be praised—no longer has sorrows to fear. . . . When you left as you did, without her seeing you, without speaking to you, she called me and said, "Sakírbaba, I will not be able to stand this sorrow!" Later came the disaster with her other son, too. Who knows? She was a good, holy woman—it turned out just as she said. You'd think every day ate away at her health and life and brought her closer to the grave. . . . Every so often she called me and asked me about the war, what I heard, and what news had come from you. But when you left, you cut all ties, and there's been no news of you until today.—I talked to her and tried to console her.

"'A diamond ring which she had on her finger seemed to her to be growing gradually dimmer and dimmer. "It's the tears in your eyes, *hanúm-efféndi*, that don't let you see how it flashes," I told her. But she didn't believe it. "I don't take this dimming as a good sign," she said. "My son's life is in danger. He's wounded; he's near death!" And as the life was gradually being extinguished from her eyes, so the ring appeared dimmer and dimmer to her.

"'One day—I recall it as if it were today—she sent for me and ordered me to tell her what news had come from the master, her son. "A man who came down from the Danube"—I told her then, just to comfort her—"brought us news that the Muscovite has been defeated and our master Selím received a medal from the King, and a high rank." "What good is this to me?" she said, and smiled with her sweet face like an angel who's sad. "My eyes have grown dark in looking at the roads from which my son will come. I can no longer tell if the ring he left me still shines!"

"'Later she took it off her white finger and gave it to the Circassian who sat at her pillow. "Here, Meléïka," she told her. "I had you as a bought slave; you loved me and you looked after me as if I were your mother. Before God and these witnesses, I make you my equal, I give you your freedom. I did not have the luck to see my darling again, my love, the bird of my heart. . . . Hide the ring I give you like your eyes! If you're luckier than I, and my son, my master, comes, I leave you in my place to love him and look after him. He's been away for a long time, and when he comes to my house I don't want him to find himself an orphan! . . ."

"'You'd think some spirit from heaven hidden in her breast had been saying these things. She said them so sweetly, so calmly, with such a divine smile on her face, that no one of us dared open his mouth and utter a word. In a little she fell asleep and I went about my work. A little later we heard women's wailings from the *selam-líki*. "Our old *hanúmissa* has entrusted her soul to God!"'

"My tears flowed like a river all the while my old servant was recounting this, and I wept a long while after he'd stopped. I wept for the dead, and I wept for myself, since I had now in fact come to live in that situation that the old man had described, orphaned and hated. I sent him to tell Meléïka, the Circassian, secretly that I'd come, to ask her for whatever could still be found of my clothes, and to bring them quickly to the public bath after me.

"When I returned home it was early evening; by now everybody knew I'd come; only my father did not. His wife didn't let them tell him, I supposed, and I sent Sakírbaba the next day and he told him.

"'Good news, *bey-effendi*' he told him. 'Your son who's been abroad has come! Your soldier!'

"'I don't have any soldier son,' he said. 'My son who was to be a soldier is not coming back again from where he went. The one who came—let my eyes not see him!'

"All the while I was being tormented in the service, all the distant travels I had suffered, I had the secret consolation that now at last I would gain my father's love. My body was covered with wounds large and small; he has only to see them, I said, and he'll understand that I inherited his courage and bravery, that I'm a warrior. I am like him at heart even though I don't resemble him in appearance. He'll surely squeeze me in his embrace now, he'll kiss me. Such things and many others like them I imagined! And I didn't reveal my name when I reached the neighborhood so his pride would not be offended by the bad condition I was in. Better a bullet had pierced my heart while I was seeking to gain his love in the turmoil of battle than for me to come and find such hate on his part after I had been bereft of those who loved me.

"Two days I stayed in the house alone; on the third they come and take me to court.

"'Many years ago,' the magistrate said, 'you were judged and found guilty because you concealed a deserter and deceived the king. The deserter was your brother, the accuser was your own father. You'll spend a year in prison because your father has reactivated the judgment against you.'

"In any other circumstance I would have known how to escape such a sentence, I would have been able to place the magistrate's two feet in one shoe. But I accepted the sentence on my head so my father's will would be done. And wasn't our house as I found it worse for me than prison? God bless Sakírbaba! He didn't let me lack for anything. Besides, I had neither shame to feel nor scorn to endure. Everybody knew I was suffering on account of my father's perversity and felt sorry for me and consoled me and looked after me as if I were their master. This I would surely not have had in my paternal home.

"So time passed; and the closer it came to the end, the more my heart constricted. My second brother had sold the properties he'd acquired from his wife and gone over to Asia Minor. So I would be condemned to live in our house. The point my father had reached made me lose hope of getting along with him. At that moment we learned suddenly that there had been a revolt in Herzegovina. I lost no time. A strong horse from the stable, a silver set of weapons, and I went!

"Sakírbaba had often found a way of praising Meléïka's beauty and kindness to me. She herself had cooked the food he brought me in prison, and she had attended to whatever else I needed from home as if my mother herself were still alive. A secret voice in my heart said, 'Your mother gave the ring to this girl, she will be your *kismét*.' But you don't know how I felt when I heard of the war. I'll go seek my *kismét* in the smoke and flame of battle one more time. Home life and joy of family has not been written for me. And I went.

"Through God's will it happened that the leader who took me into his battalion was brave and probably for this reason rather fair. When I came back after two years, I had several more wounds but also a small promotion and a medal for bravery.

"This time I could even see my father in the *selamlíki*. My father! If he hadn't sired me, I wouldn't have recognized him! What had become of his proud forehead? His flashing eyes, his broad chest, what had become of them? You'd think that all the years I hadn't seen him he'd been sick in bed. His face had yellowed, his forehead had wrinkled, and his body had sagged. His hands and knees shook like a leaf! That's how his young wife had fixed him!

"When I came in and kissed his hand, he raised his sunken eyes and took a good look at me, and two large tears hung on his pale cheeks. 'You're like your mother!' he said. 'She was my good wife, but . . . she died. This vixen, when I wrote my property over to her, she chased me out of the harem!'

"'What does this mean *afféndim?*' I asked him. 'In our family I've never heard of a woman chasing her *efféndis* out of his own house!'

"'That amazes me too!' he said with childlike perplexity. 'But again, since I love her, the sly vixen, pour me some raki so we can drink her health!'

"To such a degree had drink devastated his manly character. It was in this condition that I found and recognized my father!"

Thereupon Selím explained to me that the father's paralysis, bodily and spiritual, had brought on the financial paralysis of his family. The herds had been sold little by little; the stables had been emptied; the best of the farm properties had come into the hands of creditors and loan sharks to whose purse the old landowner ran as often as his young wife had some new whim to satisfy. One *nikiáhi* plot, that is to say, part of his mother's dowry, remained still free of obligations; Selím personally undertook the cultivation of this, as his father had once done, and within a short time he managed to improve it to such an extent that even the besotted old man marveled at it! "You're like my good wife," he sometimes said. "You're the child of my soul!"

Selím, forgetting then the old man's undeservedly harsh treatment of him, fell upon his neck and, embracing him, tried to slake that thirst for fatherly love and esteem that had for so many years possessed him. But when their kisses and embraces came to an end, Selím felt in himself the disappointment felt by the thirsty traveler who, having strayed far from his path solely in the hopes of drinking his fill from an invigorating spring he knows of, suddenly finds its stream dried up. The father he was embracing was no longer the man he had once admired and from whom a single, loving look would have made him beside himself with joy. The father he was kissing was a drunkard, an imbecilic old man besotted by abuse of alcohol to such an extent that he no longer had a clear notion of anything except whether he was drinking or not at that moment. His faculties had been devastated by vices, his heart had dried up from overindulgence—love and paternal dignity no longer existed in him.

For this reason, Selím now hastened his union with the Circassian Meléïka, his mother's freedwoman. "I could have taken a wife from a wealthy family," he said, "to replace the things my father had squandered. But my mother was a saintly woman—may the soil where she lies become musk and ambergris—the fact she gave my ring to Meléïka must mean she was my *kismét*."

It was wise of Selím to respect his mother's choice because Meléïka was in fact endowed with many virtues. She took care of her incompetent father-in-law with childlike abnegation and made Selím a partaker of married bliss, as much as this could be attained in the Turkish family. When in 1875 the latest revolt broke out in Herzegovina, Selím was a prosperous landowner and had three lively, beautiful children.

"If I had been unmarried," Selím said, "I wouldn't have waited a minute; my heart leaped so in my breast when I learned that all our efforts and the blood that was shed in '62 had gone for nothing. The children were little and my father sick, but my clothes couldn't contain me when I considered that there was war against the Sultan.

"Before long Serbia revolted, and then Bulgaria. The Kingdom called up reserves. I remember that it wasn't yet my turn; but when I learned that Russia, too, was making preparations, I didn't wait my turn, I didn't reflect, I didn't listen to anyone. You know that the Russians are considered the archenemies of our people. Water and fire can make friends with each other and stay friends; Moscow and Islam never, never! Haven't you seen Tatars and Cherkezes who have left their homes and their property and have come into the Sultan's realm naked and barefoot rather than dwell in the same place with the Russians?

"So I left my children, my wife, my goods to fend for themselves and enrolled in the reserves; goods and wife and children are the Sultan's property, and when we fight with the Muscovite, if I had seven lives, I'd lose those seven lives in the war so our *efféndis* would win! We had been fighting with Russia, as I told you, the time of the Crimean War, and we rubbed their faces in it at Silistria. The enmity and hate that I had for Russia then was intensified now that I learned they were coming back to invade our land again. They want to wipe us off the face of the earth, I said, and I'll eat them alive, if it's possible! And off I went to the war.

"At first they sent us against Serbia; there too it appeared that Russia wanted to destroy us. I don't know what was written about the Turks in the newspapers then. But I who fought at Alexinać that fall assure you that we conquered the entire country over again, as if it weren't our own! And yet what good did it do? A crummy piece of paper from the Tsar, and the *Seraskéris* ordered us out of Serbia. Ftou! May God see they get theirs! It was as if you ordered someone to get out of a house that he'd built with his own blood and bones.

"And we got out, for peace, supposedly, for concord! Such was the great wisdom of the Sultan's *Seraskéris* and the other parasites who make up the *dovléti*. The Muscovite, as you know, did what he had to do: before the wounds we got in Serbia were healed, the Russians crossed the Danube! And I who was set to go back home to get well, forgot fever and pain and changed direction. The Russians had set foot on the Sultan's land, I said; how can Selím go back and enter his house? I had a bullet wound still unhealed in my left arm, which I had in a sling. But the first place I met troops I undid the kerchief, gritted my teeth so they wouldn't know I was in pain, and presented myself to their officer. At that time, if it had been possible, they would have made soldiers even out of gravestones. I was a *tsaús,* so he accepted me without many questions, and we went off. You'd think it was written that, after so much war and so much killing in the Balkans, I should live so they could take me and shut me up in Plevna.

"Eï, Plevna, eï" Selím said with a sigh, and he continued his story pensively. "It was you, Plevna, who set my mind straight. I have God as witness that when I reached Plevna I was as if drunk, as if mad. We found the Russians dug in here and there this side of the Carpathians, and wherever we found them, we cleaned them up! It was the first time after the Crimean War I had seen them before me; each of them appeared to me seven times worse than the devil! 'Archenemy of the race, curse him!' I said whenever I met anyone wounded and helpless. And I finished him off, too, with savage delight.

"When I entered Plevna I was a platoon commander; and Plevna was famous for its first heroic resistance. Imagine, then, with what joy, with what hopes I led my men, with what excitement I held the sword in my hand, with what a cry of joy we greeted old Osman-Pasha, the hero of Plevna. We came as relief to his force, three thousand men, and the Russians couldn't stop us no matter where we went.

"'Here at last I'll slake my hatred,' I said, 'my insatiable hatred;

here I'll mercilessly have my revenge on the Russians, our fierce, pitiless enemies!'

"My excitement no longer knew any bounds when the moment came and we opened fire on them that September. I felt that every bullet we sent at them derived strength from my heart to strike its goal more deeply, to destroy more lethally. And I was one of the first wherever there was work for bayonet and sword. But what is written is written; no one changes that. A bullet in my right lung removed me from my post and put me in the hospital. A very ugly wound! Winter came, and I still couldn't move; I spat blood.

"I didn't hear much happening all that time; but suddenly one evening I realized that the doctors and the hospital personnel and all ambulatory patients had left one by one and were gone! Whispers and moans, curses and later dead silence again—I got to my feet. It was dark and I couldn't distinguish things very well, but far away troops could be heard going toward the river. That's not a good thing! The Russians had had us under siege inside the fortifications for a long time; there were no supplies left in Plevna.

"In fact, the Gazí-Osmán Pashá had been forced to withdraw! I reconnoiter; the roads are empty! No one around me; those who were left must have been like me, and worse. I took my cloak and, just as I was, in the dark, I ran after them. On the road I found other wounded, some lame and with crutches. They, too, were hurrying along as best they could, and they moaned and wept and cursed. Then my heart grew really furious. I exerted all my strength and caught up with one battalion that was moving silently forward and another that was coming down the hill toward me.

"'Turn back quickly!' an officer shouted from his horse.—He'd seen I was one of the wounded.—'They'll kill you here! Back!'

"'I'm Selím, the platoon commander,' I told him; 'how can I turn back? As long as I could raise a rifle, draw a sword, the order was "forward!" and now that I'm wounded you order me to turn back? Either you take me with you, or kill me right here! There's no one left back there. Are you sending me into the hands of our enemies?' And I stood in front of him and grabbed his horse's reins.

"'If you're a worshipper of Mohammed our Prophet,' I told him, 'draw and cut off my head! Twenty-five years a soldier of the Sultan, how can you deny me and leave me to fall alive into the hands of my enemies?'

"I didn't have time to finish, and the horse, which felt the spurs in his flanks, rushed at me and knocked me on my back. I heard a number of soldiers as they passed over me and trampled on my wounded chest. Later a sort of faint came over me . . .

"It was daybreak when I came to. The place where I found myself seemed like a dream. My knee hurt me terribly, I couldn't move it. Then I recalled the horse, my fall, and the trampling of feet that passed over me. May they get theirs from God! The heartless ones! Then I thought of all I had done in the wars for so many years, and I reflected how much better it would have been if some bullet had killed me in the line, and an inexpressible terror came over me. What can I expect to suffer now from our enemies?

"Then below, across the river, I hear cannons thundering. They've opened fire, they're being hit. *Allâh! Allâh!* No prayer will come to my lips for my brothers! I cannot say: God help them! So great was the resentment in my heart because they had left me in the hands of our enemies. I was unable to comprehend what was happening down below, but I understood that Plevna was no longer ours! Whether it was my grief and despair, whether it was my state of health, whether it was the excessive cold, there came over me a numbness, a confusion; I didn't know what I was doing. I found myself entirely weaponless; God—no, not God—my coreligionists had handed me over to our enemy as a sacrificial lamb. Now each one of them has the right to exact revenge in accordance with my deeds and my thoughts—let them come! Let them cut me to pieces for dogs to eat! . . . And, exhausted as I was, I dragged myself over and collapsed near a rock, wrapped up in my cloak.

"When I came to, I was in a mobile hospital; I learned I was a prisoner of the Russians, I and all of us who were in Plevna, forty thousand soldiers, along with Osmán-Pashá and so many other pashas!

"It's not an easy thing for me," Selím continued after a pause, "to describe what happened in my heart after that; but perhaps it will be easier for you to divine when you hear my story from this point on."

And Selím tried to describe to me the astonishment he felt when he saw the humane compassion with which the Russian doctor and his assistants, sisters of Mercy, healed his wounds within a few days, clothing and feeding him better than the pashas were fed inside Plevna. Blinded by fanaticism against the Russians, he had imagined them harsh, bloodthirsty, ready to tear his flesh to pieces raw, like wild beasts. And yet these were Russians he saw before him! And he found them now polite and attentive, trying in all manner of ways to console the captives for what had happened to them, to give them courage for the future, and to assure them that even though captives they enjoyed the admiration of the Russians and all the world because of the bravery and valor with which they had fought. Selím especially seemed to them a man of special worth because of the large number of wounds acquired at various times, the traces of which the doctor examined on his body. They gave him to understand that if only the Tsar had soldiers such as Selím, he would be Sultan of the entire world. This greatly flattered the vanity of the soldier who rarely heard an *aferím* for accomplishments that, among other nations, are rewarded in exemplary fashion. After a while Selím was sent to Russia with the rest of the captives.

From political motives the Russians lavished almost unbelievable attentions on the Turks who were captured in that war. Tears came to Selím's eyes when he recounted the kindly and loving reception that they encountered wherever they went. The Russian peasants greeted their captive enemies, addressing them as *bratushka!* that is, brothers! Wherever the train stopped they brought them tea and other warming drinks; and wherever they got out of their coaches, the natives embraced them and kissed them. All these things brought on a real revolution of feelings in Selím's basically good, sensitive heart. Were these, then, the so-called deadly enemies of his race? Were these the ones who wanted to wipe the Turks off the face of the earth? What a mistaken idea he had had about the Russians!

"I was crazy up to that point," Selím added. "That's why I told you that Plevna set my mind straight."

In Plevna Selím had seen what deprivation and sufferings the few Russian prisoners had undergone, and so he expected to undergo the same if not worse in Russia. Instead of these things, during the entire period of his captivity, Selím ate well, wore warm, clean clothes, heard sweet and encouraging words such as he never heard at home from his fellow Turks; most importantly, Selím and his fellow captives were left free and undisturbed to fulfill all their religious obligations in buildings constructed for this purpose. The enemy of Islam surely would not allow such a thing. So it's no wonder that Selím changed his opinion now as to the possibility of Moslems and Russians living together and characterized as fools those struggling against a Russian incursion into European Turkey.

"God's *dúnia* is great," he said, "and the poor Tsar has no way of accommodating his subjects. They're such good people; let them come down to our country. What does it cost the Sultan? He can live as well in Baghdad and Damascus as he can in Constantinople. Is there nowhere we can live like brothers with the Russians? *Bratushka! Bratushka!*"

So in this way Russians' political skill figured out how to bridge the endless chasm that separated them eternally from the Turks. What wasn't accomplished with the lion's skin succeeded furtively with the fox's. Approximately one hundred thousand Turkish soldiers, having been led off to captivity, were flattered to believe that they were not captives, but simply guests of the Russians; consequently they would owe them in future the same behavior and conduct that the religion of Mohammed dictates that believers exercise toward all those under whose roof they as guests have tasted "bread and salt."

As for Selím, on the other end of the bridge that spanned that chasm there stood a warning light, love's warm flame, nodding to him from afar to hasten his return to Russia's embrace.

"For one to see beauty is *haïri,*" said Selím, approaching this subject with some embarrassment. "I came to know an old officer, one of those who'd come to Adrianopole in '29; he remembered a little Turkish, and he invited me to his house to drink tea. He had a widowed daughter who looked after him—God preserve her for her father!—she was good like an angel! Her husband, a rogue, had for years and years made believe he loved her until he succeeded and got her. But you think he took her to love her? The rogue! When he'd gambled away her money at cards in five or six weeks, he took his pistol and put a hole in his noodle. The poor thing had been a widow six years then. The old man loved cards, too, and he played with Pavlóvska to pass the time, but once we became acquainted, he never let go of my collar. He told me stories of the wars he'd fought in, and with great delight listened to me praise the Russians.

"The beautiful Pavlóvska merely listened to what her father told her, and she shook her head and her finger saying that the Russians weren't good because they got drunk and played cards! Selím, who doesn't drink and who doesn't play cards—*charasso! charasso!* And

she said it in a sweet voice, and with such glances! What can I tell
you? Meleïka, my wife, was beautiful, beautiful and good, but—
what can I tell you? In our houses the best women are like sheep. I
had lived with Meleïka for many years, and we had had three small
children. Can you believe it? She had never looked me in the eye as
Pavlóvska did. Pavlóvska's gaze was not lowered before mine like a
slave who bows his head for his master to give him an order or
reprimand him. No. I felt that it entered my heart like a sweet fire,
and gave it light and warmed it and thawed it and gave it wings and
made it leap up to the skies from its joy and happiness, yet made it
feel that it would have been better to have flown into Pavlóvska's
arms. And her voice! And her singing! It's true that I didn't understand her language, but precisely for this reason I felt that she was
speaking to the deepest recesses of my heart. Is the nightingale's
language understood? And yet whoever hears it feels that it speaks
of pain and of torments and of love in its heart. God preserve her
for her father! Many's the time I lay in bed sleepless at night and
reflected and wept like a small child because God hadn't also made
my Meleïka like this, since he'd given her such beauty and such
goodness.

"But my Meleïka had the ring that my mother had given her. It
wouldn't have done to leave her. And my heart bled. And when the
time came and the war was over and they began to send us home, I
then realized that I couldn't return without leaving a piece of my
soul in Russia! . . ."

Selím, agitated now, continued: "And after such happiness in my
captivity, after the care I found at the hands of our enemies, hear
now how our own people received us, hear how the Kingdom that
we had served with our lives on the line cared for its warriors."

And in darkest colors Selím described his fate after these events.
The captives were transported by rail to nearby harbors, just as they
were, and with much attention lavished on them. Crowds said farewell to them wherever they passed, addressing them always with
the sweet name of brother and taking advantage of this last moment
to show as best they could their love for them as they departed.
Each of the captives without exception took some memento given
him by his friends; Pavlóvska and her father accompanied Selím to
the sea and hugged him and said good-bye to him shedding tears in
torrents. But the comfort of all ended there on the shore. There on
the shore each captive was obliged to leave everything Russian he

had on him, to put on those filthy rags that he had worn so long on the fields of battle. And in this way, half-naked and barefoot, they boarded the waiting steamships by the hundreds and thousands, piled pitilessly even into the space designed for ballast. And when they reached the nation's Capital, then they cursed the moment they had been summoned to return to their sweet fatherland!

The return of the captives took place in the middle of winter. Constantinople was at that time still flooded with the refugees from Bulgaria who had overflowed every public building as well as most private homes. Even the very Ottoman mosques had fallen into the possession of women and children right up to their gates, and one saw those wild creatures—rendered still wilder from despair— camping even in the streets.

And so where were those countless captives to sleep on their return? No thought had been taken for this. The steamships disembarked them in swarms on the Galata Bridge or on the banks of the Bosporus, suffering from their frightful passage, hungry and shivering. The officers who had accompanied them as they disembarked went off to the Officers' Quarters, and the fighters at Plevna, more than forty thousand, together with so many other fellow captives, after such comforts of life in the land of their enemy, suddenly found themselves exposed to death from hunger and cold in front of the majestic altars and hearths on whose behalf they had so often faced danger.

"When I recall," said Selim, "that after so many struggles and so many accomplishments, we soldiers of the Sultan condescended to take alms even from the Jews, while delicate aristocrats with their silk umbrellas and their gloves passed by and pretended they didn't see us, my heart is torn apart! God has removed his *merhaméti* from Islam."

It wasn't long before the patience of those unfortunate creatures was exhausted, the court of the Officers' Quarters was besieged, and tens of thousands of voices sought soldiers' pay in arrears for so many years, pay for blood and suffering, so that each might go back to his home. But—in Selím's opinion—nothing remained from the extravagances of the seigneurs with which to pay the soldiers. And since they had begun to raise desperate disturbances in the streets, the authorities were forced finally to shut them up in the courtyards of the great mosques and to provide a pitiable ration, lulling them with the hope that they would shortly get what was due them! Typhoid fever had long been decimating the mobs of refugees, and the unfortunate soldiers, packed inside the same enclosures with them, began to die by the hundreds. The police, fearing the justified indignation of these men, took the precaution of removing from them any kind of weapon they happened to be carrying. And so, while Selím was lying under a kind of tent in the cold mud, very feverish, and with no one to help him, he hears one of those young men from the police demanding of him that he hand over the Russian dagger that he happened to be holding in his hands. It was only through countless precautions that Selím had managed to bring this dagger to Constantinople. It was a precious memento of his beloved Pavlóvska.

"Imagine," he told me, "what an effect that whelp's insolence had on me. That frightful illness wasn't enough for me, nor was the frightful situation in which I found myself—along comes this one to bloody my heart. I didn't hand over my weapon; and when he tried to take it by force, I leaped up, squeezed him by the Adam's apple, and shoved him down into the mud.

"'Dog,' I told him, 'from the hands of Selím the *yúzbasi,* not even the Muscovite was able to take a weapon!'"

The consequences of this desperate act on the part of the unfortunate Selím was that, though in a very bad way, he was led off that evening to the police station, was beaten pitilessly, and was not only stripped of his dagger, but also had the stripes that denoted his rank stripped from his military cloak.

"How can you wear these things in the streets and beg?" they asked him sternly; "to embarrass the *dovléti?* You're not a soldier any more, much less an officer. Get out of here! . . ."

"Now I ask you," said Selím when he had related these things in detail, "who's to blame in this world, the murderer or his victim? A horrible idea came into my head when they freed my hands, and it would not have been difficult to butcher them all on their velvet chairs. But I had lived justly and honorably up till then and I didn't want my name soiled. 'You have a wife and children back home, Selím,' I said to myself. 'If you have nothing left, at least save your good reputation for them.' And God gave me patience, and I dragged my sick body about the streets of the City for another two or three months until the snows melted and the roads opened and I could drag myself off slowly to get to my house."

"Home!" Selím repeated after a silence, and he smiled that painful, sad smile of his. "I thought that, ill fated though I am, I'm at least coming home! I am coming to my children, to my wife, to be looked after, to get well, to begin a working life again, since it wasn't written for me to die after so many ordeals. . . . My home! Where's my beloved home? Where's my dear wife, my little children?

"While we were defending the Sultan's throne and the existence of the empire beyond the Balkans, the aristocrats who stayed behind to govern the place, to protect it, joined up with the Cherkezes and the Muhatzires who were fleeing Bulgaria and overran the Christian villages and houses and destroyed much life and made off with a great deal of property. Some sort of heroic act they thought they were performing! But when Plevna fell and the Muscovite rushed in this side of the Balkans, then they knew the curse was coming to devour them, they felt that the crimes they'd committed would come out of their nostrils as vinegar, and they left their houses just as they were and rushed headlong into the City to save their lives. My father was no longer alive then, the raki he'd drunk had consumed him. God rest his soul! Prior to this time his wife had sold all our property once she'd got sole control of it and had taken the money and gone and married in the City. The *muftís* took the share that fell to me—sixty thousand *grósia*—and put it out at interest to stay for my children in case I didn't come back. But near the dry log the green one burns, too, and my poor wife—you see in order to serve the *dovléti* I'd left her helpless—when she learned that the Muscovite was coming, she too joined up with the other families and fled to the City.

"What happened afterwards you can easily infer. As soon as the Christians who'd gone to the mountains learned that the Turks had left, they came back and set fire to our houses for revenge. Of the Turks who set out in the winter, only half were left when they reached the City, and once there, not many of them survived to come back. Hunger, cold, and pestilence deprived me of my children and my wife there!" And wiping away his tears, Selím cried out: "In front of the Sultan's very throne that I had defended with my life so many times, three children and one woman died before their *etzéli* came, and they were mine . . . they were the only things left to me in this world! . . ."

The poor fellow bowed his head on his chest; a painful sadness darkened the pallor of that good face. After a little, he knitted his brows and leaped up from his seat.

"Let him come now," he said. "Let whoever was fashioned by God with a heart in his breast, let him come accuse Selím for his thoughts! God lifted his *merhaméti* from this country because of the wickedness of the *eféntides* and the *agádes*. And he made our land Russia's *kismét* because of her goodness and concern. Can't you see it for yourself? Where's Silistria? Where's Herzegovina? Where's Serbia? Where's Bulgaria? Everywhere we conquered and everywhere we lost! That's why I don't want to know anything any more. The few years God has granted me still are my *kismét*, and it's right for me to live them now as I want. How do I want to live? I haven't hidden it from anyone; look, you can see for yourself. Only they don't want to know the reasons and that's why they take me for a fool. And in all likelihood they'll take me for a coward and deserter when they hear that Selím the platoon commander went with the Muscovite."

"That no one will dare to say, I assure you," I told him. "Now that I know your story no one will say it. You're a brave man, Selím Aga! And you've been much wronged!"

"May God give you a long, happy, and joyous life!" the poor fellow said from the heart as he squeezed my hand. "My heart's been lightened today. May God repay you for it. I never knew such great delight in my misfortune! . . . I'll ask only this of you. I beg of you, when you read in the newspapers that the Russians are coming back, inform me as quickly as you can. I'll sprout wings, I assure you, to join up with them."

"I'll be going to the Capital in the next few days, and I expect to return from there in one or at most two months," I told him. "Then I'll make a point to come see you and tell you what we can expect this winter. It's certain that things are seething again in Bulgaria; Russia doesn't like their leader and very likely will find a pretext to cross the Danube once more."

"*Amín!!* May God grant it!" the Turk cried and raised his eyes to heaven.

After a few more encouraging reassurances I said a warm goodbye to Moscóv-Selím and returned from Kaïnárdza plunged in thought. There's a strange psychological wound in this man, whose

sufferings exceed every known account of Turkish soldiers' perseverance and endurance, I said to myself. By nature brave and philosophical, but brutally ignored by his father, he was cast into war as
soon as he became of age, heedless not only of his girlish upbringing
in the harem, but also of his unfortunate mother who loved him so
tenderly that she could not live on after being suddenly separated
from him. Strange, too, the parents' error as regards their children's
thoughts and feelings. Concentrating on external similarity only,
they both judged prematurely; the father especially was responsible
for the utter ruin of his house on account of this. To tell the truth,
Selím united in himself all that was fair and good in his parents'
separate temperaments. The fearless and brave in his character, his
sense of honor and pride—what were they if not his father's virtues? But while these virtues were corrupted in the old man's soul
by the brutality of his spirit and his inhumanly harsh, unnecessarily
strict nature, Selím, inheriting in addition to those virtues a mild
nature, an innate understanding, patience, and goodness of heart,
had become a person who compelled respect and admiration.

It seemed to me a comic quirk of nature that the warlike, mag-
nanimous Selím had inherited from his gentle and peaceable mother
not only a heart extraordinarily vulnerable in some respects, but
also an unusually lively imagination that served that vulnerable
heart. Selím had created for himself a Russian life in that Hellenic
land because his lively imagination, perverted by his passion for
Russian things, filled in the gaps in that life so that what for the rest
of us was comic and ridiculous disappeared from before his eyes
in exactly the same way that that good hanúmissa had created
through her own imagining a girl child by dressing and making up
the extremely manly Selím as a daughter.

In this way I spent the entire length of the road discovering in
Selím's character its individual psychological components, components that had already pre-existed separately in the opposed natures
of his parents. That the exclusiveness and religious fanaticism of his
race had not only disappeared once and for all from the consciousness of one born of such parents, but had even developed into a
point of view diametrically opposite, seemed to me understandable
of itself. After the sacrifices that he had offered on behalf of the
leader of the nation and religion, after the horrible spiritual wounds
he'd received from his own people when placed in the balance with

those superhuman sacrifices, it seemed to me that my friend's every moral obligation to them had been discharged forever. Then another thought occurred to me.

I had often heard it said by our people that the Turks have never regarded the Ottoman Empire's possessions in Europe as actually belonging to them. On the contrary they believe and admit that their natural homeland is the East, and that, when the time comes, all will take their women and children and cross the Bosporus silently and calmly, reverently returning to us the keys of Byzantium as a sacred heritage. And to be sure, the facts of history oppose to this truly Byzantine hope a long series of notably superhuman, desperate, ferocious struggles in which the Turks step by step contested the integrity of their empire in Europe against every attack or revolt. But hadn't Selím himself indicated it? Of what avail were the many victories and the many accomplishments of Turkish arms? Didn't what was fated to happen happen? Once the iron hand of the Greek Revolution had shaken the Sultan's realm in Europe, it introduced cracks that could no longer be joined and welded, either with abundance of blood or with the countless bodies that the faithful eagerly put at its disposal for this purpose.

One after another, Montenegro, Serbia, Roumania, Bulgaria itself, Bosnia, and Herzegovina fell away. Almost everywhere the naive Turks made war, triumphing over and subduing and occupying those lands again, and yet always they saw themselves thrust out of their own possessions by the intervention of Europe, and especially of Russia. Why is it strange, then, if a person like Moscóv-Selím felt that that fated hour is now at hand in which the Caliph must remove his throne to Damascus or Baghdad?

When I returned to the county seat, V., from the Capital this past September, the coup that deposed Battenberg had already been carried out by the Bulgarians. As soon as I arrived people thronged to my lodging in order to hear the news of the matter from European papers, which they supposed I must have read, since the local press was not allowed to publish such news. Among those who came along was the municipal physician, a thin gentleman with a degree from the University of Athens, an insatiable seeker of the new and an ardent political observer. When I told him Selím's story before I went back to the Capital, he cried out with his natural liveliness: "They're all *démoralisés,* my friend, all of them. Association with foreigners has by now taken away their fanaticism. At the first blow in the future they'll all act just like Selím. No one will obey the Sultan, all will desert to the enemy."

Seeing the doctor again after the events in Bulgaria, I said to him, "Early tomorrow I'll offer you a coffee by the streams of the local Castalia."

"Who'll brew it for us?" he asked bewildered.

"Moscóv-Selím, of course. I don't believe he can have left for Russia yet; he doesn't have the fare. They won't give him *teskéres,* so he's waiting for me to bring him news about the coming of the Russians, and he'll wait a long time yet."

"Oh! the poor wretch!" said the doctor with compassion. "Some idiots have his life on their conscience."

"Why?" I asked.

"As soon as the Bulgarian coup became known," he said, "they went and assured him the Russians had come. The next day the Municipality sent me to visit him—I found him half paralyzed! Clearly he must have suffered a stroke from an excess of joy."

The next day, a little late, we both went over to visit him. We found him lying in his dark cottage on a worn straw mat. His pleasant face had become almost unrecognizable. His pale flesh now seemed still more swollen and slack. A certain fierce gloominess dominated it, a gloominess that became all the more pronounced because his mouth and one of his large eyes slanted to the right. His arm and right leg had become difficult to move, as the doctor had said; after today's examination, however, he was convinced that the evil would pass this time, so improved did he find the invalid's condition.

When he saw me, poor Selím tried to smile that unforgettable sad smile of his; my body shuddered. His expression had become so hideously savage from the morbid distortion of his features! Tears came to my eyes, and when Selím noticed them, he began to cry like a child, hiding his face in his hand. I sat beside him, took his hand in mine, and said, "What's the matter, good friend? God will make you well!"

Up to that moment Selím had not uttered a word; and my heart was torn apart when I heard his voice, thin and whining in any event, now sounding as if it came from some grave that lay beneath his mat. "Glory be to God!" the unlucky fellow said with a moan; "you see what's happened to me!"

"It's nothing," I told him. "The doctor *éféntis* assures me that the worst has already passed and that you'll be well in a little while. But how did such an awful thing happen to you? How did you hurt yourself? Is such great joy possible again, and so in vain? The doctor tells me you suffered this on account of your joy!"

"Don't say that!" whined the sick man with a disapproving gesture. "I wish it were joy!... For me, God wrote that I'll die from my sorrow!... In fact I, too, thought I'd rejoice... but it cannot be."

And collecting his weak powers the Turk continued speaking in that mournfully failing voice of his and with his painfully sad gaze fixed on my eyes: "My father and my mother were Islam... I and all the *Osmanlís* are the Sultan's property.... Does blood ever become water?... How can I deny my blood?... Betray my master?... Go with the Rusians?... This frightful idea tormented me one night, all night long.... One night, all night long my mind wrestled with my heart.... At daybreak... out of my grief, out of my pondering, it came to me..."

The doctor's astonished eyes met my own, which were no less astonished. When Selím had regained his strength: "But what need is there, then, my good fellow, what need is there for you to agonize so? It was no business of yours."

"The Russians have come back to Bulgaria!" he said indignantly. "Haven't you heard that yet?"

"Oh! The liars, the villains!" I cried out then. "They almost destroyed a man's life. Didn't I promise you I'd bring you the only true reports? So, my friend, learn from me that the Russians have neither come nor will they ever come back again into the Sultan's land."

"For the love of your God!" shouted the Turk excitedly but sorrowfully. "Really, they haven't come? Come, let me kiss you!" His eyes shone ghastly—"For the love of your God! They won't come again?"

The doctor came between us quickly and abruptly shoved me away from the invalid's bed and addressing Selím seriously said, "My friend, you need more rest; leave the Russians be and look after your own health."

Some incoherent words of Selím's reached our ears; I heard the cry *Alláh! Alláh!* distinctly.

When the doctor got up from the invalid's bedside and looked at me; his face was white as a sheet and his eyes wide from terror. "He's gone," he stammered with trembling lips. "His joy killed him! . . ."

A second onset of the disease had put an end to the old soldier's trials, and the Turk remained a Turk to the last.